SCANDAL AND THE RUNAWAY BRIDE

DONNA ALWARD

THE COWBOY'S PROMISE

TERESA SOUTHWICK

D1464362

MILLS & BOON

First Published in Great Britain 2020
by Mills & Boon, an imprint of HarperCollinsPublishers,
1 London Bridge Street, London, SE1 9GF

Scandal and the Runaway Bride © 2020 Donna Alward
The Cowboy's Promise © 2020 Harlequin Books S.A.

Special thanks and acknowledgement are given to Teresa Southwick for her
contribution to the *Montana Mavericks: What Happened to Beatrix?* series.

ISBN: 978-0-263-27899-6

1020

Printed and bound in Spain
by CPI, Barcelona

SCANDAL AND THE RUNAWAY BRIDE

DONNA ALWARD

To the Real Sisterwives, Barb, Shirley, Jenna and Renee—brainstormers extraordinaire and the best besties in the world.

CHAPTER ONE

Surrey, mid-July

WILLIAM PEMBERTON HELD the folded sheet of cream paper in his hand and clenched his jaw. Just beyond this room, in the Chatsworth estate chapel, his elder brother, Stephen Pemberton, the Earl of Chatsworth, was waiting for his bride. The guests had already filled the pews and the organist was playing quietly, though the wait had been so long now she was starting to repeat pieces. The bridesmaids were lined up at the entry doors, dresses and bouquets perfect, and William had been discreetly dispatched to find out what was keeping the bride.

What he'd discovered was no bride at all, and a note instead.

I'm sorry. Please forgive me.

William fought to contain the rage and contempt racing through his veins. His brother was a good man, and deserved better than this. Especially after his previous broken engagement—though the rest of the family wasn't aware of the circumstances of Stephen's breakup with Bridget. Only William, who'd found his brother soundly inebriated in the Chatsworth study one night last February, knew the truth. The whole sordid tale had come out over far too much gin.

And while William had thought that Stephen's marriage

to Gabriella was also a mistake, this was too much. Who did Gabi Baresi think she was? There'd been ample time to change her mind. Instead she'd left it to the eleventh hour, when it was sure to humiliate Stephen—and his family— the most. Rage simmered in William's veins. This wasn't just going to hurt Stephen, it was going to be a PR nightmare for Aurora, Inc.

He let out a breath. Okay. His job right now was damage control. There would be no wedding today and he had to think fast to keep it from being an utter scandal, splashed all over the tabloids. The Pembertons and the company didn't need that. Not now, so soon after William's father's death.

He folded the paper in little squares, tucked it into his pocket, and then set his shoulders, preparing for the horrible task ahead. His shoes clicked on the stone floor as he made his way through the back door to the chapel, where Stephen looked over at him with a questioning brow. William gave a jerk of his head and Stephen hurried to his side, still beaming his happy groom smile. That was, until they were behind a gigantic display of roses and lilies. William nearly choked on the overpowering scent.

"What is it?" Stephen asked. "You look like you're ready to murder someone."

"Not far off," William whispered. "Listen, Gabi's not coming. But I have a plan, so please don't go off half-cocked until you hear me out."

Stephen's face paled and his lips thinned. "My God. What do you mean, she's not coming?"

"She left a note, saying she's sorry and to forgive her."

"Let me see it."

William had learned long ago to never disobey that tone in his brother's voice. He took the note out of his pocket and unfolded it, careful to keep it out of sight of any guests. Not much worry, though. There were so many flower arrangements that the chapel had become a veritable bower of blooms. One only had to duck behind a single install- ment of blossoms and greenery to be completely concealed.

Stephen swore.

"My thoughts exactly," William said. "Now, here's what you're going to do, and it's going to take all your acting abil- ity. You're going to go up to that altar, incredibly concerned that your bride-to-be has fallen horribly ill. You're going to ask to be excused, and you're going to go back to the house. No one is going to see you, and once I've found her we'll figure out a plan to contain the damage. It'll be on so- cial media within the hour, so we have to watch our steps."

"You're going to find her."

"Oh, yes," William promised darkly. "I don't care if we have to call it food poisoning or the flu, but she is going to disappear for a while to 'recuperate' until this is under control. Then you can decide if you still want to go through with this farce."

"William—"

"I know. Sorry. We'll talk more later. Right now, you give the performance of your life and get back to the house. I'll smooth things here and then find Gabi."

Stephen gave a brusque nod. If William had ever had any doubts about his brother's feelings for Gabi, they were put to rest. He was angry, but he wasn't heartbroken like a man should be when his bride pulls a runner. It was small comfort, but it was something.

Stephen went to the altar and cleared his throat. "Ladies and gentlemen, I'm so sorry to say that there won't be a wed- ding today. Gabi has fallen horribly ill. I thank you all for coming, and I'm sure we'll set a new date once she's feeling better. Right now, I'd better go look after my...after Gabri- ella." He put on an expression of appropriate concern and affection that even William nearly believed.

Then Stephen brushed past him and stormed through the door, looking to the rest of the world like a worried fiancé. But William knew that look. And when Stephen wore that expression, his mind was set. No matter what Gabi said now, this "arrangement" was over. Maybe that was a blessing, even if it was a mess to be cleaned up.

Their mother, Aurora Germain Pemberton, hastened forward, concern flattening her normally soft, ethereal expression. "William, what is happening?"

He met her gaze and kept his voice low. "Gabi ran. Stephen's going to the house as if she's ill. I'm going to find her, and then I'm going to find us a way out of this mess. Can you handle things here? Say as little as possible?"

She scoffed. "Of course." Then she looked up at William. "I wish I could say I was sorry, but I'm not. She was not the woman for Stephen, and they do not love each other. But, *mon Dieu*, I wish she'd done it another way. What a mess."

"I know, *Maman*." He risked a little of Stephen's secret. "You know he wanted a happy occasion. Something to make you look to the future, instead of grieving so much."

Aurora looked into William's eyes, and he saw the sadness lurking in the gray depths. "Grief is what it is, darling. I will always grieve for your father. No wedding can take that away."

"I'm sorry."

"Don't be. It is life." She smiled a little and kissed his cheek. "Now, don't worry about a thing here. This is not my first PR crisis."

She walked away, head high and so very poised. His mother was an incredibly strong woman.

One of the bridesmaids was standing back, twisting her fingers in her bouquet and biting her lip. Gabi's younger sister, Giulia, who had traveled from Italy to be in the wedding. William beckoned her forward.

"Giulia, right?" he asked.

She nodded, chewing on her lip even more. She was young, maybe twenty-two or so. And Gabi had abandoned her, too. William might have felt sorry for her except he didn't have the luxury of sympathy at the moment. A young man hovered just behind her—well, maybe Giulia wasn't totally alone. She'd brought a plus one with her, though Will couldn't remember his name.

"Is my sister all right?"

"Did you speak to her this morning?"

Giulia nodded quickly. "Yes, of course. She was nervous, but who isn't on their wedding day?"

William searched her face for any hint of lying and found nothing. He was generally good at reading people, and he wasn't sure this sweet young woman had it in her to be manipulative or a liar.

"Come with me," he said, putting his hand on her arm. "Where we can speak more privately."

The young man stepped forward, but Giulia gave a quick shake of her head and he halted. Her heels clacked behind William's black dress shoes as he led her out of the chapel and into the room where he'd found the note. He shut the door behind him and looked her square in the eye. "Your sister isn't sick. She left a note and ran."

"Oh, *Dio mio*!"

William lifted an eyebrow. "That's a common sentiment at the moment." So far he'd heard it in three languages.

"Do you know where she is? Oh, no." Giulia's hand was now over her mouth, her bouquet dangling from her opposite hand. "I need to go to her…"

While William believed Giulia's upset was genuine, he wasn't swayed by her distressed voice. "Actually, I was hoping you might know where I could find her. This is quite a mess. We don't want news to get out, do we? Did she say anything to you? Anything at all?"

"I don't understand." Giulia gave a sniff, and William patiently went to the desk and retrieved a tissue for her.

She dabbed her nose and eyes, and then William started again. "Giulia, your sister and my brother were getting married for appearances only. We both know they are not in love. Marrying Stephen meant that your family's struggling company would benefit from an alliance with Aurora. Surely you must see how that won't happen now."

Her eyes widened and he felt like the world's biggest heel. He hadn't said anything that was a lie, but he was being cold and calculating right now. It wasn't his usual way of doing things. This was what came of having had to do far too much crisis management since his father died.

"But… Mama and Papa…this isn't their fault."

He gentled his voice. "No, of course not. But until I find Gabi and we sort this out…" He let the thought hang, and watched as Giulia sorted through the ramifications on her own.

"William…" She said his name hesitantly, as if unsure if she was being too familiar. "Please, I…I do want to help. She is my sister."

"There are two ways you can help," he said firmly. "The first is to not breathe a word about this to anyone. If it gets out that she left Stephen at the altar, I promise you there will not be a deal with your family. Ever."

She nodded quickly.

"The second is to help me find her. Do you know where she might have gone? Is there anyone she would go to or a place that comes to mind?"

She shook her head rapidly, then paused. "London. She'd try to hide in London. She always said that a person could get lost there. We laughed about it. Our city is much smaller."

"That's not a lot to go on."

Giulia met his gaze. "I don't know. She joked all the time about staying at the Ritz like Julia Roberts in that movie, you know? Where she always used a cartoon character as a fake name?"

William fought the urge to roll his eyes. Yes, *Notting Hill*. His sister Arabella had watched it often enough.

The Ritz wasn't a lot to go on, but it was a place to start.

He ripped a corner off the note and grabbed a pen from the vicar's desk. "If you hear from her or think of anything, please let me know." He jotted down his mobile number. "I can't help her if I can't find her."

And he did want to help her. Only because that was the singular way to help his family.

And he'd do anything for them.

Gabriella's hands trembled as she lifted the demitasse to her lips. If they were at Chatsworth Hall, Stephen would have called for restorative tea. But tea wasn't for Gabi, not at this moment. What she required was several jolts of espresso so she could make a better plan.

She'd left him. Fled Surrey in her wedding dress and in Stephen's car. She'd left the car at the train station, taken her bag and changed into regular clothes before hopping on the train for London. She had never done anything this impulsive in her life—and that included agreeing to marry Stephen in the first place.

Her couture dress was stuffed into a garment bag and was hanging in the closet where she couldn't see it. So far the only thing she'd been capable of was getting to the room and ordering coffee. Her hands wouldn't stop shaking and her stomach quaked as she thought about what she'd done and the consequences.

What would happen to Baresi Textiles? Her parents? Her baby sister, whom she'd left behind at the estate? Though at least Giulia had Marco. She wasn't alone.

Gabi put the small cup down on the table and rested her forehead on her hands. She'd ruined everything. But how could she have gone through with it? Marriage to a man she didn't love? An agreement to bear a child...to divorce... all for financial gain?

It had been a dumb idea. She should have had the courage to say no from the beginning. She'd been so very worried about her father and hiding her own broken heart, but that was no excuse for making stupid decisions. At least she could try to make things right now.

When she thought of Stephen, her gut twisted again. He wasn't a bad man. He was nice, and incredibly handsome, and he'd always treated her with respect and kindness. He'd been easy to like. But not love. The chemistry wasn't there. And maybe that had been the clincher. He had been very open about wanting a child to inherit the title that he'd inherited himself only a year ago. In the end, she hadn't been able to bring herself to sleep with someone she didn't at least desire.

Was it selfish? Maybe. It didn't really matter now. It was done. She'd ruined the wedding and Stephen's plan and his guarantees for her family's business.

And worst of all, she really didn't like herself at this moment. It had been a coward's move, and a panicked one. For a woman who considered herself strong and reasonable, jilting a groom at the altar was incredibly out of character.

Maybe, just maybe, that was indicative of her level of desperation, and not a horrible character flaw?

She'd just lifted the cup to her lips again when there was

a knock at the door. Gabi frowned; she hadn't ordered anything else from room service and she hadn't told anyone where she was going. Not even Giulia.

A peek through the peephole showed William Pemberton, and her stomach turned to ice.

"Gabriella, I know you're inside. Open the door."

She swallowed against the lump in her throat.

"This is a hell of a mess you made. I'm here to help you."

"I doubt that." She finally opened her mouth and the words came out stronger than she'd anticipated. Good.

"Minimizing the damage from this helps you *and* Stephen. Now let me in."

"Is he with you?"

"No. Now open the door."

She did, because the last thing they needed was to be having a conversation with a door between them, where anyone passing in the hallway could hear.

He stepped inside and she shut the door behind him.

"Nice room."

She met his gaze. Oh, he was angry. So very angry, and he had a right to be. But she would stand her ground, too. Maybe it was messy but she'd done the right thing.

"I took a basic room, and not a suite, William."

"Still put it on my brother's card, though, didn't you?"

"Is that how you found me?" She didn't deny the card. Stephen had given it to her several weeks ago, to pay for things for the wedding. She'd planned to use it to get back to Italy and then pay him back every penny. She'd kept all the receipts.

"No," he answered. "I spoke to your sister."

Her gaze snapped to his and held. "I didn't tell her where I was going."

"She's your sister. She remembers things. Apparently there's a movie you like quite a bit, Cinderella."

The way he said it wasn't a compliment. And she supposed she deserved it. She'd run from her wedding like Cinderella had run from the ball. Only the prince wasn't the one roaming the countryside to find her. It was the younger brother of an earl.

"I couldn't do it, William. I couldn't marry him. Not when I don't...when we don't..." Her voice caught and she turned away, suddenly exhausted despite the injection of espresso.

He let out a sigh behind her. "Dammit, Gabi, I'm angry as hell. I like you, you know. I think you're a good person. I thought you two were making a mistake, but really? The day of the wedding, after everyone got to the chapel? Why wait so long?"

Tears pricked at her eyes. "I thought I could do it. Mama and Papa...they needed me to go through with the wedding. Having Aurora step in meant security for the business while my father is fighting..." She couldn't finish the sentence. Even saying the word *cancer* sent a sick feeling through her body. "Now I've ruined it all."

Afraid of losing her grip on her emotions, she went to the window and looked out over the city.

Daylight was softening, and she took a moment to breathe deeply and regain control. Then she turned around. "What happened at the chapel?"

"Stephen told everyone you'd fallen ill. It's to buy us some time before we need to make an announcement about rescheduling."

Alarm skittered down her spine. "Rescheduling? No, William, no... I can't do that. No, the wedding is off. I promise I'll pay back what I spent and...and..." And she thought about her ailing father going through cancer treatments, and how they'd stayed in Italy because he was too sick to make the trip for the wedding, and she finally broke down in the way she hadn't let herself in the weeks leading to this day. What if they lost the company? What if... he died?

Large hands settled on her shoulders and guided her to the table where the coffee service was set up. She sat in the chair and tried to regain her composure. Will sat opposite her and poured himself a cup of the espresso. "Take your time," he suggested. "I'm guessing you need to get that out."

She looked up at him through eyes blurred with tears. "Oh, so now you're nice?"

His dark gaze was steady. "Make no mistake, Gabi. I'm furious. But if you were upset enough to run from the wedding, I'm guessing there are some hefty emotions that need to get out. I'd prefer you do it now so we can make a plan without that messiness getting in the way."

So not so nice. Instead he was a cold, arrogant jerk. Hah. And she'd always thought him the fun one, and Stephen the serious one. No such luck.

He took out his phone and tapped in a message while she wiped her eyes on a thick white napkin. "What are you doing?"

"Telling Stephen to keep up the story that you're ill. And then I'm messaging your sister to tell her you're safe. You left her behind, too, you know. In a strange country where she doesn't know anyone."

She wasn't sure it was possible for a human to feel guiltier than she felt at this moment. "She has Marco with her, and a return ticket for Monday," she reminded him.

"Yes, and they are now staying at our house. How do you think she feels?"

Gabi got up from the table and spun away, irritation flaring. "Fine, William, I'm a horrible, horrible human. Is that what you want to hear?"

But neither tears nor temper fazed him. "All I'm saying

is that there are a lot of moving parts to consider. As far as the world knows, you got food poisoning and were too sick to attend the wedding. We'll feed snippets to the press. And no one here will talk. I took care of that."

She resented him even more now. The Pembertons had the money and status to pull all that off, didn't they?

"Well, I guess you have it all under control." Even if she'd wanted to, she couldn't keep the sarcasm out of her voice.

"Not quite. Making this work means keeping you off the radar and away from the paparazzi. And that means you packing your bag again. You can't stay here."

She laced her fingers together, trying to control the unease trickling through her at his tone. "And where do you suggest I go?"

"Not you. *We.* I'm not letting you out of my sight. So why don't you order us some dinner while I sort out the arrangements?"

He turned away, effectively dismissing her. If she'd felt that her life was out of her control, she felt it even more intensely now. She was at the mercy of William Pemberton and his family. But she wouldn't be forever. She'd make sure of it.

CHAPTER TWO

IT WAS DARK when Gabi showed her passport and then followed William to the Aurora, Inc., private jet. Of course they wouldn't risk flying commercial and being seen. She was being escorted away like a dirty secret, hidden away until there was a plan to "deal" with the situation. The situation being her, of course.

She wanted to be angry about it. And maybe she should. But the truth was, this was a PR nightmare. And she was the one who'd caused it.

The inside of the jet was familiar, yet tonight she felt like an interloper. She'd flown in it before, of course. As Stephen Pemberton's fiancée, she'd flown from her home in Italy to Paris, and Stephen's luxurious flat there, and of course to London, where it was a short commute to Chatsworth Hall. Indeed, the plane had been fueled and ready for the honeymoon trip, a week on Malta.

She paused and William came up behind her, letting out a breath of frustration. "What is it now?"

"Sorry. I'll take my seat. Where are we going again?"

"To the château."

Right. He'd said France. She should have remembered, but she was exhausted and distracted by everything. As she sank into the buttery leather, she bit her lip. "For how long?"

He shrugged. "A few days, a week? Hard to say."

A week. She frowned. As long as she could be back home for her father's surgery, it would be okay.

William had been calling Stephen and the pilot and whoever else he'd needed to call. Gabi had only made two calls. One to her sister, and then one to her parents.

On the first call she'd been completely honest and apologized to Giulia for leaving her stranded. Giulia said the Pembertons were looking after her and not to worry. Of course that was what Giulia would say. She was the peacemaker of the family and would do anything to avoid conflict.

Her parents had been another story. She'd lied to them, and it had hurt. She'd perpetuated the story of her illness and setting a new date. The illness angle kept the call mercifully brief. The guilt, however, had settled like a lead weight in her stomach, and she wasn't sure it could ever be dislodged. She'd done so much more than lie to them today. She'd thrown away the chance to save their company. If she couldn't manage in her father's absence, they might have to sell, which would break his heart. Going into an early retirement was not his plan at all. The partnership with Aurora would have kept it financially stable while he went through his treatments and recovered. She was twenty-eight years old and held an accounting degree—how was she supposed to manage the entire company and navigate it through a tough economy?

Her throat closed over with emotion. She was going to disappoint people, and that hurt her heart.

"What are you thinking?" William asked, sitting across from her and reaching for his seat belt.

"I'm thinking that I've ruined everything. My parents… my arrangement with Stephen would have kept everything going and kept the company in my father's name. Now we're probably going to have to sell." She met William's gaze. "I feel like the most selfish woman on the planet.

Even though deep down I know marrying Stephen would have been wrong."

"Would it have been so bad? Being a countess?"

"Maybe you don't believe me, but I don't care about those things. What is being a countess when one is miserable? Not that your brother is awful," she hurried to add. "But I'm not in love with him, and I can't imagine being married to someone I don't love. Even temporarily. I thought I could, but..." She turned away. "Oh, maybe I'm just naive. I probably sound silly and stupid."

"No, not that," William said. "I'm mad at you about the mess. But personally, I agree with you. The engagement was foolish. I can't actually believe that Stephen came up with the idea. He doesn't usually buckle to pressure. Not even from our mother."

The plane began to taxi down the runway and Gabi fastened her seat belt across her hips. "He loves her, and he loved his father. She's grieving for Cedric so much. He wanted to give her hope. A wedding and...and a baby. A grandchild to carry on her husband's legacy. Is that so bad?" Stephen had made a compelling case. Plus she'd always liked him. They'd first met three years ago. She'd been working with the Baresi accountant with the goal of taking over the financial aspect of the business eventually, and Stephen had been looking in on Aurora suppliers as he took on more responsibility within the company. Stephen had been charming and kind and they'd become friends. On his last trip, she'd confessed her worries to him over a glass or two...or maybe three...of Chianti. He'd come up with the plan.

And he'd said he trusted her because they were friends.

Her cheeks heated, though. Perhaps that was the clincher in the whole decision, really. A marriage of convenience she might have been able to go through with. But bearing

Stephen's child… She wanted children, of course she did. Very much. And Stephen was an honorable man who would honor his promises. But…

But. It always came down to the lack of actual love between them. It was completely platonic on her end, and she suspected on his, too. It was the one thing she couldn't talk herself around.

"It's not bad, as an idea. As a plan, though, it's very… I don't know. Like something out of those period dramas that Charlotte loves to watch."

His twin sister, Charlotte, was a doll. "I like your family very much," she said softly. "They've been very good to me. They must hate me right now."

"As far as they know, you've broken Stephen's heart and caused a scandal."

"Are you always so blunt?"

"Yes." But he smiled a little, and a light flickered in his eyes. "There isn't much room for misinterpretation when one speaks clearly and honestly."

"I'm not sure if I like it or not. But I thank you for not yelling at me. Or being…too angry."

They reached altitude and William unbuckled his seat belt and rose, moving to the onboard bar. He took out two glasses and poured a good splash of cognac in each. As he handed her the wide-bowled glass, he smiled. "I think you both dodged a bullet today. This, darling, is simply controlling the story. A week or so in Provence will keep you hidden away from the paparazzi. After that, you can set a new date." She was about to protest when he held up his free hand. "A date which will never happen. After an appropriate amount of time, the wedding will be quietly called off, you'll go your separate ways and that will be that."

So neat and tidy. Should she be grateful that William was taking care of all of it, or angry at having her life dictated yet again? "And what about Baresi Textiles?" she asked, lifting her chin.

He took a healthy sip of his cognac and lifted an eyebrow. "You'll have to ask Stephen his plans. And maybe wait until his pride's not in the toilet."

She sipped her drink, and it made her feel warm and slightly drowsy. She and William didn't talk anymore. He had taken out his phone and kept rapidly typing in messages. She was unbearably curious, and kept sliding glances his way.

He looked a little like his brother, but there was a difference, too, in the square set of his jaw. His hair was dark brown and cut short and neat, and if he would smile more his eyes would soften from a hard, cold golden brown to something that made her think of waving grasses in autumn fields, a little green, a little brown, but never quite one or the other. Right now he was still in his tuxedo trousers and shirt, though he'd undone the cuffs and rolled up the sleeves, and ditched the tie. The unbuttoned collar drew her eyes to a V of skin, right at the hollow of his throat.

She guessed him to be somewhere around six feet, and like the rest of his family, he had a lean legginess that led to a trim waist and a broader chest and shoulders.

All in all, the Pembertons were a good-looking family, and William was no exception.

It would have been so much easier if she could have actually loved Stephen. But then, he didn't want to be loved, so it didn't really matter.

She drank the last drop of cognac and leaned back against the soft seat. It wasn't long at all and her eyelids were drooping…

William frowned as he looked over at Gabi as she fell asleep. There was no big shifting to a comfortable position or snuffling or anything. She sat back, her lids grew heavy and she was gone.

Stephen was a fool. Gabriella Baresi was a beautiful woman: smart, a little shy, but what she'd done today? It was an almighty headache, but damn, it was brave. She would have made Stephen a great wife, if he'd let her. But Stephen was an idiot right now, still stinging from his last relationship gone wrong. While most would consider her last question to be cold and calculating, he didn't think so. She had been going through with this out of a sense of family loyalty and responsibility. Her father was ill. Aurora would have partnered with Baresi for the finest Italian cashmere, in exchange for her father still maintaining control of the company. Stephen had agreed, with his own preposterous conditions.

William shook his head. The pair of them, trying to live up to parental expectations in the most misguided way. Not that he didn't understand. He owed everything to both Stephen and their father. His life had been on a dangerous path until the two of them had stepped in and saved him. He hadn't deserved it. He'd acted like the typical "spare" to the heir, partying too much, getting attention the wrong way, getting in over his head. Stephen could have washed his hands of Will and his antics, but instead he'd stepped in and been Will's biggest support.

Saint Stephen. The old nickname flitted through his brain, and he frowned. Stephen always did everything right. Will constantly had to prove himself. But he'd brought that on himself, so he shuttered the feelings away and studied the sleeping woman across from him again.

He'd met Massimo Baresi. William seriously doubted that the man knew what bargain Gabi had struck to save their business. He was a proud, smart man going through a horrible time. No, Gabi had taken this on herself, and he thought back to his crack about being a countess. He didn't think she'd done it for her own personal gain. She'd accepted Stephen for the good of her family, a self-sacrifice. Misguided, but admirable.

He swallowed tightly. She *was* beautiful. There was no harm in admitting that; it was a fact and he was a fan of facts in general. A piece of hair curled around her heart-shaped face, the same sable color as her thick eyelashes. Her lashes were full and curled up slightly at the ends. Her mouth was relaxed in sleep, delicate lips a soft pink now that she'd chewed her lipstick off.

He'd learned she chewed on her lips when upset or nervous. She'd done it a lot today. Choosing to run hadn't been easy for her. He rather suspected she'd been pumped full of adrenaline all day. No wonder she'd crashed.

In an hour or so they'd be in France, headed to the Germain château, surrounded by lush gardens and lavender fields. It was the most beautiful place he'd ever been, and now he was going to be there with her for the next week.

At this point he didn't know if that was a curse or a blessing.

Coffee. The rich, thick, beautiful scent of it woke Gabi from a deep sleep. She blinked and then rolled over and gasped at the sight of a maid depositing a tray on a small table.

"Oh, excusez-moi, mademoiselle." She stood and wiped her hands on her apron.

"You brought coffee. No need to beg pardon. You have my undying gratitude." She sat up a bit and pushed her hair back. "What's your name?"

"Suzanne," came the reply.

"Merci, Suzanne. I can't face the day without coffee."

They shared a smile and then the maid slipped away, closing the bedroom door with a click.

Good heavens. She didn't realize there'd be a maid. But then, the château was huge. Of course there was staff.

She barely remembered arriving last night. William had awakened her on landing and they'd been ushered into a car and then into the château sometime around two a.m.— or was it three? She reached for the coffee and inhaled its strong aroma, took a bracing sip and sighed as she leaned against the enormous headboard. Someone had guided her to this room and deposited her bags as well. The bags, still packed, now stood by a gorgeous wardrobe. She'd unpack this morning after...

She didn't know what after. She was supposed to be sick, wasn't she? And she highly doubted William wanted anything to do with her.

He'd have to, though. Because she insisted on knowing about the mysterious "plan." Maybe she didn't have much control over what happened next, and for good reason, she admitted to herself. But she wasn't about to sit back and be quiet as a mouse about it, either.

She emptied her cup and filled it again, then sampled the flaky, rich croissant on the plate and picked at the fresh berries in a china bowl. Last night she'd barely touched her dinner, and now she found herself quite hungry. It wasn't long before the food had disappeared, the coffee had kicked in and she was ready for a shower and a fresh start.

It was amazing to think that yesterday at this time she'd been preparing to put on her wedding dress. It seemed as if it were days ago, and not a mere twenty-four hours.

She'd showered and dressed and was putting cream on her face when she realized she hadn't seen her mobile this morning.

She dashed back to the bedroom and ripped through her handbag. No phone. She lugged her suitcase to the bed, threw it on top of the coverlet and opened it, tossing clothing aside looking for the tiny piece of tech that kept her connected to her life. Nothing. She hung the garment bag that held the wedding dress, now crumpled, in the wardrobe and tried to calm her heartbeat. Had she left it on the plane, perhaps? In the car last night? She tried to remember where she had it last and couldn't think.

"Good heavens."

Her head snapped up at the sound of William's voice. He stood in the doorway, staring at the state of her room, his mouth agape. She followed his gaze.

Her clothes were strewn all over the room. Dresses and skirts littered the fine silk of the coverlet, shoes and trousers were scattered all over the floor, and her cheeks heated as she realized a few of her very fine and pretty underthings were tossed over a tufted chair.

She lifted her chin. "I'm unpacking."

William lifted one eyebrow and she would swear his eyes twinkled with amusement, despite his stern expression. "An unorthodox method."

She wouldn't laugh. She was too vulnerable right now to attempt to share any sort of camaraderie with him. "I'm sorting."

He bit down on his lip and looked down, and she started to smile, before quickly wiping the expression away.

"William, have you seen my mobile? It's not in any of my bags."

His gaze caught hers again. "Ah. That explains the mess. As a matter of fact, yes. I have it."

"Oh, thank goodness. Could I have it back, please?"

"Not quite yet."

She blinked. "I beg your pardon?"

He had the grace to look uncomfortable. "Look, Gabriella, the last thing we need is for you to post on your social media or something. Our PR department is looking after this. Our job is to lie low for a few days while they control the messaging. That means not being online."

Gabi clenched her fists as she stared at William. How had she ever thought him the fun brother? Stephen was somber but he wasn't stuffy or bossy. But William…this was infuriating! Who did he think he was?

"Then tell me that. Do not confiscate my phone like I am a disobedient child. I demand you give it back to me."

"So you can text your sister or parents? Do you have any idea how leaks happen?" He ran his hand over his hair. "I like your sister very much. She seems like a sweet girl. But she could get your family out of its financial bind by selling this story to the tabloids."

Gabi's mouth dropped open for a solid five seconds. And when she spoke again, her voice trembled with barely contained outrage.

"I don't know how your family does things, but that would never happen. I would trust Giulia with my life."

"And yet you didn't trust her with the truth yesterday."

Gabi sat heavily on the bed, the fight gone out of her, at least for the moment. Deep down, she didn't blame William for being cautious. She had given him no reason to trust her. And yet…this was a most uncomfortable situation. Why should the two of them be at odds? They could work as a team, couldn't they? It didn't have to be a battle *royale*.

William finally moved from his spot by the door and came further into the room. He pulled up a small footstool and sat on it in front of her, resting his elbows on his knees. "I'm sorry," he said on a sigh. "I know I'm being harsh. I just…"

He sighed again, and Gabi got the feeling he wanted to say something but was holding off. "You just what?"

"I would do anything to protect Stephen. And that means this going to plan. He's been through enough."

"If you mean his relationship to Bridget…"

Hazel eyes caught hers and his mouth thinned. "You know."

"Of course I do." She kept her voice soft and even. "Stephen and I are friends, you know. At least we were. Until I panicked."

"Are you prone to panic?"

"Not really. I'm not prone to lying, either, so yesterday was a choice. I could lie to the world, but then I'd be lying to myself, too. And I couldn't live with that. So I panicked and I ran. I'm not proud of it, but here we are."

"Indeed."

"You're very loyal to your brother."

"I owe him a great deal." He smiled faintly. "I was on my way to being a big disappointment when he stepped in. I literally owe him my life. So yeah…you being angry that I took your phone isn't really going to shake me that much."

She should be mad, but the way he spoke about Stephen was so moving she couldn't hold on to her anger. She had no idea what Stephen had done, but clearly it was something huge. All the knowledge did was make her feel worse about what she'd done. Stephen hadn't deserved any of it. She should have spoken up sooner.

Except there'd been the afternoon when they'd walked around the Baresi villa, soaking in the sun. He'd told her then about his parents' love story, about how his father's death had affected them all, about how the indomitable Aurora Germain Pemberton was grieving. He'd been grieving, too, so much. As a friend, it was hard to refuse him comfort in that moment. A few weeks later he'd visited her in Italy and had presented her with his plan.

She looked at William and compared him to his brother. He wasn't quite as imposing as Stephen, but there was a strength about him that was reassuring as well as being infuriating. He'd lost his father, too. And he'd had his own grief to deal with. Maybe not the same pressures as Stephen, who was the eldest and the heir. But grief and adjustment all the same.

"I'm sorry," she said quietly now. "I'm sorry about your father. It must have been hard for you as well."

His eyes softened with sadness and pain. "He was a good man. Losing him was unexpected. We all managed to step into new roles in the company with only a few bumps. But living without him…that's different. So many times I've wanted to call him and ask his advice, and I can't."

"But Stephen's been the one in the spotlight. I hope you and your siblings haven't been forgotten."

He smiled a little. "Forgotten by the press? That's a blessing."

Of course. And if anyone found out they were here together, he'd be in the press and…it explained why he was holding on to her phone.

"Compromise?" she offered, her voice deliberately light. "You let me check my phone. You can vet any messages I send. And I will give it back to you. You trust me a little, and I'll trust you."

He considered for a moment, his gaze holding hers. Something strange swirled through her belly at his close examination. It was as if he could see right into her and her thoughts and feelings. She didn't really trust him at all. It was something he'd have to earn. But this might be a start.

He reached inside the back pocket of his jeans and pulled out her phone.

"You had it with you the whole time?" Gabi couldn't help the censure that colored her words.

And then he smiled. Smiled for the first time all morning. Had he smiled at all yesterday? She was hard-pressed to remember. But this one…oh, that swirly feeling came back with a vengeance. It lit up his face and made his eyes sparkle with impishness. Wasn't this inconvenient? The last thing she needed was to find her ex-fiancé's brother attractive.

"Of course I had it with me. And I was going to suggest what you just did. I don't want you to be a prisoner, Gabi. I just want this whole thing to be done cautiously and correctly."

"To protect Stephen."

"And the family. The tabloids will jump on any little thing, and while my mother is as strong as they come, I'd like to keep her from salacious speculation."

"You're very loyal," Gabi murmured, impressed despite herself.

"I protect people I care about," he admitted. "I didn't always, but I do now."

"In addition to managing part of the family business."

"That, too. It's been a big learning curve."

He handed her the phone and she cradled it in her hand. It was warm from being in his pocket and the knowledge felt more intimate than it should. "Thank you."

"After that, you're welcome to explore the château and the gardens. Just please don't leave the immediate property. As far as I know, no one knows we're here."

On one hand it was lovely to know she wouldn't be cooped up in the house. On the other, closeting her away felt strange and wrong. But it was only for a few days. That was what William had said.

And William, she was quickly realizing, appeared to be a man of his word. So far.

CHAPTER THREE

WILL PRESSED THE phone to his ear and closed his eyes. "Yes, I know. No one knows we're here, Stephen."

His brother went off again, and Will told himself to be patient. He understood Stephen being upset. He'd been betrayed, and if the truth got out, he'd be utterly humiliated. This wasn't the first time. Being rich and an earl made him desirable. But he was also very human, and right now his pride was understandably smarting. He'd never truly gotten over Bridget's betrayal. That was driving his emotion now more than Gabi, so William took a breath and stayed calm.

When Will could finally get a word in, he interrupted. "You should know that she's very contrite. She panicked. She didn't do this to create problems for you."

Why he was defending Gabi was a mystery. Maybe it was the soft look in her eyes this morning. Or how she'd offered a compromise and had stuck to it, no tantrums or pouting or trying to renegotiate. He pinched the skin above his nose and sighed. "Stephen, it was a stupid idea in the first place. And if you think she was using you, perhaps you need to look in the mirror. You were using her, too."

There was silence on the other end.

And then a click.

The beginning of a headache began behind his eyes now. Great. Stephen was mad, and Will didn't like that they were at odds. Meanwhile, he was stuck in France babysitting Gabi. Truthfully, that wasn't much of a hardship. She was rather lovely. Stephen would remember that when he got past his hurt pride.

He tucked the phone into his back pocket and stared out the window of his bedroom. There was very little of himself here; the rooms were professionally decorated and he'd always stayed in this room when they were in residence. His flat in Paris was much more his style. And yet he had to admit the light-colored walls and airy draperies contributed to the overall atmosphere of Château Germain: restful and calm.

The windows overlooked the terrace gardens, and always gave him a measure of peace. At twenty-eight, he was young to be in charge of an actual division of Aurora, and at times he wondered if it was what he really wanted. But there'd never been any question that he'd be part of the business, just like all the Germain-Pemberton children. His mother had put him at the helm of the fashion side of the business six months ago, which still struck him as humorous. But as she pointed out, he didn't need to know fashion to know business.

And what he knew was that Aurora, Inc., would never compromise on quality. The Baresi family had been their supplier for cashmere for nearly two decades. It was in Aurora's best interest to maintain that relationship.

How convenient that a member of the Baresi family was under the same roof.

A movement caught his eye, and he discovered Gabi walking through the terraced garden that led to the larger park beyond. His throat constricted as he tried to swallow. She wore the same dress she'd had on this morning, something simple with blue flowers on a white background, in a cut that emphasized her trim figure. But what really got his attention was her hair. This morning she'd been just out of the shower and it had been wound up in some sort of knot. But now it flowed down past her shoulders, a curtain of rich mink, thick and wavy. The kind of hair a man itched to sink his fingers into. He imagined doing so and hearing her sigh with pleasure…

But Gabi was not for him. He wouldn't do that to Stephen. Besides, they were all trying to avoid a scandal here.

She stopped by a rosebush and he caught himself smiling as she leaned forward to smell a blossom. Could he be more of a fool?

He wiped the smile from his face and decided to join her in the garden. There was no reason why she couldn't have what she wanted. A deeper alliance with Baresi was a solid business move for Aurora. Stephen had attached conditions to his offer. William would, too, but it wouldn't require anyone to sacrifice their principles or integrity. He'd do this for the company, and for Baresi, and let Stephen worry about procreating and providing an heir and a baby for their mother to bounce on her knee.

The garden reminded Gabi of home.

Provençal climate meant many of the plants, shrubs and flowers were of the Mediterranean variety, and very unlike the English garden back at Chatsworth Hall. Boxwoods, olive trees and cypress flanked flower and herb gardens that cascaded down each terrace. The smell was incredible. She was sure she sensed the tart aroma of lemons and perhaps the softer scent of nectarine…was there an orchard somewhere on the grounds? In the garden proper there was rosemary and thyme and of course lavender, the savory scents soothing her frayed nerves as she made her way to the gurgling fountain in the very center.

The fountain was a little oasis, with a few Aleppo pines providing a bit of shade and wicker furniture placed around it for a wanderer to take a moment to rest. She did, easing herself into a chair with a creak. It was exceedingly comfortable, and Gabi let out a long, slow breath. Her anxiety had been on high alert for hours. She needed to decompress, so she focused on breathing, checking in with each of her senses.

The feel of the chair, beneath her bottom, the armrests beneath her fingers, warm and dry and textured. The perfumed, soft air. The way the light breeze fluttered nearby leaves ever so gently, a susurrus of sound that shivered along her nerve endings, inviting her to relax. The sun on her face, and William, walking down the terrace with long-legged grace.

William!

So much for relaxing. She'd already agonized over her reaction to him this morning. Up until two months ago, she hadn't even met Stephen's brother. At the time she remembered thinking how handsome looks ran in the family, but she'd been so distracted by her father's test results and Stephen's proposition that he'd been relegated to the background.

He wasn't in the background now, and she still hadn't figured out how to handle him. Or if she even should try.

She reminded herself to relax her muscles, so that when he arrived by her side, she looked for all the world as if she were enjoying a sunny afternoon in a spectacular garden.

"I see you discovered the gardens. They're lovely, aren't they?"

"Some of it reminds me of home," she replied, smiling up at him. "But the lavender…it weaves its way through everything, doesn't it?"

"You can't see them, but there are fields nearby. And we always have some in the gardens."

"It's supposed to be good for anxiety." She laughed lightly. "My own little aromatherapy afternoon."

He looked over his shoulder and then back at her again. "If you need help relaxing, I did ask for some wine to be brought out. I'd like to talk to you about something."

Unease centered in her gut. So far, William had been honest, telling her exactly what was on his mind. She respected that. She could deal with that. She couldn't deal with half-truths and angles and trying to pretty something up that was downright ugly. She'd been through enough of that already. She'd been willing to agree to Stephen's offer because Luca had strung her along for two years before shattering her dreams. She wanted marriage and a family. Stephen had offered both. Luca, on the other hand, already had a wife. A wife she'd known nothing about until she'd had her own pregnancy scare. Then the truth had come out. Luca had broken her heart and made her feel stupid in equal measure.

But she also reminded herself that Will had his own agenda, which was about what was good for Aurora, Inc. She forgot that at her peril.

"All right." She sat up straighter, encouraged when William grabbed a nearby chair and pulled it over closer to her. At least he wasn't going to stand over her in a very obvious position of power. Power which, of course, he had. She'd lost her only bargaining chip to save her family.

A maid approached, carrying a tray with wineglasses and a chilled bottle. With a small smile she set the tray on the little table. William nodded and smiled at her. "Thank you, Angeline. I can pour for us."

Gabi had no doubt the wine would be excellent, and she was of two minds about the motivation behind it. William might be trying to broach his topic in a convivial manner. Or he might be lulling her into thinking that, using it to his advantage. Either way, she was on her guard.

He handed her the glass, touched the rim with his own and said a quiet, "Cheers."

She sipped, enjoying the taste of the liquid on her tongue. *"Grazie,"* she said softly. "It's very good."

"You don't speak Italian much."

She smiled. "I do when I'm angry. And with family. But business...that's mostly in English."

"You've been working for the family business for some time now."

She sipped again, and then casually responded, "As have you."

"Did you always want to?"

How could she answer that? Truthfully, no. She hadn't grown up with this burning desire to take over her father's business. In fact, the agreement with Stephen had benefited her as well as her father. With Baresi under the Aurora, Inc., umbrella, she would have been free to move on once their marriage ended, if she wanted to. Now she was going to be responsible for the company whether she liked it or not.

She shifted uncomfortably.

"It's a big world," she finally answered. "But I also love my family and it's a good job."

"But not your calling."

She sighed. "You're talking about something different, a vocation, yes? A higher purpose?" A frown tipped her lips downward. "I don't know. Running the company has never been a driving force for me."

"If you could do anything, what would it be?"

She met his gaze. "I don't know. I figured that if I found it, I'd know."

He nodded, his brows pulling together. "I think we might be more similar than we thought," he murmured. "Both of us love our families. We're in the family business. And yet we wonder if there's something more."

"There's not for me, not right now, and that's okay." She figured she might as well be honest, just in case Stephen hadn't given him all the particulars. "My papa…he's very ill. The doctors say the survival rate is promising, but the treatments…without him, Baresi can't survive. He *is* Baresi. Now that I've messed everything up, I'm going to have to go home once this PR nightmare is over and do my best to keep it alive until he returns." She swallowed against the lump in her throat. She refused to think the words *if he returns*.

William's keen gaze locked on her face. "Maybe that's a way to ease out of the engagement publicly. Say that you've returned home to care for the family business while your father is ill."

"It would tie it up neatly, but no. I'm not using my papa as a…what's the word? A scapegoat."

His eyes glowed. "Damn, Gabi. That made me like you a little bit."

She laughed in response, because it was so unexpected. "You didn't like me before?"

"I didn't know you. I just had impressions and what Stephen told me. But I'm forming my own opinion. As much as you've landed us in this mess, I cannot argue with your principles." His lips turned up in a smile. "Just your timing."

"I'm so glad my principles measure up," she replied. And took a healthy sip of wine, because the twinkle in William's eyes made her think they had somehow made the switch to flirting. How could she be doing that a mere twenty-four hours after fleeing the Chatsworth chapel? And when they didn't trust each other?

His phone buzzed and she watched as he leaned forward and removed it from his pocket, then swiped his finger over the screen to unlock it. His smile turned to a frown and he sighed. "I asked my assistant to keep me updated on what's happening online."

He handed her the phone so she could see. His assistant, whoever she was, had included links. So many that Gabi had to scroll with her finger—twice—to see them all.

"So many," she whispered.

"It'll go from here to some of the tabloids by tomorrow, I think. And within a week or so it'll quiet. We have to outlast the news cycle, and not create a new one."

"It's a lot. But I'm a nobody. Why is anyone interested?"

"Because Stephen is an earl and because our mother is Aurora Germain. She's known all over the world."

"She must hate me right now."

"Not hate. My mother doesn't hate people. But I can guarantee she's not happy."

"Should I talk to her?" It was the last thing she wanted to do, but she'd been the one to make the mess. She should be the one to reach out. Even if the thought made her the teensiest bit sick to her stomach.

"Not now." He took the phone back and tucked it away. "Listen, look at this week as a vacation. The château is lovely and you have the run of it and the gardens. The library is packed with books. There's a theater room with a huge movie selection. This'll be over before you know it."

And she'd be bored to tears. But as consequences went, she couldn't complain. There were so many worse things than boredom.

So why did she feel like crying all of a sudden?

She looked away and sniffed, tried to keep her lower lip from wobbling. She wasn't a crier and she definitely didn't want to lose her grip in front of William, especially since she'd broken down briefly yesterday. And yet somehow the urge would not go away. A tear trembled on her lashes and snuck down her cheek.

"Gabi?" His voice was hesitant, surprised. "What's wrong?"

How could she explain? There were so many emotions roiling around inside her she didn't know where to start.

She sniffed again, but it was no use. Now that she'd started, she had the feeling she was going to have to cry it out and get it out of her system.

"What is it?" he said gently, and he put his hand over hers on the wicker armrest.

His fingers were warm and strong as they enveloped hers, and another emotion bloomed in her chest, adding on to the complicated feelings she was already battling. Oh, he shouldn't be nice to her. This wouldn't do at all. She had to keep the wall between them standing strong.

"I'm fine," she tried, and sniffed again. Why wouldn't her nose stop running?

He took his hand away, much to her relief, but it was short-lived as a moment later he held out a handkerchief.

She dabbed her eyes and nose and laughed a little. "Seriously? I didn't think men carried these anymore."

"Maman always insisted we have one for emergencies. It stuck. Comes in handy for damsels in distress, too."

She dabbed again and met his gaze. Her eyes must be red now and the tip of her nose, too, but she didn't care. "Despite all appearances to the contrary, I do not need to be rescued."

"Good. I'm glad." He put his hands on his knees. "It means you're made of strong stuff. Stiff upper lip and all that."

She chuckled. He sounded so perfectly English in that moment.

"Here," he suggested, and topped up her glass. "Take an hour and let yourself feel what you need to. Drink wine. Soak in the garden. I'm sure you've got some thinking to do. And when you're ready, come find me. We can talk about what comes next."

He got up from the chair and prepared to leave.

"William?"

"Hmm?"

"Why are you being so nice to me?"

His hazel gaze locked with hers, and that strange feeling came over her again. Ugh! If only she could have felt like this when Stephen looked at her, she wouldn't be in this predicament!

"Because being a jerk rarely accomplishes anything. And because you nearly went through with a fake marriage to save your family. That's brave. So was walking away from it. Don't get me wrong, I was furious yesterday. It's a hell of a mess to try to control, but I don't think you did it maliciously. You've got a strong character, Gabi, and I respect that a lot."

She was pretty sure her mouth was hanging open at this point. "I…thank you. I don't really know how to respond to that. Except that I'm so glad you understand why I did what I did. I'm so sorry I've caused so much trouble."

"Stephen bears some of the blame, too," William replied. "And I've told him so. He didn't like it."

She laughed again despite herself. "No, he wouldn't. He's stubborn." She sighed. "I've probably ruined any friendship we had. I regret that. Your brother is a very good man. There just weren't any—"

She stopped abruptly. There was no way she was going to talk about sexual attraction with William. Not considering the way her pulse leaped every time he appeared.

"Sparks? Fireworks?" he filled in for her.

Her cheeks, which she imagined were already pink from crying, heated.

William laughed, presumably at her discomfiture. "No

need to be shy now. And to be honest, I'm kind of glad to hear it." He stepped away. "Enjoy your afternoon, Gabi."

He turned and walked back on the cobbles, his shoes echoing through the peaceful afternoon. She watched him go, let out a breath that she hoped would calm the beating of her heart. What had he meant just now, that he was glad to hear it?

Why would he be happy there'd never been any chemistry between her and his brother?

CHAPTER FOUR

By WEDNESDAY, GABI was going crazy. She'd read three books, watched two movies, wandered the gardens, slept, ate delicious food and drank excellent wine. For the first day, it was lovely—as William had said, it was a vacation of sorts. And who didn't want that? But on Tuesday she'd found herself restless. And by Wednesday afternoon, she was ready for a change of scenery. Not that the château staff wasn't lovely; they were. But she'd hardly seen William, either. Once a day they had a meal together, but he spent a lot of time in a downstairs office, working remotely.

While she had no purpose at all beyond staying out of sight. And presumably out of mind, too.

This morning she'd popped down to the kitchens to ask a favor, since she wasn't allowed to go into the nearby town. She'd given a simple shopping list to the cook and now she was heading downstairs to whip up her own dinner. She needed to do something with her hands and to keep her mind occupied, and cooking was just the thing. She needed a taste of…home.

She was homesick. She missed her apartment in Perugia, family meals at the villa, even the Baresi offices where she did most of her work. But most of all she missed Mama and Papa, and their ready smiles and hugs. Right now her papa was preparing for surgery followed by chemotherapy. And she was stuck here, unable to go to him or even tell him what was happening. She was lying. And if anything happened to him and the lie stood between them…

The kitchen was quiet when she entered, and she found the ingredients she'd asked for in the massive refrigerator. Before she began, she opened the bottle of wine that she'd placed in the fridge earlier. Since William had said she could have full run of the château, she'd made a trip to the wine cellar and had been delighted to find an Orvieto that looked to do the trick. A little taste of home.

The first thing she did was put an apron on over her jeans and top. Even though she'd dressed casually, her first job had the potential to be a messy one. She rinsed the cherries and put them in a bowl, and then went to work pitting and slicing them in half. Juice stained her fingers and now and then one of the cherries would squirt as she removed the pit. She popped one in her mouth at the end, then put red wine, sugar and orange zest in a pan to heat. Poached cherries was one of her favorite desserts growing up, and so very simple to make.

Once that was on the go and set aside, she turned to her vegetables.

Vignole was something she remembered from childhood, particularly when spring came and everything was fresh and new. The tension started to unwind in Gabi's body as she prepared the artichokes, leeks, peas and fava beans. Garlic and onion went into the pot, and broth, and then the artichokes.

There would be far more than she would be able to eat, but she didn't care. This felt right. And it felt, in some small way, like something she could control when everything else was out of control. She raised her glass in a toast to herself and took a long, revivifying drink.

As everything bubbled and aromas rose in the air around her, she drizzled honey into a bowl of mascarpone, to go on top of the cherries. Her mouth watered just thinking about it.

"Hullo! Madame Gosselin…" Gabi turned as William entered the kitchen, releasing a torrent of French that she didn't understand.

"Oh," he said, breaking off midsentence and staring. "I didn't know you were in here. I was looking for Madame Gosselin."

"She gave me use of her kitchen," Gabi said softly.

"I see that. You cook."

"Of course. If I didn't cook, I'd starve." She laughed a little. "I needed something to do, and I was missing home and my mama's cooking. So here I am."

He relaxed and came farther into the kitchen. "What are you making? It smells amazing."

"*Vignole*—it's a vegetable stew. Nothing heavy. Lots of vegetables and broth and a little pancetta. There's fresh bread from this morning."

He leaned over the pot and inhaled the steam. "Mmm. And what's in here?"

She reached for the copper pot and took it off the burner. "Poached cherries to serve with a bowl of mascarpone cream for dessert."

"A feast," he said, and smiled at her.

Oh, no. Not the smile again. This was why it was good he'd hidden away in the office for the past few days. Every time he smiled at her she forgot who she was for a brief second, and who he was, and why this was so very inadvisable. If a runaway bride was a mess, this situation would be catastrophic.

So it made absolutely no sense that she smiled in return and said, "There's plenty for both of us, if you'd like dinner."

"I'd like that. Don't tell Madame Gosselin, but my tastes are a little more simple than what she puts together."

"Surely you had your share of French food growing up."

She waved a hand, gesturing to nothing in particular in the kitchen. "Between here and Paris."

"Yes, but I also lived in England a good part of the year. And the family has properties all over."

She stirred the stew and he came up behind her and looked over her shoulder into the pot. She was startled at having him so near; she could smell his cologne and the lighter fragrance in his hair from his shampoo. Unsettled, she moved away so she could slice the bread.

"So what's your favorite meal in the world?" he asked. "If you could have absolutely anything?"

She thought for a moment, her hand paused on the bread loaf. "There's a restaurant in Perugia that I adore. My parents took me there for my eighteenth birthday and now I go every year. They make the most amazing pasta with a butter truffle sauce. Every time I go I swear I'm going to have something different, but then… I always go back to it."

"Mmm…sounds delicious."

"What's yours?"

"When I was in uni, there was a curry takeaway just around the corner from our flat. I'd eat anything from there any day of the week." He frowned. "I don't even know if it's still there."

"You should go back and find out." She grinned at him and put down the knife. "And you surprise me. I expected something elaborate and fancy."

"Not me. If I can't have that, I'll take a traditional English breakfast all the way. I get that from my father."

"You miss him." She'd been reaching for the olive oil, but she hesitated and met his gaze evenly. "I really am sorry."

"None of us expected it. He was only in his early sixties, you know? He should have had more time."

She swallowed thickly. At twenty-eight, she was the

oldest. Giulia was only twenty-one. Her father was only fifty-four. What if he didn't make it? She bit down on her lip and remained silent.

"You said your father's prognosis is good. You need to hold on to that."

It surprised her that he'd guessed the path of her thoughts. "I know, but there's always that other number that sneaks up and reminds you that not everyone is lucky. The business aside, I don't know what we'd do without him."

William came around the table where she was working and took her hands. "When is his surgery?"

"Next week. Stephen and I were going to stop for a few days on our way home from Malta, but now…" She tried not to think about him touching her, but her fingers tingled from the contact. Oh, this would not do at all…

A strong finger tilted up her chin. "Now you're not in Malta. But I'll do what I can to get you home so you can be there, for him and for your family. Will you let me arrange it?"

That he even offered filled her heart with joy and relief. "Oh, William, that means so much to me. If I can be home when he has his operation…" She took his hand in hers. "When can I tell Mama?"

His eyes clouded a bit. "Not yet. I don't want to set something in stone until the rest of the week plays out. Can you trust me? And not because you don't have a choice, but because you know I'll do my best?"

She wanted to trust him, and that scared her to bits. Look at what had happened the last time she trusted someone. Maybe the problem wasn't with trusting others, maybe it was trusting herself. Because twice now she'd landed in "relationships" that were nothing but lies.

"You haven't given me a reason not to. Yet."

"I'll endeavor to keep your good opinion of me," he said formally, and it made her smile again.

"Come on, then. I think this is ready, and you can eat a very Umbrian dish tonight instead of Madame Gosselin's heavy sauces."

"Music to my ears," he said, and went to find bowls and plates.

Will looked across the table at Gabi and knew he was asking for trouble.

The candlelight lit her face, and when she laughed it was like music. The meal she'd prepared had been fairly simple but amazingly delicious. For dessert, he'd headed to the basement for an appropriate wine. Not a dessert wine, but a red that would complement the cherries and also be drinkable throughout the evening.

Right now Gabi was pushing her remaining cherries around her bowl with a spoon. "Full?" he asked, dipping his own spoon for one more scrumptious bite.

"Very. Madame Gosselin really knows how to bake bread."

"Once, when we were kids, Charlotte and I snuck into the kitchen at night and toasted a whole loaf. We spread it with Nutella and nearly made ourselves sick. The next morning there were chocolate fingerprints on everything."

She laughed, a light, lovely sound. How had Stephen thought he could marry her and not fall in love with her? What was wrong with him?

"Your mother had her hands full with twins."

"Yes. And you know, despite being 'the' Aurora of Aurora, Inc., she spent a lot of time parenting us. Both our parents did. We had a nanny, but we were never made to be out of the way. We were…are…a family."

"I like your mother. She frightens me, but she's lovely

just the same. She has this aura about her that is so strong and capable."

"She is," William agreed. "But she has her weaknesses, too. No," he corrected, "not weaknesses. Love is not a weakness. She has a wonderful soft side. I think that's why Stephen felt so pressured to marry. After he broke with Bridget, Maman was devastated. She'd put a lot of hope into that relationship. It's horrible seeing your very strong and capable mother reduced by grief. It was like she'd lost her husband and then the family hope for the future, too."

There. He'd brought Stephen back into the conversation. That should help steer his thoughts away from where they shouldn't be. On Gabi and her smooth skin and gorgeous hair and musical laugh.

Gabi reached for her wine, sat back, took a drink and licked her lips. And Stephen was quickly forgotten.

"I should go do the dishes," Gabi said, a little reluctantly. "Confession. I love to cook. Hate cleaning up."

"I'll help. It's the least I can do since you fed me."

They stacked their dishes and made their way to the kitchen again, but when they arrived it was sparkling clean and one of the maids was putting away the copper pots.

"Oh! We were just coming to tidy!"

The maid smiled and replied in French. William said a quick *merci* and *bonne nuit* and then put down their dishes and guided Gabi out of the kitchen. "What did she say?" she asked.

"She said it was no trouble and that if we left the dishes she'd put them in the dishwasher."

"Oh. I'm not used to that."

"Now you're free to enjoy the evening." Which he guessed would be without him, and he knew it should be even as he hoped it would not.

She sighed. "I'll confess, I've had my fill of peace and

quiet. I wish I could go and *do* something." She turned her gaze up to his. "But I understand why I cannot. I don't mean to complain. I know I brought this on myself."

Will thought for a few minutes. So far, their PR strategy had worked perfectly. They'd leaked a few lines about Gabi being ill, recuperating at Chatsworth, and despite gossip to the contrary, they'd set a bogus new tentative date for the wedding. It looked as if there was no trouble in paradise as far as communications from Aurora went. Soon there would be another story with different celebs, and this delicious little tidbit would be mostly forgotten. Taking her back to Chatsworth wasn't possible; she wasn't exactly welcome there and he understood why. But if he took her home to Italy next week, he could probably leave her there, safe with her family. And temptation would be firmly out of his way.

Which did nothing about her boredom this evening.

"We could take a walk in the lemon grove," he suggested, suddenly inspired. "I know I've insisted you stay in the garden, but I don't think anyone suspects you're here. It's a gorgeous night. I know it's not a night on the town, but it's better than nothing."

"I'd like that."

The day's heat held in the air as they left the château through the garden. The sun was retreating but the moon wasn't out yet, and the sky was a soft blend of blues and pale pinks announcing the beginning of sunset. A smear of cloud carried the colors across the horizon, and William took a deep breath. There was something so different in the air here, as distinctive as terroir to a grape. It was the combination of earthiness, the proximity to the Mediterranean, the vegetation and, for lack of a better word, the utter *Frenchness* of it all. Tonight there was nowhere else he'd rather be than walking through the stone gate from the olive-bordered gardens to the orchard beyond, where the leafy trees provided a shadowy canopy as they ambled along.

"Better?" he asked, breaking the silence.

"Much. What trees are in here?"

"Oh, lemons, and some oranges, and over in that corner are some nectarines."

"Was it ever farmed?"

"Maybe? I don't know for sure. My parents bought this place when I was very little. It hasn't been in the family that long, you know?" He shrugged. "We have a gardener. He cares for the groves now and picks the fruit."

"And the lavender?" She stopped and pointed over the hill to the sloping purple fields below. "Do you own those fields as well?"

"No. But we source it for our fragrances. However, that is not my department. I'm trying to learn more about fabrics and fashion these days."

"Like cashmere."

"Exactly."

"In that case, let me help." She grinned up at him. "You can't find better than Baresi."

He paused for a moment, wondering if now was the right time to broach the topic. Gabi could have thrown a tantrum about this week. She could have made things difficult. Instead she'd done everything he'd asked in order to minimize the damage to his family, even knowing that the chance of saving hers was gone.

Except it wasn't.

The twilight deepened and he reached for her hand. "Come with me for a moment. I want to talk to you about something."

There was an old bench down the path, almost forgotten among the grass and shrubs. But William knew it was there. He knew because when he was fourteen he'd spied on his sister one day when she'd gone walking with a boy and they'd sat on the bench to kiss. Charlotte had given him half her pocket money for the holiday to keep him from telling their father.

Now he sat on it with his brother's ex-fiancée. He wondered what price Charlotte would demand if she knew, and he laughed a little.

"What's so funny?" Gabi sat beside him and tilted her head a little.

"I was remembering something from my childhood. It involved my sister, a local boy and extortion."

"Oh, my." A warm smile bloomed on her face. "I love stories like that. Those are the kinds of shared family memories that last, aren't they? I hope you weren't too demanding."

"Half of her allowance for the six weeks we were here. I spent it unwisely and it was the most fun I've ever had."

"Poor Charlotte. She's too sweet for that."

"Don't let her fool you."

They sat for a moment and then, when the silence drew out, Gabi said, "What did you want to talk to me about?"

He turned on the bench so he was facing her. "This business agreement with Baresi... I know Stephen set it up as a mutually beneficial arrangement. But the thing is... I think it's mutually beneficial, even without the marriage. I've looked at our history with Baresi. I've looked at the quality. There's no reason we can't enter into some sort of agreement that benefits us both." He held her gaze. "Without you having to marry someone you don't love."

Her cheeks pinkened. "But..." The word trailed away. He could see the question in her face, though, and he didn't have a good answer.

"I don't know why Stephen wouldn't have just made the deal. Maybe it was pressure from our mother—she can be very persuasive. Or his way of dealing with his own broken heart—to give it to someone where it would be safe from harm." He met her gaze steadily. "If you're not in love, you're safe from having your heart broken."

"That seems a bit poetic for Stephen."

"Maybe. I can't speak to my brother's motives, but truthfully…in my opinion this would be a sound deal, period. There's no reason why we can't partner with you. It gives us a steady supply of top-quality material, and to be honest, it would elevate Baresi's status in the industry."

She stared at him. "I didn't have to marry him."

"No. And he shouldn't have asked it of you. I love my brother, Gabi. I'll do what I can to protect him, always. But that doesn't mean I agree with all his actions, and in this he was wrong."

There was one sticking point, and he felt duty-bound to bring it up. "It's not a sure thing yet. I'm head of the division, but Stephen is head of acquisitions. He'll have to approve it."

He watched carefully as her face fell. She tried to hide her disappointment, but it was impossible. "And he hates me right now."

"*Hate* is a strong word. Besides, I'm positive that he's going to come to the conclusion that you saved him from a very big mistake. Let me handle Stephen. You worry about your family."

Her eyes widened as she reached out and touched his hand. "Why are you doing this for me? Why aren't you as mad as Stephen?"

She was so beautiful in the fading light. Her eyes were soft velvet, her skin luminous. He couldn't remember another woman capturing his attention this way, which complicated everything. He had to keep this just business, and when she looked into his eyes like she was right now, it was impossible to think in terms of dollars and cents. Yes, getting her back to Italy and leaving her there was a very good idea. Out of sight, out of mind.

"I wasn't the groom, Gabi. My pride wasn't crushed. I was called in to do damage control."

"I know. It just baffles me." She looked away. "You should be angry. I deserve for you to be angry."

"No, not angry. Look at it this way. If I had the chance to make things right and maybe save *my* father, I'd do it. I can't save him now. My father is gone. But yours isn't. Why wouldn't I want to help?"

Her eyes misted over as she looked back at him and squeezed his hand. "You're a good man, William Pemberton. Better than I realized."

"We barely knew each other before Saturday night," he observed, keeping his voice light, but the compliment struck him right in the heart. If he was a good man it was because of his brother's support and his father's patience. He tried to remember that every day and let it guide his actions. His days of making messes were over. Now he tried to clean them up. Be someone his family could depend on. That person he was before could never be resurrected. He looked at Gabi, so forbidden to him, so beautiful. She could make him forget for a few moments, and that was dangerous.

"We should probably get back," she said quietly after a few minutes of silence. The air was soft and the world around them seemed colored in muted pinks and periwinkle as the sun slid closer to the horizon. It was the time of day for whispered secrets and hidden smiles, forbidden touches and soft sighs. That in between time when possibilities were waiting to be plucked like fruit from the tree, and romance bloomed around every corner.

Their gazes held, and for the space of a held breath, they drifted close together. His heart pounded as his gaze dropped to her ripe lips. And then William broke the spell and stood abruptly.

"You're right. We should get back. I want to start drafting a proposal and also work on travel arrangements."

Gabi's face shifted back to impersonal and friendly, thank goodness. He wasn't sure he had the strength to resist her if she'd pushed their…intimacy. Was that what it was? This feeling that kept coming over him? She felt it, too, didn't she? All the more reason to keep his distance now and get her back to Italy as soon as feasible.

"Of course," she answered, also rising. She started back along the rows of the lemon trees, toward the château towering in the distance.

Maybe it had been a mistake bringing her here. William had only been thinking of privacy and seclusion. He hadn't thought of the unintended consequences of being here together, yet alone.

They could be friendly. And friends. But anything more was impossible. He could never betray Stephen that way. Even if his brother wasn't in love with Gabi, it would be wrong, wouldn't it? Besides, if a runaway bride was a PR nightmare for Aurora, imagine what would follow if William suddenly showed up with her on his arm?

"You go on ahead. I'm going to…check on something." He knew he sounded lame, but walking through the gardens and into the château together meant separating there and he wanted to kiss her so badly he could nearly taste her lips just from the mere thought.

"Thank you for the walk. And letting me get out a bit more."

"Thank you for dinner," he replied, and then made a turn on the path and headed in a different direction.

It was the best way. It was the only way.

CHAPTER FIVE

THE WALK IN the garden had been a mistake.

For the first time since her arrival, William had given her access to a laptop. "You need to see what's happened," he'd said, his voice brittle. He hadn't shown her any tabloid links since that first day. Now, though, he'd given her full access. "I trust you won't make this worse by responding to anything." There'd been barely concealed anger in his tone. "This wasn't your fault. It was mine. I should have anticipated this would happen."

But she stared at the picture and knew she wasn't blameless. How could she be? A photog's massive lens had done its job. Their identities were clear as they sat on the stone bench. And so was the fact that her hand was on his and they were gazing at each other dreamily. She could pass it off and say it was nothing more than gratitude, but she'd be wrong. She liked William, a lot. And that walk had been ridiculously romantic.

She muttered a stream of words in Italian that she hoped William couldn't translate. He was on the other side of the room, talking on his cell, but his eyes never left her. Flat. Assessing. Because now she'd become another problem that needed solving.

For the first time since arriving, she got angry. Angry at Stephen for suggesting their crazy arrangement. Angry that he could have helped her without coercing her to marry him. And really, truly angry at herself for going along with it, and not being stronger in the face of her own personal crises. That was really why they were in this mess. It was up to her to get them out of this conundrum. She was done being a pawn in anyone's agenda. And she was done reacting out of fear and distress.

And yet her heart seized as she thought of Baresi Textiles. If she made a misstep, it could all go wrong and she could add to her father's burdens rather than solve them. But she had cards to play, didn't she? And she could use them. For a week she'd been docile and nice and sweet and full of self-blame. Where had the self-assured, proactive woman she'd worked so hard to become gone? She didn't like that when things went sideways, she'd made weak decisions. Well, no more. She was going to go home and she was going to handle the business until her father was well enough to come back.

She closed the browser, making the photo and the accompanying headline disappear. The fact that the article asked if the wedding had been called off because she was "cavorting" with the groom's brother was too much.

It was time to go back to Perugia.

She rose from her chair and stood tall, then crossed the library to where William stood. "When you're done your call, I want to speak with you."

Then she turned and walked away. She was tired of doing everything on Pemberton terms. William had been kind, there was no doubt about that. And there were far worse things than spending a week in a château in Provence. But it hadn't actually solved anything. Her guilt over leaving Stephen at the altar had prompted her to go along with the plan. That guilt was diminishing by the day.

The important thing was to get through this so that Baresi ended up in a strong position. That was the only consideration now.

She went to her room, that lovely, airy, restful room, and got her suitcase out of the wardrobe. Then she started packing it, piece by piece, folding each item carefully, the exact opposite of what she'd done on her arrival. She looked at the garment bag holding the wedding dress and closed the door of the wardrobe. She would leave it behind. There was no use for it now, and it was nothing more than dead weight to carry around.

William knocked and she latched the wardrobe door before saying, "Come in."

He looked at the suitcase on the bed and his brows pulled together. "Going somewhere?"

"Home. This is ridiculous. I should have gone home in the first place. It's where I belong."

"I know this is a setback, but we're dealing with it."

She put her hands on her hips and let out a sigh. "William, I don't want to be something you have to 'deal with.' I did everything you asked without complaint for the better part of a week and it changed nothing. If anything, it made things worse." She tried to ignore the niggling fact that the press had picked up on some sort of attraction between them. One they wouldn't act on but that was there just the same.

"It's my fault. I suggested the walk. It had been quiet, and I didn't consider someone would be out there with a massive camera lens. I got careless."

"Would it be so bad if we told the truth? That I decided we didn't suit and took the blame?"

He gave his head a shake. "Are you serious? Then the story becomes all about what possible deficiencies Stephen has, since it clearly isn't his money or position."

Gabi spun away, frustrated beyond belief. "But they're going to spin it no matter what! So why can't we, I don't know, live our lives?" She turned back to face him. "Stephen is a big boy. Why do you have to handle everything?"

"Because I owe him," William shot back.

"Owe him for what?"

"Saving me from myself, all right?"

Silence fell over the room. Gabi wondered what in the world that meant.

"I understand family loyalty—"

"You have no idea," he interrupted. "I owe William, and my father, everything. I can never repay our dad. But I owe Stephen this. I'm no longer a mess to clean up, you see? I'm the one who does the cleaning up. That's how it is now."

She didn't even know what that meant. "Then we're right back where we started. I'm the mess. So let's take me out of the equation. I'll go back to Italy and my family. Completely out of your hair."

William ran his fingers through his hair. "Are you mad? You think they won't find you there, either?"

"So what's your brilliant idea? How are you going to control the story this time?" She raised her voice in frustration, and he did the same.

"I don't know, all right?"

Was it absolutely bonkers to feel like crossing the room to kiss him right now? What was wrong with her?

And then *he* did it. William took a half dozen long strides, pulled her into his arms and pressed his mouth to hers.

There was a brief moment of surprise and then she wrapped her arms around him, sliding her fingers into the hair just above his neck. Excitement jangled from her belly up through her chest, catching her breath as she responded to the feel of his lips on hers. His arm settled at the hollow of her back and pulled her tightly against his hard body.

Oh, *magnifico*. The word slipped into her brain on a sigh as her body ignited against his fit physique.

She nibbled on his lower lip and he moaned, then pushed her away and stood back, his chest rising and falling rapidly as he stared at her. His hair was slightly mussed and his lips swollen, and his jeans… She swallowed thickly. *Magnifico*, indeed. *Fantastico. Splendido.* And about a hundred other adjectives she could think of.

"That was a spectacular mistake," he ground out, his voice gritty with frustration.

Gabi straightened her shoulders and reminded herself to be calm, despite the crazy beating of her heart. "Oh? I'm glad we got it out of the way. It's been brewing all week. At least now I don't have to wonder."

"Wonder? What are you talking about?"

She tucked her hair behind her ears. "I got the feeling there was some chemistry between us. Then I wondered if I'd imagined it. Now I know."

"Chemistry!" he exploded.

In another situation she might have laughed at the astounded expression on his face, as if she'd said something both preposterous and unsavory. But this was a serious situation. It made the mess even more complicated.

"We ignore it at our peril," she advised, trying to sound logical. It was difficult, though, because he looked so utterly delicious and the taste of him was still on her lips. "That picture caught us in a vulnerable moment, Will. It looks bad because we *were* gazing at each other." She wiped a hand over her face. "It's annoying and problematic, but the worst thing we can do is pretend what just happened never happened."

His expression darkened. "Stephen is my brother." His voice was low and seemed to hold a warning.

"I know that."

"Less than a week ago, you were going to marry him."

"Thank you for the recap."

His eyes sparked, more green than hazel at the moment. "Stop that. You're being…troublesome."

"After last weekend? Also not news. And your finely executed plan didn't exactly work. Here I am in the tabloids again." She glared. "I trusted you and your precious plan, and look where it landed us. I won't make that mistake again."

He clamped his lips shut.

"I am going back to Italy. I'm going to be with my parents as my father prepares for surgery. And you're going to help me do it."

"You're hardly in a position to make demands," he shot back, shoving his hands in his pockets.

She took a moment to breathe, swallow and stand tall even though inside she was quivering. She lifted her chin and met his gaze. "I'm in a perfect position to make demands. Because if you don't, I'm sure the press would be interested in a few details from the past week."

Gabi hated the words immediately after saying them. Extortion wasn't her style, and neither was deliberately hurting someone. But William had to believe she'd follow through. It was the only way to regain control of the situation. The only way to go home. That was all she really wanted to do now. Be with her family. Get back to her life and start rebuilding.

"You wouldn't."

"I don't want to, but I would. I've played it your way and all it's done is keep me closeted away and bored for a week."

The green in his eyes dulled as he stared at her. "Gabriella."

"You're very displeased. You always call me Gabi."

"I thought we were becoming friends."

She huffed. "Don't try that, Will. Friends don't kiss like we just kissed. What am I to you? Forbidden fruit? You don't want to betray your brother. I get that. Believe me, I understand family loyalty. And while running from my wedding does not demonstrate the best judgment, I'm really quite smart. It made sense for me to lie low for a few days. Now I need to start controlling the story instead of hiding from it."

"I don't like it." He moved to a chair and sat down with a sigh. "When you control it, it means I don't."

"Ah, yes." She smiled faintly and sat across from him. Now they were getting somewhere. "And you don't trust me. I don't blame you. I haven't given you much reason to. Except that I've followed your every instruction all week." She raised an eyebrow.

"You have," he admitted.

"I promise that if you let me return to my family now, I will keep to the original story. I fell ill and recovered for a few days, then took some quiet time at the family château. I'll frame it as you and I are friends, as we should be as future in-laws. I'll even hint at the new wedding date. But I'm not going to stay hidden away like a princess in a tower."

"I'm going with you."

"That will only fuel the rumors."

He ran a finger along his chin. "Too bad. That's my condition." He frowned, his brows pulling together. "In fact, what makes the most sense is for Stephen to meet us there."

Her head shot up in alarm. "Stephen? Whatever for?"

"Because you should be seen with your fiancé. And because if Aurora is going to make a deal with Baresi, he needs to be part of it."

She sensed she was now losing the bit of control she'd had, but she had to be smart with this. "Not if. When. The deal with Baresi will happen, William, because if it doesn't,

I'll tell all." She hoped he couldn't see the lie in her eyes. The truth would also hurt her family.

His fingers gripped the arms of the chair until his knuckles turned white. "You wouldn't. You're too…sweet."

Her eyebrows shot up at his choice of words. "Sweet? I was going to enter into a loveless marriage as a business deal. Not sure how sweet that makes me."

"But you didn't go through with it."

It was a fair point. She stood, folding her hands in front of her. "You're protecting your family, and I'm protecting mine. Whatever was between us that night in the garden, and ten minutes ago in this room, can't exist, can it? We both know it. So let's focus on what's important. Our families."

She went to the bed and began folding clothes again, placing them in her suitcase. She certainly hoped that William couldn't tell that her hands were shaking.

Because Gabriella Baresi was terrified. Terrified of what she'd felt only minutes ago, being held in his arms. And terrified that she'd have to make a decision to make good on her threat. In her heart she knew she never would. Never could. Stephen didn't deserve that, and neither did William. Neither did her papa.

She only hoped William didn't call her bluff. Because that would ruin everything.

She'd called him Will. Twice.

Over the last twenty-four hours he'd tried to push that thought aside and failed. Why should it matter so? And yet the sound of her voice, soft and yet strong, speaking the truncated version of his name, repeated over and over. She'd gotten into his head, hadn't she? Into his blood, like a drug he needed more of. The thought sent a shaft of panic through his veins. All those years ago, he'd been looking for thrills, adventure, and the element of danger had been attractive. The reasons why he'd gone off the rails didn't matter. What mattered was that he was worried that reckless person was still inside of him somewhere, waiting to emerge and undo all his hard work.

Was that the real reason he'd insisted he come along? To get his Gabi fix? It couldn't be. No. He was being careful. Protecting his family, like he'd promised to do four years ago. And Gabi was not to blame, not for this. Not for the undeniable attraction and…dammit, need for her. She'd done absolutely nothing to try to tempt or manipulate him. He wasn't sure she was capable of it. No, this was all on him.

Now they were in a rented car, climbing the hill to her family's villa outside Perugia. Umbria was not a region he'd traveled to often, and he was captivated by the rolling hills and abundant olive groves. Gabi drove at eye-watering speeds through the turns, and more than once his fingers tightened in his lap while Gabi seemed perfectly serene.

Perhaps she was. She was getting her way, after all. Except for one sticking point. Stephen would be arriving on Tuesday.

He and his brother had had a huge argument about it. First about the photo, which he'd had to explain as best he could, leaving out the truth that Gabi had so plainly revealed during their argument yesterday. They *did* have chemistry, and a lot of it. She was also right that to ignore it would be a big mistake. Nothing like that scene on the bench—or yesterday's kiss—could happen again.

Once he'd calmed Stephen down, he'd put forward the case for him visiting the Baresi villa. He'd expected it to be a harder sell, but once they'd shifted into business talk Stephen had been far more amenable. It came down to what was good for Aurora, Inc., and the rest be damned.

He loved his brother, but even William was losing patience with Stephen's cold, calculating manner. He'd treated his wedding like a business merger. No wonder Gabi had fled. She deserved better. Even if she'd threatened to reveal the truth to the press, he understood an act of desperation when he saw it. She wasn't mercenary. She was fighting back. He admired that, even if it made her a pain in his neck.

And once more, he was the mess cleaner-upper. Which meant he had to keep her from making good on her threat. He was feeling pulled in about six directions, but he could manage. Finding the right thing to focus on and then coming up with solutions was something he'd discovered he was good at during his time in the trenches at Aurora. It was why his mother had put him in charge of the division, or so she said.

Clean up the mess. Run a division. Make everyone happy. No pressure at all. He'd redeemed himself and proved he was up to the task.

"William?"

"Hmm?" He turned toward her, found her smiling. The sight shouldn't affect him at all, but her full lips curved happily and a light in her eyes sent a warm sensation through his chest. When she was happy, she was breathtaking.

"You weren't listening. Look. You can see the villa from here." She pointed out his window.

A stone villa stood proudly atop the hill. Even at this distance he could tell it wasn't massive but was a good size, tall and strong. Massimo Baresi had built his business and provided for his family. As they wound their way up the drive, he noted healthy-looking olive groves and slopes of leafy grapes. Dust swirled up from their tires as they neared the house, and when they pulled to a stop, a woman who had to be Gabi's mother stepped outside the door, shading her eyes with her hand, a huge smile breaking over her face.

Gabi barely waited for the car to stop before she jumped out and rushed across the gravel, calling, "Mama!"

They hugged tightly for several seconds before Gabi stepped back and turned toward the car.

William took it as his cue, so he opened the door and got out, then shut it carefully behind him.

Signora Baresi said something in Italian as her gaze traveled over him, assessing. William lifted an eyebrow as Gabi laughed, but she gave her head a little shake. He'd ask her later what her mother had said, but there was a twinkle in the older woman's eye so he guessed it couldn't be anything too bad.

"Signora Baresi, it is so good to meet you."

She looked up at him, her eyes sharp. "We were surprised that you were coming with Gabi, and not Stephen."

"He'll join us on Tuesday."

Signora Baresi let her gaze slide to her daughter. "Oh, well, that's good."

Gabi's smile was weak. "It's the first he could get away."

"Get away? You were supposed to be on your honeymoon this week!"

At Gabi's panicked look, William stepped in. "I'm afraid that's my fault," he interjected as smoothly as possible. "I asked Stephen for help on a project. I thought it would keep his mind off things."

Signora Baresi looked at Gabi again. "And you're feeling all right?"

"I'm fine now. Is Giulia here?"

"Tomorrow. She's been staying with friends in Rome since the wedding. I mean, since the wedding was canceled."

Gabi flinched. Clearly the Baresi family had been in favor of the marriage, and the delay wasn't going over well. William quickly realized that Gabi had wanted to come home, but she'd also known that she'd have to keep up the lie of why the wedding didn't happen. She loved her parents. Lying to them had to be killing her.

Did they realize how much she would sacrifice for their well-being?

"It is good to have you home," her mother decreed. "Your father is inside, and I'm making *pollo arrabiata* for dinner."

"Mama. You know that's my favorite."

"Sì, gattina." Her smile was warm as she touched Gabi's face. "I know." Then she looked at William again. "Come. I will show you to your room, Signor Pemberton."

Will tried winning her over with a charming smile. "Please, call me William. Or Will, if you like."

She smiled politely, but William got the idea that he had some work to do where she was concerned. Normally mothers were not his problem. His bank account and the Pemberton charm usually worked fine, but maybe not so much in Italy.

The villa was gorgeous and homey, with oak beams creating an old-country look throughout. Signora Baresi's decorations were warm and welcoming, and Will could understand why Gabi had wanted to come back here. The château was lovely, but this was a home.

Signor Baresi was in the kitchen, fixing a plate of what Will assumed was *antipasti*. A broad smile spread across his face as he saw Gabi enter the room. "Gabriella," he said softly, opening his arms.

"Papa." The way she said it went straight to William's heart. There was so much affection there, so much love. She went to her father and embraced him, and Will watched as the man closed his eyes and hugged his daughter in return. It made Will miss his own father intensely. Not that they'd ever been the hugging type, but the unconditional welcome? That was familiar, and Will missed it horribly.

"Papa, this is William, Stephen's brother. William is in charge of the fashion division at Aurora."

"Signor Baresi. It's a pleasure to see you again. We met, once a few years ago. And of course, Gabi has told me so much." He held out his hand and Massimo Baresi shook it firmly, not like a man who was about to undergo cancer surgery. But there was something in his color that was off, and he looked tired around the eyes.

"*Benvenuto a* Villa Baresi, William." Massimo glanced at Gabi. "I was sorry to hear that the wedding was postponed, but selfishly I'm hoping that when it is rescheduled I'll be well enough to walk my daughter down the aisle."

"I'm sure she would like nothing more," William replied, smiling at Gabi. "Stephen will be joining us on Tuesday. We want to assure you that nothing will harm your relationship with Aurora. You need to focus on your treatments and recovery."

Massimo wagged his finger at Gabi. "You are marrying into good people, Gabriella. But then, you have never disappointed us."

Gabi's cheeks pinkened. William wondered why. There was something frightening about being put on a pedestal, wasn't there? Stephen had told him that once. Or maybe Gabi was feeling guilty for lying about her relationship with Stephen. What would her parents think if they knew the truth?

He looked at Gabi closer. For all her "I'll tell the tabloids the truth" talk, he realized that if she did that, she'd also have to come clean with her family. Was she bluffing? He frowned. Maybe. Or maybe she'd risk their disapproval to ensure their business's security. He somehow thought she would. After all, she'd been willing to marry his brother for that very reason, giving up her own life for a few years, and even bearing him a child. She would have been tied to Stephen for life.

He wondered how shaky the Baresi foundation was, really.

"Papa, I'm going to show William to his room. When I come down, I am going to devour that platter with you. I'm starving. William hasn't tried the local prosciutto and salami yet." She kissed his cheek and then looked at him closer. "Are you still allowed to eat it before your surgery?"

"A little, for now. Go. This will be ready soon."

William nodded at Massimo. Signora Baresi went to her husband's side with a smile and wrapped an arm around his waist. The Baresis were a loving and affectionate family, and William liked it. The Pembertons weren't as physically demonstrative, even if love had always been evident and abundant.

"Come on, Will," Gabi said quietly, leading him away. "Your room is up here."

She led him to a guest room on a third floor. An open window let in a warm breeze and there were doors leading to a small balcony. The headboard of the bed was solid wood and sturdy, like the beams of the pitched ceiling. There were flowers on a table, too, and he wondered if they were always there or if they'd been placed especially as a welcome. Overall, it was relaxing and charming. And hot. But he could live with the heat. He was so used to cold and damp in London that he welcomed the Italian summer.

"We don't have air-conditioning. Sorry." Gabi ruffled her hair off her neck. "The villa was built centuries ago, and my grandfather renovated it. We keep at Papa to put in air-con, but so far..."

"It's fine. And quite lovely. Don't worry about me."

"There is a pool. It's especially lovely in the early evening." She smiled softly. "I often swim before bed. I find it cools me off and I sleep better."

His brain instantly conjured up an image of her in a bathing suit, slick with water from the pool, and he knew he would have to avoid an evening swim.

"Thank you." He put down his bag and rolled his shoulders. "Your parents love you very much. It's easy to see. It must be difficult lying to them. I'm sorry about that."

Her face clouded, but before she could answer, there was a knock on the doorframe. "Gabi?"

The disturbed expression gave way to one of joy. "Giulia! You *are* here!"

"Marco and I just got back early from Rome and I came straight here. Are you okay? Truly?" She rattled off something in Italian. William picked up a few familiar words, something about the wedding and Stephen and an apology.

"It is not your fault, not even a little bit. I shouldn't have left you there. I didn't know what else to do. But William has been very helpful." She gave her sister a stern look. "Please don't breathe a word to Papa and Mama, okay? I'm going to fix everything, I promise."

Giulia looked at William and her smile faded. "You were very angry the last time we met."

"I was very panicked the last time we met." He tried a sideways smile, and was gratified when her lips curved a little bit. "Thank you, Giulia, for helping that day, and for your discretion since."

"She is my sister." She said it as if it explained everything, which to William, it did.

"Mama and Papa think there will be a wedding in the future. I don't want them to know any differently. Especially with Papa going for his operation. We can count on you, right?" Gabi pressed forward with the importance of secrecy.

William was surprised Gabi had used the term *we*. But he supposed they were in on it together.

"Of course."

"How is he, really?" Gabi's face fell with worry as she reached for her sister's hand.

William stepped forward. "Why don't you two go and get caught up? I'm fine here. I assume there's internet I can connect to?"

Gabi nodded. "I'll text you the password in a few minutes. And thank you. I'm really quite worried about my father."

He put his hand on her shoulder and squeezed. "Gabi, that's why we're here. You need to be with your family. So go do that. I don't need a nanny or babysitter."

Giulia laughed. "I guess you don't."

For some reason that small joke made William blush, heat traveling to his cheeks. Gabi's cheeks pinkened, too, and they couldn't have that. Giulia couldn't have any idea that there was an attraction between them. Every time they were within two feet of each other, it felt as if sparks lit in his stomach.

"I'll come back and get you for dinner," Gabi said, offering a small smile. "But if there's anything you need, text. I won't be far."

"I'll be fine. Go. Catch up with your family." He leaned over and whispered in her ear. "If you keep your secret, I'll keep my end of the bargain. Remember that."

Her gaze darted up and met his evenly. "How could I forget?"

CHAPTER SIX

"Gabi." Giulia's voice held the kind of significance only a sister knew how to use. "What is going on between you and William Pemberton?"

Gabi fussed with a perfume bottle on her sister's dresser. "Nothing. Don't be ridiculous."

"I'm not." Giulia spun Gabi around with a hand on her arm. "We both know you're not marrying Stephen. So did you leave him because of that very gorgeous man upstairs?"

"No!" She said it too loudly and tempered her voice. "No, of course not." Instead she took a few moments to give Giulia the highlights. "In the end I couldn't do it. Not even for Papa."

Giulia shook her dark curls. "I'm younger than you but even I know that Papa would be furious if he knew you'd made such a bargain."

"You won't tell him, will you?" Gabi lost some of her confidence and looked her sister fully in the face. "I don't think I could bear him being angry at me before his surgery. What if…?"

She let the thought spin out, and knew Giulia felt the same when tears filled her eyes.

"I meant it, Gabi. I won't breathe a word," Giulia promised. She sat down on the bed and patted the mattress beside her. "You are so…good. I feel like a horrible daughter. At least you tried to do something to protect the family. I never came up with such a scheme."

"My idea flopped, so who's the horrible one? Oh, Giulia, how sad is it that I thought it would be better to marry Stephen than have to run the company myself?" Gabi gave a little laugh, but inside guilt was eating her up. Giulia thought she was so good, but before Stephen arrived on the scene she'd been ready to leave everything for a man, with dreams of a wedding and babies in her eyes. She'd been a naive fool. He hadn't been free for either of those things. And it had almost been too late. No, she wasn't the good daughter at all.

"I can't imagine stepping in." Giulia worked in their human resources department. "Don't be too hard on yourself."

"I'm afraid of failing. Of letting Papa down," she confessed.

Giulia reached over and took her hand. "I understand," she said softly. "But you will do fine. You're smart and strong."

She meant the words to be supportive and encouraging, but it added to Gabi's worry that she'd disappoint Giulia, too. She was the older sister, and supposed to set the example.

"How is Marco?" Gabi changed the subject, needing a little levity.

Giulia blushed. "He's fine. Working in the family business. He'll never leave this valley. Which in a way is okay, but in another way…"

"You want to see the world a little?"

She nodded. "Which is silly. We had the most wonderful time in Rome with friends. What's wrong with me?"

"You're both young. What if you spent a year somewhere, working? Like Paris or London?" She wondered if there would be a spot somewhere in Aurora where Gabi could intern. She was a smart girl, and poised. Often underestimated because she was so pretty, but she had a good head on her shoulders.

Of course, asking William—or Stephen—for another favor probably wasn't wise. Still, though, it was something to think about.

"I don't know. Maybe." She shrugged. "I do love him, though. I'm just not ready to settle down."

"You're barely twenty-two. There is lots of time." Gabi squeezed her hand. "At this rate, you'll be married before I will."

She would be stepping up to manage the company, wouldn't she? How much time would she have for relationships and love?

"Not for a while yet," Giulia assured her. "And first we need to look after Papa. And Mama. She is going to find this very difficult. I know I should move out again, but I might be able to help while Papa is sick."

"I'll be staying at my flat in Perugia," Gabi said. "Once the surgery is over and we know where things stand I have to be back to work." She looked into Giulia's eyes. "I screwed up the deal that would help us. So I'm going to do everything I can to make sure Baresi Textiles weathers this storm."

"Maybe William will help you even if Stephen won't." Giulia's gaze was sly. "He couldn't take his eyes off you."

Gabi laughed, even as her cheeks heated. "That's because he's terrified I'll go to the press or do something to hurt Aurora's image."

"Like the photo in the garden?" Giulia's eyes sparkled. "It certainly looked romantic."

"That walk was his idea. And boy, does he regret it." Gabi got up from the bed and rolled her shoulders. "Let's put all of it aside for tonight and enjoy the family being together. Mama's cooking and Papa's jokes and lots of good wine. William needs some Umbrian hospitality." She patted her tummy and laughed. "And after a day or two of Mama's cooking, maybe he will come up with a way to help us."

An hour later, Gabi went to William's room and knocked. At his easy "come in," she opened the door and found him sitting in a chair, laptop on his knees, typing away on the keys. He smiled at her. "Hi there. Did you catch up with your sister?"

"I did."

"You're close."

"Of course we are." She laughed a little. "We drive each other crazy sometimes, but when it comes down to it, we will always have each other's backs."

"Sounds familiar," he agreed. "Let me send this email and I'll shut down."

She kept her hand on the doorknob. "Papa has food downstairs and you're probably hungry. We could have a little antipasti and I can take you on a tour of the villa, if you like. Dinner will be later."

"Actually, that sounds perfect."

She waited as he typed for a few more seconds, then hit a key with finality and shut the lid on the laptop. "There. I'm all yours."

I wish, she thought, and was glad she hadn't said it out loud. She'd been thinking of him far too often, and long before the kiss happened back in Provence. If he hadn't pushed her away, she might have fallen into bed with him. Giulia's teasing observations had only heightened her awareness. Why couldn't she have met him first, and not Stephen? This story might have had a completely different ending.

The rest of the family was already downstairs. Papa was sitting on a stool nibbling on cold meats and crostini.

Giulia was mixing something in a bowl and Mama was checking on her chicken. The smells were unbelievable, and so very much *home*.

"Are you sharing, Papa, or keeping the whole plate to yourself?" He smiled widely and she went forward and kissed his cheek. "Save some for William. And for me. I haven't had good *capicollo* for some time." She reached around him and plucked a piece, popping it into her mouth.

"By all means," he said, sliding the plate over.

Gabi selected a few things for herself, but mostly sipped her wine and enjoyed watching William try the different foods as he chatted to her parents. He was so at ease, so perfectly lovely. He laughed at something her father said and his face lit up as he nodded and smiled. She didn't even know what they were talking about. It didn't matter. Her family had made him feel welcome and he'd let them. No airs, no awe. He was just as—or nearly as—rich as Stephen, even without the title. William was...

Perfect. He was perfect. Except that he was Stephen's brother. That was starting to matter to her less and less, and it worried her. At some point she'd let her guard down and started to trust him. Was she wrong to?

Her wine was nearly gone and she'd helped herself to another crostini with truffle pâté when she heard her mother say, "Please, you must call me Lucia. Signora Baresi will not do."

Gabi turned around to find her mother beaming up at William. "All right, Lucia. This was delicious."

"Wait until later. My Lucia makes the best *pollo arrabiata* in Italy." There was a world of pride in her father's voice, and her throat tightened. He had to be okay. He just had to. She looked over at him and realized how exhausted he looked. His skin was pale and there were shadows beneath his eyes. Had the commotion of company tired him out so soon? He tired so easily now. And he'd lost more weight. It wasn't a good sign.

"Maybe William needs a walk to work up his appetite," Gabi suggested, putting down her empty glass. "Would you like me to give you a tour?"

"Very much," he replied, turning his warm gaze from her mother to her. It made her a little weak in the knees, and the warm glow from the glass of wine wasn't helping.

It was a little easier to establish some distance between them once they were outside. First she took him along the patio and pool, and then the gardens.

"Your father was getting tired," William observed, his voice somber. "You suggested the walk to give him time to rest, didn't you?"

She nodded. "I'll be glad when the surgery happens and we can get on with his treatment. I can't help thinking that every day we wait erodes his chances at recovery."

"A few more days, that's all," William reassured her. He reached for her hand. "Stay positive. He'll need that."

"I know you're right. And I don't mean to bring down the mood. I'm supposed to be giving you a tour." She smiled and removed her hand from his clasp, which had felt far too good. "These are Mama's vegetable gardens. She used to tend them by herself, but now she has a local boy come in two days a week to look after the grass and weeds." Most of the vegetables that graced their table came from their own gardens. It was a point of pride with Lucia.

"If that snack was anything to go by, your mother is a marvelous cook," William said as they ambled along, graciously accepting the subject change. "And you've inherited her talents, haven't you? The meal you made at the château was delicious."

Gabi thought for a moment. "We're not poor, and we've never been poor. This is a lovely villa and my parents have renovated it through the years as the business grew and things got easier. But we haven't had staff or servants, either. Mama taught both of us how to cook and how to clean. By the time I was twelve I was doing all my own laundry. I've been helping in the kitchen since I was old enough to stand on a little stool to see the counter. I'm glad of it. I have my own flat in Perugia, and I enjoy keeping it and cooking for myself. Even if cooking for one can be a bit lonely."

Particularly since her relationship ended. At least once a week Luca had come over for dinner and...

Gabi didn't like to think of it now. She'd been so foolish and trusting.

"Surely you haven't been too lonely," William ventured, chuckling. "You're a beautiful woman, Gabi. And accomplished."

"Since you're prying, I'll tell you that I was seeing someone for quite a while. It didn't work out."

"I'm sorry."

"Not as sorry as I am." The words were bitter and sharp.

He halted and faced her. "What happened?"

Gabi lifted an eyebrow. "Well, if I'm honest, I was a fool. I wanted forever. A wedding and babies and a family. I really thought that was where we were heading. But he already had those things...with his wife."

She'd shocked him. His lips dropped open and his eyes widened with surprise. "Oh. From how you said that, I'm assuming you didn't know."

"No. But I should have, looking back. There were red flags I ignored. So I got my heart crushed and felt incredibly stupid all at the same time. Life lessons, you know?"

"When did this happen?"

"Last winter."

It didn't take a rocket scientist to figure out that this had happened only a few months before her engagement to Stephen. "I see," he said quietly, and started walking again.

She caught up with him within a few steps and sighed. "Yes, I can see you do. I was bitter and jaded and Stephen and I had been friendly for a while by then. So fool me twice. Instead of being smart and using my head, I let my emotions carry me into another bad situation."

"But for honorable reasons," William added.

They were at the olive groves now, and out of view of the villa. "Perhaps. Or perhaps that was my excuse. Stephen was offering me what I thought I was going to have—a big wedding and a baby and security. And I was so angry and disillusioned that for a while I figured love didn't matter. It got in the way. It...hurt."

"But it does matter."

She shrugged. "To me it does, and it took me getting an hour from the altar to realize it. Either way, I have to have my eyes open now. No more foolish decisions."

William sighed and put his hands in his pockets. They had paused at the top of a hill, and the olive trees sloped down and away from them, running into a long, green valley. "It's beautiful here."

"Isn't it? I understand Mama and Papa never wanting to leave, although they've been talking about moving closer to the city, into something smaller, for a while now. Even more so since Papa became ill. The ironic thing? They had a house in Perugia and they sold it when the economy shifted. The villa was more important to them." She knew her voice sounded sad, but she couldn't help it. She loved the villa and the rolling hills surrounding it. "But it's a large house with large grounds and a lot of upkeep."

"And they either need help with it, or need to change their situation."

She nodded. "And I'm not sure they want to hire help. It's

not just the cost. I think it would seem less...theirs some-how. I don't know if that makes sense."

"Not really. I was born with the proverbial silver spoon. But just because I'm different doesn't make their perspective any less valid. It's a shame. I can tell you love it here."

"It's home," she said simply. It was the place she came back to even as she loved her life and flat in the city. There were so many memories here. And so much love.

William held out his hand. "Let's keep walking. We can circle around the grounds and make room for dinner."

She hesitated, then put her hand in his. It fit so perfectly, her fingers clasped in his slightly larger, stronger ones. That curl of awareness was back, and she was once again unsure what to do about it. The situation was far too complicated to make it more so by getting involved romantically. But nothing bad would come from holding hands, would it? She thought back to her time spent with Stephen. Holding hands had never been his thing.

"You're different from your brother," she said.

"How so?"

She shrugged. "I don't know how to say this without seeming uncomplimentary. He's very polite and charm-ing, but also a bit..."

"Cold?"

"Reserved," she amended.

"He's always been a little more somber than the rest of us. I think it's a first-child thing, really. And something about the burden and weight of expectation. He's the first son, heir to a title and estate. He feels responsible not only for our mother and the legacy he's left with, but us, too. Honestly, it's a burden he places mostly on himself. But you know the old saying, right? Heavy lies the head that wears the crown?"

She did know it, and nodded. "We are...were, anyway, friends. I like him very much. But he's not really easygoing."

"No. I'm trying very hard to understand his motives in all this. I guess his whole world was upside down and there was nothing he could do to make it right. The one thing he thought he could fix was Mother. He was determined to see her through her grief."

"And I was part of his plan."

"Stephen is a great one for making plans. Usually they're good ones. This one was not. But only, I think, because it came from the wrong place. A broken place."

"You're very understanding. And...thoughtful. Not many men I know would understand those feelings so well."

He squeezed her fingers. "I have a big soft spot for my brother. I see his flaws but I know the heart underneath. He would do anything for his family." He looked away over the valley and Gabi saw his throat bob as he swallowed. "He saved me, you know. Gave me tough love and support and a shoulder to cry on, too."

"He did?"

"Four years ago. Seems like a lifetime away now. I was twenty-four, done school, wasting my life, partying all the time. I had no direction, so I drifted in the wrong one. Hung around with the wrong people and did wrong things." He paused. "I think deep down I'd always resented him being the center of everything and me being...less important. I started thinking of him as Saint Stephen, and I was determined to be what he wasn't. I wasn't the heir. I could do what I wanted."

"You thought no one cared what you did."

He didn't look at her, but she took his silence for agreement. He was quiet for so long Gabi thought that was going to be the end of the story.

Finally he sniffed and rolled his shoulders. "He found

me one day, in my London flat, still high on drugs and booze. I'd promised him I'd stop and it had lasted two whole days before I scored again. Stephen came in, put me in the shower, cleaned up my flat and took me to rehab. He was with me every step of the way. And so was my father. When I was clean, my father offered me a job at Aurora. Put his faith in me even though I didn't deserve it. There was only one way I could repay both of them. I had to live up to their faith in me because I loved them, too."

Tears had sprung into Gabi's eyes as William told the story. "Addiction is a terrible thing."

"Getting clean has been the hardest and best thing I've ever done. I told you before that I can't repay my father. That's true. He's gone now." His voice was thick with emotion, and Gabi realized he was still grieving, too. "But it's also the reason why I have been so determined to make this right for Stephen. He saved my life. Saved me from myself. I owe him everything."

She paused, tugging on his hand. "So this thing between you and me, this 'back and forth, ignore it most of the time and acknowledge it occasionally' attraction, it's eating at you because of your loyalty to Stephen."

"Exactly."

"And it eats at me because of my father, and the company. Because that's where my allegiance lies."

"It's damned inconvenient, isn't it?"

But he wasn't scowling this time, not like he'd been in France.

"I really am sorry about that photo on the bench."

"I wasn't really angry at you, Gabi. I was angry at myself."

"I know."

The soft admission swirled around them. It had been barely over a week and already she felt she knew him better than she'd ever known his brother. She looked up into his eyes and melted a little. "This is going to sound awful and complicated and a million other things, but I really wish I could kiss you again, Will."

He drifted closer, his head blocking the sun from blazing onto her face. Instead it created a halo around his hair. She wanted to run her fingers into it, pull his face down to hers. But she wouldn't. She'd issued the invitation. She'd let him decide if he wanted to take her up on it.

"You shouldn't say things like that."

"It's very inadvisable. And I just finished telling myself I was done with wrong decisions." Her voice was barely a whisper. Somewhere in the olive groves birds sang, and she faintly registered their lilting song, but her sense of touch was overriding everything, making her attuned to his every move and breath.

"And I'd be a wrong decision."

"After what you just told me? Don't you think so?"

"A kiss," he said, his voice uncertain. "That's all we're talking about here."

"There are no photographers," she whispered. "No one will know."

"I'll know," he answered, even closer now, so close she was dying to close the gap and press herself against his strong chest.

"Then it'll be our little secret."

"Damn you."

His hand curled around her neck, but not in anger and frustration as it had the last time. This time it was a caress, a strong, yet tender touch as his fingers slid beneath her hair to press against the muscles of her neck. Before she could think, she tilted her head into his touch, her eyes drifting closed as the sun washed over her face. The light was gone again as he followed her movements, touching his lips to hers.

At the moment of contact, her mouth followed his lead, like a sunflower arching to the morning sun. *Girasole*, she thought, opening her mouth wider beneath his, letting the kiss blossom and grow. She was the flower, he was the sun, and she couldn't get enough of his light and warmth.

"Gabi," he whispered, then trailed his lips from her mouth to her jaw, and then back to the sensitive spot just below her earlobe. "You taste so good, Gabi."

Every single nerve ending in her body was alive. "Mmm," she answered, stretching into the contact. "You feel good. You're warm and hard and…" She couldn't finish the thought. His mouth skittered over the tender skin of her neck and she gasped. "Will," she murmured, turning fully into his arms, and they kissed again, a little wilder now.

He walked her backward until she stumbled a little, and then he did the most amazing and surprising thing. He lifted her against him so that her feet dangled inches off the ground, and carried her to the shade of an olive tree. The bark was warm and hard beneath her back, providing a bolster as Will pressed close again. Not close enough. Never enough. But enough for now. It had to be.

He kissed her for long minutes, until it seemed their control hung by a mere thread. He'd unbuttoned the top of her dress and kissed his way to her cleavage, though he'd stopped at her lace bra, much to her relief and disappointment. Her hair was a mess from rubbing against the tree trunk, and she was sure she had whisker burn down her jaw and neck. The simple cotton skirt she wore had stayed in place, but the thin material had done little to hide his desire.

And Gabi had explored, too. Her fingers had skimmed up his ribs and then pulled his shirt out of his jeans so she could explore the warm, hard body beneath. She'd splayed her hands over his back and shoulder blades, pulling him close, wanting things she had no right to want. She was on fire and didn't care. Nothing could have prepared her for this. Everything was different from anything she'd ever known. Chemistry, sure. But more than that. There was a connection between them that went deeper than attraction.

"We need to stop," he murmured, stilling his hands on her arms. "Gabi, we need to stop now."

"I know." Her breath caught as she tried to slow it. "Will, this is so complicated...what I said back in Provence..."

His golden gaze clung to hers. "You needed to come home. I understand. And you played your cards to get here. I respect that, too, even though it meant I didn't get my own way."

"It's going to be okay, though, right?"

He lifted his hand and brushed a finger over her cheek. "I want to say yes, but this is too..." He growled. "It's such a damned mess. If only it had been anyone but you."

"If only I'd met you first..."

He reached down and gripped her fingers tightly. "Don't say that. We have to focus on doing the right thing here."

Her heart hammered as her chest rose and fell with breathlessness. She knew what he meant—minimizing the fallout from the wedding, and to secure Baresi Textiles to the benefit of both companies. He was right, but that didn't address the very real problem of them. "And what about us?"

He looked away and his jaw tightened. "Gabi, I don't see how there can be an us. It would be better if we could be friends. And business associates." He swallowed tightly and his gaze touched hers again. "We leave sex out of it."

Sex. For a flash of a moment that word pulsed through her, leaving an indelible impression of what that glorious event might be like. Sex with Will. Desire flooded her body but she tamped it down ruthlessly.

She stepped away from the trunk of the olive tree and heaved a sigh that was full of frustration and resignation.

"Even if I know you're right, I don't have to like it." Gabi kicked at a small rock with her toe. "I have such a talent for meeting men at the exact time they're unavailable."

William chuckled a bit, relieving some of the tension around them. "Everyone has a skill," he said, and she couldn't help but laugh despite herself.

"I'd like to develop a different one." She lifted her chin. "So what, we go back to the villa and that's it, friends only?"

"I think we have to. For everyone's sake, including ours. It's messy, but I also don't want to hurt you, and I think I could."

She wondered if she could hurt him. She doubted it. And that alone was reason enough to walk away. Her eyes burned with regret and sadness. "We should get back, then."

"Can I kiss you once more?" His eyes pleaded with her. "I don't want the last time to be, well, the last time. One more to take away with me."

Torture. This was torture of the sweetest kind.

She lifted her face and opened her lips slightly. "One more."

He cradled her face in his hands and kissed her with such gentleness she wasn't sure what to do with all the feelings that crowded her heart. Why did it have to be this way? Why did the perfect guy have to show up now and be completely unavailable? Why did he have to be so damned ethical and loyal?

He pulled away, leaving her empty and bereft. Without speaking, and now without holding hands, they made their way back toward the villa, where her parents and sister waited. The day after tomorrow Stephen would arrive. The day after that her father would have his surgery. And then the Pemberton brothers would walk out of her life forever.

CHAPTER SEVEN

WILLIAM COULDN'T REMEMBER the last time he'd had such a wonderful meal.

It wasn't just the food, though that was spectacular. The chicken was to die for, and he sopped up the sauce with the most amazing bread. Then there was almond cake for dessert, and the most delicious wine to go with it all. But the real wonderfulness was in spending time with the Baresi family.

Giulia's boyfriend, Marco, was there, so the table rounded out at six. It was clear he'd been close to the family for a while, and Will grinned at how he teased Lucia and made her laugh and how he'd wink at Giulia and make her blush. Despite his illness, Massimo's laugh was big and booming, and Will could tell they were a family who enjoyed being together.

The Pembertons were like that as well, but it had been different since his father's death. Not so much laughter. An empty spot at the table when they were all together. Cedric had died and taken a lot of the family joy with him. Will had missed it, he realized. And if anything happened to Massimo, the Baresi family wouldn't be the same, either.

He pushed away his plate and looked across the table at Gabi. She was smiling and watching her family, too, and her gaze slid to William's and held. She was thinking the same thing, wasn't she? She loved them so much. Perhaps her agreement with his brother had been impulsive, but he still believed she'd done it for her family. She'd do anything for them.

Massimo laughed and her gaze was diverted for a moment, but when she looked back again, he saw the certainty in her eyes. Even without help from Aurora, Inc., Gabi would do whatever she could to keep the business going. She had that kind of burning passion inside her, didn't she? He should know. He'd had to turn it away earlier in order to do the right thing.

Stephen was an idiot.

When dinner was over, he pulled Gabi aside. "Tomorrow, I think we should meet to discuss Baresi's current situation and go over the notes I made. When Stephen arrives, I want to present him with a plan he can't say no to. One that will keep Baresi profitable and stable, enable your father to take the time off to have the treatment he needs, and that also benefits Aurora."

"One that keeps the majority of ownership in our hands?" she asked.

"That's never been a question. Of course. I want Aurora to invest in it. And I want you to be able to use our resources so you're not trying to do this alone, Gabi, but you would still have control."

"All right. Tomorrow morning, after breakfast."

He nodded.

"We should join the others." The family had taken drinks out to the patio, where the breeze was refreshing, and Gabi turned on her heel and walked away. William followed her outside and took a seat with everyone else. But his earlier joy had dissipated. Gabi had followed his guidance impeccably—friends, business, but no intimacy at all. It was what he wanted, and what had to happen.

But it left him distinctly unsatisfied, because his heart didn't always follow logic a hundred percent. After this afternoon, his heart wanted more. He was dangerously close to falling for her, and he wasn't entirely sure it wasn't because she was supposed to be off-limits. Worse, he knew she could be a huge distraction, when he'd carefully built a new life and wanted to keep on the right course. All in all, Gabriella Baresi did not fit into his life.

So he stared into his cup and frowned, and after a few minutes, excused himself to go back up to his room.

Gabi wasn't sure what to expect when she saw Stephen again, and her chest was cramped as anxiety took hold on Tuesday morning. He was scheduled to arrive around eleven. The last time she'd seen him, the last time they'd spoken, was the night before the non-wedding.

Will had been the buffer all this time. She hadn't even had to speak to Stephen on the phone. And today Will had offered to be there for her first meeting with his brother. But Gabi said no. She had to face Stephen on her own, if she were to have any self-respect and any agency with him at all.

Besides, she and Stephen had been friends. Their friendship demanded she be honest and up front with him, and not hide behind his brother. It wasn't fair to put Will in the middle any more than he already was.

Ever punctual, Gabi saw the cloud of dust announcing Stephen's arrival at precisely seven minutes to eleven. Her stomach was in knots. Will had agreed to remain upstairs until Gabi had a chance to talk to Stephen, and Giulia had gone to work. That left her parents, and the awkward realization that they still thought that Gabi and Stephen were going to set a new date. Things had been easy between her and Stephen before. She hoped they wouldn't be overtly awkward now.

Oh, *mea culpa*.

Stephen parked his rental and she stepped to the doorway, feeling as if she might throw up. What a stir she'd caused. And now he'd come all the way out here. There was no way he was happy about it.

When he stepped out of the car she remembered how different he was from Will. Only slightly taller, but with darker hair, darker eyes and a squarer jaw. When he smiled he epitomized tall, dark and handsome. But right now he wasn't smiling. He wasn't really showing any emotion at all as he looked at her. Then he shut the door and stepped around the hood to approach the house, and his mouth softened the smallest bit.

"Gabriella."

"Hello, Stephen." Always Stephen. Never Steve. Or any other endearment. That just occurred to her now, and yet in a short amount of time she'd found herself shortening William to Will…in her head, and sometimes that's what came out of her mouth, too.

He leaned in and they bussed cheeks. "Do your parents know?" he murmured, before pulling away.

She met his gaze, her stomach quaking. "No," she whispered.

His dark eyes cooled. "So they think we're still engaged."

Gabi swallowed against a growing lump in her throat. "Y-yes. Are you able to…you know…pull that off?"

He smiled then, warm and lovely. "My dear Gabriella, I've spent a lifetime smiling at people I don't know or don't like. It won't be a problem. The bigger question is, will you be able to act like a convincing fiancée?"

She wanted to weep. His words were delivered with a smile but were so sharp and cutting. "Stephen, we were friends, remember? I'd like us to stay friends."

"You left me at the altar," he said quietly. "I deserved better."

She held her tongue because, first of all, he was right. And secondly, she desperately wanted to call him out on insisting on the marriage in the first place, but right now she needed him on her side. Tonight her father would be admitted into the hospital. Later tomorrow he'd have surgery. The question of the company needed to be settled.

"Let's not talk out here. Come inside to the library where we can have some privacy."

They entered the house and right away her mother was there, greeting Stephen, offering refreshment. He switched on the charm and accepted a drink of something cold; Massimo came forward to shake his hand and the two spoke warmly. It couldn't all be an act, could it? Stephen was angry with her but he'd always been so great to her parents. When Massimo mentioned how good it was for him to be here for Gabi while he had his operation, Gabi wanted to choke. She didn't want solace from Stephen, not anymore. But she'd love to have William beside her, she realized. How things had changed in such a short time.

After pleasantries, Gabi led him into the small library, which was really a home office with several bookshelves. She shut the door and let out a breath. "Thank you."

"I have no problem with your parents, Gabi. They're innocent in all this."

"But I'm not."

"No, you're not." He put his glass down on a table and turned to face her. "If you were going to bolt, why the hell did you say yes in the first place?"

It was hard to breathe, but she had to own up to everything. "Because I wanted security for my family. Because we were friends and I trusted you. And because I'd had my heart broken and my dreams shattered and I thought I could have what I wanted without the messiness of being in love."

His mouth dropped open. "What?"

It was the thing she'd confessed to William, but hadn't to her own fiancé. "I loved someone, Stephen. I thought I was pregnant and while the timing wasn't great, I was happy. I want a partner and babies. When I told him about it, he was so angry. You see, he was already married. Thank God the test was negative."

Stephen ran his hand through his hair and shook his head. "Why didn't you tell me this?"

"I was afraid. And at the time I was really focusing on Baresi and doing what I had to in order for us to weather my father's illness."

When he said nothing, she spoke again. "Our motivations were the same, weren't they? You'd had your heart broken, too. You wanted to put your mother's mind at ease. Give her something positive after your father's death. I don't blame you for that."

His gaze sharpened. "But you do blame me for something, don't you?"

Heat rushed to her face. "What good does blame do? You have every right to be angry with me. In the end I couldn't go through with it, and I ran. I panicked. I caused a great deal of…inconvenience. And I'm sorry for that. I truly am."

"You're sorry."

"Yes! And wanted to tell you that in person."

Stephen was quiet for several moments. He picked up his glass and drank again, then wandered around the room, glancing at shelves, making Gabi more nervous by the second. What was he thinking? Why wasn't he saying anything?

When she was ready to burst, he turned back to her. "But that's not why I'm here, is it? For apologies?"

She bit down on her lip, considering her response. "I know you were hurt before, and I'm sorry that I added to it by my actions."

His nostrils flared, the only outward sign that her words had hit some sort of sore spot. "Don't worry, Gabriella. We both know this wasn't going to be a real marriage, with love and hearts and flowers. You didn't hurt me."

Maybe not. But she'd caused him great embarrassment, and she sensed that was almost as bad. Maybe worse. Feelings you could hide away from the world. Public humiliation was out there for all to see. And, in his case, comment on incessantly.

He stepped closer. "So I'll ask you again, Gabi. Why am I really here? It's not to make amends. I know that. Particularly since it wasn't you who invited me. It was Will."

Her annoyance came bubbling up and she spoke before she could think better of it. "Would you have taken my call?"

"Probably not. Will seems to think that Aurora should still invest in Baresi. I disagree."

Cold ran down her body. She hadn't thought this would be an easy meeting, but she hadn't expected a downright refusal. "Please," she whispered, "don't punish my father because of what I did."

"I like your father. But this is business, *cara*."

The way he said the endearment made her want to slap his face. "This is not business. This is taking it out on me. Punishing me."

He shrugged and her temper flared again. "A shrug? That's your answer? Doing business with Baresi is good for Aurora and you know it! Making a deal wouldn't have been any sacrifice on your part, just the opposite. But you tacked on the condition of marriage as a way of 'helping each other.' That isn't business. That's personal. And you're making it personal again now."

He was silent again. How could he do that? How could he stay so calm and implacable?

"Well," he finally said, drawing out the word for emphasis, "I'm the head of acquisitions. So it doesn't matter if it's personal or not. I still have to sign off on it. Our contract with Baresi remains the same, don't worry. I'm not canceling it. I'm just not furthering our investments."

For a moment, it felt to Gabi as if her heart stopped. Baresi was struggling; not in danger of closing its doors—yet—but the last few years had been difficult. No one knew the business better than her father. But his surgery, recovery and then rounds of chemotherapy meant he'd be out of the office for months. They couldn't afford a further decline. And Gabi would do her level best, but if anything happened to Baresi Textiles, how would her parents live? Papa wasn't old, but he wasn't a young man, either. He and Mama needed to be thinking about working less and enjoying each other more.

The cold knot settled in her gut. "So that's it, then," she said, taking a step back. "I've ruined everything." She was angrier than she could ever remember being in her life. "Because I couldn't go through with a sham marriage. I thought we were friends. I see how wrong I was."

She turned to walk away, and had almost reached the door when he called out, "What are you going to tell your parents?"

"I don't know. I'm not going to cause Papa any more worry today, not when he has surgery tomorrow. But don't worry, Stephen, I'll figure it out. I'll figure it all out."

She swept out of the room, biting her lip so hard she thought it might bleed. Then she went straight for the stairs.

She couldn't talk to her parents like this. She had to get herself together. And William needed to speak to Stephen, too.

Will's door was shut and she knocked quietly. There were footsteps, then he opened the door and his face blanked with shock. "What the hell did he say? You look ready to commit murder."

"I need to calm down and I don't want to rant at you because he's your brother and you love him. So please, go speak to him about whatever you need to and leave me here to calm down."

"You asked him about the deal and he said no, didn't he?"

"He said a lot more, too. He's very angry at me, Will. And I'm very angry at me. I put myself in this position and now my family is being punished for it. Please, let me lick my wounds in private."

He nodded, but as he moved past her in the doorway, he squeezed her hand. "Wait here. I'll come back and we'll talk."

"All right."

He left and she shut the door quietly, then went to the chair he'd been sitting in and sank into it. He'd left his phone, and his laptop was on a small table, still open. He really did trust her, she realized. While she hadn't always liked Will's decisions or attitude, she could say this for him: he'd always been honest with her. Always.

He'd always displayed impeccable integrity and loyalty. But then, so had Stephen, or so she thought. Was she being foolish, trusting Will?

She leaned her head back against the chair and sniffled. She didn't know what to say to her father. He'd been so happy when she'd announced her engagement. "I know he'll make sure everything is all right," Massimo had said. "He'll look after you." And in looking after her, Massimo had known that Stephen would ensure nothing would happen to Baresi. That was all gone now.

Her father had trusted him, too, because she'd let him. Maybe it was time to stop being angry at Stephen and take responsibility for her part in it. And that meant coming clean with her parents.

The timing sucked. But if anything happened to her father tomorrow, she didn't want their last words to be based on a lie.

CHAPTER EIGHT

WILL STARED AT his brother. "So your answer is no. Even though I've given you the numbers that prove this could be profitable for us, and not an act of charity. And by the way, even if it were an act of charity, it would be the right thing. Aurora has done business with Baresi for over two decades."

"My answer is no."

"Because of your pride."

Stephen stared at William for a long moment. "Why do you care so much?"

Will struggled to keep his face schooled. What he felt for Gabi wasn't any of his brother's business, especially since it wasn't going to go anywhere. "Because she's a nice woman who got caught up in a lot of stuff. Because she did the right thing in the wrong way, and now you're making a point of punishing her entire family for it."

Stephen's expression darkened. "What do you mean?"

Will met his brother's eyes and unease slid through his gut. In four years, he'd never really been at odds with Stephen. To be so now hurt, and he still very much felt like the younger, less wise brother. And yet he knew, deep down, that Stephen was wrong.

"You know I love you. But I can't pretend that this whole arrangement was okay. I told you that at the beginning. I admire her for not going through with it. It shows an integrity that you didn't, Stephen. And yes, she could have done it differently and caused less fuss. But you're punishing her for doing the right thing."

"Oh, my God. You love her." Stephen cursed and wiped a hand over his face. "Ten days. Has it even been ten days? And she's wrapped you around her little finger."

Will tamped down his anger. "My loyalty is with you, Stephen. It always will be. It doesn't mean I always have to agree with you. You told me when I screwed up. Well, you screwed up this time. Do the right thing here. Buy an interest in Baresi. It's right for Aurora."

"I'm heading back to Rome, and then home. And, William? Don't issue an order for me again."

Will's heart lurched, hating that their relationship was suffering, and yet certain in his gut that his motives were in the right place. "If that's the way you want it."

"It is."

"Fine. I'll handle everything here."

Stephen laughed bitterly. "There's nothing to handle."

Will went to the library door and held it open for his brother. His disappointment was profound. It was so unlike Stephen to be petty and mean. William had to believe that it was pain and pride wrapped up into one.

"If you think that," Will said quietly, "I'm disappointed in you." And just like that, their roles were reversed.

Stephen stopped at the door and met Will's gaze. "Don't lecture me, little brother."

Then he left—straight down the hallway and out the front door, without saying goodbye to anyone. Why had he even come?

William wasn't just mad. He was horribly, horribly disappointed in his brother.

Lucia came to the library door. "William? Has Stephen left? Did Gabi go with him?"

"No, Mama." Gabi's steady voice sounded behind her

mother, and Will looked over Lucia's shoulder to catch Gabi's gaze. Her chin was set with a determined tilt and there was no biting down on her lip. Her eyes were dry. When she'd gone to his room, he'd thought her on the verge of tears. The woman in front of him was anything but.

"I don't understand." Lucia looked from Gabi to William and then back again.

"You will." She went forward and hugged Lucia tightly. "I need to talk to you and Papa. In the kitchen, okay?"

"All right," Lucia said, but her eyes were worried as she moved off to find Massimo.

Will looked down at Gabi. "Are you sure you want to do this?"

She nodded. "It's time I told the truth. There should be no lies between Papa and me tomorrow." Her gaze locked with his. "You do not have to be there for it, but I would appreciate the support if you want to give it. I understand if not. Stephen is your brother, and I know where your loyalties lie."

Will clenched his teeth. "I won't go behind my brother's back and go against his wishes. That's true. But I can certainly stand beside a friend when they do a difficult thing."

"You're a very decent human being," she murmured.

"I try to be. Stephen taught me that. That he's somehow forgotten hurts me. But I'll sit with you today. And tomorrow, too, if you want me to. I know it's going to be a long, rough day."

He didn't want to have to choose. In fact, he refused to. Being there for a friend during a difficult time should not be a crisis of loyalty. And if it was, he and Stephen were going to have even bigger words once Will was back in Paris.

Gabi sat at the table, with William beside her and her mother across from them. Massimo shuffled into the room and settled himself in a chair with a sigh, his jovial face tight with concern. Gabi met her father's gaze and said, "I'm sorry, Papa. It's time I told you and Mama the truth."

"It has to do with Stephen?"

"Yes, and me, and a foolish mistake that I'm going to make right. I haven't been honest with you, and I don't want there to be lies between us."

Their gazes held a long time, full of unsaid words. She knew he understood when he answered softly, "Me, either, *gattina*." Oh, how it hurt for them both to consider his mortality like this. He couldn't die. He just couldn't.

Will sat beside her and put his hand over hers for a brief moment. She was so glad he was here.

"Mama, Papa..." She looked at both of them and felt her heart in her throat. "I wasn't sick the day of the wedding. I ran away because I couldn't go through with it. The Pembertons made up my illness so there wouldn't be a scandal. Or as much of one, anyway."

Gabi had expected the shocked looks on their faces, so she carried on, since that was just the opening and not anywhere near the worst part. "The truth is, our engagement wasn't what it seemed. It was more of an...agreement."

Massimo and Lucia looked at each other, then back at Gabi. "You mean you were not in love with him," Lucia said, her voice low.

"No, Mama, I wasn't. And I'm not. We were friends. Or at least I thought we were. Now I'm not so sure." Her nose burned a little, but she wouldn't cry. She'd screwed up but Stephen had disappointed her, too. Maybe she was a horrible judge of character.

But then she looked over at Will and saw the reassurance in his eyes, and her confidence returned.

"But why?" Massimo asked. "Why would you agree to marry him if you didn't love him? Your mama and me...

oh, Gabriella. You were raised in a house where there was always love. Why would you settle for less?"

"I know, Papa, I know!" The words came out in a flood. "In the end, that was why I couldn't do it. I couldn't marry someone I didn't love, even if it meant having all the security in the world."

Massimo's face changed. "Security?"

"Papa." She reached across the table and took his hand. It was still so strong and warm, as it had always been. "I agreed to something I shouldn't have, and I'm sorry. Please listen before you get angry."

"I don't like the sound of this, Gabriella."

She sighed. "I know." Will's hand rested on her shoulder, giving her courage. She sent him a look of gratitude and then faced her father again.

"You know as well as I do that Baresi has been struggling. Not desperately, but the market has been tough and we've felt the pinch. I'm an accountant, Papa. I know how to read the sheets. Then, with your diagnosis, and the long treatment ahead of you...all I could see was a ship without a captain, no one to take the wheel. I started to fear for our financial situation, so when Stephen and I became friends, I might have told him a little of what we were facing. He was the one who came up with the plan, Papa, but he's not to blame. I considered it and agreed to it, which makes me just as guilty."

"What plan?"

The question was delivered with a sharpness that stole her breath. Still, she deserved her father's anger and disappointment and so told them everything.

Silence fell around the table when she was done. Lucia's mouth had dropped open and Massimo's brows were pulled together so tightly they nearly met above his nose.

She couldn't stand the silence so she carried on. "Papa...

Baresi is everything. I wanted to do this so the legacy wouldn't be threatened. But it was the wrong thing, and I couldn't do it."

"Thank God for that," Lucia murmured.

"Did you not trust me to make sure the company was in good hands?" Massimo asked, and it killed Gabi to hear the hurt in his voice.

"Of course I trust you! Papa, you have never let me down. I was just so scared. When the doctor said it was cancer, all I wanted to do was look after this for you. To make sure Baresi flourished so it would be waiting for you when you were better." Her eyes burned. "I was so afraid of messing up and not being up to this challenge. You put your faith in me to step in but I'm not sure I can do this."

Will's hand still rested on her shoulder and she reached up and clasped it briefly. "I'm sorry, Papa. I lost my head for a while and made some stupid decisions. But I've got it back on right now. Tomorrow you're going to have your operation and I'm going to make sure the company thrives, even without Aurora's backing. It's time for me to step up and I'll do everything in my power to make sure I don't let you down."

"*Gattina*, why did you not talk to me? To your mother? We would have worked through this together."

Lucia leaned forward. "You didn't have to take this all on yourself. We're a family."

"I thought you had enough to worry about. I didn't want to be a burden." She sniffed now, as relief at unloading the secret started to creep in. "Papa, I wasn't going to tell you the truth because I didn't want to upset you before your operation. But today I realized…it isn't right to have lies between us. I failed but I won't again, I promise."

Massimo's eyes softened. He got up from his chair and came around the table, and Gabi rose and went into his arms. His safe, warm, strong arms that had always been there for her since the day she was born. A bit weaker now, certainly, and she tried not to let the fear take over.

"Gabriella Angelica Baresi, you have not failed anyone. I believe in you. I should have told you this before, but I didn't want to add any pressure when you were planning a wedding." He laughed a little, and stepped back so he could look into her eyes. "You know I made all the necessary arrangements at the office for the month I am recovering. I also had papers drawn up. If anything does happen to me, Gabi, the company is yours. You might be a numbers woman, but you're smart and resourceful and you love what I've built. I trust you to look after your mother and sister. And I didn't tell you because I felt it would be a huge burden on your shoulders while you were on your way to marry Stephen."

"You said you were glad I'd be taken care of."

"It put my mind at ease. I knew if anything happened and you took over Baresi, Stephen would be able to look after *you*. I was never expecting him to look after my company. You might not have faith in yourself, but I have faith in you. And you could not let me down. Ever."

She put her shoulders back. "I can look after myself."

"She sure can." Will finally spoke.

Massimo looked over Gabi's shoulder. "And what's your part in all this? You're Stephen's brother. You said you were here to check on local business interests and to escort Gabi home until Stephen could join her. Clearly that's not true, either."

Will shook his head, but Gabi admired his calm. "No, it's not. Well, some of it's true. I did escort Gabi home, at my insistence, not hers. And I have been checking up on local interests. Baresi is one of them. Initially I took on the role of damage control after the wedding didn't happen. Giulia helped me find Gabi, and then we went to the family châ-teau in France to wait out the media storm. Over that time I've come to see how stupid my brother has been, both in suggesting such an arrangement and—"

It was if he'd suddenly realized he'd said something wrong. Will pursed his lips and frowned.

"And?" Lucia prodded him.

"And I like your daughter," he said, almost as if dar-ing them to defy him. "She's a good person who wanted nothing more than to take care of her family, and she was willing to do it at her own personal cost. While the idea was flawed, her loyalty and love were not. I presented my brother with a proposal to partner with Baresi, something that would benefit both you and Aurora. He turned it down, because of his pride. But if there is anything I can do to be of help, I will. I won't go against my family, but as I told Gabi before this conversation, I'm definitely willing to help a friend."

His gaze went to Gabi's. "And despite the unorthodox circumstances, I do believe we've become friends."

She nodded, overwhelmed by his speech. "Yes, we have. Thank you, Will."

"You're welcome."

Will looked up at Massimo. "*Signore*, if there is any-thing at all you need, I hope you will ask. My brother is head of acquisitions, but I'm the head of my division, and I'll do what I can to ensure Aurora's relationship with Baresi remains intact."

"I appreciate that."

"And your daughter can come to me at any time for help if she needs it." He glanced at Gabi and grinned, shoot-ing a dart of sunlight into her soul. "Though she probably won't. She's smart and she's stubborn. And hopefully she now knows that she's worth more than anyone has ever given her credit for."

Oh, dear heavens. It was like he'd been dropped, completely perfect, into her lap. Once again, she was reminded of the fact that she never seemed to meet the right guy at the right time. Either the timing was wrong or the man was. Having him on her side but not being with him was going to be torturous. And yet she wasn't in any position to turn him away. He was too valuable an ally, in business but mostly in friendship.

Gabi hugged her father again. "Are you angry with me, Papa?"

He chuckled. "I don't know what to say. It seems so unreal and... I don't know. But I'm not angry. I'm sorry you ever felt you needed to go to such lengths."

"I'd do anything for you, Papa. You know that."

"And I'd do the same for you, and your sister, and your mama." He squeezed her tight. "This isn't going to beat me. I'm going to fight it. So please don't worry."

She nodded against his chest. Why had she worried so much? Her father had always been willing to forgive any transgression. She shouldn't have taken this burden on alone.

"You should get some rest before you have to leave for the hospital. And I'm going to pack a bag. I'll be staying at my flat."

"I'll drive you," Will said. "I need to return the rental, anyway, and I want to make sure everyone is all right before I fly back to Paris."

Paris. Of course he would be leaving now. The tabloids had quieted, no one had come looking for her, and Will had to know by now that she had no intention of spilling the actual story to the press. Because he trusted her.

Oh, she was going to miss him.

"It looks as though everything is sorted," Lucia said. "Massimo and I are leaving around three."

"Mama, you can stay with me at my flat if you like."

Lucia shook her head. "*Grazie*, but I am going to stay with Zia Isabella. She lives closer to the hospital, and I haven't seen her in a while."

Will rose from his chair. "If that's the case, I should go upstairs and wrap up some business I was working on. Signor and Signora Baresi, thank you for your hospitality the past few days." He held out his hand to Massimo. "And the best of luck to you tomorrow."

"You are welcome here anytime," Massimo replied, shaking Will's hand.

He left and went toward the stairs, and Gabi waited until she heard his footsteps above her. Then she let out a huge breath.

Lucia looked at her with a crooked smile and a raised eyebrow. "Any hope there?" she asked. "Of the real kind?"

Gabi shook her head. "No. It's too messy." She met her mother's gaze. "But I'm a bit sorry about that."

She stood on tiptoe and kissed her father's cheek. "I'll see you before you go," she said softly. "And again tomorrow at the hospital."

"*Ti amo, gattina,*" he said, kissing her cheek in return.

She escaped to the stairs before he could see the tears in her eyes. No one had ever loved her as unconditionally as her parents. They loved each other the same way.

Why had Gabi ever even considered that she could settle for anything less?

CHAPTER NINE

WILLIAM KNEW HE should hop on a plane and fly back to Paris. It would be the smart thing to do at this point, and it was what was expected. He'd had a sharply worded email from Stephen, and another from his mother that was less angry and more concerned. Why was he still in Italy? He should forget about Gabriella Baresi now that the media story seemed under control, and get back home and to work. The family, who'd congregated at the manor for the wedding, were now all back in either London or Paris for work, and he should be, too. According to Aurora Germain Pemberton, anyway.

But he couldn't leave yet. Not while Gabi was sitting with her mother and sister, waiting while Massimo was having surgery to have a section of his colon removed. Marco was there, too, and right now had gone to get coffee for everyone. Will found he quite liked the younger man, who seemed bright and energetic but now, at a serious time, stepped up and provided support for Giulia. According to Gabi, they'd been seeing each other off and on for some time, though it had only recently become a steady thing.

He went to the chairs in the waiting area and sat down beside Gabi. "How're you holding up?"

"Okay. It's taking so long."

He knew. The surgeon had estimated the surgery to take about ninety minutes, and then of course Massimo would be taken to recovery. But it was already five in the afternoon. It had been three hours already, and no doctor, no word.

Of course everyone was thinking the worst. Were there complications? More cancer than they realized? Had it spread?

Will's father had died suddenly, from a heart attack. There'd been no waiting around for results, no hope. One minute Cedric had been alive, then next he was gone. It had been excruciating, but watching the Baresi women worry, he wasn't sure this was a better alternative. He hoped that it all worked out right in the end, and Massimo would be going home again.

Marco returned with coffee and a bag of pastries for everyone to share. "You need to eat something, Mama Lucia," he said, pressing a paper napkin and a sweet into her hand.

"*Grazie*, Marco," she whispered, but Will saw that her face was pale and her eyes dull with worry.

Will leaned over and whispered in Gabi's ear. "Eat one, and maybe your mother will, too."

She nodded, then looked up at Marco. "I'll have one, thank you."

Giulia rose and put her arms around Marco's waist. "Thank you for being here with us."

"I wouldn't be anywhere else, *cara*."

Gabi nibbled on her bun and Will sat back, sipping on strong coffee, wishing the doctors would hurry up.

Gabi had been a wreck. Not outwardly, of course, but he'd noticed how quiet she'd been. Last night, after Lucia and Massimo had left for the hospital, she'd barely eaten. Instead she'd gone into the library to work for a while, she'd said. Giulia had come home and they'd spoken for a bit, and Will had been the one to venture into the kitchen and throw something together for dinner and make sure she ate. It was the same this morning, before they'd left for Perugia.

He'd made sure she'd eaten breakfast so she had something in her stomach to get her through the day.

He knew how he'd feel if this were his mother, or any of his siblings. He'd be sick with worry and waiting. So he sat beside her and when she tilted her neck to release tension, he put his hand on her back and gently rubbed, trying to help ease the muscles.

"I'm glad you're here," she murmured.

"Me, too. I could have flown back today but I would have worried the whole time." He tried a smile. "Who would have thought that I'd stick around for moral support, huh?"

She smiled back. "When I opened that hotel room door in London and you were there, you looked ready to kill."

"I was angry."

"You had a right to be."

"I wasn't angry for long. I think I stopped about the time you fell asleep on the plane."

"I wanted to be angry with you, too, but I knew you were trying to help. It was a lot of hating you for bossing me around and knowing I deserved it because it was my fault."

He nodded, then started to chuckle a bit. "It was a pretty unorthodox way to get to know each other. But…" He looked up at her and the connection between them was strong and sure. "I don't regret it. Not a moment."

"Me, either. I appreciate you trying to help with Stephen, too. But don't worry about Baresi. I'm going to figure everything out."

"I know you will. Now eat. You need something since you refused lunch."

The coffee was gone and the pastries half-eaten and discarded when finally, finally, the doctor came through the doors toward the family.

Everyone stood together.

"The surgery went well, though not without complication," he said, not mincing any words. "The tumor was a bit bigger than we anticipated, and Signor Baresi had some bleeding that we needed to get under control, which extended the length of the surgery. We removed lymph nodes that we'll send for testing to see if the cancer has spread."

The family seemed to be collectively holding their breath.

"But overall it was a success. He'll be in recovery for some time, and access is restricted."

"The bleeding…was it serious?"

The surgeon looked at Giulia, who'd asked the question. "Serious enough, but he's a strong man and healthy for his age. I don't anticipate further postoperative problems, but we'll wait and see."

He looked at the rest of the group. "He's going to be on some pretty strong pain medication. It'd be better for you to try to see him tomorrow. I understand you'll want to wait to see him, though, Signora Baresi."

He said his goodbyes and left. Will sensed the collective relief of the family as if they had all let out a giant breath. "Well, that's good news," he said, and he looked over at Gabi. She looked ready to drop, so he put his arm around her shoulders and pulled her to his side. "First hurdle over, yes?"

She nodded, and he saw she was blinking quickly. His heart melted a little and he turned her into his arms. "It's okay now," he said gently, rubbing her back. "He made it through the surgery. You can breathe again."

He looked over and saw Marco holding Giulia's hand and Lucia watching William and Gabi with tenderness lining her face. His feelings were so transparent, weren't they? He really did need to get back to Paris, before he did something foolish.

But not tonight. Right now Gabi was crying softly into his chest and he would make sure she was all right and that Massimo got through the night okay. As long as everything went well, William would be on a flight from Rome to Paris tomorrow afternoon, back in his flat tomorrow night and in the office on Thursday.

It sounded horrid and dull, and he rather suspected it was because she wouldn't be there.

"Come, now," he said softly, rubbing her shoulder. "It's all right. Your mama is going to stay and be with him when he's awake. You need some food and some rest."

She nodded against him, and lifted her chin as she pulled away. "Sorry. I think the relief hit me."

"It's no problem."

Gabi looked at her sister and said, "Do you and Marco want to stay at my flat tonight? I have room."

Giulia looked at Marco, and then back at Gabi. "Marco and I are going to drive home. But we'll be back tomorrow. The drive isn't that long. Call if there's anything..." Her lip quivered. "You know."

Marco nodded. "I'll have her back here in no time."

"Whatever you want," Gabi said. "Mama?"

"I'm staying with your father, but I'll go to Isabella's later."

"Promise you'll take care of yourself. I can stay with you..."

"No," Lucia said firmly. "Will is right. I bet you hardly slept last night. Go home. You're only minutes away and I will call if there's a change. But I am fine, I promise. Now that he's through the surgery, I'm fine." She smiled tiredly. "Now we fight."

"Oh, Mama, I love you," Gabi said, and she went for a hug.

Will waited while everyone said their goodbyes, and

told Lucia to give Massimo their love. By the time they finally left the hospital, it was nearly eight p.m. Will had awakened at six that morning and had heard Gabi already up and about. She had to be ready to drop by now.

"Let's get you home, and then I'll head to a hotel," he said. "You need sleep."

Gabi looked up at him and shook her head. "You don't need a hotel. I have a spare room. You can stay with me, and go straight to the airport tomorrow. If you want to."

And just like that she'd put the decision on him. He knew what he wanted and knew what he should do and they weren't the same thing at all. Sleeping in her spare room, knowing she was there, too, in a bed alone, was a torturous thought. Going to a lonely hotel was no better.

"Let's get you home first and maybe some actual dinner, and then we'll see."

Once outside she took a deep breath and let it out, as if shaking off the weight of the world. She rolled her shoulders a bit. "Do you want me to drive?" she asked. "I know the city. My flat is about ten minutes away."

"Sure, if you want to." He dug in his pocket for the keys, and before long Gabi was behind the wheel, navigating her way out of the hospital and through the city streets.

It seemed no time at all before she pulled up in front of a building and parked on the street. "This is me," she said, looking up at a nondescript three-story building with affection. "My flat is the top two floors. I got lucky with it. The neighborhood is quiet and lovely, and it's a nice walk to the historic center. The offices are on the other side of the city, so I drive or take transit. But I fell in love with this place and I've lived here for four years, ever since I started working at Baresi."

He got out and started to open the back door for his bag, when she said, "No, wait. Before we go up, I need food. I haven't been home in weeks. The cupboard is most definitely bare and there's nothing in the refrigerator. Leave your bag. We'll only be a few minutes."

It was only a short walk to a street with a smattering of cafés, a few markets and one pizzeria that smelled heavenly. "You can get pizza if you want," she said, "but my favorite thing of all is their *porchetta* sandwiches. Let's get the basics first and come back."

At the market they stocked up on coffee, bread, butter and, at Will's insistence, eggs. "I'm dying for a mess of eggs," he confessed. "I could make you an omelet. I need cheese, and good ham—"

"You're in the right part of Italy for good ham," she replied, and their basket got fuller. Tomatoes and mushrooms followed, and Gabi insisted on truffles, and then there was wine. By the time they paid, they were both carrying two bags each.

"Now for sandwiches," she said, and they popped into the pizzeria. Will stood back while she talked and joked in Italian with the young man behind the counter. He could only pick up a few words, because they were speaking so fast, but he didn't mind. Gabi's face was relaxed and animated. She'd needed to come home, he realized. Not just to the villa but to the home she'd made for herself. For the first time, he felt like he was finally seeing the real Gabi, and he liked her even more. This was her neighborhood and these were her people. They knew her and liked her. A young woman, very pregnant, came around the counter and gave her a hug. Will picked up enough Italian to know she asked about Massimo, and Gabi answered briefly.

The young man handed over a bag of sandwiches and then a separate bag with a wink. When Gabi protested, he waved his hands and walked away. *"Grazie!"* she called out, and then they were headed to the door again.

"What's in the other bag?" Will asked as they stepped outside again.

"Tiramisu that Bianca made this morning. Bianca is his wife. Expecting their third baby any day now. I probably eat there more than I should, but…"

He nudged her elbow. "They're your friends. It's lovely. Remember that curry place I told you about? I felt the same way. I walked in and it felt like being welcomed into their family."

"It's nice, isn't it?"

"Very."

They were already back at her door. "Let's take this up first, and come back for the bags."

He followed her up the stairs to the third floor. There was no elevator, but he didn't mind. She unlocked her door and they stepped inside. It was hot; the windows had been shut up while she was gone, and as soon as she put her bags on the counter, she went to the French doors and opened them to reveal a small balcony. Fresh air rushed into the flat. "Phew, that's better," she said. "It's stuffy in here."

It was lovely. He remembered she'd said the flat was two floors. What he could see was a small but well-equipped kitchen, an airy living space with a sofa and two chairs and a small powder room off to one side. "How many bedrooms?" he asked, curious. It was really quite a lovely space.

"Two," she replied, opening the refrigerator. She put the tiramisu inside, and then started to put away the perishables from the market. "I have the extra for Giulia or Mama and Papa."

"Your father…he commutes?"

"Yes. But the offices are closer to the villa than we are now."

"They sold the house in town for financial reasons, right?"

Gabi paused and met his gaze. "Yes. Not as an emergency, but as a way of…streamlining. But I can't be sorry they kept the villa. It will always be the first place I think of when I think of home."

He wiggled his fingers for the keys. "You do this, and I'll get the bags. I'm starving."

She nodded and handed them over. Will jogged down the stairs and retrieved their bags. Gabi's suitcase was huge, and by the time he reached the top he was breathing heavily.

Gabi laughed at him when he stepped inside, and he grinned. "What do you have in here, bricks?"

"It's what I had at Chatsworth and what I was taking on my honeymoon. I really don't keep my things at the villa. Here, sit down outside and I'll bring you the best sandwich you've ever eaten."

He was expecting wine, since she seemed to prefer it, so he was surprised when she brought the sandwich on a plate and a cold beer to drink.

It was perfect in its simplicity. Crusty bread, sliced pork…and nothing else. But the *porchetta* was like nothing he'd ever eaten. There were flavors of rosemary and then the crispy skin and the tender flesh that all combined into something extraordinary.

"Oh. I get it now."

She grinned, the smile spreading from ear to ear. "See? I told you."

"This is amazing. How do you not eat this every day?"

She laughed. "I like vegetables. But I won't lie, I buy one of Gio's sandwiches once a week as a treat."

He took two more bites and the gnawing in his stomach started to ease. He sat back a bit and toyed with his beer bottle, and looked at the view. "This is incredible. You can see so much of the city from up here."

"I fell in love with it," she said quietly. "It was the view that sold me. I don't need a large place for just me, but I stepped out here and took a deep breath and that was it. It's an entirely different view, but it reminds me of looking down over the valley from the olive groves at the villa. It felt familiar, and I liked that."

"It's the feeling, not the actual view," he said, understanding. "It's how I feel in the orchard at the château."

"You mean at the bench where we…" She blushed a little and turned away. "You took me there on purpose, didn't you?"

"I needed the calm and I thought you did, too. Caused us some bother, though, didn't it?"

She laughed. "You know, if someone took a photo of us now, I don't think I'd mind as much as I did then."

He took another drink of beer, met her gaze and said, "Me, either."

They were quiet for long minutes, finishing their sandwiches, enjoying the solitude, not feeling compelled to make conversation. It was comfortable. Wonderful. William had never experienced anything like it in his life. Not with any of the women he'd dated or in any relationship. He'd always felt he had to be "on." Sparkling conversation. Endless charm. This being easy and comfortable with each other was new and he liked it. A lot.

Gabi got up, took their plates and went inside. When she came back, she had the dessert with her and two forks. He really didn't need sweets, but it looked too gorgeous to turn away.

Gabi tasted hers, then said, "So, I haven't asked you this before, but…there's no girlfriend, is there?"

His head lifted sharply. "What? No. Of course not. I wouldn't have…especially at the villa…if there were."

"I'm sorry. I didn't mean to offend you."

"You didn't. Surprised me, yes. But considering your

last relationship—Stephen not included—you have a right to ask."

"Do I? What right? We're friends. That's all."

He wasn't sure he was ready for this conversation. He should have flown home. Avoided this whole thing. Because he was probably going to have to lie to her, and he hated that. Still, after Stephen's abrupt departure, Will really didn't want to create a big rift in the family. Not when they were already fragmented by his father's death.

"Gabi...we both know this is more complicated than either of us like. Not just the situation, but...feelings." He was stopping and starting so much he figured he sounded like an idiot. "Maybe I should get a hotel for tonight."

Her eyes widened. "What if I don't want you to get a hotel?"

Her question surprised him. "What are you suggesting? We established that we were friends—"

"Even you can't fool yourself into believing that," she interrupted, twisting her fingers together on the tabletop. "This isn't easy for me, either. But tomorrow you are leaving. We both know it. You have a life to get back to, and Papa...he's through his surgery. I have a company to run and so do you. But tonight..."

She turned quite red as she chanced a look up at him. "Tonight you're here. And no one else is."

"Gabi..."

"If you don't want to, that's fine. We'll part as friends and that will be that. But if you do...want to, that is, I—I'm..." She was stuttering a bit now, nervous and insecure. She shouldn't be. He couldn't remember ever wanting a woman more.

"No one needs to know," she finished. "I mean, we can be discreet."

It felt like sneaking around, hiding things, when in reality he wished it were different and they could try being together. "And then what?" he asked, his voice hoarse. He didn't know why he was giving her a reason to change her mind, other than he wanted her to be very sure this was what she wanted.

He did. So very much. It wasn't just that she was beautiful, though she was. It was how she loved her family. How she stood up to Stephen. Even the warmth and grace with which she spoke to her neighbors. He liked her as a person, desired her as a woman.

"I don't want you to have any regrets," he said.

"My only regret would be letting you walk away tomorrow without taking this chance." Her voice was soft and rode over his nerve endings like silk. "It isn't just chemistry, Will. You're the right kind of man at the wrong time, but at least I might be able to keep the memory of a wonderful night."

"Gabi," he replied, knowing she would have her way. Why not, when it was what he wanted, too? He was tired of the heavy weight of his loyalty dragging him down. She was right. She was also the right kind of woman at the wrong time, and he wished with all his heart that he might have met her first. But he hadn't, and so if tonight was all they'd have, he'd make sure it was a memory worth keeping.

Were they being crazy? Reckless? Probably. Was it a bad thing? Maybe, maybe not. After their kisses against the olive tree, he'd known this was what he wanted. "Here," he said, tapping his lap. "I want to hold you in my arms and watch the sun disappear."

"Oh, Will…"

"We have time, Gabi. If this is our only night, I don't want to rush it."

Gabi perched on his knee, then leaned back against his shoulder. The evening air was cooling but Will was so perfectly warm. His right arm came around her, holding her in place. The light was soft as it touched the trees, gaps in the green tops punctuated by ancient buildings in the town's historic center.

This was her favorite place on a summer evening, and to share it with Will made it even more special.

He was so unexpected. So perfect. But she tried to imagine walking into a Pemberton family function on his arm and knew it was impossible. This really was all they had, and she wanted to soak in every precious second.

His fingers grazed down her arm, stroking back and forth, as she pointed out the general area of landmarks like the Arco Etrusco and the Piazza IV Novembre. How she wished she could keep him to herself for a few days, walk the cobbled streets, take him to the gallery. Show him the city she called home. An emptiness opened up inside, knowing it could never be what she wanted.

She couldn't think that way, not now. They must embrace and enjoy every moment they had together.

"Is it strange that just sitting like this is wonderful?" he murmured, his lips close to her ear.

Goose bumps rose on her arms at the warmth of his breath on her neck. "I was thinking the same thing. It's as close to perfect as I can think of right now."

He shifted, so her knees were over his lap and her arm was around his neck. "Gabi, these last two weeks—not even—have been the craziest and best I have ever had. How is that even possible?" He shook his head with wonder. "I was so angry with you, and then I admired you, and then I couldn't stop thinking about you."

"I know," she answered. "I feel the same. And I felt so wrong, too. Because you're Stephen's brother. I was supposed to be the problem and you were supposed to be the enemy, and honestly, after about twenty minutes I couldn't think of you that way."

"My brother's a damned fool."

"Let's make that the last time we mention your brother tonight, shall we?" She curled in closer. "Tonight is about you and me. Only you and me."

And then Gabi leaned forward and touched her lips to his, something they hadn't done since the olive grove.

He tasted like beer and hints of espresso and cream from the tiramisu, and a particular flavor that was just Will. His lips opened and invited her in, and she made a little noise of surrender as she pressed herself closer, looping her knees over the arm of the chair and wrapping her other hand around his neck. He leaned forward a little, bracing her back with one strong arm, and deepened the kiss.

And still he didn't hurry. Instead they took their time, kissing on her balcony, letting the lights of Perugia come on, blinking and twinkling as darkness settled.

His hand slid out of her hair and over her shoulder, then down over her breast.

"Mmm." She arched into his palm, loving the sensation. "That feels so good."

In response, his thumb flicked over her nipple, and she gasped into his mouth. "Will…"

"We should go inside, before we give your neighbors a free show," he suggested.

She knew he was right. Once inside, she led him through the flat to the stairs, and began the climb to her bedroom. The air was warmer as they approached the second floor, and once inside her bedroom, she went to the window, opening it wide to let in the cooling air.

"I'm sorry it's so warm," she apologized.

"Don't be. It'll be cooler with our clothes off." He grinned at her again, and she figured her whole body flushed at his suggestion. Goodness, she wasn't some green virgin. Why did he have the power to embarrass her so?

"Are you nervous, Gabriella?"

"A little."

"Me, too."

"Why are you nervous?" she asked.

"We may only have tonight," he said, "but it feels important, don't you think? I don't want to screw it up."

"Oh, Will. You couldn't. I promise." She went to him. "You're the most decent man I've ever met. You're handsome and sexy and kind and funny and you make me crazy. I want to touch you everywhere and have you touch me. I want you to kiss me like you never want to stop. I want you to make love to me, Will. Because I trust you. I trust you with me, and that isn't something that happens very often."

Especially not now, after living a lie for so long. But Will...he was different. She knew it deep inside, where it mattered.

He didn't answer. He gathered her in his arms for a passionate kiss that emptied her brain of anything but him. She fumbled with the buttons of his shirt; he pulled her top over her head, leaving her standing in her bra and trousers. Wordlessly she reached for the button and zip on her pants and let them drop to the floor, stepping out of them to stand before him in lacy peekaboo panties that matched the bra. His nostrils flared as he looked at her, his eyes glowing in the twilight of the room. Then he undid the button of his jeans and took them off, so he was standing in a pair of dark boxer briefs.

"Touch me, then," he invited, and she closed the distance between them in a nanosecond. His breath hissed as she pressed against him, skin to skin, and cupped him in her hand.

"God," he groaned. "I didn't expect that."

"I'm not shy," she replied, moving her hand. "I want all of this, Will. I want to give and I want to take. Oh, your skin is so warm." Her abdomen grazed his, and she marveled at the beautiful feeling of skin against skin. Was there anything sexier?

For a while they took their time exploring, touching here, kissing there, learning what the other liked, where the sensitive spots were. He reached behind her and unclasped her bra with one hand, and she wrapped her arms around his neck so that she was pressed firmly against him. She couldn't get enough of that feeling. There were no barriers between them, not physically and not emotionally, either. Gabi couldn't remember a time when she'd been this naked with someone. She'd been too afraid. Too worried about trying to be "right." She didn't worry about that with Will. He seemed to want her just as she was.

He scooped her up in his arms and carried her the short distance to the bed, then laid her down and stretched out beside her, on his side so that his left hand made trails over her breasts, her belly, the tiny bit of fabric between her legs. He braced his weight on his right arm and let his lips follow the path of his hand, until she wasn't sure how much more she could stand.

When she thought she might weep or else somehow come out of her skin with wanting, he shed his briefs and skimmed her panties down her legs. "In the drawer," she whispered, turning her head to look at the small stand beside the bed. "There should be a condom in there."

He opened the drawer and found the tiny foil packet. Then there was nothing holding them back. They met equally and enthusiastically. If Gabi were only going to have this one chance to be with him, she wanted to make it something to remember.

There was no particular rush; once Will paused and gripped the pillows beside her head, clenching his teeth. "Not yet," he ground out. "I want it to last."

"Mmm, me, too," she answered, but subtly moved her hips, teasing, tempting. She wasn't ready for it to be over, either, but there was something alluring about challenging his control.

"Minx," he growled, and the next thing she knew he had pulled out and slid down her body, taking revenge. She could hardly breathe as he loved her with his mouth, and she cried out, saying his name as she climaxed.

She was still sensitive and pulsing when he slid into her again, and this time he didn't hold back. Their skin grew slick in the heat, and she tasted salt under her tongue as she kissed his shoulder. A bead of sweat dropped from his forehead to her breast, and when he finally came, he growled out her full name—Gabriella—and held her gaze, making her heart tremble. It couldn't be more clear that they hadn't just made love but they'd made love to each other. It was more than sex and desire. To Gabi, it was as if all the missing pieces of her life clicked into place when she was in his arms.

And in a matter of hours he was walking away.

Will caught his breath, collapsing on the bed beside her. "Well, damn."

She laughed. "I was thinking the same thing."

"Give me a minute." He got up and disappeared into her bathroom, then came back again, stark naked.

Gabi rested on an elbow, admired him as he walked back to the bed and said, "Now that's a better view than the one from my balcony."

"I'm glad you think so."

"You're making fun of me."

"No, I'm just happy. Tonight I'm going to let myself be happy. Tomorrow is enough time to worry about…what I need to worry about."

"Cleaning up messes?"

He chuckled, lying down beside her so they were face-to-face. "This time I get to clean up my own mess. This wasn't supposed to happen."

"I know. None of it was, Will. Maybe I should be sorry, but I'm not."

"Me, either."

"I wish…" She halted, wondering if it was right to put what she was feeling into words, but knowing if she didn't she'd probably regret it. "I wish I had met you first. Your brother is angry with me right now, but I know he's a good man underneath. We didn't have this kind of connection, though."

"I'm glad." Will's face darkened. "It's selfish of me, I know. But I'm glad it wasn't like this with him. And yet…" He sighed. "This still feels like a betrayal."

"Because he's your brother. And even if I didn't break his heart, I hurt him just the same. And your loyalty is to family. I understand, you know. I do."

"I'm glad, because I'm not sure I understand."

She thought for a moment, then smiled softly. "I remember this American show I watched a few years ago, and they were talking about the 'bro code.' It was between best friends but I understood. There are just some things that you don't do to a friend or brother. I'm pretty sure this would qualify. So I do understand. I'm just going to miss you."

"I'm going to miss you, too." He traced a fingertip over her arm. The room was still warm, the summer air caressing their skin, and Gabi had no desire to get under the covers. Right now her legs were twined with Will's, her hand resting on his rib cage. There was nowhere else she would rather be.

He looked into her eyes. "Will you let me know how your father is?"

Why did he have to be so caring? Didn't he have any flaws whatsoever? For a moment she hesitated, a cold thought settling in her stomach. What if he wasn't this perfect? What if she was missing something?

"What is it?" he asked, frowning. "What's wrong?"

"Nothing," she answered, pushing the thought away. "And of course I'll let you know about Papa. It seems a little selfish that he's in the hospital tonight and we're here. Until this moment, I hadn't given him a thought."

"You're allowed a little time to yourself, you know. You've been worrying about him constantly."

"Would you mind if I checked my messages? He should be out of recovery by now."

"Of course."

She slid off the bed and grabbed a light robe from the back of her door before slipping into the kitchen and grabbing the phone off the counter. She pressed the button and it lit up in the dark. Sure enough, there was a text from her mother that she'd sent to both Gabi and Giulia.

Papa is awake and in his room. He is very groggy but doing well. Please get some sleep and we will see you tomorrow.

Get some sleep. Gabi thought of the man currently in her room and wondered if they'd sleep much at all. And even if they did, she knew she'd lie awake, wishing, wanting things she couldn't have.

But it didn't matter, anyway. The responsibility of Baresi was on her shoulders right now. That had to be her focus. Her personal life—what there was of it—could wait.

CHAPTER TEN

THE LAST THING Will wanted to do the next day was get on a plane and fly to Paris. But here he was, sitting in the airport in Rome, waiting for his flight, missing Gabi already.

Ten days. They'd spent ten days together and already his life felt permanently altered.

This morning had been torture. Oh, Gabi had put a good face on it. She'd made coffee while he'd cooked her an omelet, and they'd made love one last time before he'd jumped in her shower and dressed for the flight.

He'd left her at her door, both of them trying to smile, but he'd seen the brightness in her eyes as he'd prepared to say goodbye. It was amazing to him that she cared about him that much.

In the end he'd said nothing, just dropped a light kiss on her lips and turned to walk away, straight to the car. He'd had to get away, out of sight, so he'd driven three blocks before pulling over and setting up the GPS so he could find his way to the airport.

And if his eyes had been misty, too, then so be it. Maybe he was the guy who cleaned up the messes and lived on the straight and narrow these days, but he still had feelings, dammit. And he cared for her a lot. If fate was really a thing, it seemed a cruel joke that he met her too late.

For a while he'd wondered if the attraction had been because she was exactly the wrong person. In earlier years, he'd made those foolish decisions, and he'd caught himself at times over the last week and a half, wondering if he was falling into old patterns.

But he was not. It wasn't that Gabi was dangerous and risky, or that she fit some sort of rebellion against the family. Those days were gone. He cared about her because she was, quite simply, wonderful.

His flight was called and he went to the gate, then boarded and found his business-class seat. The in-flight Wi-Fi meant he could start catching up on the work emails he'd missed the past two days. He might as well get stuck in the thick of things. It was probably the best way to forget.

It was raining in Paris when he landed, and the car service took him from the airport to his apartment in the heart of the city. He loved Paris, perhaps even more than London, maybe because he'd spent so much time here as a child as his parents built Aurora, Inc., into the massive enterprise it was today. Even in the rain Paris was beautiful, with its shiny pavement and magical streets.

His apartment was a sprawling thing, with a wall of windows overlooking the river. He dropped his bag and went to the windows, looking out over the city he called home, and thought about all the times he had stood with Gabi in special places. In the lemon grove, on top of the hill at the villa, last night on her balcony. Places that reso-nated with them both, and he wished he could share this one with her now.

But she was back in Perugia, getting on with her life, and he was in France, doing the same.

But damn, he missed her.

He sent an email to the family announcing his return and then went to his bedroom to unpack as his phone started blowing up with requests for meetings.

The old routine, back again.

But he sighed and looked out the windows again at the

glistening, wet streets. It was different now because he was different. And all the keeping busy in the world wouldn't change it.

Gabi was used to being front and center in the financial aspects of Baresi Textiles, but in the days that followed her father's surgery, she found herself in the midst of the full-on operations of the company. To say she was overwhelmed was an understatement, but the employees all knew her well. For the most part, everyone was helpful and asked about Massimo's recovery daily.

As she sat at her desk, wading through emails, she realized that her father had built a company where the employees were contented and invested. That was saying something. She owed it to them to do a good job now. Captain the ship in his absence. And ask for help when she needed it.

After three days of back and forth with one of their main accounts, though, she felt she needed some advice. Massimo was at home and still on pain medication; once he'd healed sufficiently he'd start a grueling chemotherapy regime. She could ask him. Thought she probably should, but didn't. Instead she sent an email and sat back in her chair, wondering if she'd done the right thing.

Five minutes later her phone rang.

"Hi," she said, thrilled at the fast response, anxious to hear his voice again.

"God, it's good to hear your voice," he said, and she thrilled at the sound, so deep and soft.

"Oh, you, too. Things are okay in Paris?"

"Busy but fine. And you? You said you want my opinion on something."

She hesitated. She was about to reveal things about her business that made her vulnerable. But he'd also said if she needed help or advice to call him. It came down to trust, didn't it? And though she'd had misgivings at first, she trusted him. He hadn't done one single thing to make her think otherwise.

"It's one of our clients, actually. He's been with us for over fifteen years, but now he's making noise about not renewing his contract."

"Any particular reason?"

She sighed and pinched the bridge of her nose. "He says it's because he can get the same quality product cheaper elsewhere, but I don't think that's it. It's no secret that Papa is ill. I think he's worried that the company will be in trouble without Papa here. That he doesn't trust...current management."

"I'd laugh if I didn't think it was absolutely possible. Some people's opinions are still archaic. But really, what it comes down to is trust. Trust in your product and trust in you. Not Massimo, but you."

"But I've been doing this job for ten minutes. Know what I mean? How do I get him to trust me?"

Will's voice was warm in her ear. "You go see him, in person. You remind him that you grew up in this company, that you've worked in the family business and that you're completely capable of sitting in that chair while your father is taking care of his health. You look him in the eye and shake his hand. And you go armed with quality samples and numbers. Make sure he knows you've done your homework. A face-to-face meeting can change everything."

"You make it sound so easy."

Will laughed. "Oh, it's not. But you have to learn how. If you're going to sit in the big chair you have to be worthy of it. What would your father do?"

Gabi let out a breath, knowing he was right. "He'd go see him in person."

"Now you're getting it."

"But...what if I do all that and he's still determined to leave? It's a big contract, Will. If we lose it, it'll hit us hard."

Will sighed. "Sometimes that happens, too. Sometimes despite our best efforts, we fail. And so we pick ourselves up and find other solutions. You can do this, Gabi. I have faith in you."

"More than I have in myself, obviously. But thank you for the advice. I needed some common sense, I think."

"Of course." He paused and then his voice softened. "And how's your father? Doing better?"

"Home from the hospital, and thank you for asking. He's cranky at not being able to do much, which is an improvement from before the surgery, because he was too tired and not his old self. The more he drives Mama crazy, the more relieved she is."

Will chuckled and then sighed. "And you? How are you? Other than working all the time?"

"I'm fine." But the truth was, she was lonely. And not lonely in general—lonely for him in particular. "And you?"

"If 'fine' is the same as missing you, then I'm fine as well."

"Oh, Will." Still, his words lit something inside her. She'd needed to hear them desperately. To know that the ache left in her chest wasn't hers alone.

"I miss you, Gabi."

"I miss you, too. Crazy when you think about it, but... yeah."

"I'm terribly glad you emailed. I like to think that we're friends. That you know I'm here for you if you need something."

There was that word again...*friends*. They'd used it after the kisses in the olive grove, and for a few whole days they'd managed to not act on their desires. Until they were faced with parting. Then those cautions and assurances had gone right out the window. She probably should regret it, but she never would.

"I like that, too, Will. Everything is okay there? I keep watching the magazines and internet, but I haven't seen anything recently. It looks as though it's forgotten."

"There was a brief mention somewhere about Stephen visiting you…that we might have planted. No one wants to read about rescheduling the wedding. They want a scandal."

"If they only knew," she said, and laughed a little. His warm chuckle came across the line and she closed her eyes, wishing she could hear it in person.

"I've got a meeting in five minutes, but I hope that helped," he said, and she felt a bit of letdown knowing their conversation was coming to an end.

"It did. Sometimes it just feels as if I'm doing this alone. Your advice has given me some confidence, so thank you."

"Will you call and let me know how it goes?"

"If you want me to."

"I do, Gabi. There's no reason why we have to stop talking to each other."

Wasn't there? They weren't going to be together. They both knew it. It hadn't even been on the table as an option. And yet hearing his voice today was like having a lifeline, something to keep her going when she got overwhelmed with the responsibilities in front of her. She didn't want to let her father down, or anyone else for that matter.

"Then I'll let you know how it goes. Good or bad."

"I'm sure it'll be fine. I believe in you."

Oh, great. Another person she didn't want to disappoint.

"Thank you, Will. Go to your meeting. I'm fine."

"Take care, Gabi."

"You, too."

She hung up the phone and sat back in her chair. Was she torturing herself by talking to Will? Could they possibly be just friends?

Two days later she was in Milan, as nervous as she'd ever been, waiting to see Giacomo Corsetti. Giacomo had been her father's client for a decade and a half. The Corsetti brand was more high street fashion than couture, but it prided itself on exceptional quality. Gabi had dressed to impress: a splendidly cut pantsuit in navy and off-white, matching shoes and a designer bag that held several reports and an iPad so she could bring up data in real time if she needed. She'd put up her hair—more businesslike—and been subtle with her makeup. Overall she was going for a stylish but competent look.

If only her insides were as confident as the outside looked.

"Gabriella!" A jovial voice echoed across the marble floor and she turned to see Giacomo approaching. He wasn't overly tall, and his mustache was grayer than when she'd last seen him. "*Buongiorno*, Gabriella. How good it is to see you." He came forward and kissed both cheeks, making her realize that he was, indeed, a good inch or two shorter than she was. Perhaps the heels were a mistake.

"It's good to see you, too, Giacomo." She smiled at him.

"Last time I saw you, you were starting university. You've grown up a lot."

She had to dispel the image of her as a child, so she held her smile and replied, "Yes, I have. I've been working with the company for several years now."

"Learning at the elbow of the master?"

"Just as you say. It made perfect sense for me to step in as Papa is recovering."

Giacomo gestured toward the hall, and they began walking, Gabi's heels clicking on the cool marble. "How is your father? Such a sad thing, the cancer."

"He's doing well. He's home from surgery and starts chemo in a few weeks. The prognosis is encouraging." She looked over at Giacomo and added, "He looks far better now than he did before the operation, in fact."

"I'm very glad to hear it."

He led her into a large office in a modern design. For all his old-school attitudes, Giacomo knew how to keep up with what was fashionable. He went to sit behind a large desk, but Gabi halted and swept out a hand. "I have some figures to show you. Why don't we sit at your table where we can spread them out?"

If he sat behind his desk and she in front of it, she'd feel like a naughty student in the principal's office.

"Of course, of course."

Once they were seated she proceeded to take out her spreadsheets and make her case. Giacomo listened politely, but when she was finished, he tapped his fingers on the table.

"You see, Gabriella, I can get product much cheaper elsewhere."

"Ah, but it's not Baresi quality. Corsetti has always prided itself on its quality. What is it you say? Couture quality at high street prices?"

"The market is changing."

She hesitated for a moment, then met his gaze. "Yes, it is shifting, which is why I outlined some options for a new contract, to give you some flexibility. We want to work *with* you, Giacomo. What's good for Corsetti is good for Baresi."

"I'd have to be able to source at a lower price." He named a number that was bordering on insulting. In fact, it was insulting considering their long history of doing business together. To concede to such a price would obliterate any profit margin for Baresi.

"Come now, Giacomo. You know that's not possible. If you're trying to negotiate up, that's a very low place to start." She held his gaze. The whole time she was thinking, *What would Will do?* She knew he'd stand his ground and do what was right for Aurora. And so would she.

"It is my offer," he said firmly.

Gabi started to get mad now. Did he think she was stupid? She gathered up her papers to give herself time to decide what to say. Finally she folded her hands on top of the table, looked him in the eyes and said, "If my father were sitting here, you would never have asked such a thing. We both know it."

"Signorina—" he started, but she lifted a hand.

"No, Giacomo. I am the head of Baresi Textiles right now. I am young and I am a woman, but I am not green. You know my father. You know he would not have entrusted this responsibility to me if he did not think I was fully capable."

She said it, and then suddenly realized it was true, and she sat a little taller.

"On a short-term basis," he replied.

"On any basis."

Giacomo sighed. *"Mi dispiace*, Gabriella. But that is my offer. I'm hesitant to stay with Baresi with the instability at the moment."

Her heart sank, but she wouldn't show it. Instead she plucked a sheaf of papers from her stack and handed it over. "You won't get the quality you want at that price, Giacomo. And if you start compromising there, your brand will weaken. Take this. Look it over. There are several options I've outlined here to, as I said, give you some flexibility and versatility. Baresi would very much like to remain your supplier. No matter if I'm sitting in the chair or if my father is."

She stood and straightened her suit jacket, then tucked her files away in her bag. Giacomo rose, too, looking a little flustered. Did he think she would stay and negotiate away all Baresi profit? If so, he had another think coming. She was stronger and smarter than that.

"Let me take you to lunch," he suggested. "We can catch up on family."

That was the last thing Gabi wanted, after attempting to establish herself as a businesswoman. "Perhaps another time, and Maria could join us?" She remembered the name of his wife—the second wife—and then added, "Or when Papa is feeling better. I know he'd enjoy seeing you both."

"I'll walk you out."

"Grazie."

She left him with a smile and a handshake—no bussing of cheeks again. And now she had a choice. She could leave and go back to Perugia right now, or she could stay in Milan for a few hours and take an afternoon off. The hotel was already booked for tonight. Why not?

It was no contest. Taking the afternoon off won.

Corsetti was located right on the edge of the Quadrilatero della Moda—Milan's fashion district. Gabi had spent hours here as a child and then a young woman, staring in the windows, admiring the fashions even though her Papa couldn't afford to shop there. Instead it was his fabrics and, in particular, cashmere that graced the elegant windows. The Baresis had a good life. A very comfortable one, but not at this level. Not at… Pemberton level.

She had her flat and there was the family villa, which was very nice, but it was certainly no château or indeed the manor house in Surrey. Still, now and again she splurged on a nice piece. Shoes, for example, or the bag she carried today, which she'd bought as a Christmas present to herself two years previous and rarely used. Today had been an appropriate occasion.

The sun was warm on her face and she slid her sunglasses over her eyes, and then ambled along the street. Via Montenapoleone was home to the biggest brands on the planet, housed in gorgeous buildings with huge arched windows and stone balustrades above. She walked past giants like Vuitton and Versace, Prada and Hermès. The store she stopped in front of was Aurora.

It wouldn't hurt to go inside, would it?

Three hours later, Gabriella had made her way out of the district and into a cab to a modest hotel. She carried a signature black-and-white bag with a splurge for herself—a soft pink cashmere sweater and a small bottle of perfume. Visiting Aurora had been fun, but it was time to get back to business.

The room was perfectly adequate, and Gabi ordered up a light meal and some wine. She set up her keyboard with her iPad and figured she might as well do some work. Her heart gave a little leap when she opened her in-box and saw an email from William.

Did you have your meeting yet? How did it go?

She wasn't sure what to say. She felt she'd stood her ground, and she thought she'd handled herself well. But she was totally unsure of the outcome.

I don't know yet. I was strong, though! He lowballed me and I told him he'll pay the price in quality if he goes elsewhere.

She waited a few minutes, read a few other emails, then his answer came back.

Good for you. Baresi has a strong product. It's why we've used you as a supplier for so long.

   She laughed to herself.

That's what I said. I also gave him some options that were more cost-effective, so we'll see. I'd hate to lose a big client.

   Her email was quiet for several minutes. Her dinner arrived, and she munched and sipped on the crisp wine. She had just poured a second glass when her mobile buzzed. A quick glance showed it was William.

   She should ignore the little jump in her heart knowing it was him, shouldn't she?

   "Hello?"

   "Emailing was annoying. I thought a call might be better. Where are you?"

   "In a hotel in Milan, and then starting for home early in the morning."

   "You're driving?"

   "It's faster than the train, even if it's not as comfortable."

   "I'm glad you're not driving back tonight."

   "Me, too. I drove up this morning, and ten hours of driving in one day is a lot. I'm glad I did, though. You were right about the face-to-face meeting. If nothing else, I gave him something to think about before walking away."

   There was a pause, and Gabi frowned. What was William having trouble saying?

   "Gabi, is…is Baresi in trouble? Seriously?"

   She let out a breath. He'd seen her statements and nothing had changed. "No, not like that, Will. And I hope we don't get to that point. I just think if a client as well-known as Cor…as this one walks away, others will follow." She made the correction midsentence. There was no need to bring companies and sensitive information into it. There was trust and then there was professional discretion.

"Will you let me know if you ever get close to that point? Please?"

"I can manage, Will. I think I know what you're getting at, but no. Agreeing to that sort of proposition is what got me in trouble in the first place. Baresi will get through this."

"All right. The door is open should you need it."

"I appreciate it, but we're doing all right."

Just all right. Her worry about others following if Corsetti left was a real one. They could withstand the loss of one major client. Maybe two or three, even. More than that and the books were going to take a major hit. She put her forehead on her hand, feeling the beginning of a headache start. Maybe the best thing to do when she got back to Perugia was to hold another meeting with the sales team.

"Gabi, are you still there?"

"Yeah, I'm here." She needed to change the subject. "Do you know what I did after my meeting?"

"No, what?"

"I went into the Aurora shop. And I bought things."

"Ooh," he said. "What sorts of things?"

Some of the tension rolled off her. "A gorgeous sweater from the new fall line. And I saw the most amazing dress… a black evening gown. The attendant said that it had been designed for one of the family and then added to the fall line. Bit out of my price range."

"Ah, yes, the halter back, right? Charlotte wore that to the BAFTAs in February. It's lovely, isn't it?"

"I also bought a bottle of scent that reminds me of the garden at the château. Lavender, but also spicier notes of rosemary and thyme, and then something else…something gentler and more floral. It was like the day I sat in the garden with the sun on my face. I closed my eyes and just felt everything. The world was a million miles away."

"That's lovely."

"I would go back there if I could. Odd, but true. I felt half like a prisoner and half on vacation, but it really is the most beautiful, restful place."

"Now you can travel back when you have that scent memory," he suggested. "Maybe I need to get a bottle."

"I'm not sure it would smell the same on you," she laughed.

"No, but I could smell it and think of you," he replied, and she went quiet again.

"Will…"

"I miss you," he said bluntly.

"Will…"

"No, let me say this. I know our time together was strange and screwed up. But what I felt…what I feel…that's real. I don't know what to do about it, Gabi, but to deny my feelings feels so wrong. I wish… I wish we had time to explore what's between us."

She did, too, but it was impossible, wasn't it? And if she agreed with him, it would only make it more difficult. "Maybe we should make a clean break, Will." It killed her to say it. "This talking and emailing makes it harder."

"Because you feel the same? Be honest."

"It won't help anything to have me say it."

He let out a huff of frustration. "It'll help me feel like I'm not alone in this. Damn, Gabi. I feel so alone."

Hearing him say that hurt her heart. "You have your lovely big family," she said. She closed her eyes and felt like crying. "But if you told them you wanted to be with me, it would cause a total uproar. None of them know of my agreement with Stephen. As far as they're concerned, I walked out on him on our wedding day. They all think

I broke his heart. Will, we've been over this. You say you want this now, but it would mean turning your back on your family, and they mean everything to you. You'd end up resenting me, and I'm not sure I can take another heartbreak."

He was quiet on the other end.

"Say something," she whispered.

"My head knows you're right. My heart doesn't want to believe you. If I told Maman the truth…"

"There's no winning here. If you told her the truth, then I haven't broken Stephen's heart but I was willing to marry him for his money. Either way I come out of this looking like the kind of woman she will not want for her son."

"Gabi, I've never felt like this before. I'm heading toward thirty and I've had girlfriends but none have made me want things I never thought I'd want."

"Why? Because I'm forbidden? A challenge?"

There was another bald silence, and she knew she'd upset him. But still, these were important questions to ask. Someone had to play devil's advocate here.

"If you really think that of me, then maybe you're right. Maybe a clean break is best."

There it was. The opportunity to walk away, do the sensible thing. It was exactly the opening she was hoping for. And instead of reaching out and grabbing it, she found herself wiping tears off her face.

"I'm sorry." She sniffed. "That was unfair of me. Oh, Will, you're the most ethical person I know. I don't think that of you. I'm just so afraid."

"Afraid of what?"

"Of…of falling for you. Of having my heart broken again. Of screwing up, just when I am starting to get myself together."

"You're falling for me?"

She choked out a laugh. "Come on, that can hardly be a

surprise. Not after…" She halted as her throat closed over. That night in her flat had been so magical.

"I know," he said softly. "Gabi, I think of you all the time. I can't stop remembering what it's like to touch you. To taste you."

The air in the hotel room grew heavy. She remembered all those things, too. And then some.

"Would you consider coming to Paris for a few days?"

To what end? she wondered. What would it accomplish? And yet the idea of spending time with Will, just the two of them, sent a shaft of longing through her she couldn't deny. "I shouldn't want this so much," she whispered into the phone. "Not after such a short time. Not when it's so complicated."

"Love doesn't make sense," he replied, his voice husky. Had he used the word *love*? This was going so much faster and deeper than she knew what to do with.

"Come to Paris," his low voice persuaded. "Please. Spend a few days with me so we can sort this out face-to-face. I thought leaving you would be the end of it. I thought friends would be fine. But it's not fine, Gabi. I haven't been able to let you go."

How many women could refuse such a plea?

"Not this weekend. Next weekend. I'll fly Friday afternoon and will have to be back Sunday night."

"I'll take it. I'll take whatever time with you I can have, Gabriella."

She felt the same. And knew deep down that this weekend might be their one and only chance.

CHAPTER ELEVEN

GABI FLEW IN to Charles de Gaulle Airport early Friday evening and tried to contain the nervousness centered in her belly. She'd brought only a carry-on with her, and she shouldered the bag as she walked toward the doors leading out of the secure area. When they slid open, Will was waiting there, his eyes searching for her, and she knew.

I love him.

Then his gaze found her and connected and he smiled, and she knew a second most important thing: he loved her, too. It was on his face, in his eyes. In the connection that jolted to life the moment they laid eyes on each other. Oh, this was going to be so complicated.

"You're here." He said it when she was close enough to hear. "You're really here."

"I told you I was coming," she said, unable to contain her smile.

There was a moment where they hovered, considering a kiss. The urge to touch, to be close to him, was overwhelming, but common sense prevailed and Will stepped back. "Do you have another bag? Do we need to collect it?"

She shook her head. "No, this is it. I can pack light for two days, you know."

He laughed, the sound happy and free. "Come on, then. I have a car waiting."

Of course he did. No run-of-the-mill taxis for the Pemberton family. She found herself ensconced in black leather luxury as a driver drove away from the airport.

Will reached over for her hand. "How is your father?"

"Recovering well and getting stronger every day. The cancer hadn't spread, so that's very good news."

"I'm happy for you, and for your family. And Lucia? Giulia? Marco?"

"Mama is fussing over Papa. Giulia, I'm discovering, is very good at her job in human resources, and Marco is getting more besotted by the day. I'm not sure what's going to happen there. Giulia isn't ready to settle down."

"Is he willing to wait for her?"

"I think so. I hope so." She met Will's gaze. "I hope she's not throwing something away that is pretty incredible."

"Hmm," he said, and Gabi knew what he was thinking. They shouldn't throw away their chance, either, even if neither of them knew how to navigate the situation.

"I didn't even hug you when you arrived." Will's face took on a boyish pout and she laughed. And then he lifted his arm along the back of the seat, and she wiggled over to the middle and settled into his embrace, grateful for the tinted windows.

She closed her eyes. This was where she wanted to be. Always. Warm and loved and secure and accepted. He kissed her hair and tucked her head into his shoulder. "Oh, Gabi," he murmured. "This feels so right."

"I know."

"We're not even at my place yet, haven't even spent any time together, and yet I know what I want. I want to be with you. Really with you. Not sneaking around but a part of your life and you part of mine. I want us to own our relationship."

"I'm pretty sure my family wouldn't have a problem with that," she admitted, his words both thrilling and terrifying her. "They love you already. The day I told my parents the truth and you went upstairs? Mama asked if there was 'any hope there.' My family isn't the problem."

"I have to believe mine won't be, either, if we tell them the truth. Everyone liked you so much before."

"Yes, before I ran out on Stephen. Before they knew I was lying to them. Let's be realistic. And there's still the press to consider. Being seen together would rekindle that story."

They were quiet for a while, sitting with their own thoughts. Gabi hadn't been to Paris in a long time, but she didn't care to look out the window at the city moving past them. She kept her eyes closed and held on to Will and the fragile bond between them.

The driver dropped them at Will's apartment and Gabi tried very hard not to be overwhelmed. She had an idea what to expect—she'd been to the château and the manor, after all—but this was different. This wasn't a family space, this was Will's space, and his alone.

The first thing she noticed was the wall of windows that overlooked the river. "That is stunning." She looked at the view and then turned back. "What is it with us and views, anyway?"

"It's freedom," he replied, putting down her bag. "It's open space and possibilities and calm and a million other things that call to us. I've wanted to share this one with you ever since I got back."

And then he finally kissed her, the way she'd wanted to since first seeing him at the airport. His arms tightened around her and his mouth was sure and soft, claiming and seducing, loving and teasing. Nothing in the world was as lovely as kissing William Pemberton.

The living area before the windows was open and furnished in soft whites and grays. It took no time at all before they were on the plush sofa, wrapped in each other's arms. "I've missed you so much," Will said. "That night in Perugia…it wasn't enough."

"I didn't want to miss you, but I did," she replied, then kissed his neck. "Oh, Will." Their lips met again, and then he pulled away and looked into her face.

"I love you, Gabriella."

It felt as if her heart expanded in her chest as the words filled her with joy, and yes, even fear. Love was such a big emotion, filled with such risk. But she couldn't stop the words from coming. "I love you, too, Will."

"We'll figure it all out. I swear we will," he promised, and somehow she believed him.

Will woke early. The sun was up but still held that thin, morning light quality to it. He slid out of bed and left Gabi sleeping on her side with her glorious hair fanned out on her pillow, the sheet tucked beneath her arms and revealing the top of her breasts. As quietly as he could, he grabbed a pair of pajama bottoms and pulled them on, tying the drawstring loosely around his hips, and then padded quietly to the kitchen. He'd start some coffee. Enjoy the quiet moments, knowing that the woman he loved was in his bed.

The water was heating and he took a few moments to quietly tidy the remnants of last night's late dinner. They'd made love first, on the rug in his living room, an urgent, hurried coming together after so many days apart. Then he'd ordered in steak frites for two, opened a bottle of wine, and they'd eaten, talking as if they'd never been apart, perhaps even freer now that they'd confessed their feelings. And then they'd made love again, slower, with a reverence that had shaken him to the core.

She didn't know, but he'd never told a woman he loved her before. At least not since he'd been seventeen, and in his mind, that really didn't count. It wasn't a love like this.

He was still trying to figure out how to bring up the matter with his family, but it was no longer a question of if but of when. He did not want this to cause a rift, but his feelings couldn't be denied, either.

But that was for later. Today he was going to enjoy every moment with Gabi that he could. She had to go home tomorrow.

He poured the first cup of coffee and had sipped away at half of it when he heard a key turn in his lock and he froze.

Charlotte, his twin sister, popped into the apartment and looked at him with surprise. "You're up! I figured I'd have to wake you. I brought breakfast. I thought we could talk about the designs for the fashion week show. I want your approval before I finalize everything."

Oh, God. Charlotte was here. Gabi was in his bedroom, wearing nothing at all. He had to get his sister out of here.

"You should have called, Charlotte." His voice held a low warning. "We didn't make plans for this. It's barely eight on a Saturday morning."

"I know, but it's coming up soon, and—"

"We can do it another time. I'll call you. It's really not a good time for me."

Her eyes widened. "You have a woman here. Oh, *mon Dieu*, I'm so sorry." Then her eyes twinkled. "Anyone I know? Is it serious?"

"Charlotte." His voice was firmer now as worry settled in his gut. "Please."

"Mmm, is that coffee I smell?"

Will froze. Gabi shuffled out of the bedroom wearing nothing but panties and one of his T-shirts. Charlotte gasped, and Gabi suddenly looked very, very awake.

"Oh," she breathed.

Charlotte's normally sweet gaze darkened. "What the

hell is going on here? Will? Gabi?" She put an emphasis on Gabi's name that was more accusatory than surprise.

"I said you should have called." Will's voice was firm and none too pleased. "Now you'd better come in."

Charlotte glared at Gabi. "I can't believe this. Isn't it bad enough you jilted Stephen?"

Gabi glanced at Will, her faced tense with apology and anxiety. "I'm going to put some pants on. I'll be back." Her gaze told him she didn't expect him to handle this alone, though he was more than prepared to.

"I'll get us all some coffee," he said, and then looked at his twin. "You'd better sit down."

To his surprise, she did, but not before she dropped the bag of pastries on his counter, her lips pursed in a judgmental knot. He'd wanted to do this on his own time, when they were ready, when they'd figured out exactly how they wanted to handle his family. For heaven's sake, they'd only just said I love you to each other.

He hadn't been ready to fall in love. He certainly wasn't ready to deal with the family fallout.

He poured coffee, fixed Charlotte's and Gabi's the way he knew they liked, and as he took the mugs to the dining table, Gabi came out of the bedroom dressed in yoga pants and still in his T-shirt. He liked that she hadn't changed. In some way, keeping his shirt on seemed like maintaining ownership of their relationship. Not hiding away, when it would be so easy to.

He sat down with his own mug, looked Charlotte in the eye and said, "Yes. Gabi and I are together. We weren't going to tell anyone yet because it's new to us, too. But I'm not going to lie to you, Charlotte, and pretend this is something it's not."

Charlotte looked at Gabi and scowled. "So you left one brother for another. Nice."

Gabi curled her hands around her mug and met Charlotte's gaze. "I never should have agreed to marry Stephen. We were never in love, Charlotte. We made a big mistake, getting engaged."

"How convenient for you."

Gabi laughed a little. "Trust me, this is anything but convenient." Then she looked at Will. "Your brother was sent in to do damage control and…it just happened. Despite both of us saying it couldn't and shouldn't." She smiled a little, and Will reached over and put his hand over hers.

"Oh, yuck." Charlotte was not convinced. "And you, doing this to your own brother. I'm disgusted with you."

"It isn't what it seems, Charlotte."

"What does that mean?"

"It means you should ask Stephen about his relationship with Gabi. I love my brother. God, you know I do." He held her gaze and knew she understood. She knew what Stephen had done for him. "You know I would never hurt him. But what am I supposed to do, throw away the best thing that's ever happened to me because it's messy?"

"Will." Gabi's voice was soft and full of amazement, and he tore his eyes from Charlotte and looked at her instead.

"It's true," he admitted. "I've never felt this way about anyone."

"Me, either."

Charlotte made a sound of disgust and stood. "Ugh, I can't do this. Gabriella, I liked you when Stephen brought you home. But since then you've left him at the altar, caused a PR disaster, apparently seduced my other brother, and now you're both creating another scandal. I don't understand you."

"I know it looks that way," Gabi replied, "but you've only got part of the story. It's not my place to reveal Stephen's secrets. And you're quite right that I'm not innocent in all this. Let me just say that not marrying Stephen was my attempt to make things right, not cause trouble. And falling for Will was pure accident."

"That makes no sense at all."

"I know, and I'm sorry. The truth is, Will and I haven't had a chance to figure out how we wanted to tell your family. So I'm saying less than I might otherwise, out of respect for both your brothers."

Charlotte stared at Will, and looked angrier than he could ever remember. "If you think I'm keeping your dirty little secret, you're sadly mistaken."

"I don't expect you to. Hoped you might, but don't expect it."

"Don't try to guilt me, Will."

"I'm not."

"And you." She stared at Gabi. "If you think this is another way to get your hands on Pemberton money, forget it. Maman will never allow it."

"That's enough, Charlotte." Will stood now. Anger he understood. Of course Charlotte wouldn't understand, especially when appearances were so damning. But he also wouldn't stand for Gabi being abused.

"It's okay, Will. It's no more than I expected."

Charlotte grabbed her handbag and headed for the door. "I've heard enough. If you can dig your head out of your little love nest long enough, I'd like a meeting early this week. In my office."

"I appreciate the summons."

With one last scathing look, his sister slammed out the door.

He looked down at Gabi, who was sitting looking a bit shell-shocked. "I'm so sorry. She let herself in with her key and you came out before I could get her to leave."

"It was bound to happen sometime. And like I said, I

expected it. And more. Stephen will lose his mind and I'm sure your mother will be equally angry."

"Arabella might be okay. She's more the type who listens to all sides and makes up her own mind. Not that it won't be weighted against us. I know that. But Bella is reasonable. And Christophe...he tries to please everyone. He'll stay quiet and out of the drama."

Will knew his cousin had never quite felt like a brother, even though he'd been practically raised by Aurora and Cedric. Mostly he tried to not make any extra waves, which Will thought was a shame. His cousin was smart and far more savvy than most gave him credit for.

Gabi slumped in her chair and took a drink of cooling coffee. "So what do we do now?"

"I don't know. Let's sit tight for a while and see what happens. For once, getting ahead of the story might not do us any favors. Charlotte is probably already on the phone with Stephen. Let's see how this all plays out before we make a plan to change minds."

She put down her cup and looked at him sadly. "It is worth it, right?" she asked, her voice wobbling. "I do love you, you know."

"It's worth it," he confirmed, sitting next to her again. "I won't let you have to make a choice."

His heart warmed. "Oh, darling, I know that. If anyone forces a choice, it'll be my family. And that makes me sad. But it can't stop me from loving you. I never had a choice in that."

Still, the atmosphere in the apartment had turned to one of sadness and worry. Will had made all sorts of romantic plans for the day, but pushed them aside. What they needed now was to stick together. And so they went back into the bedroom, crawled under the covers and held on to each other while they waited for the storm to break.

CHAPTER TWELVE

IT DIDN'T TAKE LONG.

First Bella called, asking if Will was sure about what he was doing, at least attempting to be fair as she agreed that there seemed to be more to the story than a runaway bride and the groom's brother. Will hung up not quite sure he had an ally, but at least one person who was willing to listen.

The next phone call came early in the afternoon, and was from his mother. It didn't go as well as the call with Bella. It became clear to Will that Stephen had not enlightened anyone as to the original agreement between himself and Gabi. It was very difficult to hear Gabi spoken about in unfavorable terms, and to have his own family loyalty questioned. Gabi was right about one thing. The truth about the fake marriage would end up making her look like a gold digger.

Gabi was unusually quiet, her face pensive. Their romantic weekend was a disaster. Would their entire relationship be this way? Could they handle it, especially living so far apart? Will listened to his mother's voice in his ear and closed his eyes, pinching the bridge of his nose. He and Gabi were supposed to work this out gradually. Tell people when they were ready, when they had a handle on their relationship. Will, who prided himself on his ability to clean up messes, now found himself in the middle of the biggest one yet, and no clue how to fix it, other than let Gabi go.

He pondered it for exactly two seconds, before his stubborn nature rose up and rebelled. If he buckled under the pressure now, he'd regret it forever. He was not the same boy who'd been rash and impulsive and seeking attention. He was a grown man who'd worked very hard to become who he was. He wouldn't let anyone put him back in that box.

"Maman, what I'm saying is you need to talk to Stephen. Can you do that and then we can talk again?"

He listened to her for another moment, then replied, "Because it is his story to tell, not mine." William had never been, and never would, be a tattletale, even now that they were grown men.

The call ended and he sighed deeply.

"I'm so sorry, Will. I should go home. This is causing nothing but strife."

"I can handle it, but I understand if you want to go home. This is not the weekend I promised."

Instead of getting out of the bed, she slid closer and wrapped her arms around his middle. "It was going to happen eventually. We just thought we had more time."

"It's a lot of pressure on a new relationship."

She nodded against his chest. "Yes, but we're not exactly conventional."

He chuckled at that. How did she have the ability to make him laugh in the midst of such a horrible day?

His phone buzzed and he looked down. It was a text this time, not a call, but it hurt his heart more than any conversation he'd had thus far today.

So much for loyalty.

He put the phone aside, regret weighing heavily.

"From Stephen?"

He nodded.

"I'm sorry. Maybe this is a mistake, Will. It isn't fair

to put you through this. I'd rather walk away than see you lose your family. I can't imagine if this were my papa and mama and Giulia."

He thought back to the day she'd confessed the "plan" to her parents at the villa. There had been instant forgiveness and acceptance. Why did his family not trust him the same way? He understood they were trying to protect him, but why could they not give him the benefit of the doubt?

Was it because despite all the hard work of the last four years, he was still the screw up who'd fought an addiction and nearly tossed his life away?

For the briefest of moments he let those feelings in. Feelings of being a disappointment and a failure. Feelings of being a burden. And then he sniffed, sat up a little taller. He'd changed, grown, and had worked so hard to make up for the worry he'd caused. That was the man his family needed to see. Not the troubled boy.

"Will?"

He turned to her. "Stay. Forget about my family for twenty-four hours and stay with me. Love me. They can wait. We get to decide what we want, so let's do that."

"If you're sure…"

"I'm sure." In fact, he'd never been surer of anything. "Let's get out of here, get a hotel and hide away."

"That sounds a lot like running away."

He shook his head. "No, darling. It's a tactical retreat. Sometimes you concede the battle to win the war, and we're going to win them over, you'll see."

Gabi sighed, tucked her hair behind her ears and, for the first time in her adult life, considered day drinking.

Corsetti had not renewed their contract. When word got out, two smaller clients pulled their agreements as well. Massimo was home after his second round of chemotherapy and going through the full gamut of side effects. Her job was to save the company, not chase all their clients away.

And she didn't even have Will here for moral support. He'd visited the weekend before last, spending two days at the villa with her and her parents. He hadn't minded sleeping in his own room, he'd assured her. So they'd kept to separate rooms, but swam in the pool and walked the grounds and spent time together free of criticism or pressure.

Basically she'd spent forty-eight hours in denial about the mess of her life.

She looked at the financial projections again and sighed, then called the head of sales and set up a meeting for the following Tuesday. Tomorrow would have been preferable, but this time she was flying to London. Will was meeting her there and they were going to Chatsworth Hall together, for Aurora's birthday.

Gabi was so nervous about it she'd barely eaten in three days and was constantly nauseated. It was her first time back at Chatsworth, first time seeing the family again, and it was the matriarch's fifty-sixth birthday. No pressure at all.

At the end of the workday, she made her way home to her flat and packed her bag for the weekend. She would have to dress smartly, even when she wasn't at the party. She had her favorite standby little black dress for that occasion, and fine heels that would put her closer to Will's lovely height.

And then she sat on her bed and wondered if she could get on the plane, after all. If she was strong enough.

Her phone dinged twice, indicating a text message. She lifted it and laughed. How could he know? One short sentence was all it took to give her a smidge of courage.

Don't even think about canceling.

She typed back.

How did you know?

The reply came across the screen and she laughed when she saw it.

LOL. I would.

But she wouldn't. For all her insecurities, she trusted that Will wanted to be with her. He was the master at making things right, wasn't he? And so he would again, somehow. If he was brave enough to stand up to his family, she would match his courage by being by his side.

The last time Gabi had flown into Heathrow, she'd taken the Express into the station and then cabbed it to Stephen's house in St. John's Wood. This time, however, she flew into Gatwick and Will met her there. They made the drive to Chatsworth Hall in Will's car, a peppy little thing that made her wonder how he could ever fit behind the wheel with his long legs. It was drizzling, and the drive was not as picturesque as she remembered. The traffic on the A281 was heavy and Gabi's nerves made her muscles tense. She wasn't sure how she could make it through a whole weekend like this.

"It's going to be okay," Will promised. "The family will come around."

"You're optimistic," she said darkly, but he reached over and took her hand. "They need to know the truth, that's all."

Gabi knew he thought that, but she'd had a different thought. They didn't just need to know the truth, they needed to believe it. And in the weeks since Charlotte had walked in on them in Will's flat, Stephen had not once of-fered any additional information.

"So what's the plan for tonight?"

"A quiet dinner on our own. Tomorrow is Maman's party. Just family, but she's planning a lavish meal and it's cocktail dress."

"I brought something suitable." She was at least confi-dent in her dress and appearance. That was the only thing she was confident about.

"If you like, we can go out riding tomorrow. Or into Bramley to browse around."

"Let's not make anything firm. Being locked into plans makes me even more nervous."

"Sweetheart. We're in this together."

They drove on for several minutes before Gabi spoke up again. "Do you ever wonder if we're being crazy? Fall-ing so hard, so fast?" Her heart hammered in her chest. "What if they're right, Will? What if we're being foolish?"

He glanced over, his lips thin, though he kept his voice carefully even. "Do you think we're being foolish?"

"Maybe." Her stomach somersaulted as she said it.

"Do you think what we have is real?"

She blinked against sudden tears. "I'm sure it is. I've never felt this way. Not even with Luca."

"Then relax. The course of true love never did run smooth."

She reached over and gave his arm a little punch, but she smiled a bit. It was three days. Not even three whole days. If they could get through this, they could get through anything and it would be smooth sailing.

The lane to the manor finally appeared and Gabi felt a bit of déjà vu as they drove up to the house. She'd come here only weeks ago, and while she had changed, the house and the gardens had not. Oh, perhaps a few blooms had gone out of season and others had taken their place, but everything else was as majestic and perfect as she remembered.

"Home sweet home," Will murmured, and despite his light words, she saw his jaw was set.

He stopped the car and killed the engine, then reached over and took her hand as he looked in her eyes in one last private moment before going inside. "Together," he said firmly. "We do this together."

"Together," she echoed, though she thought she sounded far more confident than she felt.

The only one at home was Arabella, and they encountered her only five minutes after entering. She was coming down the stairs just as they were preparing to go up, and halted on a small landing where the stairs made a turn.

"Bella," Will said, his voice unsure.

Bella looked from Will to Gabi, and back to Will again. "You have guts, I'll give you that," she said, but then she smiled and gracefully descended several more steps to meet them. She held her hand out to Gabi. "Gabriella," she said quietly. "Welcome back to the lion's den."

Gabi gasped and laughed at the same time, and Bella's eyes twinkled a bit. Gabi understood that while she was on notice, this woman could be a potential ally, and that wasn't something she took lightly. "Thank you, Bella."

"Stephen is in London and coming down tomorrow. Christophe will be here late tonight, and Charlotte and Maman are flying in together from Paris in the morning." The itinerary gave Gabi an idea of what to expect when, and from whom. "Tonight it's just us. You can breathe a bit easier. I'm trying to keep an open mind and be Switzerland."

"Thank you, Bella. That means a lot."

She pinned Gabi with an assessing look. "I do expect some sort of an explanation, though. With this sort of family drama, it's hard to go on faith, you understand."

Gabi nodded quickly. "I do, and of course."

Will squeezed her hand reassuringly. "We'll scare up some food in the kitchen in a bit. But maybe a glass of wine later?"

"That sounds perfect. You go get settled. It's going to be a bumpy ride."

As Bella continued down the stairs, Gabi and Will continued up, Will carrying their bags. "You're staying in my room," he decreed. "I'm not leaving you alone for any sneak attacks."

Gabi tried to keep a sense of humor as he led her down a long, carpeted hall. "Hmm. So you've gone from my jailer to my protector. Interesting."

"Isn't it just?" He opened a door on the left and drew her inside, then closed it and pinned her against the solid wood, kissing her so thoroughly she was quite breathless. "I've been wanting to do that for an hour and a half," he growled, and then feasted again on her willing mouth.

"Okay," she said when they finally came up for air. "We've established that we're still wildly attracted to each other. It's a good start."

He laughed and gathered her into his arms for a massive hug. "You are a joy," he murmured in her ear. "And a gift. I'd be a fool to let that go. Remember that when things get tense, okay? Joy. Fool."

She nodded against his chest and wrapped her arms around him. It would be okay. Will wouldn't let anything bad happen.

Gabi took some time to unpack, though it only took a few minutes as she'd packed lightly for the weekend. Will had arrived that morning, and his things were already tucked away. Including a tux for the following night, she noticed. "A tuxedo?"

"For birthday celebrations? Always." He grinned. "Have you seen me in a tuxedo? I'm really quite dashing."

She met his gaze and frowned. "The day of the wedding, remember?"

He slapped his head. "How could I have forgotten?"

They were still chuckling about it when they made their way down to the kitchens and Will fixed them thick sandwiches with sour pickles and then jam tarts that their cook had made that morning. As they ate, they caught up on more "normal" things, like work and her father's health.

"You've had a rough go with your client list lately. Have you told your father?"

She frowned, her brow wrinkling. "No, not yet. When he's had his treatment and feels awful, it seems wrong to add to it. And when he's perked up before his next treatment, it seems unfair to ruin it by giving him bad news."

Will bit down on his pickle. "You should, though. He'd want to know what was happening."

"I know. I'll find a way to tell him when I get back."

"He might welcome a chance to be part of the business, you know. Feel useful and connected."

"You mean, instead of not worrying, he might be worrying about what he doesn't know?"

Will shrugged. "Maybe. How many have you lost?"

"Three big accounts, a few smaller ones. Baresi was already feeling a pinch. I'm worried, Will."

"Any new accounts? How's your sales department doing?"

"We've picked up a few new ones, but certainly not enough to make up for the losses."

He nodded sagely, and seemed lost in thought for a few minutes. "What are you thinking?" she asked.

"Just pondering solutions. I'll let you know if I come up with anything."

"Thanks."

They tidied up together, and then went to the drawing room. Will wandered through and then stopped at a small table set up with a chessboard. "My father used to play with anyone who would take him on," he said, warm reminiscence in his voice. "Do you know how?"

"I haven't for years, but yes." She went to the table and pulled out a chair, settling in. "You'll beat me, but I can take it."

"I never beat Papa. Not once."

"It wouldn't be right to trounce the earl."

"No, it damned well wouldn't."

They played for a while. Gabi held her own, but Will was more strategic and she was losing ground when Arabella entered, still dressed in her casual pants and the soft green sweater that skimmed her arms to the wrist. "I brought a good, full cabernet from the cellar," she said, holding a bottle aloft. "Anyone interested?"

"I will, because your brother is about to beat me soundly. Now we can call it a draw."

"Not if you concede."

"Hah," she answered, but grinned at him.

Bella went to a side table and uncorked the wine, then decanted it. "You really do care about each other, don't you?"

"What makes you say that?" Will moved to get three glasses.

"How you talk to each other. How you look at each other. It's the real deal."

Gabi put her hand on Bella's arm. "That's the nicest thing you possibly might have said, and I appreciate it."

"Oh, you still have some explaining to do." Bella started to pour wine in the glasses. "But at least I believe that you care for each other. Either that or you're a hell of an ac-

tress, Gabi. I mean, we all thought you loved Stephen."
She looked Gabi over with an eagle eye. "But you look at
Will differently."

The three of them settled down together. Gabi took a
sip—it was truly excellent—and then took a breath. "Will,
I think I should be the one to tell her the truth. After all,
I'm the one who ran. I'm the one no one trusts."

"If you're sure."

Gabi looked at Bella. "You've been fair so far. If I have
to do this again tomorrow, I'd like to at least make a first
run at it with someone who is open to listening."

Bella lifted her glass in a small toast. "Go on, then."

Gabi took a drink of wine and then laid out the entire
timeline, right up until the morning of the wedding. As she
got to the part about Will showing up at the hotel, he interrupted. "I told her that her timing left a lot to be desired, but
not the decision. It was a crazy plan and I never liked it."

"You knew?" Bella's lips dropped open.

"I knew. About Bridget, about his plans for Gabi." He
leaned forward. "Why else do you think I was the one to
go clean up the mess?"

Bella sat back on the sofa and sighed. She met Gabi's
gaze. "So you're double damned. If the family doesn't know
the truth, you've jilted Stephen at the altar. If they do, then
you were marrying him for the money. You don't come out
looking good, no matter what."

"Just so." This time Gabi lifted her glass in a mock salute.

"Except you don't have Stephen or the money," Bella
pointed out.

"No, but I've moved on to his brother. Charlotte pointed
that out."

Bella nodded. "Except this time it's real."

Gabi turned her head and looked at Will. He was watching her with such adoration she melted. "Oh, yes," she agreed. "It's so very real."

Bella got up and grabbed the wine bottle, then topped up the glasses. "Will, you are the most honorable man I know. I believe you," she said firmly. "But, so help me God, if I'm wrong, I'm going to strangle you both. And then throw you to Maman."

CHAPTER THIRTEEN

THE BIRTHDAY PARTY of Aurora Germain Pemberton was small but a sparkling affair. She would never have it any other way, and William gave one final tug on his bow tie before turning to look at Gabi, who was nervously twisting her fingers as she waited for him.

William wanted to tell her to relax, but he knew it was an impossible request. Tonight she truly was walking into the lion's den, as Bella had put it. The entire family was here: Aurora, of course, and Bella, Stephen, Christophe and his current girlfriend, Lizzy, Charlotte and of course Will and Gabi. Will hoped that the presence of Lizzy meant everyone would be on their best behavior, but there was no guarantee of that.

Gabi looked stunning, though. The little black dress skimmed her curves beautifully, and her black heels were simple but he recognized the quality. He'd come to notice something about Gabi. She did not have an endless wardrobe but what she chose was high quality and classic. Since those were the basic principles behind his mother's fashion dynasty, there was nothing to fault in her appearance.

"You are so beautiful," he murmured, holding out his hand. "I'm the luckiest man in England."

She laughed a little. "You're foolish, but I appreciate the compliment."

"It's going to be fine," he said, more confidently than he felt. But one thing he was sure of: he would stand beside her. She hadn't cowered; she'd come to face them all, and at the scene of the crime. That took a lot of strength.

They made their way down to the drawing room for before-dinner drinks. Gabi clutched his hand so tightly his fingers hurt, but he wouldn't say a word about it. She was entitled. When they walked in, a hush fell over the room as several pairs of eyes landed on them.

And then the conversation sparked up again as they were...ignored.

"Let's get a drink," Will suggested.

"Just soda or tonic or something for me," Gabi whispered. "I think I'll go light on the alcohol tonight."

"Fair." He kept his voice low. He headed to the bar and poured himself a gin and tonic and added a fresh wedge of lime. Bella appeared at their side and smiled, though her eyes were troubled. "Here we go," she said. "Gabi, would you like a drink?" She said it loudly enough that others might hear her being at least polite. Will appreciated her trying to set the tone.

"Maybe a white wine spritzer?"

"Good choice. I'll get it." Bella adeptly poured some wine in a glass and added club soda. "Lime?"

"No, thank you." She accepted the glass. "Thank you, Bella," she whispered.

"Don't thank me yet."

Will and Gabi held their drinks but it soon became clear that the family strategy was to pretend they didn't exist. Will took Gabi's hand and led her to his mother, whom he wished happy birthday. She kissed his cheek but her eyes only glanced over Gabi and she said nothing to her. The snub was brutally obvious, though subtle.

Charlotte looked their way and then turned her back, talking to Stephen, who stood with his hand in his suit pocket, being ever the earl, commanding the room almost as much as their mother.

Resentment burned in Will's veins. They weren't even making an effort. He wanted to call them out on it, but he wouldn't give them the satisfaction. He would not ruin the party or make things more difficult for Gabi. He would choose his moment.

Christophe finally took pity on them and approached with Lizzy, a model from London who, while no stranger to celebrity, seemed very shy and lovely. Will sent Christophe a look of gratitude, which his cousin acknowledged with a slight nod. Lizzy was the perfect buffer, at least for now. She and Gabi chatted easily.

They went into dinner and Gabi and her ally were separated, being seated at different sides of the table. Will noticed that Gabi picked at her food but really didn't eat much from each course. The conversation was never directed their way, and William's anger multiplied. He was still a part of this family. He put his hand on Gabi's thigh under the table, a small gesture of togetherness. She put her hand over his and squeezed, then looked at him and smiled weakly.

She was here and she was trying. And Will's anger continued to bubble.

After several courses that Will couldn't remember tasting, the cake was brought in, a beautiful white cream cake with fresh fruit. Corks popped as champagne was opened to accompany the cake, and it was sliced and served beautifully on the Pemberton china.

If his father were here, he wouldn't have stood for this. Will knew it deep in his soul. Cedric Pemberton had been a fair man, always willing to listen, to give people a chance even when others were against them. Look at Maman. She came from humble beginnings and had married an earl, and if Will remembered correctly, his grandparents hadn't been overly fond of the idea, either.

He was just about to say as much when Gabi touched his elbow. "Will you excuse me for a moment, Will? I need to go to the powder room."

"Of course." He smiled into her eyes. "Are you coming back?"

She lifted an eyebrow. "I'm not running away, if that's what you're asking."

"That's my girl," he replied. "I'll be here."

She slipped out of the dining room while the rest of the family rose from the table and circulated with their champagne. The formal part of dinner was over. If they could get through the next thirty minutes or so of mingling, they were in the clear.

Gabi locked the powder room door and let out a breath as her chin dropped. It had been a good ninety minutes of constant tension and being under a microscope. Bella had been polite, and Christophe's girlfriend was a godsend, but she hadn't been able to completely ignore the standoffishness of Stephen, Charlotte and Aurora. It was like she didn't exist.

Five minutes. She just needed five minutes of peace to regroup and then she could face the rest of the evening. She sat on the closed toilet lid and closed her eyes, then took several long, slow breaths.

When she felt she was ready again, she opened the door, only to find Stephen leaning against the wall on the opposite side of the hall.

"Oh," she said, immediately wary and confused.

"I wanted a chance to talk to you alone. I wasn't sure William would let me, he's so protective. Though I can understand that, considering his motives."

She frowned. "Motives? You mean not leaving me to

the wolves? You said what you needed to say at the villa, Stephen." She started to walk away, but Stephen's voice called her back.

"He's using you."

She turned back, angry that he would try to drive a wedge between them. "William has been nothing but wonderful, even while his family has shunned him because of it."

"He doesn't want you. Why do you think I turned down his plan? At least I was honest about what I wanted out of our...alliance. Will is making you think he's in love with you, when what he wants is control of Baresi." He stepped away from the wall. "I said no to the acquisition to protect you, not punish you."

Gabi stared at him. It wasn't true. She didn't believe him. "This is sour grapes, and so beneath you, Stephen. We were friends once."

His gaze sharpened. "Yes, we were."

Nausea rolled in her stomach again, and it had little to do with the rich sauce she'd eaten earlier. It was the tiniest bit of doubt. "You're wrong."

But in the back of her mind she was thinking about all the things she'd told Will. He'd been supportive in his comments but hadn't really offered firm advice. She'd told him about clients they'd lost, their financial situation, how new clients were hard to come by...all the information he'd need if he wanted to move in and make an offer.

No. She would not believe it of Will.

But then, she'd believed a lot of things. She'd believed Luca wanted to marry her and have a family. She'd believed in Stephen, too, and while his words were causing her great concern, she realized she didn't trust him. What if he was right about Will? Her father had put Baresi in her hands. He'd trusted her with everything. Had she misplaced her trust by trusting William? And then she thought back to all the times when her gut had said she maybe shouldn't trust Will, and she wondered if she might be sick. What if her intuition had been right?

"Be careful, Gabi."

"I don't believe you. You haven't even told your own family the truth of our engagement."

He stepped forward then, holding her gaze. "You know I don't let people into my intimate business."

"You're letting them think I'm with Will for his money."

"You're really in love with him. God, he's played this perfectly."

Her heart took the hit. She didn't want to believe it, but she'd been played before. She would be a fool to not consider the possibility now. Not with so much at stake.

She should have been talking to her father about the business, not Will. Fear clogged her throat.

"Please think about it, Gabriella."

He walked away then, as nonchalantly as ever, in his perfectly tailored tuxedo. She had trusted him and he had done nothing to break that trust, really. She had been the one to run from their wedding. At the villa he'd been angry and hurt and humiliated. And rude, but…to her knowledge, he'd never outright lied.

Stephen was gone when Will came around the corner, his face wreathed in concern. "Are you all right? You've been gone a long time."

She wanted to cry. She loved him, she did. She didn't want to believe what Stephen had said, but he'd planted the damned seed and she couldn't help herself. "I'm not feeling very well, it turns out," she replied. "I was going to find you and make my excuses. I think dinner was a little too rich."

"Are you sick?"

She bit down on her lip. "Close."

"Of course. We can leave the party now."

"Not both of us. Just me, William. You should stay. It's your mother's birthday."

"Then I'll follow shortly, after saying my goodbyes." He leaned forward and kissed her cheek. "You're cold," he murmured.

"I'm fine. I just need to lie down."

"I'll be right along, I promise." The concern on his face scored her heart. Why, why had Stephen made her doubt even the smallest bit?

He squeezed her hand before turning away. "Go put on something cozy and rest," he advised. Then he met her gaze again. "I love you, Gabi."

If he didn't go right now she was going to burst into tears. "I love you, too," she answered, knowing it was true, wondering if it was wrong.

He smiled, and she memorized every feature of his handsome face. He couldn't be guilty of what Stephen said. He couldn't. Will strode back toward the dining room, and she stumbled toward the stairs, fighting tears. The moments they'd shared, making love, the soul-to-soul connection... it had to be real.

She opened the bedroom door and then rushed to the bathroom and was sick. Not from the food, but from the stress and the possibility that she had once again made a bad decision. She'd believed that she and Luca had had that connection, too, and he'd been a liar and a fraud and a cheat.

What she needed now was time and space. To think. To decide what to do now. She washed her face and put on the nightgown she'd brought, one that was much too sexy for the situation but she'd brought nothing else to sleep in. She was sitting in bed, with earbuds in her ears, when Will came in.

She pulled out the earbuds.

"What are you listening to?"

"A meditation."

He instantly went to the bed and sat on the edge. "I'm so sorry about how my family reacted." He smiled. "I'm used to their dramatics. I promise it'll pass eventually, when they see we're committed."

"I'm not sure of that," she replied, looking down.

"They will. Bella is already halfway there and I can always count on Christophe." He put a finger under her chin and lifted it, tried a winning smile, but she didn't have it in her to give one in return. "Sweetheart, what is it? Is it my family, or your family situation? You've been under so much stress. Damn that Stephen. If he had only agreed to my proposal, so much of this burden would have been lessened for you."

Her stomach clenched. "It isn't for you to save Baresi. I can do this on my own."

"I've been giving it more thought the last few weeks," he said, sliding further onto the bed so they were face-to-face. "We don't need Aurora to officially invest. I have my own money. I can help you."

The proposition struck her speechless for several seconds. Had he mentioned this to his brother? That he was planning to go off book and make an offer himself?

"No, William." She slid out of the bed and went to the closet to take out her robe. She slid it over her shoulders and tied the belt firmly. "I don't want your money. I'm going to deal with this on my own."

"But, darling, it could make things so much easier for you. Like we planned at the villa, remember?"

She remembered, and she'd felt desperate at the time, with her father's surgery still looming and so much uncertainty. Now, even though she was struggling in her new position, she wasn't nearly as afraid of it. Not so much that she was willing to cede control to anyone. Not even Will.

"Maybe I don't need easy. Maybe I need to accomplish this myself. And I certainly don't need you coming in and taking over."

He stood and stared at her. "Taking over? Who said anything about taking over?"

"It would be a great addition to your own business interests, wouldn't it? And then you could be the one to negotiate with Aurora and you'd be padding your pockets from both sides." She shook her head. "I can't believe I didn't see it before."

His mouth dropped open. "I can't believe you just said that. Gabi."

"Maybe I've been gullible this whole time. What a perfect mark I was, trying to avoid a scandal, vulnerable because of my father...you could swoop in as my rescuer and achieve what Stephen could not."

He swore quite thoroughly. "Who the hell got to you? What did they say? This is ridiculous!"

"Is it?" Fear and desperation nudged her forward. "You always said that loyalty to your family comes first, particularly to Stephen." She thought back to that day at the villa when Stephen and Will had fought. "What happened between you at my house?" she asked. "Did Stephen not like your plan?"

Will ran his hand through his hair, clearly frustrated. "This is unbelievable. An hour ago we were united against the world. And now you're accusing me of using you to take over your company? Someone must have said something to you. What I don't understand is why you'd believe them."

Gabi heard hurt in his voice and didn't know what to believe. He hadn't actually denied it, but he hadn't confirmed it, either. And Stephen had been convincing, playing the friend card. She shook her head. "Do you know what? I don't trust any of you right now. I don't know who to believe."

"So someone did get to you."

"It doesn't mean they were lying."

He stared at her, and the longer he did, the more confused she became. Why couldn't she trust him? Why couldn't she believe him? And then she remembered telling Luca she might be pregnant and the look of horror on his face as he crushed her future beneath his heel. She remembered the horrible sick feeling as she waited for the pregnancy test results, and the combined sadness and relief she felt. She remembered the panic of her wedding day, and dashing off in Stephen's car to hide away in London, knowing she'd been foolish to agree to his plan in the first place.

The truth was, she had a history of making bad decisions, and there was too much at stake to do it again.

"I don't trust my own judgment," she said, her voice as even as she could make it. "I don't know who or what to believe. And if that's the case, I think… I think I need some time and distance away to think things through."

"You're giving up on us."

"I'm choosing what I know is real. I need to go home. And I need to sort through my life. This was all such a mistake."

And yet her heart cracked as she said it. The pain nearly stole her breath. Her heart was screaming for her to trust him and remember all the ways he'd been there for her. Her head was challenging her to think about his motives.

"Please, don't do anything rash. We can talk about this tomorrow. Think about what you're saying, and don't let fear or my family's meanness drive you away. Please, Gabi. This is too important to throw away."

"I think I need to sleep alone tonight, Will. I have a lot to sort through."

He hesitated, and she hoped he wouldn't insist. The idea of lying beside him in the bed, trying to hold her emotions in check, was overwhelming. She needed to cry, and then to really sort things out.

"I'll go to another room," he acquiesced, though he sounded upset about it. "If that's what you need."

"I do."

"And we'll sort this out in the morning."

She nodded.

He paused, and she wondered if he was going to try and kiss her or hug her before leaving the room. In the end he sent her a complicated look of love and fear and left, shutting the door quietly behind him.

She went back to the bed and sat on the edge, expecting to cry. Instead her eyes remained dry as she sat for long minutes. For the first time ever, her emotions were too big for tears.

She needed to go home.

CHAPTER FOURTEEN

WILL WOKE AND went to the room where Gabi slept. He knocked on the door, but there was no answer. And he knew what he would find before he finished opening the door.

She was gone.

A helplessness overwhelmed him as he stared at the room. The bed was perfectly made, as if no one had been there at all. And on the night table was a folded note. God, just like last time. For a second he felt played and understood how Stephen must have felt that day at the chapel. Except Stephen hadn't loved her. Will did.

He picked it up carefully, as if it might bite, and unfolded the thick cream paper. *Dear Will*, it began, and there were several lines beneath the salutation.

At least it was better than Stephen's brief *Please forgive me.*

> *Dear Will,*
> *I know you're going to be furious that I've run again, but I have to go home. I have to sort out what is real and what isn't in my head. I do not know who to trust. Maybe I've been manipulated too many times, or maybe I'm a horrible judge of people. I just don't trust myself to make the right decision.*
> *I'm afraid, Will. Afraid that I'll do the wrong thing and in doing so ruin everything.*
> *I want to believe everything between us was real,*

*but I can't. That doubt is there, and I can't shake it.
And that is no way to have a relationship. I'm sorry.
Gabi*

He folded the page into quarters and tucked it into his pocket. She hadn't doubted him until last night when she'd excused herself, so what had happened in that fifteen minutes? He tried to think of who might have spoken to her, but they were all mingling and enjoying cake and champagne at the time. He'd been talking to Christophe, and couldn't account for everyone else at the time.

But someone had, and he was going to find out who.

Within three minutes he'd banged on everyone's door and announced a family meeting immediately in the library. This was going to end now. No more secrets. No more maneuvering. And no more putting up with sneaky behavior in the name of loyalty. It had to work both ways, and he was owed some, too.

It took half an hour for everyone to congregate. Bella was cool as ever, in jeans and a sweater, her hair up in a top-knot. Christophe's hair, on the other hand, was smushed on one side and he had a good bit of stubble on his chin. Lizzy was still in bed, he said, and out of the family drama. Charlotte looked supremely annoyed and attended in her silk pajamas and robe, and Aurora, as ever, was fully dressed, hair perfect, and her "day" makeup on.

"No coffee?" Charlotte complained, and Will silenced her with a look.

He took the note out of his pocket and held it up. "If someone helped Gabi catch a ride to the airport, I'd like to know right now."

No one said a word, but Aurora lifted one eyebrow and Stephen looked slightly smug.

"You're probably amused that I, too, got a runaway

note," Will said, glaring at Stephen. "But I'm going to say this. Gabi has been manipulated, and not by me. One of you spoke to her last night and portrayed our relationship as one of opportunity and not love. And I'm here to say that whoever did that has betrayed me in the biggest way because I love her. I love her and she loves me and someone has made her doubt that."

No one spoke.

"Charlotte? You've been against this since you found out in Paris. Was it you?"

"No." She nodded at the note. "But I'd say that note is evidence that whoever did, did you a favor."

He was so angry. So very, very angry and afraid. What if he couldn't figure out a way to get her back?

William looked at his mother. There was something in her eyes he didn't expect. Compassion. He knew it wasn't her. She might not approve, but she wouldn't actively poison the well. She knew what it was like to be distrusted and disliked by a man's family. And so that left...

Stephen.

"You're my brother. I can't believe you'd be this malicious."

Stephen met Will's gaze. "It was business."

"Like hell it was."

"Face it, Will. Your proposal would have put you in a fine position to take control of Baresi. I just said that I couldn't let that happen."

"Stephen." That was from Aurora, a stern admonishment. "Will would never do that."

"No, I wouldn't." If they weren't in his father's library, and if his mother weren't here, he'd be tempted to take Stephen down a notch or two.

"But see? She doesn't trust you. You're better off," Stephen said. "I'm just looking out for you, little brother."

"No, you're not." Bella stepped in this time. "Stephen, I know about your stupid agreement with Gabi. If you start with the 'left at the altar broken heart' thing, *I'm* going to knock you into next week."

Three sets of eyes looked from Bella to Stephen.

"Are you going to tell them or shall I?" Will asked.

"Tell us what?" Aurora's voice was soft but imperious, a tone they'd all learned to take very seriously.

Stephen's dark gaze hardened as he stared at Will.

"Fine," Will said. "Stephen knew Gabi's company was struggling and that her father had just heard he had cancer. He made her a deal that Aurora would invest and save the company, in exchange for a sham marriage." He looked at his mother and his gaze softened. "For Stephen's part, he was worried about you. You have grieved so hard. He thought, rather foolishly, that a wife and perhaps a baby would help with your grief."

Aurora rarely looked shocked but she did now. "Stephen. If that was the case, why didn't you marry Bridget?"

Stephen's voice was as cold as chipped ice. "Because she was a money-grubbing liar who wanted Aurora, Inc., money and a title to show off."

"Bridget was the one who broke Stephen's heart, not Gabi," Will said. "And I was sent to clean up the mess after the wedding. Only Gabi and I...we fell in love."

Stephen made a scoffing noise that had every person in the room looking at him.

Bella spoke softly. "Just because you're hurt doesn't mean everyone else deserves to be."

Will swallowed against a lump in his throat. "I know you're thinking Gabi should trust me, but there are reasons she doesn't that have nothing to do with me. Those are her secrets and she entrusted them to me, which she is probably regretting at this moment. Stephen, I told you in Italy that family is first, and that I will always owe you a debt because of what you did for me years ago. But this…what you did last night did not put family first. You put your hurt feelings and pride first. I'm ashamed of you, Stephen. And it kills me to say that. You're my big brother and I love you."

"I got you out of that flat in London so you could make something of yourself."

Will stood taller. "And I did. And I'm sorry if you don't like who I've become, or if it threatens you in some way. But I'm never going back to being that person. I will always owe you a debt but not on these terms, Stephen. Not when you're so very wrong."

His insides quivered as he faced down his brother, but it was time. Time he stepped into his own power and agency.

"You have every right to be angry, Will." This from Aurora.

"You all should know that after Stephen spoke to Gabi last night, I made the error of offering to help Baresi out of my own wealth. She turned me down flat. She's not in this for money."

Charlotte got up and went to Will, and hugged him. "I was so awful to you two in Paris."

"We expected it. Falling for each other made everything so complicated and messy."

Christophe finally chipped in. "What are you going to do now?"

"I don't know." He finally sat down and wilted a bit, now that the truth was out and the family knew it all. "I've never…damn. I've never felt like this."

Stephen walked out of the room.

Aurora sighed and looked at Will. "I'll talk to him later. He's hurting more than I realized. It doesn't excuse his behavior. I had no idea, William." She looked over the rest of the children. "I miss your papa every day, but please, do not make any more decisions to protect me or somehow coddle me. I'm fine."

She got up and went to sit beside Will. "I confess I have my doubts. The whole situation is unorthodox. But I am the last person to judge. If you love her, that's good enough for me."

"*Merci*, Maman." He fought the urge to lean in to her shoulder like he would have as a child.

"You really love her?" This from Charlotte.

"Yes. And she loves me, except she doesn't trust herself."

"Then leave this to Bella and me. What this needs is a grand gesture. And if there's anything this family is good at, it's grandeur."

"I'm not sure I want to trust my future happiness to my sisters."

Bella laughed. "Don't worry. We're going to do the dirty work, but you're going to be in it the entire way. You just have to follow our instructions to the letter."

One week later

Gabi stepped into her office and put down her briefcase, ready to start her day. While her heart was bruised and aching, she was feeling ever so much better about Baresi. When she'd returned to the villa, she'd told all to her father. She hadn't wanted to burden him before, but something Will had said once kept coming back to her. About how being involved might be exactly what her father needed. He'd been right. Massimo had been fretting while she'd been trying to protect him. Now they consulted on everything, with her in the office to execute, and she was discovering they made very good partners.

There was a knock on the office door and she went to answer it. She had no meetings this morning, so she wasn't sure who to expect. Opening it to find Charlotte and Bella in front of her was a shock.

"Please hear us out," Charlotte said, stepping just inside the door. "I owe you the biggest apology. Bella and I are here to help."

Curiosity won out, particularly if the antagonistic Charlotte was apologizing.

"I'm not sure there's anything to help," she replied, but she gestured to the two guest chairs in her office. She went to hers behind the desk, needing its protection and illusion of power.

"Stephen was wrong. We all know he spoke to you the night of the party and made you doubt Will. And that Will unwittingly played into the problem by offering to help with Baresi. We're here to assure you that Aurora isn't going to give you one penny." Charlotte grinned. "You're a strong, smart woman and can handle this on your own. What we need help with is handling Will."

Bella jumped in. "He's moping around like someone kicked his dog. You broke his heart, Gabi. He keeps saying he understands why you don't trust him and even Maman has had a go at Stephen for meddling and being a git."

Gabi didn't know what to say. "I don't think it's that simple," she replied.

Bella's dark eyes were sympathetic. "Will says you have a good reason for not trusting people, but I want you to think back over your relationship. Other than the night of the party, had he ever given you any reason to doubt?"

Gabi knew he hadn't. It was part of what scared her so much.

"I know I was awful to you in Paris, but I didn't know all that about your engagement to Stephen."

"I should never have agreed to it. In the end, I couldn't go through with it. I couldn't marry someone I didn't love, not even to help my family. I thought that was the only way, you know? But now…" She looked around the office. "I have a bit more confidence in my business abilities. My personal life? Not so much."

"Trust is a hard thing to fix," Bella agreed softly. "But if any Baresi involvement is off the table, and Will still wants to be with you…would you be willing to work it out?"

She wanted to so badly she ached with it. In the days since, she'd had a chance to think about it, away from the drama of the Pemberton family. The only person who ever seemed to have an agenda was Stephen, and she was disappointed in him. But even though he'd had an agenda, he'd never lied to her. Not until that night. The arrangement had been clear and she'd agreed to it. His behavior the night of the party had been awful, but Will…she was starting to think her trust hadn't been misplaced. Indeed, she'd rather felt she'd ruined everything since he hadn't even called since she left Chatsworth. After all, she'd leveled him with an accusation and then…run. Again.

Charlotte leaned forward. "Gabi, we have a plan. If you're willing, we're pretty sure we know how you can get Will back…if you want him. You just need your passport, a plane ticket and a killer dress." She handed over an ivory envelope. "You're invited to the Aurora party at the Four Seasons."

CHAPTER FIFTEEN

WILL HAD BEEN a bundle of nerves all day. As head of the fashion division, Paris Fashion Week was a big deal, particularly to Aurora's bottom line. Charlotte had shouldered much of the work on the ground for the first time, and she'd done a fantastic job. The show had been a success and the applause spectacular as Aurora had taken the stage beside a team of designers at the end. As Will watched, happy to be in the background, he realized what a dynamic, strong, amazing woman his mother was.

No wonder his father had fallen for her. She'd taken an idea and made it into an empire. Sure, being married to the Earl of Chatsworth had helped. But he knew that it came down to her vision and strength.

It reminded him of someone else he knew.

Charlotte and Bella had gone to visit Gabi and put their plan in motion, this grand gesture that they seemed to think would fix everything. His palms started to sweat as fear made its way through the elation of the day. What if she didn't come? What if she said no?

He'd missed her with a keenness that robbed him of breath. If she said no now, if it was over for good, he wasn't sure he'd ever be able to breathe again.

After the show, William slid inside the limousine with Aurora, who was glowing, and they departed for the Aurora, Inc., party at the Four Seasons in the massive, ornate ballroom.

"You look beautiful, Maman." She'd chosen an elegant gown in white that draped and shimmered beautifully against her creamy skin. He recognized the Pemberton diamonds at her throat and felt a tightness at his own as he thought of his father. He reached over and took her hand, then kissed the top of it. "I'm so proud of you. Papa would be, too."

"Likewise, darling. I know you doubted I'd put you in the right spot, but look at what we achieved tonight."

"I wish Papa was here to see it."

"Me, too, darling. Me, too. But let's have fun tonight, yes?"

His mother didn't know what he had planned, or she wouldn't have suggested something so lighthearted. His future lay in the balance.

They got out of the limo at the hotel and were immediately faced with camera flashes. A few waves and smiles and they were inside, moving toward the party. There was just one thing missing for Will...or rather one person. Having Gabi here tonight would make it complete.

They were in the foyer before the ballroom, surrounded by icons and the highest fashion in the world, when a simple black dress caught his eye.

And there she was, standing between Charlotte and Bella, wearing Charlotte's black gown—the one Gabi had seen in Milan. It suited her perfectly. The jersey draped over the curve of her hips and fell to the floor in soft folds, and the halter neckline highlighted the column of her throat and her strong, beautiful shoulders. Her hair was up and... he swallowed thickly. Bella had loaned her jewelry. He recognized the diamond-and-pearl teardrop earrings that their father had given her on her eighteenth birthday.

She'd come.

Charlotte gave Gabi a gentle nudge, and she looked startled for a moment, but then began walking across the foyer toward him, her dark eyes wide and unsure, her lip…oh, she was biting her lip. Did she not realize he would welcome her with open arms?

He glanced to his left… Aurora had melted away into the background. Out of his way.

And then Gabi was there, before him, so incredibly beautiful he wasn't sure he knew how to breathe.

"You're here," he said, feeling at once stupid and awestruck. "You never said for sure if you were coming."

She laughed. "I wasn't sure. But then I decided that I had to stop running away. Though I might have had some help with that." She looked over her shoulder at his sisters, who grinned ridiculously and gave them a thumbs-up. She laughed, and he thought he'd never heard such a gorgeous sound in his life.

"My sisters can be persuasive."

She met his gaze. "I didn't want to listen. I was afraid to listen, Will. And the more I thought about it, the more I realized I'd panicked because of my insecurities, and not because of you."

"I would never… Oh, Gabi. I would never seduce you for business. It's just not in me. Every feeling, every kiss, every touch…it was all you. None of it was part of my plan. I only offered what I did to help. Not because of what Stephen said. He lied to you. He said so in front of the entire family."

"In front of everyone?"

"When you left, I called a family meeting."

Her gaze widened. "Your sisters never told me that."

"I should have done it earlier. I should have spoken up the night before when everyone was being so awful. I didn't stand up for you, Gabi, so I can hardly blame you for doubting me."

She touched his hand and her fingers shook against his. "I was so afraid. That evening was so hard. And then Stephen... It hit on a weakness and I was already vulnerable. I should have been stronger for you, like you were for me. I'm so sorry, Will. Sorry I ran instead of staying for us to work it out like I said I would."

"If Stephen hadn't—"

"No," she interrupted. "That's my fault, not your brother's. The truth is, I'm stronger than I realized and a good deal of that is due to you. I hope you..." She cleared her throat. "I hope you forgive me."

"Of course I forgive you. I love you."

"Oh, Will, I love you, too. I'm so sorry I was such a fool."

Will no longer cared about scandals or paparazzi or public displays of affection. Right now, the only thing that mattered was the woman in front of him, and he cupped his hands around her face and kissed her, the ache in his chest replaced by a sweetness he'd never known.

She was here. She still loved him. Charlotte and Bella had done their part, and now it was his turn. He looked over his shoulder at his mother, standing ten feet behind him and smiling. Another look around showed Christophe and Lizzy next to Bella and Charlotte. The only one missing was Stephen, and for that Will found he was a bit sad.

But the time was right. He felt it in his heart.

"Gabi?"

"What is it?"

He took her hand in his. "I love you, you know that, right?"

She nodded, her eyes warm and affectionate.

"And we've already shown we can make it through high-pressure situations."

She laughed then. "Oh, one or two. Never mind the pictures that will probably be online in about five seconds because you kissed me in a public ballroom."

He reached inside his pocket and took out a box. It was white satin with black trim around it, the classic Aurora packaging. It had taken him three hours to decide on the one he wanted, and his heart beat frantically in his chest at what he was about to do. "Will you do me the honor of marrying me? Because I don't think I can do this alone anymore."

He opened the box and inside was nestled a stunning oval engagement ring with channel-set diamonds on either side.

For three whole, torturous seconds, Gabi stood with her hand over her mouth in stunned surprise.

And then her arms were around his neck as she hugged him close. "Oh," she cried softly. "Oh, William. I didn't expect this."

"Is that a yes?" His arms tightened around her.

"Yes." She let him go and moved back enough that she could look up at him. Her eyes were wet with tears but her lips were smiling. "Yes. But please, can we not get married in the Chatsworth chapel?"

He laughed. "Deal." And then he took the ring out of the box and slid it over her finger as a cheer went up from the crowd.

"This is so not going to be discreet," she lamented.

"This time, I don't give a damn." He kissed her hand. "I love you and I don't care who knows it."

They spent a few minutes accepting congratulations from the family, and others who seemed more curious than anything. Finally Gabi pulled on his sleeve. "I should call Mama and Papa and tell them the news," she said. "They both thought I was crazy for leaving you, anyway."

"Of course."

She was just about to head to a quieter spot when he tugged on her fingers. "Gabi? We won't set a date until we're sure your father can walk you down the aisle. In Italy. The wedding will be in your home." Then he thought of the villa, and how they'd truly fallen in love in Italy, and he added, "In our home."

And when she walked away to share the good news, he knew all the missing pieces suddenly fit together.

* * * * *

THE COWBOY'S PROMISE

TERESA SOUTHWICK

To readers who adore happy endings as much as I do. Without you I couldn't do the job I love. Though it doesn't seem like enough, this thank-you comes from the bottom of my heart.

Chapter One

There's no place like home. And for Erica Abernathy home was Bronco Heights, Montana—where everyone had an opinion, and not always a positive one.

She was driving her loaded-to-the-roof SUV down the road to the big house on the Ambling A Ranch, where she'd grown up. The trip from Denver had been long, but now that she was so close, she wouldn't mind a couple thousand more miles between her and what was coming.

She loved her family, but wasn't looking forward to their reaction when they saw her. There would be so many questions.

Although that happened every time she came

home for a visit. Usually some variation of "Do you like *city* life in Denver?" Or "Are you dating anyone? Getting serious about a special man?" And the ever popular, "Can we look forward to an engagement soon? We can't wait to be grandparents." Erica glanced down at her pregnant belly that was getting closer to the steering wheel every day.

"You're going to make them grandparents, little one. But they are not going to be happy with me."

Erica stopped her car in front of the large home constructed from Canadian red cedar and native Montana rock. The building materials were a salute to pioneers and the generations of Abernathys who came before and settled this land. Sturdy logs supported the second story roof over the front entrance. The sun had just set, and inside lights blazed through the tall windows.

There was a chimney sticking up over the pitched roofline and smoke drifted out of it. She could picture the fireplace in the great room, where flames would crackle and snap. That wasn't about providing atmosphere. Montana could get darn cold, and it wasn't unheard of to have a freak snowstorm the beginning of October. Shivering, she pulled her poncho up more snugly around her neck.

She'd missed this place. In spite of what her family thought about her choosing a career in Colorado over it, she did love the ranch, the land, the mountains. And after twelve years, she was back to stay, just like her parents always wanted. But when Angela and George Abernathy saw her, they were probably not going to ask about city life in Denver. They would have way too many other questions.

She sighed. Procrastination wasn't going to make this first step any easier. "Here goes nothing…"

She walked up to the front door and rang the bell. It was her childhood home, but she hadn't told them she was coming. It didn't feel right to simply walk in.

Suddenly the front porch light flashed on, the door was opened and Angela Abernathy stood there. She was in her early fifties with dark blond highlighted hair. Her blue eyes widened and she blinked once, then smiled with pleasure. "Erica! Sweetheart, what a surprise."

"Hi, Mama."

"This is wonderful. Don't stand out here in the cold. Come inside. Please tell me you're staying. And for more than a day this time."

"Big fat yes." She forced cheerfulness into her voice. "I definitely am."

"Is there a holiday I don't know about?"

Boom, there it was. First judgment. The subtext was that since her grandparents' funerals five years ago she only showed up on holidays and hadn't visited since last Christmas. And her mom hadn't yet noticed the main attraction.

"Why didn't you tell us you were coming?" She

pulled her daughter close for a hug, then backed away, looking shocked. "Erica?"

She walked farther into the brightly lit entryway and pulled her poncho off over her head. Her mother's eyes went wide and her jaw actually dropped. In her rebellious teens, there was a time when Erica might have taken pride in pulling off the miracle of rendering her unflappable mother speechless. Not so much now. Or like this.

"You're pregnant." Her mother stated the obvious. "*Very* pregnant. Why didn't you tell us you're going to have a baby?"

Her token teen mutinies were small potatoes compared to this, but every time Erica had disappointed her parents, it ripped her heart out. This was, pardon the pun, the mother of all rebellions and no matter how old she was, or how much career success she had, making them proud was always her intention.

"I was going to tell you—" No points for good intentions. She lifted her hands in a helpless gesture. "I couldn't figure out how to say it."

Angela's gaze dropped to the ring finger on her left hand. "Is there a marriage you couldn't figure out how to tell us about either?"

Erica flinched at the words. Not that her mother's tone was sharp, but because it wasn't. The hurt in her eyes and reproach in her voice were like pokes in the chest, jabbing her heart. This was why she'd put off the conversation. The problem was, the longer she had dragged her feet, the worse it got. That was her bad, just one on a very long list.

"No, Mama. I'm not married."

"Is it Peter's baby?"

Erica should have expected the question but hadn't. "No. I told you we broke up over a year ago."

Regret was stark in her mom's eyes. "You did but I just thought—" The breakup had stunned Erica because they'd dated for a long time. Peter Barron was handsome, smart, fun, successful and she'd really cared about him. They had a relationship that was the envy of all their friends. She'd been so sure he was The One. So, she brought up the subject of having children. His answer was adamant and unequivocal: he didn't want any kids. Ever. And he wasn't going to change his mind.

She'd tried to tell herself it didn't matter. She could be content, fulfilled and live a happy life with Peter while having a successful career of her own. It could be enough. But every time she saw a pregnant woman or a baby in a stroller, she got a knot of emptiness and longing in her stomach. Like a protest from her uterus. The yearning for a baby, the ache to be a mother, just wouldn't go away.

"Erica, who is the father?"

The quiet question snapped her back to the present. "I don't want to talk about it."

The anxiety in her mother's blue eyes increased,

and her face went pale. "Did something happen to you?"

"No." She reached out, took her mother's hand and Angela squeezed it hard. "I didn't mean to scare you."

She'd given her poor mother a lot of shocks since she walked through the front door. Maybe she should tell her the truth. It was possible that she would understand. Angela Abernathy had two babies in two years, a boy and a girl. She thought her family was complete. Then right around the time she turned thirty, she accidentally got pregnant and realized how very much she wanted another baby. But she miscarried and the loss was devastating. After several more tries and losses she was told she couldn't carry a baby. It nearly destroyed her.

When Erica was suddenly staring thirty in the face, she remembered her mother's difficulty with pregnancy. Erica had no potential husband material on her horizon and worried that the inability to carry a baby at a certain age was genetic. She wasn't willing to wait and hope for a man to come along. She wouldn't risk what might be her only chance and pulled the trigger on going the single mom route. A big part of her hadn't believed IUI—intrauterine insemination—would work, but it did, and she was thrilled.

If anyone would understand the primal longing to have a baby, it was this woman.

"Mama, I really want to talk to you about this—"

The sound of heavy footsteps coming closer stopped her. Before she saw him, Erica heard her father's voice.

"Angela? What's taking so long? Who was at the door?" And then George Abernathy walked into the entryway and saw her. Emotions swirled in his eyes from pleasure to shock.

"Surprise." She'd always been Daddy's little girl, but she'd never seen him look at her quite like this before.

He was fit and tan but the color drained from his face. "Good Lord, Erica. What in the world—"

"You're going to be a grandfather, Daddy." She tried to smile, but her mouth was trembling and her heart was beating way too fast.

"Did you come here alone?"

"You're asking if I'm married. The answer is no."

He waited for several moments, then rubbed a hand across the back of his neck. "Are you all right? You look well."

Erica was pretty sure telling him the details would make things worse. Her father was old-fashioned and set in his ways. She knew her brother, Gabe, had butted heads with him over trying progressive ranching techniques. *Stubborn* was her dad's middle name, and Gabe finally gave up. Now he was more involved with real estate wheeling and dealing than the ranch. No, admitting to her father that she'd gone to a sperm bank was the last thing she planned to do.

"I'm fine, Daddy."

He looked down for a moment as if gathering his thoughts. Then he met her gaze and his eyes churned with confusion and hurt. "We're your parents and we have concerns—"

"I know. And I love you both very much," she interrupted. "But please believe me when I say I'm fine. Obviously I'm going to be a mother and more happy about this pregnancy than I can even put into words. I will do my very best to do as spectacular a job with my child as you guys did with Gabe and me. When the shock wears off, I hope you'll be as excited about this baby as I am. I know how much you want to be grandparents."

Neither of them responded to her impassioned speech but simply stared at her. Then they looked at each other and seemed to exchange silent agreement not to say anything more.

Finally her mother asked, "How long are you staying?"

"Would it be all right if I lived here until I find a job?"

"Of course you can stay with us—" Then her father stopped as her words sank in. "Wait. You left Barron Enterprises?" George Abernathy didn't shock easily, but this was the second time in five minutes he'd looked completely bewildered.

Erica was on a roll apparently. "I was fired actually."

"I don't understand. Not long ago you got that big promotion," her mom protested.

"I did." To chief administrative officer. In the last few years, these two had been so busy quizzing her about her marriage prospects, she hadn't been sure the move up the corporate ladder had even registered with them. "But Mr. Barron Senior, called me into his office to tell me I was being transferred to the Miami office. I didn't want to go."

"Why would he do that?" her dad asked. "Doesn't the chief administrative officer work out of the corporate office in Denver?"

Wow, she thought. He really had been paying attention. She'd been hoping to gloss over this part. "Peter married one of the receptionists at work. And she's pregnant." Even though she didn't love him anymore, that news had come as a blow. The lying bastard. "His wife has been a little hostile to me, since everyone at the company knows he and I were together for a long time."

"You said he's not the baby's father," Angela reminded her.

"He's not. But the woman apparently had a problem seeing me every day."

"So, Peter's father fired you because the new wife is an insecure twit?" her mother scoffed.

Erica was glad they seemed to be annoyed with someone besides her. "Apparently."

"That's wrongful termination," her father chimed in. "You can't let them get away with that."

"Way ahead of you, Daddy. I already have an appointment with an attorney."

"Good for you," he said.

"The thing is, after I moved in with Peter I sold my condo and banked a nice profit. When we split up, I rented an apartment while I figured out what I wanted to do." And how big a place she would need *if* she got pregnant. "I have savings, but no job means no income until I can find another one. There's no telling how long that will be, so my savings have to last."

Her father nodded his understanding. "And if you file a lawsuit against Barron Enterprises, it could be a long time until there's a financial settlement."

"Exactly. So, I was hoping you guys wouldn't mind if I stayed here until I get back on my feet," she said.

"Of course." He didn't hesitate. "You're back where you belong. Even if it means coming home with your tail between your legs."

Erica refused to flinch at the words. Her father was right. She'd thought she had everything figured out and was thrown a big curve. She refused to call it a mess because that reflected on the child she was carrying, and the choices had been hers. The way it had played out made her feel like crap, and now she needed help from the family she'd neglected.

"Thank you, Daddy."

Her dad nodded, held out his arms to her and she stepped into them for a much needed hug. "I love you, honey. I think I speak for your mother when I say we're glad you're home, but we aren't finished talking about this baby's father."

Erica was finished, but wisely chose not to say that. The line was drawn in the sand, and she knew which side of it she was on.

Her dad helped her unload the car and take some things upstairs to her old room. She appreciated that very much and knew all of this must be hard for him. After that, she felt an overwhelming need to see her big brother. Fortunately his house was on the ranch and was located not far from her parents, so Erica walked over.

For the second time that day, she knocked on a door and waited to shock the person who opened it. But she was the one who got a surprise when a pretty, petite woman with long, straight blond hair stood there instead of her big brother.

"Hi. I'm Melanie Driscoll."

"You're the woman who's going to marry my brother. I'm Erica." She couldn't believe they hadn't met. "Mom called me right after he proposed, and she said the ring is fabulous."

"I think so." Melanie held out her left hand with a platinum band supporting a spectacularly large diamond.

"Gorgeous." Erica smiled. "When's the wedding?"

"Next summer."

"I'm so glad to finally meet you."

"Same here." The other woman's gaze dropped to her belly. "And I hear congratulations are in order for you, too. Your mom called."

"I figured."

Melanie shrugged. "Gabe is still on the phone with her."

"My ears were burning," Erica said wryly, and slid off her poncho as she stepped into the warm house.

Melanie gave her the once-over. "I've known you all of a minute but I have to say, you're positively glowing. The baby bump is so cute and you're beautiful."

"You should probably get your eyes checked. I'm as big as a barn."

"Hardly. When is the baby due?"

"November."

"You look fantastic," Melanie said. "How do you feel?"

"The first three months were a little rough with morning sickness. But since then I've been great. Not too tired. I love being pregnant." She smiled at the other woman. "I've known you all of a minute, but I have to say this. I'm so glad my brother has the good sense to marry you."

"I'm the lucky one. I'd given up on finding someone and then, there he was." She turned an adoring gaze on the man in question when he came up beside her.

Gabriel Abernathy was a tall, broad-shouldered force of nature. When he looked at Melanie, his blue eyes were flirty. Then his gaze landed on Erica and turned serious.

"I just got off the phone with Mom."

"Hello to you, too," she said.

"Come here." He held out his arms.

She walked into them and sighed when he hugged her. "I'm so glad to see you."

"Same here. But I have to ask—what the hell are you doing, Erica?"

"I'm having a baby." She put her hands protectively on her belly. "And I want this child more than anything in the world."

"Mom told me you won't say who the father is." With his hands on his hips and looking all serious at her, Gabe looked a lot like their father.

It had been a long, emotional day, and Erica was just about at her limit. "Don't you start on me. I left for Colorado to go to college. I stayed to have a career. Every time I make a decision, I'm being judged in a bad way. And you all wonder why I don't come home more often."

"It's not judgment. It's just that—" he dragged his hand through his spiky dirty blond hair "we miss you. Me. Mom. Dad. Grandpa Alexander. Gramps."

Guilt zinged her hard. Gramps—her great-grandfather, Josiah Abernathy—was in his mid-nineties and had been diagnosed with dementia. The subtext of her brother's words was that no one knew how much time he had left and she'd been focused on career which didn't leave a lot of free time.

She pushed the guilt away. "I was entitled to a life that *I* chose. Not Mom and Dad. They wouldn't have been happy with anything but me marrying a local rancher. I wanted more. To travel. Broaden my horizons."

"And you did." Again he glanced at her belly. "But you've lost time with Gramps. Precious time. And he doesn't say much at all anymore."

"I'll go see him soon—" A lump in her throat cut off more words. She did love Gramps and felt badly that he was declining. There was no good excuse except that life happened. One day turned into the next and before she'd realized it, twelve years had gone by.

Erica didn't want to fight with her brother. She'd come here to get away from the tension at the big house. That thought pulled her up short. Wasn't that what they called prison? It was time to change the subject.

"So, tell me how you and Melanie met," she said enthusiastically.

"Mel moved to Bronco from Rust Creek Falls for a job. She ended up looking into the Abernathy family history. Gramps's history."

So much for a subject change, Erica thought. But Gabe was smiling lovingly at his fiancée. And this was the happiest she'd ever seen him look.

"How did that happen, Melanie?"

"It's Mel," she corrected, then her expression turned from tender to concerned. "I have a good friend in Rust Creek Falls named Winona Cobbs. It came to my attention that she and Josiah Abernathy were secretly in love when they were very young. She got pregnant. When she gave birth, she thought the little girl was stillborn and had a breakdown. But that's not what happened. The baby was alive."

Gabe jumped into the story. "It turned out that Gramps's parents forced him to leave town and put the baby up for adoption. We think somewhere in or around Bronco."

"Oh my God." Erica couldn't believe what she was hearing. "How did you find all this out?"

"When the Ambling A Ranch in Rust Creek Falls was sold, the new people found Josiah's journal in the house. There was a letter inside to Winona. Somehow he found out who adopted their daughter, Beatrix, and promised he'd find a way to bring her back to Winona."

Erica was holding her breath. Waiting for the happy reunion part of the story. When it didn't come, she said, "And?"

"Because of the dementia, he can't give us any information. A friend of mine who's really good with social media did an internet search with what information we have and got a hit." Melanie looked up at Gabe, and disappointment was all over their faces. "It turned out that was just someone looking for money."

"People like that make me so angry." Not only that, Erica was feeling even more guilty about neglecting her great-grandfather. "What now?"

"Good question," Mel said. "So far we've only turned up frauds and weirdos."

Erica looked at her and saw concern. "There's more, isn't there?"

"Winona was hospitalized recently. She's ninety-three and frail. I'm worried that if something doesn't break soon, we'll lose her before we can reunite her with her daughter."

"That would be awful. What are we going to do?" Erica demanded.

"What's this 'we' stuff?" he asked.

"I want to help."

"Really?" Gabe looked surprised.

"Yes, me. I'll do whatever I can."

"Why?"

"He's my great-grandfather." And that wasn't her only reason.

Erica was definitely shocked that Josiah had a
daughter out of wedlock that the family never knew
about. But she felt a parallel to his story. Her own
secret. She was having a baby, and no one was going
to know how this child came to be.

"I love him," she said simply.

"I know that." But his tone and expression were
skeptical, as if he didn't expect her to stick around.

And why would he? She didn't come home enough
when her life was going great. Until it fell apart, she'd
acted as if she didn't need any of them.

"I know I should have made more of an effort to
visit. But I'm here now and I want to do whatever I
can to help. I've certainly got time—"

Gabe's expression turned sympathetic. "Mom told
me about Peter and his father."

Erica saw the blaze of fury in his eyes but knew
that it wasn't directed at her. She loved him so much
for that.

She let out a sigh. "It's been an emotional and
eventful couple of weeks."

Mel put her arm around Erica. "You've been
through a lot recently. Everyone needs a minute to
get used to the new normal. It's all going to be fine."

"Listen to her, baby sister. She's a smart lady." He
smiled tenderly at the woman he was going to marry.
"And I'm taking her out to dinner tonight."

"Why don't you come with us?" Mel asked her.

"I don't want to intrude."

"You won't be. Right, Gabe?" She turned her big blue eyes on him.

He nodded. "Definitely, you should come. There's a new restaurant in town. Barbecue but better. DJ's Deluxe."

"I'm the CFO now and have connections," Mel said. "Come with us. A change of scene will be good for you. We could all use a distraction."

"I could sure use one."

"It's settled then," Mel declared.

Erica watched her brother hold his fiancée's jacket for her to slip on. He put his arm around her for a quick hug, then took her hand and laced their fingers together.

Oh man, he's got it bad, Erica thought. *The bigger they are, the harder they fall.*

She didn't for a moment regret that she was pregnant, but seeing Mel and Gabe together, loving each other, made her a little envious. On the upside, her baby was going to have the best aunt and uncle in the world.

Chapter Two

Morgan Dalton walked into DJ's Deluxe and went straight to the bar. He needed a beer, and if a woman came along after that, he wouldn't complain. A woman would sure take his mind off his problems.

The place was crowded tonight, but he found a spot at the bar. DJ Traub himself was tending it and delivering food. The man was in his forties, handsome, a friendly guy with a face you could trust. The restaurant owner, who looked like he could just as easily round up a herd of cattle, had dark hair, brown eyes. He put a plate of potato skins deluxe in front of the blond woman sitting beside Morgan.

"This looks fantastic," she said. "Even better than

the supermessy wings I just ate. Everything you give me is better than the last."

"You keep eating, I'll keep the food coming. It's the least I can do for Bronco Heights' newest full-time resident and my CFO's future sister-in-law."

Morgan was eavesdropping, but it wasn't his fault. She was close enough that he could smell her super-sexy perfume. And he liked her voice. There was something low and husky and sensuous about it that made him sit up and take notice of everything she said.

DJ noticed him and said hello. Morgan had been a regular since the place opened, and they'd struck up a friendship.

He angled his head toward the woman beside him, a signal that he'd like to be introduced. The other man nodded slightly, an indication that his message was received.

"Hey, Erica," DJ said. "Since you're new to town, I thought you'd like to meet my friend Morgan Dalton."

Still chewing a bite of potato, she full on looked at him for the first time. That face... *This is what it must feel like to get zapped with those paddle things when your heart stops.*

She was beautiful. He'd seen his share of beautiful women in his thirty-four years, some of them on a movie screen. But this one sitting so close to him was more than a wow. He liked women, they liked him and he did his share of dating, although it was never serious and never would be. But he was dead certain that he'd never had such a strong reaction to a female the very first time he laid eyes on her.

"Hello, Morgan," she said. "I'm Erica."

"Nice to meet you." He barely noticed when DJ put a glass of beer in front of him. He wanted to say *where have you been all my life* and was afraid the words had come out of his mouth. But she didn't look afraid, so he figured he hadn't made a fool of himself yet. "So, you're new to town?"

"Not exactly. But I haven't lived here for twelve years. What about you?"

"I've been here a year." Why did it feel so much longer? "My father bought Dalton's Grange. My four brothers and I work there with my dad."

"There are four more at home like you?" she teased.

Her smile was as spectacular as a Montana sunrise, and he swore his heart got zapped again. "Yes, ma'am."

"How do you like it here, so far?" She cut into the potato skin and ate a piece.

"Prettiest country I've ever seen. But a little on the chilly side." He took a sip from his beer glass. "Could just be me, but there are some folks who consider us new money, without deep roots or any legacy. A couple of families have been here for generations. The Taylors and Abernathys. If you're not one of them, you get some funny looks."

"Really? Thanks for the warning." She nodded her head, but there was a twinkle in her pretty hazel eyes.

"So where are you moving from?" he asked.

"Colorado. Denver. My parents have been wanting me to come back and I had a change of circumstances in my career."

"Oh?"

"I got fired."

Morgan wasn't sure how he knew, but some instinct told him it was not a just termination. "Whoever fired you was clearly an idiot."

"I think so. But that's very nice of you to say, considering that we just met."

"The length of our acquaintance doesn't make my comment any less sincere. I just know. Because... Where have you been all my life?" He couldn't believe the words actually came out of his mouth. "Wait. Forget I said that—"

"No way. I love it." Erica was laughing. "That was quite possibly cheesier than these potato skins."

"I take it back—"

"And without a doubt the sweetest thing a man's ever said to me," she added.

"So that didn't make you want to head for the exit?"

"I'm made of sterner stuff." She smiled her punch-to-the-gut smile again. "Besides, I happen to like cheese."

He met her gaze over the corner of the shiny teak bar that separated them as they sat at a right angle to each other. "That makes two of us."

"So tell me, Morgan, why don't you have a beautiful woman on your arm tonight?"

"I wouldn't say *you're* on my arm exactly," he answered, "but you're talking to me. And you're definitely beautiful."

Her smile was suddenly shy and a little sad for some reason. "But we're not together. A good-looking cowboy like you, in this place all by yourself, is a dozen kinds of wrong. So what gives?"

"I thought I made that clear. I've been waiting for you." He knew he was only half kidding.

"Are you flirting with me?" There was the cutest expression on her face, a look that said the flirt factor might be going both ways.

"Maybe a little," he admitted. "And that makes me want to ask for your phone number. It's not every day a man meets a woman like you."

"That statement is true in more ways than you realize," she said wryly. "And it's becoming clear to me you didn't notice that I'm—"

"What?"

She swiveled her bar stool sideways toward him. The good news was they sat close enough that her legs were touching his. The jaw-dropping news was that she was very much with child.

Morgan glanced from her round belly to her eyes a couple of times before blurting out, "You're pregnant."

"Really?" Her look was wry as she put her hands on her stomach. "I hadn't noticed. But that would explain why I've been eating my weight in food that DJ keeps bringing me, even after I ate dinner."

"I didn't mean it like that. It's just— I didn't mean to offend you." He automatically looked for a ring on her left hand.

"I'm not married or offended." There was laughter in her voice.

"Erica, you have to know that I've never hit on a pregnant woman in my life. I apologize."

"Well, Morgan Dalton, I'm thrilled to be your first. And speaking for pregnant women everywhere, it's quite flattering to be flirted with." She stopped and studied his face. "But maybe I should apologize to you."

"For what?"

"You're white as a ghost."

"And you're enjoying that quite a bit, aren't you?"

"Yes."

She pushed away the plate with food still on it. Either she was finally full or had suddenly lost her appetite. "But I should have said something sooner. It's been a long day and coming home is hard."

"Oh?"

"My great-grandfather has dementia. And my family is kind of upset that I haven't been back to visit him in a while."

"I'm sorry."

"Thank you. And today I found out that said great-grandfather, Josiah Abernathy, had a baby out of wedlock and no one in my family knew about it."

He wasn't sure about turning white when she pointed out her pregnancy, but he felt the color drain from his face now. This was a bad time to find out he never got her last name before bad-mouthing her family. "You're an Abernathy?"

"Guilty." She put her hand on his arm, a consoling gesture. "Don't feel bad. I didn't take it the wrong way. I understand where you're coming from. People in this town don't deal well with change. And my parents are no exception. They respect tradition, passing land down to their children."

"Like I said. We're new money."

"Yeah. It kind of makes you an outsider." She looked down at her stomach and sighed. "They also aren't thrilled that their daughter is pregnant and not married. It's been a long time since I lived here, and I feel a lot like an outsider, too."

"What about the baby's father?"

"Don't you start judging me." Her eyes flashed with anger. "It was bad enough coming from my parents and brother, but I barely know you."

"I wasn't judging," he assured her. "And we just met, but we've shared a lot of information over potato skins and beer."

"Technically, and for the record, I'm drinking club soda with lime."

"That doesn't change the fact that we've bonded over being outsiders."

She thought about that for a moment, then nodded. "Okay. You win. We've bonded."

It was nice to have a friendly conversation with someone. Morgan was just about to ask for her phone number when he saw her expression change. He hadn't known her long but would swear her guard went up. He glanced over his shoulder and saw Gabe Abernathy and Melanie Driscoll walking toward them. Morgan had run into him in town, at events, and the man had been cordial but not overly friendly.

Looking wary, he stopped beside his sister. "Are you okay, Erica?"

"Of course. Why wouldn't I be?"

"Mel and I didn't mean to be gone so long. We ran into some friends and got to talking." He gave Morgan another careful look. "I'm sorry we left you alone."

"It's okay. Morgan kept me company." She looked back and forth between them. "Have you two met?"

"Yes," Gabe said in his best "don't get any ideas" tone.

Erica's eyes narrowed as she looked at her

brother's fiancée. "Mel, you're pretty new in town, aren't you?"

"Yes. And I love it here," she said, as chipper as could be. "People have been so friendly and welcoming."

"I guess that happens when you're engaged to an Abernathy." Morgan maintained a friendly tone, but never looked away from the other man.

"It helps," Gabe said. Then he looked at his sister. "We're leaving. Are you ready to go?"

"Yeah. I'm tired. It's been a long day." From her perch on the high bar stool, she looked hesitantly at the floor. "I just have to get down from here first."

Instantly Morgan got up and took her arms to help her down. Touching her seemed to short-circuit his brain, because he couldn't stop looking at her mouth. With an effort he pulled himself together and said, "Gracefully done."

"Thanks to you." She gave him a grateful look. "It was really nice to meet you, Morgan."

"The pleasure was mine." And he sincerely meant that.

"Good night," Mel said. "I'll see you around, Morgan."

"You will."

Then he watched the three of them walk away. Mostly he watched Erica. From this view it was impossible to tell she was pregnant. She had on leggings and cowboy boots with a sweater covering her hips and butt. What he could see was damn shapely, and her face and smile would steal a man's heart and have him grateful for it.

That's when he remembered he hadn't gotten her phone number. Now that he could think straight again, he realized how idiotic the thought was. Why would he even consider it? But he knew the answer to that. He felt comfortable with her, and that hadn't happened to him in a long time. Clearly she wasn't looking for a relationship but that could be *why* he felt so comfortable with her. He wasn't looking for a relationship either. He'd fallen half in love with Erica Abernathy before realizing she was going to have a baby. And that complicated things in a way that would keep him from making a romantic fool of himself.

The next morning Erica was in the best mood. A man had flirted with her! Granted, when he started, he didn't know she was pregnant. What pleased and surprised her the most was that he didn't seem to lose interest when he found out.

Another surprise was how nice it felt waking up in her old room. Her mom kept it the way it was when Erica left for college. She slept in her queen-size bed with the brass headboard. Across from it was a cherrywood dresser and matching dressing table where she did her makeup. Lace curtains crisscrossed the window that had a spectacular view of the mountains. The walls were painted a pale lavender, with white doors and trim. And the room came with an en suite bathroom. The whole effect was soothing.

Except for the part where she couldn't get last night out of her mind. A man like that—those shoulders, that voice and face. His blue eyes twinkled with humor and he was tan, evidence of a rugged outdoor life. And he admitted flirting with her and wanting her phone number. In an alternate universe, where she wasn't pregnant and as big as the *Queen Mary*, she'd have seriously flirted back.

So it was probably a good thing she had her own personal speed bump. After being dumped by the man she'd thought was The One, then watching him take up with another woman so soon after, her self-esteem had been pretty battered. Last night made her feel better.

After showering, then doing her hair and makeup, she slipped on a dress she hoped projected confident professionalism. Then she went downstairs.

Erica heard voices, which was unusual at this hour. She'd only expected to see her mother, as her father was almost always busy with ranch work by now. Not today. And she got a bonus surprise. Her brother, Gabe, was there, too. And Grandpa Alexander. She kissed his cheek and gave him a hug.

"It's good to see you, Erica." The silver-haired man smiled, but there were questions in his eyes.

"How come you guys aren't out working?" She

was practically positive the four of them had been talking about her, because they clammed up when she'd walked into the room. Now they all looked guilty. "What?"

"Good morning, sweetie." Her mother set the spatula she'd been holding on the granite countertop beside the stainless steel stove. "Did you sleep well?"

"As well as can be expected, what with being as big as a house." She made eye contact with each one of them. "Don't let me interrupt. Feel free to continue talking about me."

Gabe snorted. "What makes you think we were talking about you?"

"Oh please." She put a hand on her hip. "Since when are you and Daddy and Grandpa not doing ranch chores at this time of day? I grew up hearing that there's always something to be done around here. This looks very much like a family meeting. And it's not a leap to figure out that I'm the topic of discussion, since my presence on the Ambling A is the only variable."

"Why don't you let me make you a plate of food?" her mother suggested. "You need to keep up your strength."

"Thank you, Mama. Something smells wonderful. But first I'd like to know what's going on." She looked at her brother pointedly, and he squirmed under her gaze.

"You know I've always had your best interests at heart," he started.

"That's how you start when someone isn't going to like what you're about to say. Does this have anything to do with last night at DJ's?"

He pressed his lips together and wouldn't quite meet her gaze, confirming the theory. "Do you always chat up strangers at a bar, sis?"

"Obviously you're talking about Morgan Dalton." Just saying his name brought to mind a very appealing image of the man, and it made her tummy flutter. This was something she hadn't felt in a long time. Or maybe ever. "He seemed to be a very nice man. I liked him a lot."

"Looks can be deceiving," her mother said.

"Do you have something against him?" Erica asked the question and looked at all of them for a response.

"The Daltons are new to Bronco Heights," Grandpa Alexander said.

"No one knows much about them." Her father planted his feet wide apart and folded his arms over his chest.

She remembered what Morgan had said about local folks being a little standoffish.

"Has anyone bothered to get to know them?" she demanded.

"There are rumors. You know how this town is." Her mother didn't actually answer the question.

"Mel's friend Amanda is engaged to his brother. I heard something about the father cheating on his wife. No one knows how they got the money to buy the ranch."

"If it wasn't legal, I'm sure someone would be in jail." Erica wasn't sure why, but she felt strongly about defending Morgan. She met her brother's gaze. "Does Mel think her friend is making a mistake marrying Morgan's brother?"

Gabe shifted his feet before meeting her gaze. "She said he's a good man and a terrific father."

"Well, what do you know?" Erica looked at each of them in turn. "Amanda found out that one of the Daltons is a stand-up guy because she got to know him."

"People change," Erica continued. "They mature. Let them screw up first before you put their picture on a Most Wanted poster at the post office."

"But, sweetie, you're pregnant," her mother said.

"Not a news flash, Mama."

"He's after something," her father declared.

"Not my money." She was unemployed and her savings wouldn't last long. "I don't have any."

"But your family does." It seemed her father had already made up his mind.

"His ranch seems to be doing fine, no?" she asked them.

"No one knows for sure," Gabe said. "The smart move would be to stay away from him."

Erica looked from her brother to her father to her grandfather. "You know, I find this overprotective streak of yours equal parts adorable and annoying. You do realize that for the past twelve years I've been taking pretty good care of myself."

"Except for the part where you're having a baby without a husband." Her mother didn't pull any punches.

The zinger hit its mark, and Erica heard the message loud and clear. "Thank you all for your advice and I know it comes from a place of caring about me." It was also worth what she'd paid for it, no matter their good intentions. Wasn't the road to hell paved with them? "I'm not very hungry after all, Mama. And I have to run. I have an appointment in town with an attorney."

"Could you do me a favor since you're going into town?" her father asked. "I called in an order to the building supply store. It will fit in your SUV and you be sure to have one of the guys there load it up for you. That would save me a trip. Since I'm behind on work today..."

Because he'd felt an obligation to warn her away from Morgan. Defensiveness didn't trump her sense of obligation to do as he'd asked. "Not a problem, Daddy."

Erica walked away before anyone, including herself, could say another word. She'd grab something to eat before her appointment. More than one friend in Denver had suggested she might have a case to sue Barron Enterprises for wrongful termination, so she'd made the appointment before moving home.

After stopping for a fast-food breakfast sandwich, she was early for her ten o'clock slot at Randall & Randall, attorneys at law. It was a brother-sister firm located in the Bronco Heights business district. The receptionist was somewhere in her fifties, with stylishly cut short brown hair and brown eyes. The nameplate on her desk read Mrs. Frances Randall. *All in the family*, Erica thought.

She introduced herself and was politely asked to take a seat in the expensively furnished waiting area. Charlotte Randall would be with her shortly.

"Can I get you anything?" Mrs. Randall asked. "Water? Coffee?"

"Nothing, thanks."

A few minutes later a pretty young woman with red hair and brown eyes opened the door to the back offices. "You must be Erica Abernathy. I'm Charlotte Randall. It's nice to meet you."

"Likewise." Erica stood and shook hands.

"Let's go to my office and you can tell me why you're here."

They walked down a hall, then turned right into a large room with a desk full of files and a laptop buried in the middle of it. Floor-to-ceiling windows looked out on the gorgeous mountains while diplomas and certificates hanging on the wall proudly displayed her impressive credentials.

Charlotte sat behind the desk. "How can I help you?"

"I'm not sure you can, actually." She took a deep breath. "Until recently I worked for Barron Enterprises in Denver."

"I've heard of it. Big media company headquartered there. Powerful."

"Yeah." Erica fully expected to be told there was no point in wasting time because Barron had an army of lawyers. They would fight any settlement by every legal means necessary and drag out a lawsuit, making it too expensive to continue. "I was fired."

The young woman nodded thoughtfully. "Colorado is an at-will state. That means either an employer or employee can terminate an employment situation at any time without consequences."

"So, you're saying I have no recourse?" Though it was expected, her heart fell. She could practically hear the thud.

"Not necessarily. Were you given a reason for the dismissal?"

"No." She thought for a moment. "I was called in to see the company president. He told me I was being transferred to the Miami office."

Erica went on from there, explaining everything. Dating the boss's son. Their breakup. His relationship with another company employee. "I wanted to quit even before I was called on the carpet."

"Why is that?"

"Peter and that employee's sudden marriage and baby announcement. After that his wife became increasingly hostile as my pregnancy began to show."

"It's a good thing you toughed it out. If you'd quit, you would have lost any standing in the court to file a lawsuit."

"The transfer came out of the blue and I'm in my third trimester. The job I had was traditionally done from the home office in Denver. I pushed back. My boss got angry and said I was fired."

"I see." Charlotte's eyes narrowed a little dangerously. "So there was no misconduct on your part? No job performance issues like habitual tardiness?"

"No. I'd been with the company for eight years and had a spotless record. In fact, before the work environment turned hostile, I was promoted to chief administrative officer."

Charlotte nodded, her expression reflecting respect for that higher management job. "So you want to sue Barron for wrongful termination."

"I believe I was unfairly let go. And that I'm entitled to a severance package at the very least. But you should be aware that my resources are limited, especially because of my pregnancy."

The lawyer smiled. "Frankly, that's what gives you cause to bring suit."

"How so?"

"Even in an at-will state there are exceptions to the rule and legal remedies that could help keep your job, if you still want it. Or go for a settlement because you were wrongfully terminated. One of those exceptions is discrimination for a number of reasons, one of them being pregnancy."

"But I don't think he fired me because I'm having a baby. Everyone knows it's not his son's. It's all about the new wife not wanting to look at me every day and be reminded I dated her husband first." What she kept to herself was that he hadn't wanted to have a baby with Erica.

"It doesn't matter what the motivation for termination was. You're in a protected class and that gives you a very good chance of winning a settlement. No matter how many lawyers the company has. And I don't think they can drag it out. The optics for a powerful media company bullying a pregnant woman are really bad. They know it, and we can use that to pressure them."

"Does that mean you'll take my case?"

"Yes." Charlotte explained that she would take it on contingency and how the attorney-client contract worked. She seemed really eager to get started. "There are laws against what they did to you, Erica. I'll put the paperwork together and have them served as soon as possible."

"Thank you, Charlotte. You have no idea how relieved I am."

Erica left the lawyer's office feeling pretty darn positive. Kind of the way she'd left DJ's last night after Morgan had said *Where have you been all my life*. The memory made her smile, but she also felt a little wistful. In her car behind the steering wheel, she looked down at the belly that prevented her from seeing her feet. She was officially a package deal, and no man in his right mind would want her.

She'd been resigned to that when she decided to take the journey to motherhood alone. But that was before she met Morgan.

It was a short drive to the building supply store. She got out of the car and walked into the cavernous interior guaranteed to make men quiver with excitement. But she was the one doing the quivering when she practically ran into Morgan Dalton standing just inside the door.

Chapter Three

Morgan had been thinking about Erica a lot since last night, but he hadn't expected to see her again. On top of that, the building supply store in town was probably the last place he would have expected to bump into her. Yet here she was. And when she smiled her beautiful smile at him, his day got a whole lot brighter. Possibly because he felt that lightning bolt to the heart even stronger than he had the first time he saw her.

"If it isn't the prettiest pregnant lady in town." Darned if she didn't blush, he thought. If she had at DJ's, the dim lighting in the restaurant prevented him from seeing. She was even more beautiful than she'd been last night, classy and stylish in her gray dress and black boots. Again his gaze was drawn to her full, sexy lips.

"I bet you say that to all the pregnant ladies."

"Nope. As a matter of fact, you're the only one I know." He steered her to the side of the doorway and out of the heavy foot traffic where she might get run into. Reluctantly, he removed his hand from her arm but couldn't stop the tingling in his fingers—or the urge to touch her and never stop. "To what do I owe the good fortune of seeing you again so soon?"

"Actually you can thank my father. I'm picking up an order for him." There was a wry expression on her face and more than a little satisfaction in her smile. "What brings you here?"

"Fencing materials. It's getting to be time to check them out and make repairs. Need to have all the supplies when that chore gets put on the schedule." When that happened, he was pretty sure his father would tag along and continue trying to "mend fences" with him. Morgan would have thought that pun was funny if it was anyone but his dad. He wasn't laughing.

"You turned very serious about something all of a sudden." That statement put a curious look on her face. "Does it have anything to do with family?"

"Why do you ask?"

"Because nine times out of ten a man looking like you do right now is having woman or family trouble.

Since you flirted with me outrageously last night, I don't think it's about a lady. That leaves family. And I have to tell you, there are rumors spreading about yours."

Folks around here hadn't given him an especially warm welcome so he was a little surprised they'd waste their breath gossiping about his family. "I don't know whether to be pissed off or proud."

"Maybe both. But one of the things they're talking about is your brother."

"I've got four," he said. "Still, my guess would be that it's Holt."

Absently she tucked a silky blond strand of hair behind her ear. "Gabe mentioned he's a good man and father."

"Yeah. He is. Ten years ago he had a brush with the law. He did community service, but there's nothing permanent on his record."

"Then that's not a rumor. It's fact."

She wasn't judging, Morgan realized, and liked her even better for it. "Holt isn't proud of it and in a lot of ways that shaped the dad he's become."

"That would make you an uncle. Niece or nephew?" Interest sparked in her hazel eyes, cranking up the green, toning down the brown.

"Nephew. Robby. He's seven. As a matter of fact, somehow my brother talked me into looking after him this afternoon. I'm taking him to Happy Hearts after school."

"I'm sorry. Happy Hearts?"

He laughed at the puzzled expression on her face. "I forgot you just came back. It's an animal sanctuary run by Daphne Taylor. Robby picked out a dog and cat from there, both rescues."

"I know Daphne. She was a year ahead of me in high school." She tapped her lip thoughtfully. "As a matter of fact, I dated her older brother Jordan for a short time the summer after I graduated. He was an older man and I was flattered by the attention. At first."

"Oh?" Jealousy pricked him a little, and that was just plain stupid. Why the hell was it any skin off his nose that she went out with the son of the richest man in town a lot of years ago? And obviously she'd been with someone since then or she wouldn't be pregnant. If, and that was a very big if, there was any skin coming off his nose about anything, it would be that.

"Yeah. I haven't thought about him for a long time. Seems like a lifetime ago." She met his gaze. "My parents made no secret of the fact that they really wanted me to marry Jordan. Partly so I wouldn't go out of state to college."

"But you didn't do that."

"Nope. There was no spark with him." She shrugged.

Damn sparks were sure inconvenient. He was pretty sure he had some for her because he was unreasonably glad she hadn't felt them for Jordan Taylor. "So, are you and Daphne friends?"

"We used to be."

"Then you should come out to the sanctuary. This afternoon maybe. If you don't have something going on."

"I don't."

"You could meet Robby. See your friend." *I could see you.*

"Maybe." She nodded thoughtfully. "Now I better see about my father's order."

"Yeah. And I have to get those supplies."

It turned out the order for her father was wood cut into short pieces and a couple bags of hardware that were already loaded onto a cart. One of the store employees started to wheel it out to her SUV in the parking lot, but Morgan offered to help.

He followed her to the car and put her rear passenger seat down flat, then slid the boards in one by one. That gave him the chance to spend a couple more minutes with her. Just in case he didn't see her later. On a one to ten stupid scale, that probably earned him a twenty.

Erica drove back to the Ambling A feeling as if she'd been on an emotional roller coaster all day. She woke up in a great mood but her family managed to bring her down with warnings to steer clear of Morgan Dalton. Then the lawyer said she had a strong case for a settlement and while doing her dad a favor she ran into Morgan.

When she saw him, she got that shivery feeling in the pit of her stomach again. The same thing she'd felt at DJ's, only stronger, especially because he kept looking at her mouth. He didn't have to mention the outing with his nephew, but he had. And, doggone it, she was curious to see him with a seven-year-old boy. Then she factored in her family's advice, the same family she was trying to make peace with.

It might be best to avoid Morgan. Not because she believed he wasn't a decent person, but because every instinct said he was. He seemed like an awfully nice man. And he was hot. In a world where she wasn't pregnant there was a good chance she'd have kissed him when he looked at her mouth. But she was pregnant, so that was that.

She drove down the long road to the ranch, turned toward the outbuildings and corral, then parked by the barn. Her father had said he would be there most of the day. She sniffed the air and savored the familiar, earthy scent of animals and hay. She'd forgotten how pleasant this all was. And inside the barn it was even stronger as she walked through. She located her dad in the tack room sitting on a stool in front of the workbench.

"Daddy, I've got the stuff you ordered from the building supply store."

"Thanks." He glanced over his shoulder. "I'll come unload it."

"Okay."

He slid off the wooden stool and walked toward her, a frown on his face. "Who loaded the car for you? Was it Jerry?"

She debated the pros and cons of telling him who had. In the end, she couldn't resist messing with him. After all, he'd warned her off Morgan, then sent her on an errand where he happened to be. Karma was funny that way. "No, I didn't lift a finger. Jerry offered, but Morgan Dalton happened to be there and he helped me out."

"Hmm." That was his only comment.

But Erica could feel the tension from him crank up. She didn't like this awkwardness and needed to try and lighten things up. She followed him out to her car, where he lifted the tailgate and pulled out a couple pieces of the wood.

"What are you going to do with this?" she asked.

"I'm building something."

"What?" she asked.

"A piece of furniture," he said vaguely.

"Something for Mama?"

"Sort of."

She walked after him back through the barn to the tack room but he didn't elaborate.

"I have a lot of good memories growing up here with Grandpa Alex and Gramps."

"Is that so?" Her dad set down the boards in an empty space on the far wall. He pulled his Stetson a little lower on his forehead. "Funny, you didn't have any trouble walking away."

It was on the tip of her tongue to explain her reasons again. How she wanted independence. And didn't want to be pressured into marrying Jordan. Or settling down in Bronco, Montana without ever experiencing another way of life. But she kept that to herself because this man had heard it all before and none of what she'd said changed his attitude.

"Do you remember that litter of kittens the barn cat had?"

"Yup." He walked past her back outside.

Erica followed behind him, just like when she was a little girl and shadowed him everywhere. "They were so cute."

"Took us forever to get rid of 'em."

"You mean find them good homes."

"Whatever," he said.

"Morgan told me about Happy Hearts, the animal sanctuary. His nephew adopted a dog and cat. If that place had been around, we wouldn't have had such a hard time getting people to take the kittens."

"Hmm." He set a few more boards down with the others, then turned to make another trip.

"I'll never forget that time we went fishing in the creek. You were trying to teach me how to cast a line."

"And you fell in." He half smiled. "Your mama wasn't too happy with us."

"No, she wasn't." As they walked through the barn, she saw the stall where her first horse had lived. "Do you remember Belle?"

"Of course. You learned to ride on her."

"Yeah." She fell off and broke her arm, too. But she was trying to lighten his mood, not remind him how he blamed himself for that accident. "She was a sweetheart."

"Gramps knew she would be. He picked her out for you."

Erica had forgotten that. Again she felt bad about not seeing him more while she could still talk to him about these memories.

"Gabe told me about the baby girl Gramps gave up for adoption. Beatrix."

"Yeah." Her father put the last piece of wood on the stack.

"He and Mel are trying to find her. Do you think they will?"

"Long shot, I figure."

"She would be your—" Erica did the family connection in her head "—aunt. How do you feel about all this?"

"Family is family. It's good to know your folks, I guess. For us and for her."

"Yes." Erica sat on the stool while he went to get the bags of hardware. When he came back she said,

"It's weird to think about Gramps having a baby and not telling anyone."

Her father's gaze snapped to hers, and irony glittered in his hazel eyes. "You didn't tell any of us you were going to have a baby until yesterday. And only because you had to."

"I would have said something. Eventually," she mumbled. This was not going at all as she'd hoped. Instead of easing the tension between them, she was making it worse.

"I don't understand this world anymore," he said. "Times are changing. I can't keep up. And not sure I want to."

"Talk to me, Daddy." That was the most he'd said. Maybe he was ready to get it out in the open. "What's bugging you?"

His gaze settled on her belly for several moments, so she braced herself for more third degree about the baby's father. When he finally spoke, she was surprised by what he said.

"You really want to know what's got me twisted up?" He set the bag down. "That damn animal sanctuary of Daphne Taylor's."

"What?" Her eyes opened wider. "Why?"

"This is cattle country. It's always been survival of the fittest. That's nature's way. What doesn't kill you makes you stronger. That's a cliché now, but it's always been the way of it on a ranch. Whether it's horses or cows, the ones that make it against the odds ensure the strength of the bloodlines to produce hardy offspring able to withstand adverse conditions. Like cold, heat, drought and anything else Mother Nature throws at us."

Erica could understand his point of view, but science made advances to benefit animals and humans. Without artificial insemination she wouldn't be having this baby. Those words would not come out of her mouth, however. Her father would never understand how very much she wanted this child. How deeply she'd longed to be a mother.

"Look at it this way, Daddy. As I understand it, Daphne takes in animals and hooks them up with someone to love them. Like an adoption agency." Or a sperm bank. "She provides a service to the community."

"If you ask me, that girl has too much time on her hands if she can take care of animals that have no practical function."

"You have dogs," she pointed out. "And you love them."

"I do. But they serve a purpose on this ranch. They herd cattle."

"Okay." Time to exit this conversation. "Just so I'm clear. Does this mean you're a no vote on Happy Hearts?"

For half a second he grinned, as if forgetting to be mad at her. As if she was the smart-ass kid he'd always called her. Then the amusement disappeared and serious dad was back.

"Have you ever seen this animal place?" he asked. "After all, you've been gone for twelve years."

She refused to engage on something she couldn't change. "No, I haven't been there yet."

"Okay, then." That meant *don't argue something you know nothing about*. He pointed to the bench where the tack was laid out. "I've got work to do."

"Right." She slid off the stool and moved toward the doorway.

"Erica?"

"Hmm?" She turned back toward him.

"How did your appointment go? With the lawyer?"

"Oh." She'd almost forgotten. "She said I have a strong case and will draw up the paperwork to file the lawsuit."

"Good. Thanks for getting my order." He nodded and picked up a bridle, effectively turning his back on her and any more conversation.

"You're welcome. See you later."

She headed outside, mulling over their talk. One positive thing had come out of it, and her dad wouldn't like the result. He was right that she was advocating for something she knew nothing about. So, she made up her mind to go to the animal sanctuary. She smiled when she realized the trip came with a bonus. Morgan would be there with his nephew.

* * *

Morgan finished feeding the horses, then jumped in his truck for the short drive to his house on Dalton's Grange. It was one of three, the other two going to the second- and third-oldest Dalton brothers—Holt and Boone.

His place had three bedrooms, two baths, living and dining rooms and a kitchen. A little more space than a single cowboy needed and this was the second largest. They'd agreed Holt should have the most square footage since he had a boy he was raising.

That boy was the reason he was in such a hurry. He was going to pick up Robby from school, then take him to Happy Hearts. While Holt was attending a cattlemen's association meeting, his fiancée, Amanda, had promised the kid an outing. Morgan was going along to provide another pair of eyes, or possibly some muscle. Robby loved to roam and roughhouse. And if Erica showed up while they were there, well, he sure as heck wouldn't turn down another chance to hang out with her.

Fifteen minutes later he was showered, changed into clean clothes and smelled pretty good, too. There was a knock on his door, and when he opened it, Holt and Amanda were there. She was a pretty little thing with long brown hair and eyes the color of warm chocolate.

He hugged her. "Hey. When are you going to get smart and leave this guy to run away with me?"

She laughed. "As tempting as that offer is, I love him."

"Hands off my woman, big brother." Holt didn't look the least bit worried. He'd loved her for a long time, and they were eager to be a family for his son.

Morgan was teasing, but if he did have a thing for her, he'd fight it into submission. No way he'd be like his father and cross the boundaries of fidelity. But he had to ask, "How come you don't think I could take her away from you?"

"Because with women you're all hat and no saddle. As soon as one gets seriously sweet on you, that's it. You're outta there." Holt grinned. "You're only interested when there's no serious danger of making a commitment."

Morgan admitted, if only to himself, that his brother had a point. But he was a little envious of Holt's happiness. "How did you guys know you were it for each other?"

"That's hard to put into words." Holt thought for a moment. "The first time I laid eyes on Amanda, I knew she was something special." He smiled down at her. "That was ten years ago. It didn't work out then, but I never forgot her. And now she's never getting rid of me."

"As if." She moved closer and slid her arm around his waist. "To answer your question, Morgan, love is when you light up in the presence of one certain person. That someone you can't wait to be with and never want to leave. It can sneak up on you gradually or hit you like a bolt of lightning. And you just *know*."

He doubted he'd find that, but out loud he teased, "That's the best you can do?"

She shook her head, exasperated. "You're impossible."

"Thank you. I try."

"And succeed nicely," Holt joked. "Seriously, Morgan, thanks for helping out with Robby today. He's always pretty active but after being cooped up in school all day he'll have a lot of energy to work off."

"Happy to help." Morgan had a deep respect for his brother, raising his son alone for the last four years. The boy's mother hadn't wanted to be a mom but Holt handled fatherhood like a pro, better than anyone could have imagined. "How did you get to be such a good dad? God knows ours left a lot to be desired in the role model department."

"Neal isn't as bad as you make him out. He's made mistakes, but he loves our mom. When she was in the hospital after the heart attack, I overheard him talking to the chaplain, promising to be a better husband. I believe he was sincere," Holt said. "And don't sell yourself short, big brother. You're really good with my kid. Just saying."

"Glad you think so."

"I know so. You are and always were a great big

brother, looking out for the rest of us. And, except for Amanda, I trust you with my son more than anyone."

"Stop," Morgan teased. "You'll make me blush, or cry. Or both."

Holt grinned. "Robby will cry if you guys are late and he's waiting in front of the school all alone."

"Let's go get him, then."

Holt kissed Amanda, then said, "I'm off to my meeting. Be home as soon as I can."

They walked outside, and before getting in his truck, Holt kissed Amanda one more time as if he didn't want to let her go. After he drove away, she and Morgan got into his truck and headed out to pick up his nephew.

When the boy was successfully retrieved from school and in the truck, Morgan thanked the good Lord for booster seats and seat belts that kept an active boy contained. It did not, however, put any limitations on the chatter. All the way there the kid talked about Bentley and Oliver, the dog and cat he'd brought home from the sanctuary.

He made the turn onto the road leading to the facility. There were two buildings—a barn and a squat structure for the smaller animals. In an enclosure, he could see goats, pigs and a variety of creatures milling around.

When Morgan parked the truck in the dirt lot, Amanda said so only he could hear, "I'm under strict orders *not* to let him get attached to an animal or under any circumstances bring another one home."

"Okay." Morgan scanned the open area and was disappointed when he spotted a few trucks and cars but no SUV with Colorado license plates.

"Is something wrong?" she asked.

"Hmm? What?" He met her gaze. "No. All good."

"Yay, we're here," Robby shouted. "I'm going to see Tiny Tim."

"That potbellied pig is his favorite," Amanda said.

"No kidding. If we brought it home, do you think Holt would ever trust me with his son again?" he teased. Then he gave the area one more look for the familiar car.

"In a word? No." She laughed, but it faded when she studied him. "Are you looking for someone?"

"No." Yes, he thought. Until he didn't see Erica, he realized just how very much he'd been looking forward to it. "Why do you ask?"

"You look like that potbellied pig just two-stepped all over your favorite Stetson."

"No. I'm good." The rear passenger door slammed shut, a clue Robby had freed himself and was off. "And we're up."

"Right."

Morgan slid out of the truck and called after his nephew. "Stay where we can see you."

"Okay, Uncle Morgan." But he continued to race

toward the animal enclosure as fast as those seven-year-old legs could go.

Amanda came around the truck and stood beside him, shading her eyes from the sun with her hand. "He'll be fine. Daphne is out there with the animals. She'll look out for him."

Behind them there was the sound of a car driving up the road. Dust trailed behind it, but the SUV looked familiar. It was the same color as Erica's, and he smiled. Although he didn't realize he was until Amanda pointed it out.

"Someone you know?" It was the tone a woman used when she knew the answer to her own question and planned to make something of it.

"Yeah. Erica Abernathy."

"And you know her—how?"

"Ran into her last night at DJ's then again today at the building supply store." With everything he had, he was trying to look indifferent.

"Well, you're lighting up, Morgan." She was definitely making this into something. "Did she know you were coming out here?"

"I might have mentioned we'd be here this afternoon."

"Hmm."

Morgan had no idea what that meant. Could be anything from "she's way out of your league" to "I can tell you're sweet on her." Oddly, he wanted both of those things to be true.

The SUV parked next to them and two women exited. Erica had brought Melanie with her.

"Mel!" Amanda squealed with delight when she saw her friend and gave her a hug.

"Hi." Erica walked around the front of her car and smiled at him, then the other two women. "I found her wandering around the Ambling A, and she had the day off. She volunteered to show me where she adopted her cat."

"Where are my manners?" Mel said. "Erica, this is my friend Amanda Jenkins. We met when I rented an apartment in the same complex as Amanda and her roommate Brittany." She looked at her friend. "This is Gabe's sister. She just came in from Colorado."

"Nice to meet you, Erica." Amanda said to both women, "I guess you know Morgan Dalton."

"Yes. He helped me out today," Erica said. "Loaded some stuff in my car."

"Aren't you the gallant one." Amanda had a shrewd expression on her face that implied she could read his mind and thought he was an idiot for trying to pretend indifference.

"Speaking of Brittany, I sure haven't seen much of her lately," Mel said. "I get short phone calls and texts. Reading between the lines, she couldn't be happier." She turned to Erica and explained, "Brittany's married to Daniel Dubois, a local rancher who's raising his orphaned niece." Then she turned her attention back to Mel. "I hear she's up to her ears in alligators what with handling Denim and Diamonds."

"What's Denim and Diamonds?" Erica asked.

"It's a black tie fundraiser," Amanda explained, then mentioned the early November date. "It's going to be a real swanky affair at the Taylor Ranch. Everyone is going to be there. You should come, Erica."

"Oh, I don't know—"

"Your folks are probably going. Gabe is too, right, Mel?"

"We wouldn't miss it," she agreed.

Erica looked down at her gently rounded belly. "Only two problems. It's the week before my due date. So…"

"I don't see that as an issue if you haven't had the baby yet." Amanda shrugged.

"You said two problems," Morgan reminded her. "What's the second one?"

She looked up at him and tucked a strand of blond hair behind her ear when it blew across her lips. After hesitating a fraction of a second, she said, "Remember I told you I dated Jordan Taylor a long time ago?"

"Yeah." How could he forget? His reaction to it was way out of proportion. But the other two women looked pretty surprised at her revelation.

"Well," Erica continued, "I met his father. Cornelius. Just a couple of times but he was always bossy and domineering. Going to any event on his ranch makes me a little uncomfortable."

"There will be so many people there he probably won't even see you," Melanie said.

"I'll be even bigger by then. No one will be able to miss me."

"You are not that big," Amanda assured her. "And we just met, so if this is out of line, don't judge. But it looks as if pregnancy agrees with you. You're radiant."

Morgan couldn't agree more, but kept that to himself. No way a guy should insert himself into this conversation. Although he could see a vulnerability in Erica that made him feel protective.

"Thanks." Erica smiled a little shyly, a lot self-consciously. "I appreciate that. And just so you know, I wasn't fishing for compliments."

"I didn't think you were." Amanda waved it off. "And you really should think about coming. It will be the biggest social event of the year. From what Brittany says, the guest list is pretty extensive. You're going, right, Morgan?"

His father mentioned an invitation and Neal Dalton had said it was a good chance to expand their ties to the community. He wanted the whole family to show up and their mother agreed with him. Morgan and his brothers would do anything for her, so that pretty much made it a command appearance.

"I wish I could say no, but…"

"So you'll see some friendly faces, Erica," Amanda persisted.

"Still," she said hesitantly, "Jordan's father can be intimidating. Facing him alone—"

"I'll go with you." Morgan was just as surprised as the three women when the words came out of his mouth.

Chapter Four

Erica held her breath, expecting any second for Morgan to grin at her and say *Gotcha*. Or *Just kidding*. She couldn't believe he'd just volunteered to escort her to the biggest social event of the year. But he looked completely serious and possibly a little embarrassed. Mel and Amanda were staring at both of them, and she couldn't imagine what they must be thinking. Actually she could see that her brother's fiancée was a little shocked—maybe even a little skeptical.

"That's awfully brave of you to offer," Erica finally said.

"Why?" He shrugged. "I don't mind running interference for you. And you'd be doing me a favor. If I have to go, the least you could do is go with me so I have someone to talk to."

"But I'm pregnant." *Nothing like stating the obvious, but... Seriously?*

"Really? I didn't notice," he teased.

"I'm not even sure I'll go." Erica looked at the two women who'd been glancing back and forth between them, like watching a tennis match.

"It's over a month away," Amanda said. "There's time to decide."

"That's true," Mel agreed a little too quickly. "Talk about it later. We came here to see the farm animals. I was going to show you around, remember?"

"And I have to go make sure Robby isn't driving Daphne crazy." Amanda headed for the farm buildings. "Mel, why don't you come with me and say hi to Daphne. There might be another cat adoption in your future."

"No more for me. But I love looking at the kittens." She glanced over her shoulder. "Coming, Erica?"

"I'm right behind you. Moving a little slowly these days."

"Okay." Mel nodded and hurried after her friend.

When they were alone, Erica turned to Morgan. "Seriously? You asked me on a date?"

"I wasn't thinking about that so much as offering

moral support. And I wasn't kidding about having someone to talk to."

"I'm not all that sure I *want* to talk to anyone at a big posh party."

They started slowly walking toward the two buildings. Robby had disappeared inside the smaller one, and she saw Mel and Amanda go in there, too. Chickens wandered everywhere, pecking at the dirt, while ducks waddled aimlessly. Goats moved around the enclosure and made bleating sounds.

"Why wouldn't you? Want to talk to anyone, I mean?" Morgan asked. "You grew up around here. Aren't there people you want to reconnect with?"

"Not right now. There's no way to hide my belly, and everyone will be curious and it's none of their business." She looked up at the tall man strolling beside her. "I don't feel like I belong here anymore. That's why I'm not sure if I even want to go."

"Okay, then. To be continued."

His black Stetson shaded his eyes, hiding his expression so she couldn't tell what he was thinking. But he must have questions. To his credit, he didn't ask, and that added to his likability points.

As they strolled, their arms bumped and brushed together. He was wearing a fleece-lined jacket against the chill in the air. But every time their bodies connected, even in the slightest way, Erica swore she could see sparks. And there was a definite fluttering in her stomach, an I-really-like-this-guy feeling. And it didn't hurt that he was helping look after his nephew and had brought him to see the animals.

"So, this is quite a place Daphne has here." Erica felt the need to change the subject to something not about a date.

Morgan told her about the glassed-off cat room inside with hay bales where the animals could frolic freely. Across from it, he explained, there was an area for the dogs that had an outside door to a fenced-in area with runs where they could roam at will.

"Before Daphne opened the sanctuary, this property sat empty for a lot of years. There are rumors it's haunted."

"Really?" She felt a shiver, but it had nothing to do with awareness of him and everything to do with being just a little freaked out.

"You never heard that? You used to live here."

"Maybe." Funny how much a woman could forget in the twelve years she'd been away. "Wasn't there a fire here?"

"That's what I've been told." Their shoulders bumped, and he looked down at her, hesitated a moment, then stuck his hands in the pockets of his jacket. As if he needed to do something safe with them. "The story is that when the barn burned down, a cowboy died along with his girlfriend and some horses." They strolled around the enclosure, and goats moved up to the fence, bleating piteously. "Story has it that the ghosts of the cowboy and the woman show up here and sometimes horses are neighing when none are around."

"Nothing creepy about that." She moved a little closer to him. "If your offer about running interference for me still stands, feel free to go for it if the ghosts show up."

"You don't believe in that kind of thing, do you?" He grinned and tipped his head enough to show the amusement in his eyes.

"I'm reserving judgment." Although not on his smile. It rocked her world as surely as if she'd seen a ghost. She felt tingles in places that never tingled before. "Speaking of judgment, my father is not a fan of a farm animal sanctuary."

"Oh?"

"Nope. He thinks farm animals should be able to pull their own weight. Work. Earn their keep and if they can't… well, let nature take its course."

"I'm a rancher, too. I can see his point."

Maybe her father's attitude about Morgan would be more favorable if he knew they shared an opinion. For some reason it mattered whether or not her dad liked the Daltons.

"So you think Daphne has too much time on her hands and should abandon the animals?" Erica asked him.

"I didn't say that. This place is important to Daphne and a lot of other folks, too. She's making it work. Live and let live, I say. But your father and mine are ranchers from a different generation."

"True." She hadn't thought about it like that. And mentioning his father opened the door on their conversation just that morning. "Remember those rumors about your family I mentioned? There were more."

"Such as?"

She wasn't sure but thought he might be trying too hard to cover irritation with nonchalance. She stopped walking and looked at the animals in a cluster close by trying to get their attention. "It was something about your dad cheating on your mom."

His mouth pulled tight for a moment as he stared at the mountains in the distance. "Although I have no clue how that became public knowledge, it's a fact."

"Are your parents still together?"

"Mom forgave him." His tone said he didn't approve. He shook his head. "He swears the women meant nothing. Just slipups when he was drinking and stressed about money."

Erica was a little surprised he admitted that. But maybe he was in the mood to share. "Speaking of money… Where did your dad get the money to buy the ranch? Please tell me you're not a reincarnation of the Dalton Gang from the Old West. They were brothers who specialized in train and bank robberies."

His mouth curved up in a reluctant smile. "Nothing illegal. He won it in Vegas. A three-buck bet on a million-dollar slot machine. On one pull he won a bundle. He sold his ranch and came here for a fresh start."

"Wow." She could feel her eyes widen. "Now you and your brothers are all here."

"For our mom. We were scattered, working ranches all over. She wanted the family together."

"I guess it's a mom thing." Without conscious thought, she put her hands on her baby bump. "It won't be long until I know what that feels like. I have an appointment with a doctor the day after tomorrow."

"Already?"

"Yeah. Because of being fired and having to move home, I had to find a new doctor."

"A lot of change in a short period of time." His rugged face was suddenly creased with concern.

"It is. I really liked my obstetrician. And to start with someone new so close to the end of this pregnancy is a little scary." Erica didn't know why she was confiding all this to Morgan. She liked him and was comfortable with him, had been from the moment they met. On top of that, she didn't feel there was anyone else she could confide in. Lately, she blamed her hormones for everything, so why not blame them for spilling her guts to this man? "The thing is, I have no choice."

"Are you going alone?"

"Yes." She was doing this whole adventure alone. Nothing had changed just because she came home.

"I thought maybe your mom would go with you. Or Mel."

She shrugged. "I don't want to bother my mom. And Mel is busy working."

He stared at her for a long moment and seemed as if he had another question. But what he said instead was a surprise. "I'll go with you to the doctor, if you want."

"Wow." Her heart fluttered a little. "Why? More running interference for me? That's getting to be a thing with you."

"Just moral support." He shrugged. "Doesn't seem right for you to go alone."

Her eyes suddenly grew moist at his sweet offer, proving her hormones were at it again. "That's awfully considerate of you, but I'll be fine by myself."

"Okay."

He opened his mouth, then shut it again. There must be a million questions in his mind but he didn't ask. That made her like him even more than she already did. And she already liked him quite a bit.

Childish laughter floated to them on a light breeze, and Morgan looked at the small animal building. "I better go make sure Amanda doesn't need help with Robby."

"I'm so sorry. I've talked your ear off," she said.

"Can't say you're not a distraction."

A good or bad one, she wondered but couldn't tell from his expression. Now they walked quickly and were just opening the door when, without warning, Robby came running outside, straight into Erica.

She was a little clumsy these days what with her body being out of proportion, and the unexpected bump knocked her back a couple of steps.

Morgan instantly caught her arm to steady her. At the same time he said, "Robby, remember what your dad says about watching where you're going."

"Yes, sir." He looked up and pushed the brown, shaggy hair out of his blue eyes. "Sorry."

"That's okay, kiddo. No harm done." Erica smiled. "You're a very handsome young man."

"Thank you," he said courteously.

"I'm Erica Abernathy."

"Nice to meet you." Apparently that was all the polite a seven-year-old who was quivering with excitement could manage. "I'm gonna look at the horses and cows now."

Morgan followed him and called out over his shoulder, "I'm on it."

Amanda and Melanie emerged from the building with another woman. Erica recognized Daphne Taylor's strawberry blond hair and doe-shaped blue eyes. The recognition was mutual and then those blue eyes took in her pregnancy.

"Oh my God, Erica! Look at you." Her friend moved closer and hugged her. "You're back."

"I am." She glanced around. "And you've got this place."

"I do. It's my pride and joy. And not without controversy." Her eyes narrowed. "My father doesn't approve."

"Neither does mine." Erica put her hands on her pregnant belly.

They smiled over shared paternal disapproval just as Morgan walked out of the barn carrying Robby and scolding.

"You'll get hurt climbing on the stalls like that, buddy. The animals spook and could hurt you without meaning to."

The boy did look remorseful as he rubbed a finger beneath his nose leaving a dirty streak. "I didn't mean to scare 'em."

"I know you didn't."

"If I promise not to scare 'em, can I go see the goats, Uncle Morgan?"

"Yes. But be careful and watch where you are." Morgan easily lowered the boy and his feet were moving before they even touched the ground.

"I've got it this time, Morgan." Amanda followed the boy, and the other two women tagged along.

"He's a cutie," Erica said. "Pretty active boy."

"That kid just took ten years off my life when he fell into the horse's stall." Exasperation laced with fear tightened Morgan's features as he shook his head. "I don't know how my brother does it. Kids.

It's one thing to watch him for an afternoon, but I don't know if I'd want to be responsible for one all the time."

Erica's warm feeling instantly cooled. For reasons she couldn't understand, she suddenly felt lonelier than at any other point on this solo journey to motherhood. When Morgan had offered to accompany her to the doctor, hope must have taken root. The idea of someone to share the experience.

But based on his reaction just now, this man didn't particularly like kids. Her disappointment about that was way out of line. She had no right to be disappointed because that smacked of having expectations of more. Because of the baby, friendship was it for them.

Two days later Erica drove to the Women's Health Center where her new OB was located in the Bronco Heights medical district. The minute she was fired and realized her only option was to move home, she worked on securing a new doctor. With the help of her Denver OB she'd found this new physician, made an appointment and had all her records forwarded even before packing up her apartment.

She pulled up to the parking structure entrance, took a ticket and the gate lifted, allowing her to drive in and look for a space. Nerves tied her stomach in knots because she was so sure she had everything figured out when she'd made her decision to use insemination to have a baby. Changing doctors during this pregnancy hadn't been part of her strategy.

She'd established a bond and trusted her Denver doctor and would barely get to know this one before her baby was born.

She found a parking space on the fifth level, then walked to the elevator. After riding it down to the first floor lobby, she checked the building directory and found Grace Turner, Obstetrics and Gynecology, Suite 100. Right around the corner.

Pressing a hand to her belly, she whispered, "Here we go, little one."

Sliding the strap of her purse more firmly on her shoulder, Erica took a deep breath and walked into the office. She checked in at the reception desk, and after filling out the forms, she looked around the waiting room. A quick glance told her she was the only expectant mother without a partner. She wished she'd accepted Morgan's offer to accompany her and would welcome his way of making her laugh.

The families around her were in different stages of development. The couple by themselves seemed to be expecting their first child and were clearly nervous. A father and mother had a brand-new tiny, adorable baby in a car seat and looked tired. The last couple had a little one running around as they prepared to add another to their growing brood. One by one the expectant moms were called back to see the doctor.

Erica was wistful but would rather do it alone

than not at all. Her first choice was the traditional way but that hadn't worked out. Her next thought was a flashback of Morgan the other day, sounding as if he didn't want any part of fatherhood. Later she'd observed him protecting Robby from overeager baby goats. Tossing the laughing child in the air. Affectionately ruffling the boy's hair. Sure looked as if he was at least a favorite uncle and enjoying the heck out of it.

The door to the back office opened and a woman in pink scrubs stood there. "Erica?"

Immediately she stood and walked over. "That's me."

"Come on back. I'm Scarlett, Dr. Turner's nurse." She closed the door and indicated the scale behind her. "I guess you probably know the drill."

"Yup." She set her purse on the chair beside it and stepped on.

Scarlett made a note, then led the way down a hall and stopped outside the ladies' room. "I guess you know the drill for this, too."

"My favorite thing," Erica joked.

After getting a sample and leaving it where instructed, she met the nurse in the hall and followed her to a room. She sat at the end of a paper-covered exam table and had her blood pressure taken.

"Good." Scarlet recorded the result, then smiled. "The doctor will be in to see you shortly."

"Thank you."

In Denver, Erica had felt just fine waiting by herself in the exam room. What was it about being back home that made her feel more alone? Probably the sad disappointment and regret in her mother's eyes every time she looked at her pregnant belly. Her happy childhood home now wasn't a happy or accepting place to talk about her baby. It always felt as if she was the elephant in the room.

Not long after the nurse left, the door opened and a thirtyish woman walked into the room. Holding out her hand she said, "I'm Dr. Turner. It's nice to meet you, Erica."

"Thank you for fitting me in. I had a change in work status and moved home. It's so late in my pregnancy, and I wasn't sure how that would all fall into place."

"Believe it or not, women change doctors in the third trimester for a lot of reasons." She was a very pretty blue-eyed brunette. "I received your medical records from your previous OB and reviewed them. I saw the early ultrasound and there's a note in your chart that you don't want to know the baby's sex?"

"That's right."

"So you want to be surprised. No gender reveal party?"

"No."

Her close friends were all in Denver. She'd been gone for so long there wasn't anyone here in Bronco she'd want to invite. Maybe Morgan. But she couldn't picture him amid a cloud of pink or blue balloons.

"And this baby was conceived with IUI using donor sperm."

"Yes."

"Okay. Is the baby moving a lot?"

"I think this child is going to be a kickboxer."

Dr. Turner grinned. "That's what I like to hear."

"It's reassuring. Although at two in the morning…"

"That's Mother Nature's way of preparing you for those night feedings." There was a sympathetic look on the doctor's face. "Go ahead and lie back on the table. I want to do a Doppler and measure your abdomen."

After Erica did as instructed, the doctor moved the instrument over her belly. She nodded. "This baby's heartbeat is strong. Everything looks good. And I think pregnancy agrees with you."

"I've never felt better," she said truthfully. "I experienced some morning sickness and was a little tired in the beginning. But now I feel great."

"It shows. I know it's a cliché, but you really are glowing."

"Thank you."

"Do you have any questions for me?" Dr. Turner asked.

"Yes, actually. I was enrolled in a childbirth class but had to withdraw when I moved. Is it too late now to do that?"

"You've got a little over a month. And it's never

too late. The more you know, the better. I can give you some information on a class that's just starting at the Health Center and arrange enrollment if you'd like."

"That would be great."

"Do you have a birthing coach?" The doctor must have seen something in her face because she quickly added, "It can be anyone—a relative or friend."

"What if I don't have one? Can I still take the class?"

"Of course. There's a lot of good information for first-time moms or even a refresher course for women who already have babies. Methods of delivery. How to know when you're in labor. What to do if your water breaks. Relaxation techniques. Pain management options. Breastfeeding. Caring for a newborn."

"Sounds like—pun intended—just what the doctor ordered."

The woman smiled. "Okay. I'll have Scarlett put together the information, and she'll give it to you when you check out."

"I was nervous about this appointment but you've really put me at ease, Doctor."

"Then I've done my job. Just relax and enjoy the rest of your pregnancy," she advised.

That was easy for her to say, Erica thought. The woman didn't have to find a job and a labor coach, not necessarily in that order.

Chapter Five

The Ambling A had a herd bull for sale and Dalton's Grange needed one to improve the calf crop, so Morgan was sitting across a desk from Gabe Abernathy. The main house was pretty impressive and this office kept that theme going. It was filled with rich leather chairs, wood beams overhead and a stone fireplace. The environment smelled of old money and reminded Morgan that until recently his family hadn't had much to spare.

The Abernathys' operation produced superior stock and they'd quickly agreed on a price, making the negotiation smoother than he expected.

"So, we have a deal?" he asked.

"Yes."

"Good." Morgan leaned forward and put out his hand, the way gentlemen did to finalize a negotiation. The other man took it.

"Okay, then."

The leather chair creaked as Morgan stood on the other side of the desk. "I guess we're finished."

"One more thing." Gabe stood up, too, and met his gaze.

"And that is?"

"My fiancée said you were at Happy Hearts the other day when she was there with Erica."

"That's right. My nephew loves going to see the animals."

"So it was a coincidence? You being there at the same time?"

Morgan sensed the other man's disapproval but he wasn't going to lie. "Actually, I ran into Erica in town. I mentioned that I'd be at the animal sanctuary with Robby."

Gabe nodded. "Mel said you and my sister were talking for a long time."

"Yeah." They'd laughed a lot, too. And Erica was the opposite of hard on the eyes. He'd enjoyed spending time with her more than anything he'd done in a long time. "She's easy to talk to."

"She's also pregnant, Dalton." There was a warning tone in his voice.

"And your point is?"

"She doesn't need someone like you complicating her life."

"Someone like me?" Morgan felt his temper flare but stopped short of telling this guy to go to hell. Mostly because he was Erica's brother. Why that should matter, he wasn't sure. But it did. He blew out a frustrated breath. "Not that I owe you an explanation, but we're friends."

"And that's all?"

"What more would I want?" Morgan's tone gave the man some of his warning back.

"You tell me." Gabe's eyes narrowed.

On some level Morgan was aware that this man was a big brother looking out for a younger sibling. He got that.

"I'm the oldest of five. I understand about keeping an eye on the younger ones. I only have brothers so I'm going to cut you some slack for being protective of your sister. I'm guessing that responsibility weighs a little heavier. So, I'll say this one more time. We're friends. Nothing more."

Gabe's look said he was going to hold Morgan to that. "Okay."

"I'll see myself out."

Morgan turned and headed out of the office, then back through the house to where he'd come in. He was frustrated and angry. How long would he have to live in Bronco Heights before he was good enough to be accepted by these people? It was a lesson, if he needed one, that money didn't buy everything. And then he saw Erica in the entryway by the front door and his irritation disappeared.

She looked fresh and pretty and made his heart skip and slide sideways in his chest. In her black leggings, long cream-colored sweater and cowboy boots, she looked beautiful. And when she saw him, she smiled with genuine warmth, which was just what he needed. Except that every time she smiled, he wondered how her lips would feel against his own.

"Morgan. What are you doing here?"

"I had some business with your brother."

She tipped her head to the side, studying him. "Did something happen?"

Other than Gabe declaring him off-limits to her? That still rubbed him the wrong way and irritated his sense of fairness. "Yes. I bought a herd bull from him."

"You don't look happy about it."

"No. It was a good deal," he said. Changing the subject, he asked, "What are you up to?"

"Just going for a walk. I've got to keep up my exercise. I used to ride horses but I can't now. It's a big no-no because of the risk of falling. That could harm the baby."

"Yeah. I can see that." He was oddly reluctant to say his goodbyes and leave. Glancing over his shoulder toward her brother's office, he frowned. Also, being warned off really bugged him, made him want to push back. "Would you like some company on your walk?"

"You don't need the exercise." She gave him a once-over and didn't seem to mind what she saw.

"A stroll with a pretty lady sounds like a healthy thing to do."

She flushed with pleasure at the compliment. "If you're sure, I wouldn't mind someone to talk to."

"Let's go." He took her jacket out of her hand and held it while she slid her arms into the sleeves. Then he opened the front door and let her precede him outside.

"Thanks."

"My pleasure." And that was the truth. She smelled really good. The scent of her hair and a certain fragrance that was uniquely her stirred in the air and burrowed inside him. *Nice* didn't even begin to describe what he was feeling. "Which way are we going?"

She pointed to a path that went behind the barn and corrals to a grass area and beyond. "Try and keep up."

"Someone's feeling pretty sassy today." He grinned.

"Yeah." Her smile faded as they headed out.

"Are you sure you're up for this? After all, you're walking for two."

"Funny. And I'm fine." She breathed deeply. "It's a beautiful day. The sun is out. It's all good."

"Okay."

They walked in silence for a while, surrounded by the sounds of nature. The birds singing, the whinny of a horse somewhere out of sight and a breeze that made tree leaves rustle.

"How's Robby?" she asked.

"Good. Rowdy. Healthy. Happy."

"Can't ask for more than that. Where's his mom? It seems like your brother was raising him alone before Amanda came into his life." She shrugged. "Women talk."

"His mother is in Colorado." But Morgan had a feeling that's not what she was asking. "She wasn't keen on being a mom. She sends presents for Christmas and birthdays but that's about it. Not hiding but not involved either."

"I see." With the toe of her boot she kicked a rock off the path and into the grass to the side. "He's a great kid."

"You'll get no argument from me about that."

"Can I ask you something?" she said hesitantly.

"Sure." But he braced himself.

"You're so good with Robby and clearly he loves you."

"I love him, too," Morgan said easily.

"But you don't want kids."

"Why do you say that?" he asked.

She looked up and the breeze blew a strand of hair across her face, into her eyes. She brushed it away and met his gaze. "The other day you seemed a little exasperated and said you don't know how your brother does it. That didn't sound like you were in favor of having the experience yourself."

"The truth is, I don't know if I'd be a very good father."

"I guess it would be hard to go for it if you have doubts." She slid her hands into the pockets of her jacket. "It was easy for me. There was no question in my mind about wanting to be a mom."

And she made it look good, he thought. But she was right. With his brother, the pregnancy happened and Holt manned up. He was all in when Robby was born, and Morgan would have done the same. But if he had a choice, it would be a tough call for him to make.

But that reminded him. "You had a doctor's appointment. How did that go?"

"Good."

Morgan hadn't known her long, but he felt as if he knew her well enough to see when something was bothering her. And that was now. He was certain of it.

"Did you like the doctor?"

"Yes. Very much." That might have been a little too enthusiastic. Compensating for something?

"Did someone give you a hard time? Was the office a dirty, windowless shack without running water and electricity?"

"It was fine."

He'd been going for the absurd to make her laugh. That was an epic fail and convinced him not to let up until she came clean about what was going on. "Tell me what's wrong, Erica. Please don't say *nothing*, because I can see different."

"Everything is good."

"I'm not buying that. Come on, this is me. Give it up." He met her gaze and saw in hers when she stopped pretending.

She left the dirt path and leaned against a tree. "I want to take a childbirth class. The doctor says it's not too late to do it."

"That's a good thing. No?"

"Yes and no." Her frown deepened. "I could use someone to go with me. A coach."

"Okay. So who's it going to be?" The baby's father? This wasn't the first time he'd wondered where the guy was. He was still curious, but it wasn't his place to push for information.

"That's just it. I don't know." She caught her top lip between her teeth.

"What about your mom?" he suggested.

She shook her head. "I can't ask her. As much as my parents nagged me about making them grandparents, their plan included marriage before motherhood. I need someone who is one hundred percent in my corner without making a judgment."

"You grew up here." From his perspective, that

was the family background someone needed to be accepted in Bronco Heights. "How about a friend?"

"I was gone so long I've lost touch with my friends. Or they've moved away." Her shoulders slumped and the sunshine in her face was all clouded over.

"What about Daphne Taylor?"

She shook her head. "We didn't stay in touch, and it seems presumptuous to ask. And Mel travels for her job. Even if that's only once or twice a month it could be inconvenient to rearrange her schedule, not to mention when I go into labor."

"There must be someone," he said.

"I don't know anyone I'd feel comfortable asking."

"You know me." Morgan couldn't hold back the words. Seeing her like this made him want to put the sparkle back in her eyes.

"You?" It wasn't quite a sparkle, but something jumped into her expression. "You do know this is a childbirth class?"

"Yeah."

"This inclination of yours to volunteer to help me out is getting to be a habit. It's very sweet, but I won't hold you to it."

Morgan wasn't sure why he felt so strongly about this. He was willing to admit that it was more than bonding over being outsiders. Mostly he just really liked her and couldn't help wanting to fix her problems.

"It's all right," he said. "You can hold me to it."

"Surely you're joking." She was incredulous.

"Nope. Dead serious."

"Why would you do it?"

"We're friends." And thrown into the mix was just a little bit of in-your-face to her brother for warning him off. "It's what friends do."

"But kids aren't your thing," she protested.

"You're doing the work. I'm being the support." He shrugged.

"But what if this baby is born in the middle of the night?" she challenged.

"It happens all the time with cows. I'm always on call."

"You didn't really just compare me to a cow," she teased. "Maybe I'm starting to look like one—"

"No way." He thought she was beautiful. "I didn't—I mean, I was just saying—"

"It's okay. I know what you meant. And I wouldn't ask you to be there for the labor—"

"What kind of friend would I be to abandon you? A coach doesn't train his players, then not show up for the game." Morgan shook his head.

"I'm completely blown away that you'd offer to do this for me. I just can't believe you would—"

"Well, believe it," he said firmly.

"I don't know what to say."

"For Pete's sake, just say yes and thank you."

"Okay. If you're absolutely sure… Yes." She laughed and looked as if a great weight was lifted from her shoulders. "I don't know why you would do this. And I'm not sure why it feels right, but it does. I'm very grateful to you. Thank you, Morgan."

When she looked at him the way she was now, as if he'd hung the moon, he would do anything for her. And it's not like this was forever. In a matter of weeks the baby would be here and his job would be done and their paths would take them in different directions. Probably he wouldn't see her and would miss that beautiful smile more than he wanted to admit.

A few days later Erica insisted on picking Morgan up for the birthing class. She knew where Dalton's Grange was and easily found his house on the property. She was early, which was a chronic thing with her because it had been drilled into her growing up that being late was rude. Now punctuality was a habit. As big as the baby was getting, she hoped this child would take after her and at least arrive on time.

Still, she wouldn't turn down the chance to check out his house. And she couldn't help being curious, especially when she noticed smoke curling out of the rock chimney and light pouring out of the windows making his home seem really warm and cozy and inviting.

She walked up to the wooden porch with the railing that spanned the front. The style was the same as the main house she'd passed, with a rock and log facade and peaked roof.

Her boots sounded on the porch as she walked up to the door and knocked. Moments later an older woman answered it. She had a blond bob hairdo, blue eyes and a welcoming smile.

"You must be Erica Abernathy. I'm Deborah, Morgan's mom."

Erica shook the hand she held out. "Nice to meet you."

It was. And it wasn't. Since he lived in his own house on the ranch, it hadn't occurred to her that she'd meet any of his relatives and have to explain her reason for being here. Especially when she hadn't told her own family about Morgan being her birthing coach.

"You are just the most adorable pregnant lady I've ever seen." The other woman beamed at her. It was the sort of look she'd hoped for from her own mother.

"I feel just the opposite of adorable," she said ruefully.

"Some women are lucky enough to barely look pregnant right up until giving birth. I have a feeling you're going to be like that." She shook her head. "This is the honest truth. I've had five babies and never looked as radiant as you."

"I'm not going to try and talk you out of that impression."

Deborah laughed. "Just to set the record straight,

no matter what it looks like, my son does not live with his mother."

"What a relief. That would be weird," she teased back.

"He was working on a project with his father and got back late, then had to feed and water the animals." She angled her head toward the hallway off the great room. "I brought him some dinner, which he wolfed down. He just went to shower and clean up."

Erica glanced around the room with a cheerful fire crackling in the hearth. Braided rugs were scattered over the wooden floor. A leather sofa and chairs were arranged on one big enough to accommodate the overstuffed furniture.

"I hope it's not a problem that I'm early." Another habit of hers was to prattle on and say too much when she was nervous. Like now. She made herself stop talking.

"Not at all. Morgan told me he's going to be your labor coach."

She felt the woman was only being chatty and nice, not fishing for gossip. To not give her a little information felt impolite. "Yes, he is. Your son is a kind, sympathetic and thoughtful man. It was the first thing I noticed about him when we met." Right after she'd rated him a solid fifteen on a one to ten hotness scale.

"He's always been that way. A sweet and sensitive little boy and a good man."

"I'll be a single mom, and I'm grateful he'll be my coach."

"He'll be a good one." The next obvious comment or question would be about the baby's father, but Deborah didn't bring it up.

Erica felt compelled to. "The baby's father isn't involved. Just so you know, there's no bad breakup or hard feelings in any way."

"Good to know." Deborah slid her hands into the pockets of her jeans.

This wasn't awkward at all. "Morgan tells me that you and your family have lived here for a year. How do you like it?"

"It's great." There was a little too much enthusiasm in her voice. "We came from a pretty small town in northern Montana. This is bigger. More civilization, I guess. Shopping, if you know what I mean."

"I do." She nodded, also with too much enthusiasm.

"My son said that you just returned to Bronco Heights."

"That's right. I went to college in Colorado and I ended up with a job there. But now I'm back home. My parents would be thrilled if I wasn't..." She looked down at her belly.

"Why do I get the feeling this homecoming wasn't

planned?" Deborah asked. Then she waved her hand and said, "Never mind. It was rude of me to ask."

"No, actually, I think you're psychic."

The woman laughed. "It's a mom thing. Gives a woman a sixth sense."

"Well, you're right. My company let me go. Coming home was plan B." Erica didn't want Morgan's mother to believe her a screwup, and gave her an abbreviated version of what happened. She wasn't exactly sure why she spilled her guts to this woman. The best thing she could come up with was that her son got his kindness and empathy genes from his mother. "In the end, my only option was to come back home."

"So your parents aren't thrilled about having their daughter back?"

"If they are, they're hiding it pretty well. They're old-fashioned."

"I'm sorry to hear that, Erica." She made an understanding sound.

"My family has expectations and I keep not meeting them."

"I'm sure they love you and just want what's best. For you to be happy."

"They absolutely do. I know that. And I want to make them proud, but I keep letting them down." Erica smiled sheepishly. "I'm sorry to dump all that on you. You're just easy to talk to."

"Your parents will come around, honey. Don't give up."

Just then Morgan walked into the room bringing with him the wonderful, masculine scents of soap and some spicy cologne. His hair was still damp from the shower and he was freshly shaved. In his plaid, snap-front shirt, jeans and boots he looked every inch the sexy cowboy he was. Erica felt that familiar flutter in her stomach, but this time her heartbeat kicked up, too.

"Sorry I'm running late," he said.

"No. I'm early." She hoped her voice wasn't as breathless as it sounded to her. And if it was, she prayed neither of the Daltons noticed. "Your mom and I have been talking. She assured me you aren't one of those men in his thirties who still lives with his mother. Although, she brings you food and that makes one wonder."

He simply grinned at the teasing. Erica got a little weak-kneed but chalked it up to simple appreciation for a good-looking man. Who was also being an exceptional friend.

"My mom is a good cook," he said. "It would be stupid to turn down a meal from her and she didn't raise any fools. It's one of her many talents. And it should be said that my brothers and I are all a little afraid of her."

Deborah laughed. "I always knew how to keep five unruly boys in line. Still do."

"I'd love to know your secret," Erica said.

She wasn't kidding. Obviously Morgan had a great relationship with his mother, and it was heart-warming to see. She wanted that with her child. It was also revealing to see him with the woman who'd raised him. She'd heard you could tell a lot about a man by the way he treated his mother. From what she could see, Morgan treated his mom with love and respect. He wasn't just a pretty face. He was a very good man.

"Please don't get her started on stories of the Dalton boys," he warned. "The naked baby pictures won't be far behind."

"I so want to make a pun out of what you just said." Erica laughed when he groaned.

"I think it's time for us to go. Now," he told her.

"Okay." She looked at his mom. "Can I drop you at the main house?"

"No, honey. I could use the walk. But thank you. I'll just gather up the dishes I brought." Deborah smiled and waved before walking into the kitchen.

Erica shivered when they went outside, and she told herself it was the chilly October evening not the nearness of Morgan. Inside her car, he was even closer, because he was tall and broad and built for a truck. Her heart did that bumping inside her chest thing again.

That made her hands shake a little and fumble as she inserted her key into the ignition. Eventually she managed and off they went, headed back the way she'd come. Past the main house with its log walls and big windows all lit up. Maybe the silence wasn't awkward, but it felt that way to her.

"Your mom is nice. Easy to talk to." Not nosy, Erica thought to herself. A good listener.

"Yeah, she's pretty great."

"I can't imagine raising five boys."

"Me either, but she made it look easy. She probably had the hang of it by the time my youngest brother came along."

"So, you told her about being my childbirth coach," Erica said casually.

"Yeah. When work ran late, she pitched in because I mentioned being late to the first class wasn't an option. Should I not have said anything?" There was a frown in his voice.

"No. Not at all. She was great about it. And didn't once share that you birth baby cows all the time."

He laughed. "Yeah. She's pretty cool about things. Always been there for me even when—"

His tone had turned sort of introspective, almost as if he'd forgotten she was there. Then he suddenly clammed up. There was a story, a personal one. Erica tried to be like his mom and not ask questions, but she was too darn curious.

"When what?" she prodded. "Something happened. Just so you know, I don't plan on letting this go. Friends talk to each other."

He was quiet for so long it appeared he wasn't going to answer. But finally he said, "I fell in love once. When I'd just turned twenty-one. I met a girl and felt the lightning strike."

That actually wasn't exactly what Erica had expected to hear. "Okay. And? There must be more."

"Unfortunately." He looked out the car window at the darkness going by. "I bought a ring, proposed, and she accepted. We set a date."

"But? I can hear one coming." She wished very much that there wasn't.

"About a week before the wedding I found out she was pregnant with another guy's baby. And she wasn't the one who told me."

"She was going to pass it off as yours?"

"She denied it, but I didn't believe her, what with not telling me and all." There was a trace of bitterness still in his voice.

That took her breath away. She shouldn't feel a parallel, because he wasn't in love with her, hadn't proposed, given her a ring or set a date. But, even though she hadn't slept with her baby's father, it surely was another man's child.

She managed to keep emotion out of her voice when she said, "So I guess you called off the wedding."

"Good guess." There was irony in his tone. "She made a fool out of me."

"Oh, Morgan, you were young and she was the

fool." To do that to a great guy like him was just really and truly stupid. "I gather from your tone that it put you off the whole notion of marriage."

"It's not high on my list," he agreed. "And that's not the only reason. My father is not anyone's example of the perfect husband."

"But your parents have overcome obstacles in their relationship and your mom seems happy. No regrets. She's given your dad a chance. Maybe you should, too."

"And maybe you should give your family a chance," he shot back.

Touché. She didn't say anything more but her mind was spinning. Such a personal and profound betrayal could explain why he was still not some lucky girl's husband and a father. That was a shame because he would be so good at both. As chances went, she would give him one in a heartbeat.

Chapter Six

Morgan hadn't planned to talk about his romantic crash and burn. A long time ago he put that unfortunate incident behind him, at least he thought he had. But suddenly the words were coming out of his mouth. One minute he was talking about how cool his mother was, and the next, he was confessing his past and explaining why marriage wasn't in his plans. All of this on the way to a childbirth class. What was wrong with this picture?

Too many things, but the only one that mattered was Erica. She was going through a tough time without a lot of support and he wouldn't turn his back on her, too.

"We're here." She turned the SUV into the parking lot of the Women's Health Center and found a space close to the entrance. "It's not too late to back out, Morgan. Speak now or forever hold your peace."

He opened the passenger door and the overhead light went on, illuminating the uncertainty in her expression. Every time he looked at her, all he could think about was fixing whatever problem she had. Tonight was no different.

"You can't get rid of me that easily," he assured her.

"Okay then." She retrieved a rolled up mat and pillow from the rear of the SUV. "Let's go learn something about birthing babies."

She smiled, and Morgan felt the power of it deep down inside. Fortunately there was no time to analyze his response because he had a feeling he wasn't going to like the results.

They made their way inside and up to a conference room at the far end of the top floor. When they walked in, the floor-to-ceiling windows revealed a beautiful view of Bronco, lights stretching to the base of the mountains.

The clock on the wall said five minutes to seven and not being late was a relief. Fixing fences had taken longer than anticipated today when he and his father had found more than one calf caught up. Freeing them without injury had taken time, and he didn't want to let Erica down, especially the first night of class. It was important to prove that she could count on him.

The rectangular room had a large open area at one end and three tables arranged in a U-shape with a lectern set up at the other. A woman in her late twenties stood there flipping through her notes. Three couples were already there, and Erica was looking around, eyes wide.

Morgan put his hand to the small of her back and fought the urge to pull her close. Only for reassurance. As a friend. "We should probably sit."

She glanced around one last time and nodded. "Right."

They found chairs at a right angle to a very young couple. The man smiled at him, the kind of look that implied sharing the ups, downs, joys and fears of this adventure, the one called fatherhood. The other two men nodded in his direction with similar expressions. Morgan noticed they were all wearing wedding rings, which made him the odd man out.

He didn't feel awkward or out of his element as much as he was relieved Erica wasn't facing this alone. But she wouldn't be if her baby's father was here. Up until now Morgan hadn't been all that curious, but this class highlighted the absence. What was the story?

That question would have to wait, because he had things to deal with now. The other people in this class probably thought he was going to be a father. There was no good reason he could think of to disabuse them of that impression. If it came up, he would let Erica take the lead. This was all about her.

The brunette standing behind the lectern glanced at the clock, then cleared her throat. "Everyone is here so let's get started. There's a lot of information to get through and you're on a deadline." There was chuckling and she waited a few moments before continuing. "My name is Carla McNicol. I'm a registered nurse and work in Labor and Delivery at the hospital. I'm also a certified childbirth educator. Why don't we start by quickly introducing ourselves."

The couple on the far side of the table started with first and last names, adding that this was their second baby. Married, as he'd suspected. The other two couples did the same. Then it was their turn.

"I'm Erica and this is Morgan. First baby," she said, "and I'm getting nervous."

"You've come to the right place," Carla assured her. "Knowledge is power. The more you know, the more in control you feel. This may be repetitious for second timers, but reminders never hurt. So, tonight I'm going to talk about things you can do to prevent preterm labor. You're all within weeks of delivery, but it's best for baby to stay put until nature takes its course."

She started with basics and Morgan was a little surprised at how very basic the things were. The importance of prenatal care. No alcohol or smoking. Prevent infections. Maybe use a condom during sex. He couldn't resist looking at Erica, and her cheeks were bright pink. The RN got as basic as taking care of teeth, keeping gums healthy. Although Carla teased that she was sure couples conscientious enough to take this class already brushed and flossed.

"Believe it or not, stress and avoiding it as much as possible is a very big factor in preventing labor too early," she pointed out. "If there's job tension, do what you can to minimize it. People who make your blood pressure spike—and we all have them in our lives—politely but firmly distance yourself as much as possible. Grandparents mean well but they can add to your tension. Do what you need to do to put yourselves first, Moms."

Carla talked about family-centered maternity care in the hospital, methods for pain management and birth options. She said there would be more information on that presented in upcoming classes.

"And the last thing we're going to do is go over relaxation techniques. I'll demonstrate tonight, but I can't emphasize this enough. Practice makes perfect. The goal is to relax your entire body while one muscle contracts. Your uterus needs to push down and retract the cervix. If other muscles are tight during contractions, you're wasting energy and oxygen. This technique also helps with stress."

She directed them to spread their mats on the

floor. Erica sat with her legs crisscrossed, knees out, while Morgan knelt behind her. Carla demonstrated deep breaths to fill the lungs, then exhaling while concentrating on relaxing other parts of the body. Doing it daily would help moms-to-be master conditioned responses to a labor coach's commands.

"I recommend practicing these techniques every night in bed," Carla said. "And that's it for tonight. I look forward to seeing everyone next week."

Erica was thoughtful and quiet as they rolled up the mat, collected the pillow and were the first ones to walk outside to the parking lot. No chatting after class. No awkward questions to be answered. He could feel her tension and remembered what the RN had said about avoiding it. She hit a button on her key fob and the rear hatch of the SUV slowly lifted.

Morgan put the mat and pillow in the car, then held out his hand. "Give me the keys."

"What?"

"Your keys," he said again.

"Why? Is this a carjacking?"

"If I was going to rip off a pregnant lady, she'd need to be driving one heck of a fine truck." They were standing under a light and he met her gaze, bracing for her stubborn streak to kick in and push back. "I'm driving. Take some stress off you."

She hesitated a moment, then nodded and set the keys in his open palm. "Okay."

Obviously she was lost in her own thoughts, because there was no conversation until he pulled the SUV into the parking lot of The Daily Grind, a coffee shop at the edge of town.

"Why are we stopping here?" she asked.

"I just thought before going home you might need to talk."

"Why would you think that?" She didn't deny it.

"Because you're not talking at all, and it's kind of freaking me out."

She sighed. "Coffee is a nice idea but I've already had my ration of caffeine for the day."

"I think this place has tea, without the kicker. Or water. Until tonight I had no idea you were supposed to drink that much." He looked over at her. "And I bet you wouldn't say no to dessert. Coach is buying."

She shook her head. "I should treat you. I had no idea—"

He put a finger to her lips to stop her words. The jolt he got from touching her nearly stopped his heart. "Arguing is stressful. My treat. End of discussion."

"Okay."

At the counter she ordered a caffeine-free herbal tea and a pumpkin scone. He got black coffee and paid for everything. They carried their stuff to a table in a far corner and sat.

He blew on his steaming cup. "So, what's on your mind?"

"I wouldn't hold it against you if you want to back

out." Her tone said that's what she expected. "I had no idea this class would be so…" She didn't finish the thought, but added, "If this experience is too weird for you, I completely understand."

"If you're okay, I'm okay."

"I am more than okay," she said. "I was very glad you were there. As long as you're sure—"

"Yes, I'm sure. We're friends. I feel as if I've known you for years." But he saw that she was still anxious. "What else is bothering you?"

She looked up, her hazel eyes more brown than green and very uneasy. "This class made it all real. There's only one way out of this. I don't know if I can do it."

"You can."

"Just like that?" she asked.

"Yeah. And there's the fact that there's no way out except birth." He shrugged. "We'll practice the breathing, go to the classes and you'll feel prepared."

"I desperately want to believe you so I'm going to." She smiled at him. "Thank you."

"Anytime."

But he was standing in for another man. That made him curious and a little bothered by the lack of information about her baby's father. The guy had to be a jerk to not be around for her.

Was she still in love with him? Morgan hoped not and the intensity of that feeling surprised—and worried—him.

* * *

When Morgan stopped at his house, Erica thanked him again for going with her, then headed home to the Ambling A. All the way she kept seeing the questions in his eyes. In class tonight he'd looked perfectly comfortable with all the information, even when she'd blushed to the roots of her hair at the mention of condoms during sex.

But when they stopped for coffee, after he'd reassured her he was her friend and would help her get through this, his expression grew more thoughtful. She knew he was wondering why he was there instead of the baby's father. Should she tell him?

That rolled around in her mind as she parked her car near the main house. No one had been around earlier when she went to pick up Morgan, so she'd left a note. The front porch light was on but she hoped no one was waiting up for her. Partly because her parents had to get up early to do ranch work. And partly because she knew there would be questions about where she'd been. Talking about anything to do with the baby seemed to create more tension.

Carefully opening the front door, she slipped inside as quietly as possible, then turned to close it. When footsteps sounded behind her, she knew stealth had been futile.

She whirled around. "Mama. I thought you'd be in bed."

"Your father is. I was watching TV in the other room. Waiting up for you."

"I'm sorry." It was sweet but sort of made her feel like a teenager sneaking in after curfew. "You didn't have to do that."

"I know." Angela stifled a yawn and pulled her long sweater more snugly around her. "But it's a funny thing. When you lived in Denver, I didn't actively worry about you coming in at night. Now that you're here, I can't relax until I know you're home safe and sound."

"But I'm a grown woman," she protested.

"Doesn't matter. You'll always be my baby." Her gaze dropped to Erica's pregnant belly. "You'll understand one of these days."

"I didn't mean to keep you up."

"It's okay." Her mom smiled. "Are you hungry? How about a cup of tea to warm you up? It's chilly outside."

"I'd love one." This was nice. It reminded Erica of the closeness they'd shared before she'd gone away to college.

They walked into the kitchen together, and her mom filled a teakettle with water and put it on the stove, lighting the burner beneath it. Erica pulled two mugs out of the cupboard and found her mom's stash of tea bags. Her father and Gabe had no use for anything but coffee, so this ritual was something only she and her mother shared.

Erica chose something decaffeinated that promised peaceful rest. She showed her mother and laughed. "I won't hold my breath about that since I'll probably be up peeing half the night."

"That's my nightly go-to tea." Her mom grinned. "But I'll be racing you to the bathroom."

Erica laughed. "It's like old times."

"I've missed this." Angela's expression was wistful. "You used to come home at night and tell me about what happened with you and your friends. Your dates. I remember the first time you went out with Jordan Taylor."

"Yeah. I was pretty stoked that a former high school big man on campus and local legend like him would even notice me, let alone ask me on a date."

"Do you think you gave him a fair shot?" her mom wondered.

"Mama, we've been over this." A few dates with the son of the wealthiest rancher in town had been part of the parental push to get her to stay home and attend a local college. "He was like a brother. There was no chemistry at all, no lightning strike."

Not like with Morgan Dalton, she thought. They had declared themselves friends tonight, but her strong feelings for him didn't fit neatly into that box. Under different circumstances she would be hoping for more, but with the baby coming, a friendship was all they'd ever have.

"Too bad." The kettle whistled and her mom filled

the two mugs. They carried them over to the table and sat, just like in the old days.

Angela blew on the steamy tea. "Your note only said that you were going out. Where were you tonight?"

Suddenly the warm, fuzzy, nostalgic feeling was replaced by wariness. Being able to go home again was an illusion. You could physically be there but emotionally it would never be the same.

The walls went up. "Oh, nowhere special."

Her mother's eyes said she didn't miss the evasive tactic. "What did you do?"

"Oh, you know—" Erica wasn't prepared to talk about this. She wanted mother-daughter warm and fuzzy, not tension and judgment.

"Actually I don't know. That's why I'm asking." Her tone hinted at hurt feelings. "Did it have something to do with Morgan Dalton?"

"Why would you ask that?"

"Gabe said he was here recently on ranch business and then you took a long walk with him." She dunked her tea bag with more force than seemed necessary. "And Mel said he offered to take you to the Denim and Diamonds fundraiser next month."

"That's true."

"Which part?" Her mother frowned. "The walk or the asking out?"

"Both, actually." Erica was not going to say more

but decided to add one last thing. "I like him. He's a good man."

"You haven't known him very long."

"Sometimes you don't have to know someone a long time. You can just tell."

"You were with him tonight, weren't you?"

She had to give the woman something. "I was at a childbirth class tonight."

"Oh." That seemed to appease her mother. "How was it?"

"Interesting. I'm a little nervous about the birth." This woman had been through it twice in addition to emotionally painful miscarriages. She knew how it felt. "Does it hurt, Mama?"

Angela's expression turned soft, a combination of sympathy and concern. "I want badly to lie and tell you it doesn't. But I can't. Yes, honey, it does hurt. But it's nothing you can't handle. And when you see your baby… There's just no feeling in the world like it. It's worth everything you go through."

That's what Morgan had said. The part where she could handle it. That helped some. "I'm still a little nervous."

"That's completely normal. Trust me, by the time this baby comes you'll be so ready to do whatever it takes to bring him or her into the world. The childbirth class will help with those nerves—" She stopped and her bonding-mom expression was replaced by something more skeptical. "I thought you needed someone to go to those classes with you. A coach."

"It's recommended." *Please don't ask more,* she silently begged.

"Do you have one?"

She hesitated and thought about a lie, but this was her *mother.* And dishonesty never ended well. "Yes, I do."

"Who?"

Erica sighed. "Morgan."

Surprise and disappointment battled for dominance in her mother's eyes. There was no sympathy or concern now. Just more hurt feelings. "Why him?"

"You and Dad and Gabe have made your negative opinion clear. I didn't feel I could ask you. Mel is a sweetheart, but I don't want to compromise her relationship with my brother. I don't know anyone else. Morgan has been there for me since I came home. There was no judgment." She shrugged. "And he offered."

"Oh, Erica—" She shook her head. Her mother sighed. "I'm concerned about you and how difficult it will be for you being a single mother."

"I gave it a lot of thought, believe me. But more than anything I want to be a mother. If I have to do it alone, then so be it. If I'd had anywhere else to go, I would have. As soon as I find a job I'll move out."

"Erica, no one is asking you to leave."

"I know. But I think it would be better if I did."

"You are more than welcome to stay. This is your home, and we love having you here. But I completely support your decision, whatever that is." Her mother stared at her, eyes suspiciously bright. She stood, leaving her now-cold tea untouched. "I'm going up to bed. Sleep well, sweetie."

"Good night, Mama." She watched the woman she loved so much walk away.

Just then the back door opened and Malone walked in. This man with the craggy face and bushy mustache was no one's idea of what a cook looked like. And he was the walking, talking explanation of why it wasn't wise to judge a book by its cover. He had a way with food. And not just meat and potatoes. His sauces were to die for and he made biscuits from scratch that melted in your mouth.

"Hi, Malone." She settled her elbow on the table and rested her cheek in her palm.

"Hey, Erica. Missed you at dinner tonight." It was dark outside, but the man still wore his tattered old hat and a bandanna tied around his neck. But the look worked with his old jeans, boots and faded plaid cotton shirt. "There's leftover chicken if you're hungry."

"I'm not." A pumpkin scone had taken care of that. "Why are you here?"

"Gonna get a head start on breakfast. Omelets tomorrow. If everything is cut up and ready I can whip them up in a jiffy." He angled his head toward her obvious condition. "If there's anything you're craving, just let me know."

"I will."

"Once knew a pregnant lady who had to have her avocados." He grinned. "And melons—cantaloupe, honeydew, watermelon—didn't matter which."

"Right now I can't say I have any cravings." At least nothing that food would fix.

"You feelin' all right? That baby giving you trouble?"

Yes, but not the way he meant. "No, I'm fine."

"Don't look like it," he observed.

"There's still some tension between Mama and I."

He sat his six-foot frame into the chair her mother had recently vacated. This man was a talker and he was settling in. "It was awful hard on your mama and daddy when you went away."

"I know. But it's my life. Shouldn't I be able to live it my way?"

"Yup. And they know that." His eyes were piercing. "It may not be my place to say but look at the view from their front porch. You come home without telling them there's gonna be a baby. Now here you are, and that little one is going to be here real soon. And their feelings were hurt. They might just need a minute or two to adjust."

She sighed. As much as she wanted to argue with him, she couldn't. When she lived here Malone had more than once put in his two cents and she'd missed his plain-spoken wisdom. "You're right. I should have said something right away. I just couldn't face what I knew I'd hear in their voices and see in their eyes. I only ever want them to be proud of me."

"They are, honey. But what with you working and living somewhere else, they didn't get much chance to fiddle with their feelings about you being all grown-up. It's hard for parents to figure out how not to butt in and try to keep their kids from making mistakes."

"This baby isn't a mistake. I've wanted to be a mother for a long time now."

He smiled and patted her hand. "And you'll be a good one, too. Just like your mama."

"Thanks, Malone." She smiled sadly. "For just a little while tonight Mama and I were having such a nice talk. Just like we used to. Then it went bad. They say you can't go home again, and I probably shouldn't have."

"Well, you did, though. And things have changed. My advice is remember the old while you're making the now new. And it doesn't happen overnight."

"That sounds like good advice."

"It is. But worth what you paid for it." He grinned, then stood up. "Gotta get going on my chores. Breakfast comes awful early around here."

"Can I give you a hand?"

"That's okay, honey. You should get some rest. The baby needs it."

She stood, too, then went up on tiptoe to kiss his cheek. "Thanks for the talk. I'll do my best to make the now new."

And until this baby was born, the new included Morgan. He was a new she could easily get used to.

Chapter Seven

Along with lawyer and doctor appointments and birthing class, Erica was busy sending out résumés. She was encouraged by quick responses to them asking for interviews. But after the second one without an offer of employment, she was forced to admit two things. Because she'd been hired at Barron Enterprises as a college intern, she didn't realize what a challenge job hunting could be. The second thing was that being very pregnant didn't make the search any easier.

This was her third interview, one she'd actually scheduled before moving back. She was sitting across the desk from Sandra Allen, the Human Re-

sources director of an energy company in downtown
Bronco Heights. This was a face-to-face meeting
for their accounting/marketing position, following a
phone interview during which this same woman had
seemed very enthusiastic. Probably Erica should have
mentioned being pregnant, but she just wanted a foot
in the door, an opportunity to display her personality
and business knowledge. One look at Erica's well-
developed baby bump had cooled off any interest.

She knew what the woman was thinking because
she'd had to deal with personnel issues like this at her
last job. She needed to get ahead of it, so to speak,
then highlight the skills she could bring to the table
in the long term.

She smiled. "You probably noticed that I'm pregnant. My due date is next month and I already have
child care arranged." That was a lie but she would
make it true. "If you decide to hire me, I'll get to
know the company, and when I return from maternity leave, I can hit the ground running." She was
going to throw everything at the wall and hope something stuck. "In my previous job, I was in charge of
day-to-day operations. I oversaw Human Resources,
accounting, marketing and IT."

Sandra folded her hands and rested them on her
desk. "You have an impressive résumé, Erica."

"Thank you." She was pretty sure she heard a
"but" in the woman's voice but hoped she was wrong.

"The thing is," she continued, "you're overqualified for the job we have. Upper management would be a better fit and we just don't have an opening right now."

"You're concerned that I'll leave if something better comes along." It was about more than that, but she was determined to leave it all on the table. "As you can see from my work history, I was hired during my college internship and stayed with the company for eight years. That shows a high degree of loyalty. If you give me a chance, I won't let you down."

"I have no doubt." The woman nodded. "But you should know that I have more people to interview. So, when that process is complete, I'll make a decision. I will call you one way or the other. Thanks for coming in."

Erica knew that was a "don't let the door hit you in the backside on the way out." She stood and shook the other woman's hand. "I appreciate your time."

She walked out of the office and left the building. It was hard not to be discouraged, even though she understood why hiring someone in her condition was a risk. On top of being discouraged, she was starving. And needing someone to listen to her bitch and moan. She knew just the place where both needs could be met and a short time later she walked into DJ's Deluxe looking for Mel. The restaurant's new manager directed her to a large office upstairs.

She found it and stood in the doorway, taking in the cushy conversation area and large desk with a computer. Mel sat behind it and was so engrossed, she didn't even know she had a visitor.

"Knock, knock."

Mel looked up and it took two beats for her to register recognition. "Hey. Sorry. I was so focused. What are you doing here?"

"I'm hungry. And I need a friendly face and sympathetic ear."

"Well, you've come to the right place. Am I wrong that you want privacy for this conversation?"

"You are not wrong."

The other woman stood and walked around her desk. "I'll get you some food. Anything you're craving? Cheesecake? Death by chocolate?"

"Call me a peasant, but a burger and fries would be just about the best thing ever," Erica said.

"Coming right up." She indicated one of the chairs in front of her desk. "Have a seat."

"Thanks."

Erica sat and closed her eyes for a moment, breathing in and out. Trying to relax the way Carla, the childbirth educator, had instructed. This scenario was not what she planned for her baby and the least she could do was try to neutralize her stress. She knew her family wouldn't put her and the baby on the street, but the judgment would always be in their eyes.

The one unexpected positive was Morgan. Literally without any questions asked, he was there for her and the baby. He calmed her when they were to-gether. And she was happy around him. He was a friendly port in a storm of tension and hormones. A bright spot in an otherwise challenging chapter of her life. Once upon a time she'd naively believed she could pull off perfect for this baby, but now she knew better. The best she could do would have to be good enough and at least she had Morgan.

It wasn't long before Mel returned with a plate. She set it on the edge of the desk. "Dig in and feed that baby."

"You don't have to tell me twice."

Erica ate a couple of the fries and closed her eyes in ecstasy. "Best thing I have ever tasted."

"That happens when you're starving. Although DJ's Deluxe sets a high bar in all its restaurants."

"I only care about this one. Right here, right now." She cut the burger in half to make it manageable.

For a few moments there was only silence in the room, if one excluded her appreciative moans. After the first half was gone, she took a break and sat back in her chair.

Erica looked at the lovely woman who was going to marry her brother. "You're a lifesaver. Almost lit-erally. I thank you, and my unborn baby, your future nephew or niece, thanks you."

"Don't mention it. Happy to help." She was sit-ting behind the desk again, frowning at all the pa-perwork in front of her. "With great power comes great responsibility. I'm grateful to you for giving me an excuse to take a break."

"It's the least I can do for family."

"That means a lot." Mel's smile was sweet and soft. "You know, before you came back home, I was a little nervous about meeting Gabe's sister."

"Me? Why?" She wiped her hands on her napkin and crumpled it in her hand.

"You're important to him. And he's important to me. I'm an only child and I lost my parents six years ago. So, I feel as if I'm not just getting the best guy in the world, but a family, too."

"Aww..." Erica felt an emotional lump in her throat. That happened a lot lately.

"You and I have hit it off even better than I'd hoped. I've never had a sister and always wanted one."

"Me, too." She reached a hand across the desk and Mel took it, squeezed affectionately. "You're going to make me cry."

"I would take that as a compliment, except I'm guessing pregnancy hormones might make you emotional if I said *the sky is blue*."

Erica laughed. "You're not completely wrong."

"Speaking of family..." Mel folded her hands and put them on top of her desk. "Have you seen Josiah since you've been home?"

Erica knew the other woman wasn't trying to make her feel guilty, but she did anyway. Gabe had told her Gramps was in Snowy Mountain, a facility north of Bronco Heights that offered a full range of services, from independent living to caring for patients with dementia or Alzheimer's. "Not yet. I've had a lot to deal with since I got home, and it hasn't been that long. I had to see a lawyer. And had a doctor's appointment. A couple of job interviews."

"I understand," Mel said. Clearly she meant that. "It's just that I'm so frustrated. We've hit a wall finding his daughter Beatrix and aren't sure what to do next. More than anything I'd like to give Winona some peace about her child, the comfort of knowing she's all right. Josiah has occasional lucid moments. Gabe and I are wondering if seeing you might just jolt him out of wherever he is and get him to give us something."

Erica sighed. "I feel so bad that I haven't visited yet."

"I know. But try to see him soon if you can." Mel nodded sympathetically. "And I'll stop now. How's the job search going?"

"Not so good."

"Is that what you wanted to talk about?" the other woman asked.

"Yes." Now it was Erica's turn to be frustrated. "I understand what's going through their mind when they look at me so pregnant. I used to deal with this situation, but on the other side of the desk, so to speak. If hired, I would work my butt off for just a few weeks, then have a baby and leave them short-handed again. I could be back to work in six weeks, if all goes as planned. But what if it doesn't? If I was making the decision and had two equal candidates for one position, but one was very pregnant, the best business decision would be to hire the other one."

"I hear you." Mel sighed. "For women, work and motherhood is always going to be a balancing act."

"That's the best you've got?" Erica was only half kidding.

"Yeah. So let's talk about something more pleasant."

"I'm open to suggestions."

"You've met Amanda, but not our friend Brittany yet. She's the one organizing the Denim and Diamonds fundraiser. Apparently it's all coming together really well."

"Great."

"Are you planning to go? If the baby hasn't come yet? I know you said Jordan Taylor's father isn't your favorite person."

"True. But I wouldn't mind seeing Jordan. He and I managed to stay friends even after dating a short time."

Mel nodded. "I can see why your folks got their hopes up. His father and uncles own Taylor Beef. Not only is he good-looking, he'll never have to worry about money."

"I should hope not. It's a big company." And suddenly flashes went off in her brain. There might be a job opening for her in that big company.

"And his father is putting on this big charity shindig to raise money for programs to help lower income families in Bronco Valley. I'm going to need a shindig kind of dress," Mel said.

Erica looked ruefully at her belly. "I'm going to need a tent."

"Oh please. You hardly look pregnant and you're beautiful." Mel toyed with a pen. "At least Morgan thinks so."

"How do you know?"

"I saw the way he looked at you that day at the animal sanctuary."

"You're imagining things."

"Am I? Because right after I noticed that, he asked you for a date."

"No. It's more like he offered to be my bodyguard."

Mel looked skeptical. "How do you explain him volunteering to be your labor coach?"

"Mom told you."

"Yeah." The other woman looked concerned. "And it makes one wonder why."

"Because he's a really nice guy."

"Your family is nice, too."

"I couldn't agree more. But they don't approve of my decision to have this baby alone. I couldn't ask my father. Which would be really weird anyway. My mother is concerned about me being a single mom so I guess I'm trying to prove I can handle the challenges that come up. And you're engaged to Gabe, who thinks I've lost my mind. So I didn't want you in the middle of it," she explained. "Morgan is my good friend. I don't feel like I fit in here anymore, and he feels as if he hasn't been welcomed into the community with open arms." She shrugged. "We get each other."

"Okay."

Erica could see the other woman still had something on her mind. "Go ahead. Sisters can tell each other things that no one else could get away with. Spit it out."

"It's just…" Mel sighed. "Things between you and Morgan seem to be moving pretty fast. I'm afraid you're vulnerable and you'll get hurt."

"He wouldn't hurt me. You'd think a man that good-looking would be a jerk, but he's not. I met his mom and can see why." She thought for a moment. "And your friend Amanda is engaged to his brother. Do you approve of him?"

"Well, yes, but—"

"No buts." Erica held up her hands. "Morgan won't hurt me. It's not like that between us. He doesn't want me that way. I'm pregnant. In fact, no one wants me."

"That's not true."

"Feels true."

After Peter, she'd given up on dating, but being with Morgan gave her a glimpse of possibilities and she had to remember that none of the possibilities included forever with him. She was almost sorry that all of it would change when the baby was born and she wouldn't have a reason to see him anymore.

When Morgan pulled his truck to a stop in front of the main house on the Ambling A, the front door opened immediately and Erica walked out. She must have been waiting for him. That could only mean tension with her family, quite possibly because of him, and she was trying to head it off. He was all in favor of steering clear of stress for her and the baby, but facing the Abernathys didn't bother him.

He'd been surprised but really stoked when she called and suggested going to the Bronco Harvest Festival, so here he was to pick her up. He got out of the truck and went around to the passenger door to open it for her.

"Hi," he said.

She smiled up at him. "You're very punctual."

"So are you." He watched her put a foot on the running board, then handed her into the truck. When she was settled in the seat, her face was very close to his. Her breath was soft on his cheek and her slightly parted lips were a whisper away.

Leaning in to see if they were as soft and sweet as he imagined would be so easy, and he really wanted to. It wasn't the first time the thought crossed his mind. But—no.

He met her gaze. "I would have come up to the door, like the gentleman my mother taught me to be."

"I was ready and waiting. Wanted to save you the trouble."

It was late in the afternoon, and the sun was setting behind the big house, putting them in shadow. Still, Morgan was almost sure her cheeks turned pink and her voice was a little too perky, even by Erica standards. "You didn't want me to come inside, say hi to the family."

She stared at him for a couple of beats, then sighed. "I'm protecting you. They've got some stupid idea that you're pretending to be interested in me because you want to take advantage of me somehow."

That burned because it was so off the mark. But showing anger wouldn't help, so he deflected with a smart-ass comment. "They're right."

"Really?"

"Yes. I'm using you. Before you, I was just a misfit outsider. Now I'm a misfit outsider who's taking the prettiest lady in Bronco Heights to the Harvest Festival."

"I'm taking you to the Harvest Festival, remember?" Her wariness slipped away and she grinned. "You, sir, are a sweet talker."

"And don't you forget it."

"Well, I'm using you right back. It's way past time

my family gets the message that I'm a grown woman. Strong and independent. They can't tell me who I can or cannot see socially." She caught herself and added, "Or who my friends are."

"So I'm your rebellion guy?" He couldn't help smiling.

"I know I'm a little old for that, but now that I'm back, ground rules need to be set," she said firmly.

"Hey, I'm just glad you called."

"It's not much," she said, "but I really want to thank you. I'm very grateful not to be the only woman in that birthing class without a coach."

"Happy to help." He closed the door and went around to the driver's side, then got in. "So, how are you?" he asked as he drove away.

"Still unemployed and guilt ridden."

"You might want to give me some context for that statement."

"Yeah." She sighed. "I had three interviews and got zero job offers. They take one look at me and it's game over."

"I'm sorry to hear that." And he wanted badly to fix her situation but kept that to himself. "And the guilt?"

"Mel reminded me I haven't been to see Gramps yet. It's no excuse, but I've had a lot to do since I moved back."

"That's the truth."

"Mel thinks seeing me might shake him up, pro-

voke a lucid moment so he'll give up something that
will help us find his daughter."

Morgan shook his head. "I can't imagine having
a child and not knowing where they are, or anything
about them."

"That child would be in her seventies now," Erica
said. "Mel wants to find her and bring her to her
mother so that Winona can see her daughter and
know she's all right. But Mel is getting discouraged
about finding a lead."

He happened to glance over and saw her put her
hands protectively on her belly. Erica was already
shielding her child. No way she'd give it up, and he
deeply respected her commitment.

"I'd sure like to help find her," he said. "If there's
anything I can do, let me know."

"Thanks, Morgan. I wish there was. But aren't
you getting tired of doing me favors?" she teased.

"No." It'd be another reason to be with Erica, and
he relished that. In fact, it was getting harder to think
the time would come when she wasn't in his life
anymore.

A short time later they arrived at the Bronco
Fairgrounds. Local law enforcement was directing
traffic, and Morgan followed the line of cars to an
unpaved field where vehicles lined up in rows.

He parked the truck and looked over at her. "You
ready to do this?"

"Yes. I haven't been to one of these since before I went away to college. I used to love it."

The sun had gone down, but large spotlights were strategically placed around the big, open field. The parking area was on a rise, and as they walked toward the festival entrance, the expanse of activities was spread out before them. There were carnival rides, booths with games and a bouncy house for the kids. Strings of white lights were hung around the whole area.

"This is bigger than I remember," she said, eyes wide.

"It's my first time, so I have nothing to compare it to."

Just inside the entrance there was a temporary enclosure holding animals. Daphne Taylor was in the middle of it surrounded by a sheep, a baby goat, a pony and the pig—Tiny Tim. She was supervising children as they petted the docile creatures. In the line of kids awaiting their turn, he recognized his brother, Holt, with Amanda and Robby.

"Hey, you guys." Morgan squatted down to eye level with his nephew. "Hi, dude. Haven't you had enough of the animals yet?"

"No." The little guy vigorously shook his head. "There are dogs and cats here, too. For adoption." His blue eyes were big, bright and eager.

Erica said hello and looked up at his brother. "We haven't met. I'm Erica Abernathy."

"Nice to meet you." If Holt was surprised about the pregnancy or the fact that Morgan was with her, it didn't show.

"Daddy, I want to adopt another dog," Robby said. "They need a good home. It says so on the sign."

"Whoa, kid." His father held up his hands. "We're here to pet the animals. That's all. Remember?"

"Yes." But the boy pointed to the separate enclosure, where several pudgy puppies were running around and tumbling over each other. "There's a black-and-white one over there, and he keeps lookin' at me."

Erica laughed. "You're in trouble now, Dad. If you can figure out how to say no to that eager little face, I'd appreciate you sharing the secret."

"Start practicing now." Holt grinned. "So, what are you two going to do?"

"Not sure yet." Morgan looked down at her. "We just got here. I figured we'd just browse and then see what grabs us." And then he couldn't resist saying, "Hey, Robby, that black-and-white pup is really cute. I think he's smiling at you again."

Holt gave him a look that could laser paint off the barn. "There will be retaliation. You won't know when or where, but it will happen."

Morgan laughed. "Bring it, brother. See you later, guys."

He put his hand to Erica's back, guiding her through the crowd. But with all the people moving every which way, they kept getting separated. So he took her hand in his. "I don't want to lose you."

"And I don't want to be lost." She squeezed his fingers and smiled up at him.

They meandered up and down the rows of booths containing food and games. She stopped by a giant ring toss game and admired the stuffed bears it had for prizes.

"Let's win one for the baby," he said.

She eyed him skeptically. "It might be less expensive to just buy one at the store."

"You doubt my skill?"

"I didn't say that."

"Not in so many words." He walked over to the woman taking money and bought five rings. Three out of five would win a prize. "I never back down from a challenge."

"You could light that money on fire and have just as much fun," she teased.

"Oh, ye of little faith..."

He turned back and tuned out distractions as he lined up his shot. With a flick of his wrist the first ring landed successfully around the neck of a bottle. Erica gasped in surprise. But his second and third ring missed their mark.

"Come on, Morgan. Just two more and the baby gets a bear. Baby needs a bear. No pressure."

He grinned, then cranked up his concentration. The shot was successful. One more and he'd have it made. Taking his time, he did a couple of flicks of his wrist, testing. Then he let the ring go. It wobbled and nearly slid off before firmly settling around the bottle's neck.

"You did it!" In her excitement Erica threw herself into his arms and hugged him.

He pulled her close and breathed in the fresh scent of her hair. Nothing had felt so good in a very long time as this woman did in his arms. He could have held her all night, but too soon she moved away.

"I was wrong about you and not too proud to admit it." She picked out a fluffy brown bear with Harvest Festival embroidered on his paws. Hugging it close she said, "I love this. The baby will, too."

"Maybe mama needs one."

"You're pushing your luck, cowboy."

"Another challenge." And it was a gamble he couldn't back down from. Maybe there was more of his father in him than he wanted to admit. "One more time," he said to the woman, handing over his money.

Five tosses later, Erica was picking out another bear. He carried it as they walked away. "What do you have to say now?"

"You are the king of the carnival games."

"Okay, then."

At the end of the row of booths he stopped and pointed to a sign. "Hayrides. What do you say?"

"I think that sounds like fun."

Her happy smile hit him squarely in the gut and

nearly dropped him to his knees. What was it about this particular woman that made him want to be her hero? She'd said more than once that he was making a habit of bailing her out. He couldn't seem to stop himself. He should be bothered by that and probably would be in the middle of the night when thoughts of her made him toss and turn.

But right now, he was going to sit close to her in a wagon with the moon shining down on them. Playing with fire was dangerous but he couldn't find the will to resist. And if he had the chance to kiss her he wasn't sure he could stop himself.

Chapter Eight

Erica waited a short distance from the hayride while Morgan took the bears he'd won back to his truck. He didn't want them to get mangled or dirty, which was incredibly sweet. And that level of sweetness after a fairly impressive ring toss performance made her realize, not for the first time, that he was a pretty impressive man in so many ways. If things were different maybe…

Nope. Not going there. Wondering "what if" was a waste of time and energy. She was going to be a mother. All the responsibility of taking care of this child would be on her, and she'd reconciled herself to that. Until Morgan, she'd never felt wistful about taking this road alone. She needed to focus on being grateful to be traveling this road at all, because it was impossible to imagine her life without children in it.

"You're still here." Morgan walked up beside her.

Erica had been so lost in thought, she hadn't heard him coming. "I told you I would be."

"One never knows. You hear those stories of an evening gone wrong when a woman heads to the ladies' room and never comes back." His look was wry. "Poor schmuck just sits there until he finally gets it that he's been ditched. And hopes no one noticed."

"First of all, you were the one who left me," she retorted. "Second, I can't wrap my head around any scenario where that has actually happened to you."

"Nope, never has." His expression was casually innocent. Maybe a little too casual?

She put her hand on his arm. "This will either reassure you or feed your ego. But what woman in her right mind would ditch the Harvest Festival ring toss legend?"

"Legend, huh?"

"And ego wins." She tsked. "Don't let it go to your head, cowboy. Your Stetson won't fit."

"Can't a guy just enjoy the moment?" he teased.

"I don't think that's going to be a problem. You're enjoying it quite a lot." She grinned. "But, seriously, that was a pretty awesome accomplishment. My little

Ichabod or Ingrid will be very impressed when he or she is old enough to hear this story."

"Shucks, it was nothing, little lady."

"Not so little, actually. And enough with the B Western cowboy imitation." He was the real deal, not an actor and way more exciting than any of them, she thought. "I was under the impression that we were going on a hayride. But here we are, standing around and talking about you."

"But that's my favorite subject—" He laughed when she playfully slugged him in the arm. "Okay. Let's go. Are you warm enough?"

She had on fur-lined boots, black leggings, a big sweater and a tightly knit fringed poncho over that. "I'm good."

Morgan offered his arm and she slid her hand into the crook of his elbow, liking the feel of him. He was tall and muscular and made her feel feminine and protected, even if it was just for tonight.

Her heart tilted a little and she didn't mind. For right now she wasn't going to question her attraction to him. Or the fact that she wasn't ready to stop touching him when they arrived at the hayride. Over her protest, Morgan paid the man for two tickets.

"A group went out a little while ago," the old guy said. "Should be back any minute. So if you'll just wait over there, I'd be obliged."

"Sure thing." Morgan took her arm and gently steered her to the side. "Don't want to get run over."

"That could ruin a perfectly wonderful evening," she agreed.

"So you're having a good time?"

"Yes." She couldn't remember the last time she'd felt so carefree and content. And just plain happy.

Just then the sound of an approaching tractor drifted to them. The machine rumbled to a stop. It pulled a big wagon with hay bales for seating. The old guy put out a step stool, and once the riders disembarked, he waved the waiting group on.

Morgan jumped up first, then held a hand down to help her. They took their seats and squeezed closer to make more room as others joined them. When the tractor slowly moved forward, it lurched enough to knock Erica into Morgan. He put his arm around her, holding her securely. It felt good, right somehow, and she sighed a little when he didn't let her go.

Smiling up at him, she said, "This is it."

"Ready or not."

She took out her cell phone to snap some pictures of the pumpkin patch they passed. Then the road curved to the right, taking them past Pine Lake, where a nearly full moon left a trail of silver light on the water. It was so beautiful, and she couldn't help thinking romantic, too.

She lifted her phone and snapped another series

of pictures, trying to take a selfie of her and Morgan. Since his reach was longer, he managed to get one.

"Let's see if we broke my camera," she said laughing.

She opened her pictures on the phone. The first one was of the lake, which came out pretty well considering the circumstances. Then she noticed something strange.

"What's this ball of light?"

"Probably just photographic artifact from the flash." Morgan took her phone and looked closely. Then he scrolled to the next picture and said, "Whoa."

Erica gasped. "Now there are three of them. I think they're called orbs. If it's from the flash, why did they multiply?"

"Good question." He scrolled to the next picture and there was just one again. "There's no reason for the change. We're not moving that fast so everything should be about the same."

"I've heard that unexplained lights can be orbs from the spirit world. Light energy. And they often collect around water."

"It's weird for sure. Could just be a coincidence, but—"

"What?" In the moonlight she could see the uneasiness on his face. "Morgan?"

"Daphne Taylor's place is just across the lake."

"The animal sanctuary with resident ghosts?" she clarified.

"Yes," he agreed. "Cue the spooky music. Evan Cruise would love this."

"Who's he?"

"A guy in town who runs ghost tours."

"He should talk to Daphne about her haunted barn." She stared at the pictures. "Maybe these orbs should zip over there, too, and keep her ghost lovers company."

"Are you creeped out?" he asked.

"Yes." She shivered and leaned into him a little more.

His arm tightened around her reassuringly. She looked up and saw an intensity in his eyes that she sensed wasn't about spirit orbs or unexplained phenomena. It had everything to do with her, and their eyes locked in a moment of acute awareness. Everyone around them faded away. It was just him and her.

Slowly he lowered his head and kissed her. The touch was sweet and almost tentative at first, until she moaned softly so that only he could hear. Then it turned into something more, an explosion of attraction that burned away rational thought. She strained for more and he was eager to oblige.

Erica had no idea how long the kiss lasted but suddenly became aware of the steady movement slowing and people around them in the wagon starting to stir.

Morgan lifted his head and glanced around. "I think we're back."

"Yeah—" Erica was in sort of a haze as the tractor slowed even more and came to a stop right where they'd started. "I guess they'll want us to get off."

The other passengers stood there waiting patiently to disembark. In front of her, a woman about her mom's age turned and smiled indulgently at them.

When she noticed Erica looking, she said, "I'm sorry. Don't mean to stare, but you two are just the cutest couple."

"Oh—" She shook her head. "We're very good friends—"

"Even better. Marrying your best friend is a solid foundation for life together. And now you're starting a family." Her gaze dropped to Erica's belly. "And look at you so pregnant and cute. Beautiful expectant mama. Doting dad. And both of you so good-looking. That baby is going to be beautiful." It was her turn to get down from the wagon, and she apologized for holding them up. "Have a good night."

Erica and Morgan were the last to get off, and he helped her down, as carefully as if she were a piece of delicate crystal. His protective attitude hadn't changed, but something else had. She could feel it.

They walked around some more, got something to eat. She chatted about the weather and any other shallow subject that came to mind. He responded in monosyllables. But they carefully avoided discussing the elephant in the room, so to speak.

After seeing all there was to see, they walked back to his truck, and Erica felt an air of tension between them, most of it coming from Morgan. Her teasing friend had disappeared and left a quiet, preoccupied man in his place. She wanted the other guy back, but that would require a conversation. Something told her he wasn't going to raise the subject, so it was up to her.

After he merged the truck into the line of cars exiting the fairgrounds, he turned onto the road leading back to the Ambling A. It was now or never.

"So—" She took a deep breath. "That was awkward. Do you want to talk about it?"

"The kiss?" He gave her a quick glance, then returned his gaze to the road. "Or the woman who assumed I'm the father of your baby?"

She'd been sort of hoping he would grin and say there was nothing to discuss. But she'd given him an opening and he made it bigger. Only a coward would slam it shut now. He'd given her two choices and she picked the latter.

"Does it bother you that people might think you're the baby's father?" She folded her hands in her lap and squeezed them tight.

"If I cared what people thought, I wouldn't have gone to childbirth class with you. People will think what they think. It's a logical conclusion and I don't blame them."

She waited for a "but." It didn't come, and yet his response hadn't relieved the tension. "Who do you blame?"

Instead of answering he asked, "Why isn't the baby's father going with you to the class? Where is he? Shouldn't he be involved?"

In a perfect world, yes, she thought. But this was so far from perfect. She'd decided on a course of action to get what she wanted and would never be sorry for that. No one was going to make her feel like she wasn't enough or that she'd done something she should be ashamed of.

"No," she said. "He shouldn't be involved. I don't need him to be."

"That's a bunch of BS." In the lights from the dash his expression was harsh. "A man takes care of his own if he's any kind of a man."

The words were confirmation that for Morgan being a father was a duty. An obligation. Cleaning up a mess he'd made. And the realization hurt her heart more than it should have.

"Look, Morgan, it's all right if you don't want to be my coach. I understand if it makes you uncomfortable."

"That's not what I'm saying." He didn't raise his voice, which made the words all the more electric. "I said I'd be there and I will. I want to be. I'd just like to know who the father of this baby is. A dead-beat or a jerk?"

For reasons she didn't understand, that made her dig in and pull stubborn around her like a blanket. "That information is on a need-to-know basis, and no one needs to know."

"That kiss says otherwise." Morgan's tone said he had his own brand of stubborn going on.

"I don't think so. Blame it on ghosts and orbs and spirit energy. And that's all I'm going to say about that."

"You're the one who asked if I wanted to talk about it." He turned onto the road leading to the main house on the ranch. "But the truth is *you* don't want to."

"I guess not."

He pulled to a stop at the front door and turned off the engine. "Erica—"

"I had a good time," she said. "Thanks. Good night."

Before he could say more, she got out of the truck and walked inside the house. She leaned her back against the door and held her tears in check. Why was he pushing this? What did it matter? She had walked through fire to have this baby, and he wasn't sure he wanted kids. That was a deal breaker. She had no business even letting it cross her mind that she liked him very much and even less business wishing this thing with them could be more.

It was too bad, really, because she had a feeling they could be good together, that he would be an exceptional husband and father. But he got burned and almost married a woman having another man's baby. Erica's baby would always be another man's. All of that took him out of the need-to-know column about how this baby was conceived.

She didn't think he would take it well and didn't want to find out she was right.

Erica pulled herself together but didn't feel up to putting on a perky face for anyone who might be awake. Still, while living under her parents' roof, she owed them the courtesy of letting them know she was home.

She walked into the great room and found her mother there alone, reading.

"Hi, Mama. I just wanted to let you know I'm home."

Her mother looked up from the book. "Thank you, sweetie."

"Is Daddy in bed?"

"Yes. He was tired." She took off her reading glasses. "How was the Harvest Festival this year?"

"That implies I can compare it to last year, but the truth is that I haven't been there in so long I can't compare it to anything recent."

Her mother closed the book, put it on the table beside her and set her glasses on top of it. "Let me rephrase. Did you have a good time?"

"Yes." Right up until that stranger mistook Morgan for her husband and the father of her baby.

"Did you see anyone there?"

"Of course. The place was packed." But that's not what her mom was asking. All she'd told her folks was her destination. Not the details. Especially that she'd asked Morgan to go. What a brazen hussy, a pregnant brazen hussy. Still, it was one thing to politely follow house rules, quite another to let anyone dictate who she could and couldn't see at thirty years old.

"I went with Morgan Dalton. He picked me up." She glanced down at the stuffed animals in her arms. "He won these playing the ring toss. One for me and one for the baby."

"So, he has skills—"

"Please don't start, Mama."

"That was a joke."

"I'm sorry." She sighed and walked over to sit on the sofa beside her mother, setting the stuffed animals between them. "I guess pregnancy hormones are making me supersensitive."

"I remember. That part is a bitch," her mother said ruefully.

"Language, Mama." She smiled. "But body chemistry does seem to have turned me into one."

Her mother picked up one of the bears and touched the plastic eyes. "These will have to come off. The baby could swallow them."

Erica had already thought of that. Since the pregnancy had been confirmed, she'd been reading everything she could find on child care.

"I'll take care of it," she assured her mother.

"I'm sure you will." Angela put the bear on her lap. "How is everything? Have you heard from the lawyer? Your father said she was going to file suit against Barron Enterprises."

"Yes, she did, but she warned me they can delay the process practically indefinitely and force me to give up."

"But you're made of sterner stuff," her mother said emphatically.

"To a point. But I need a revenue source because the money I have won't last indefinitely." She set the bear down. "I really need a job."

"How's the search going?"

"Nothing so far. I've had some interviews but..." She shrugged. "No one will say it straight out that they don't want to hire me because I'm pregnant. That would be discrimination. But... It's discouraging. I feel as if I'm stuck until after the baby is born. And it's a catch 22. I want to settle in a place of my own for the baby. But I don't feel comfortable doing that until I have cash flow again. I'm sorry that I'm putting you and Daddy out."

"Are you kidding?" Her mother glanced around the large room. "This place is huge. And we love you. You're welcome to stay here as long as you want."

She caught the corner of her lip between her teeth. "But I can't help thinking—"

"What?" Apparently sensitivity hormones were just waiting to pounce, because they kicked up again. "If only I had a husband?"

"No, sweetie. I wasn't going to say that. If only someone could see past the pregnancy. Someone who knows how smart and determined you are. You'd be an asset anywhere you worked if they could see their way clear to give you an opportunity. Those bozos are thinking short-term and that's their loss."

"Thanks, Mama." The words were encouraging and made her want to explain why she was in this situation. "I'd hoped to find a husband. That perfect someone. Get married, then have a baby right away before my eggs get old and dry up like raisins." She shook her head. "It just never happened. You were lucky with Daddy."

"I know it. He's a keeper."

Erica thought she'd found that with Peter, until she mentioned having children and they broke up. The thing was, there'd been no hole in her life when he was gone. In a lot of ways it had been a relief. She'd put in so much energy, and maybe that was just about trying to make it work because her biological clock was ticking.

Shouldn't caring about someone be effortless? The feelings just there? Like with Morgan. The thought popped into her mind and stuck. She wondered if they might have had a chance if it wasn't for the baby. But there was still the question of having kids at all. If she fell for him, it would land her in the same boat as she'd been with Peter.

"I need you to know something, Mama."

"What, sweetie?"

"Do you remember how much I loved my dolls when I was a little girl?"

"Of course." She smiled and looked as if she was pulling up those long-ago memories. "Your daddy built you that dollhouse and little furniture for your babies."

"Is it still in that storage shed in the barn?"

"As far as I know."

"Good." She pressed her palms to her belly. "I'll want to get it out if this baby is a girl."

"Absolutely." There was a soft expression in her mother's eyes. "I know there are all kinds of urban myths about how to tell the sex of a baby, and you'll think I'm being silly, but—"

"I'd never think that."

"You're carrying this baby a lot like I did you. With Gabe I was all out front. Daddy teased that it looked like I had a basketball under my shirt. From the back you couldn't tell I was pregnant."

Erica laughed. "And with me?"

"I seemed to spread out."

"Pretty soon I'll need a warning sign that says Wide Load."

"Hardly. You look healthy and beautiful."

"You're just prejudiced, Mama."

"Of course I am. You're my baby. I love being your mother. And I wanted more babies." Something flashed in her eyes. Something distant, sad and painful.

"I remember how much you did. And the miscarriages."

Angela linked her fingers around the teddy bear she still held and pressed it close to her body. "I had you and Gabe two years apart and it was hard, emotionally and physically. When you were a little older, a bit more independent, I realized I wanted more children."

"I've never forgotten the heartbreak you went through trying to have another baby," Erica said. "And now I understand, because I feel the same way. How you'd move heaven and earth just to feel that sweet warm body in your arms. And because of what happened, you should appreciate better than anyone why my life would not feel complete without a child. And why it's so important for me to do it now. Because I'm the same age you were when—"

"I get it." Still, there was a question in her mother's eyes although she didn't say more.

"I promised myself that if I was fortunate enough to get pregnant, I was having the baby. No matter what. Because later could be too late."

Angela sighed and nodded, but didn't say more or ask any questions. Talking about that painful time was hard for her, but opening up even just a little made Erica feel closer to her mother than she had in a very long time. The mother-daughter bond had suffered in the past twelve years. She took responsibility for that, and tonight was another small step toward fixing it.

She could feel how much her mom wanted her to talk about the baby's father, but now even more than before she was afraid to go there. If she confessed that she'd gone to a sperm bank, it could set their fragile bond back, even make it irreparable. And she couldn't do that. Wouldn't do that.

Neither of them broke the silence. But her mother still held that bear.

Finally she smiled. "So, you had a good time with Morgan?"

"Yes. He's fun."

"I'm glad. You've had a lot to deal with lately, and there's nothing wrong with having some fun." She glanced up. "And it's important that you're comfortable with the person who's going to coach you through labor."

The truth was she did feel comfortable with him, and he was the only one she felt that way about since coming back. She wasn't sure why she'd refused to explain to him how the baby was conceived. Maybe it was because she hadn't been ready for the question. Or she was afraid of how he would react. That's what happened when your feelings became more than they should be.

Whatever the reason, she needed to tell him the truth. As soon as possible.

Chapter Nine

A few days after the Harvest Festival, Morgan was mucking out stalls in the barn. As the oldest brother he probably could have delegated to one of the others, but the crappy job suited his crappy mood. He hadn't talked to Erica since dropping her off that night and didn't much like the way they'd left things. It didn't make him happy, but he missed her. And he was ticked off. Mad at himself for pushing. Mad at her for stonewalling him. He chucked a pitchfork full of hay and muck into the wheelbarrow beside him with more force than was necessary.

He was also mad that the evening had been ruined. He'd been having a really good time, the best since moving to Bronco. Kissing Erica was a particularly memorable highlight. Her lips were soft and eager. Her sexy, throaty sounds said she liked it, too. Then it all went sideways with that lady's comments.

Truth was, Erica was carrying another man's child. Yet all she would say was that the father wasn't an issue and Morgan didn't need to know more.

That kiss said he did and was the reason he couldn't let go of the questions. Did the father know about the baby? Did he not care? What if he had a change of heart and came after her? What if she had a change of heart and wanted to make it work with him?

Another pile of muck went in the wheelbarrow. That was followed by a string of language that made him glad he wasn't a kid anymore with his mother standing there holding a bar of soap to wash out his mouth.

He really liked Erica. It was why he'd offered to help her. But things were changing; feelings were shifting. Getting complicated. He was confused and didn't know what he wanted. But he was crystal clear that he didn't want to keep stumbling around in the dark and get blindsided by another man. He intended to see Erica through the birth of that baby, but before the next class they needed to have a chat.

Morgan heard voices and one of them was a woman's. He looked up and saw Erica coming into the barn with his father. That man being around her tweaked his already bad attitude. He rested the pitchfork against the stall's fence and stepped into the opening, watching the two of them walk down the center aisle toward him. She was smiling at something Neal Dalton said and Morgan felt the knot in his gut pull tighter.

His father noticed him there. "Hey, son."

He wanted to say he didn't need the reminder about their shared DNA. But he didn't, not in front of Erica.

"Look who's here," Neal said.

Erica smiled a little tentatively, not her usual, bright wattage cheerful expression. "Hi, Morgan."

"Hey."

"Watch your step," his father said, putting a protective hand under her elbow. "Don't want you falling, or stepping in something."

She laughed. "I'm a ranch kid. Grew up in the barn. I used to ride all the time, but that's on hold for now."

"Deb, my wife, loves to ride. After her heart attack, I got a little overprotective about her on a horse." His expression was teasing, but there was worry around the edges. "She wasn't a happy camper. And that's an understatement. Right, Morgan?"

"Yeah." His curt answer got a raised eyebrow from Erica.

Neal noticed but overlooked it and kept up the charm crusade in front of a pretty woman. "She followed doctor's orders to exercise and change her diet. Dinner isn't as exciting these days, but she's more important to me than carbs and cream sauce."

"So, she's all right now?" Erica asked.

"She is. Me and the boys are making sure of it. She put a scare into all of us." His amiable, easygoing grin disappeared. "I honestly don't know what I'd do without that woman."

"Hopefully you won't have to find out. And she's lucky to have you," Erica said.

Morgan's scoffing sound earned him another sharp look from her, but his father ignored it. After a year of working together, the man had apparently gotten used to his attitude and met it with gruffness. Morgan made no secret of how he felt and let the man deal with it however he wanted.

"No. I'm the lucky one." Neal met her gaze with a remarkably sincere look, then said, "Okay. I'll let you two talk."

"It was nice to see you, Mr. Dalton."

"Neal. Please." He politely touched the brim of his Stetson. "The pleasure is mine, Erica."

In silence they watched him walk away. Morgan knew there was a fine line between charm, flirting and just plain friendliness. He wasn't sure which side of that line his father had just walked, but women usually had a sense of those things and Erica seemed fine. He, Morgan, was the one she apparently had an issue with.

When they were alone, she said, "I know you're working. I hope I'm not interrupting."

He gave her an "oh please" look. "Yeah, because shoveling dirty hay takes a lot of concentration."

"I'll take that as a no." She twisted her fingers together. "So, your dad is nice."

"That's a matter of opinion."

"I know you told me your parents had problems, but I just saw them together. They were like newlyweds."

"Yeah." He took off his work gloves and shoved them in the back pocket of his jeans.

"How long ago was your mother's heart attack?"

"Before we moved here."

"You came for her, but why do you stay?" Her eyes narrowed. "Clearly you resent your father. I know ranch work. It's not like you can avoid him. My father and brother have a really good relationship. But Daddy is set in his ways. He and Gabe get into it when my brother comes up with some 'newfangled' ideas. My brother rebelled in his own way by backing off and getting into real estate."

Morgan thought about his recent negotiations with the man. "I don't know about real estate, but he can wheel and deal pretty well when stock is involved."

"My point is that he distanced himself from conflict and you put yourself into the middle of it. Why don't you go?"

"I stay for my mom. She wanted her family back

together, and I won't be the one to break it up. We all want to take care of her."

"That's sweet." Erica's eyes grew soft. "You're probably not going to like this, but you remind me a lot of your father. In a good way. I can see where you get your charming streak."

"I'm nothing like him." Morgan did his best to push back against the bad. But her words gave him an opening. "You're probably not going to like this. But we all have DNA. From our mothers and fathers. The baby you're carrying is no different. You know what I'm asking, and I'd appreciate it if you didn't tell me again that I don't need to know."

"I don't plan to," she said. "That's actually why I'm here. To tell you about the baby's father."

"Are you in love with him?" Morgan surprised himself with the question. He hadn't planned to ask, but the words were just right there and he couldn't stop them.

Erica blinked at him, then started laughing.

He'd expected anger or indignation, not this. "What's so damn funny?"

Her amusement faded slowly and she got serious. "There is no father—well, not like *that*. I went to a sperm bank."

He moved closer and badly wanted to touch her, but he'd been doing a dirty job and kept his hands to himself. He also wouldn't stop this flow of information. "That's not an easy thing to do on your own, Erica. If you want to talk about it, I'm happy to listen."

She nodded. "It would be a relief actually."

He angled his head toward the other side of the barn. "There's a bench over there. Something tells me this isn't going to be fast."

"Probably not—" Then she stopped and looked unsure. "But you're working. I don't want to bother you."

"Trust me—the stalls will still be there after I take a break."

"Okay." She fell into step beside him, and they stopped at the wooden bench, then sat side by side.

He met her gaze. "I'm listening."

"I dated someone in Denver. Peter. He's the son of the owner of the media company where I worked." She looked down for a moment at the clasped hands in her lap. "Things were getting serious and I thought marriage was the next step. It seemed as if we wanted all the same things—until I brought up kids."

"I take it he was a no vote?"

"Yup. And that was a roadblock for me. So we broke up."

Morgan studied her and decided she didn't seem too upset about it. So he stayed quiet and let her go on.

She told him how loud her biological clock was ticking, how she was pushing thirty and fearing the fertility issues her mother had faced at that age. How she felt it was now or never.

"Never, for me, wasn't an option. So, I went the sperm bank route. Got lucky on my first round of insemination."

Morgan saw a look on her face, part anger, part disillusionment. "There's more, isn't there?"

"Yeah. Peter started dating a receptionist at the company not long after we split. I wasn't at all hurt. Figured I dodged a bullet. But they got married and she was pregnant."

"That had to have hit a nerve," he said.

"I'm not going to lie. It did, but even that was okay. I didn't love him, and I was over the moon about having a baby." But not everything went well, she told him, when Peter's father gave her the ultimatum: transfer to Miami or get fired. She shrugged. "And here I am."

"That sucks." He heard how that sounded. "Not that you're here, but the way it happened," he clarified.

"I knew what you meant." When she looked at him, there was uncertainty in her expression. "This experience of becoming a mother isn't going at all as I planned."

"I'm really sorry you went through that. But I can't say I'm sorry to hear that some guy isn't going to turn up and arm-wrestle me to be your labor coach."

"Nope, that's not going to happen." She grinned, but wariness erased it. "But this is why I can't say anything to my folks. Daddy can't even embrace new and improved ranching techniques. I don't think the idea of a sperm bank grandbaby would go over well."

"I can see why you're hesitant. But you were the one who said we should give our families a chance."

"You first," she said.

"Touché." He laughed, then turned serious. "So you weren't in love with Peter."

"No." She caught the corner of her lip between her teeth, and uncertainly met his gaze. "Are you still in love with the girl you bought the ring for?"

"I thought I was at the time. Looking back, I don't think I ever really loved her."

And speaking of love... Morgan was awfully damn glad Erica wasn't in love with her baby's father. But that meant his feelings were turning into more than he wanted them to be. If it was anyone else, he'd walk away, but after giving his word to see her through the birth, he wouldn't back out. It would be okay, though, he reasoned. It wouldn't be long until the baby was born. He'd keep his promise, then that would be that.

The morning after clearing the air with Morgan, Erica was both relieved and full of purpose. He didn't resign as her coach. That made her unreasonably happy. Also, crying on Mel's shoulder about her job search turned out to be not all bad. She'd come up with an idea and was energized.

She'd interviewed with perfect strangers who could only see her pregnancy. They knew that shortly after starting she would be absent for six weeks. So, she needed to talk to someone who *did* know her.

It was barely nine o'clock, and she was in her room because privacy was required for the call she was about to make. And she had a strategy. She wanted to catch Jordan Taylor just as the workday started, before he was up to his neck in Taylor Beef business. After tapping in the number on her cell phone, she waited.

But she didn't get further than the receptionist.

"I'm sorry. Mr. Taylor's busy today and asked me to hold his calls. But I'll make sure and give him a message."

The woman was friendly but firm. Erica knew assertiveness was almost certainly not going to work in her favor. So, she could leave the darn message, then go camp out at his office and be the proverbial squeaky wheel. It was incredibly irritating, but the woman was simply doing her job.

Erica would admit to the tiniest bit of prejudice toward anyone in that position. Based on the fact that a receptionist at Barron Enterprises was responsible for putting her in need of a job, she had a right to the feeling.

"A message would be great." She repeated her

name, recited her phone number and said to tell him that she was back in town and would like to say hello.

She ended the call and thought about her next move to contact the man she'd gone out with all those years ago. She'd never felt they'd clicked romantically and apparently neither had Jordan. One night he'd told her he liked her, but she felt more like his little sister than his girlfriend and he hoped they could still be friends. Then they'd had a nice dinner together. It was the best brush-off she'd ever had.

Since then she'd run into him on visits home over the years, and Jordan had always been friendly. At least that's how she saw it. Hopefully he did, too, and would give her a chance to prove she had a lot to offer his company if he could see his way past the pregnancy.

Her stomach rumbled, reminding her that she hadn't eaten yet this morning. She needed fuel for this job-hunting campaign and went downstairs to the kitchen. Malone was the only one in the room.

"Mornin'," he said.

"Same to you." She looked around. "Where's Mama?"

"She left early. Said she had shopping to do. Something about a new dress for that Denim and Diamonds shindig."

"Right."

A wave of mixed feelings washed over Erica. On the one hand, with all the tension in the house right now it was kind of a relief not to see her mom. Their one talk after the Harvest Festival had made things better but hadn't completely resolved the strain. On the other hand, she missed the time when they would have made a day of buying a special occasion dress, then gone to lunch. She missed that so much.

"Are you hungry?" Malone looked at her baby bump. "Gotta feed that little one. And before you say anything, I know you're not eating for two. You don't have to double your rations."

It surprised her that he knew about not doubling up on calories when you were pregnant. "I am starving, actually."

"Okay. I can whip up some pancakes and eggs. Got some fruit cut up. Now sit. I'll have breakfast ready in a jiffy."

"And I can have one cup of coffee."

Caffeine wasn't strictly forbidden during pregnancy, but limiting it was recommended.

She did as he instructed, and he put a mug of steaming coffee in front of her. Then he proceeded to mix the pancake batter. While she watched, her cell phone rang and the ID said Private. She hoped this was who she thought it was.

As soon as she heard his voice, she knew it was.

"Hi, Jordan. You got my message." And he was returning her call a lot faster than she'd expected. Hopefully that was a good sign.

"Yes, you caught my receptionist when she was

actually working." Oddly, there was a smile in his voice. "So, you're back. Are you home to stay?"

"Yes. And that's kind of what I wanted to talk to you about."

"Okay. I have a meeting now but I'd really like to catch up. Could you meet me for lunch?"

"That would be great, Jordan. Tell me where and when." After he gave her the information, she said, "Okay. See you then."

She ended the call and saw Malone looking at her. "What?"

"That's what I'd like to know." He poured batter on the griddle and scrambled eggs into a skillet.

"I'm just meeting an old friend for lunch. I have to feed the baby, right?"

"And this old friend just happens to be the one your folks were hoping you'd end up at the altar with." That wasn't disapproval in his voice. Not exactly.

"Yes. Why?"

"He's got a reputation with women. Quantity, not quality, or so I've heard."

"It's not like that with us," she assured him. "Besides, look at me." She glanced down at her very rounded belly. "I'm so not his type."

"Still—" He finished cooking, then slid pancakes and eggs onto a plate and carried it to her at the table, along with a bowl of fruit.

"You're sweet to worry about me, but there's no

need." She was the one who wanted something from Jordan.

Which was why a few hours later she got to DJ's Deluxe and told the hostess she was meeting someone. The woman pointed him out and Erica walked over to the table where he was already seated. He stood as she approached and his eyes widened, evidence that he noticed her condition.

He gave her a hug and kissed her cheek, then held her at arm's length. "Look at you."

"Yup." She smiled. "Gonna be a mom."

"I didn't know you were married."

"I'm not."

He studied her for several moments, then simply said, "Congratulations."

"Thank you." She sat down across from him. "It's been a while. How are you, Jordan?"

"Good."

"And your dad?"

He shook his head slightly. "Same as always."

She saw a look in his eyes and said no more. The man who intimidated her also had a reputation for being difficult, and she couldn't imagine being his son. But not everything was his cross to bear. He was very tall and very handsome, with short dark hair and brown eyes that were incredibly compelling. A man that women noticed. He was also the son of the richest man in town, and women noticed that, too.

"What's new?" she asked.

"Not much." He shrugged those broad shoulders. "But you've got a lot going on. A baby on the way. Miss Independent moving back to Bronco Heights. Why?"

"Because I got fired from my job in Denver." There was no point in evading. They'd always been honest with each other, and she wasn't about to be anything less now. She told him the whole humiliating story, except for the part about how she got pregnant. Then she explained about filing a lawsuit against her previous employer.

"I think your attorney is right that you've got a good case."

Their server walked over then, and they ordered.

When he was gone, Jordan met her gaze. "How can I help, Erica?"

"I was hoping you'd ask." She leaned forward. "I need a job. The money I've saved won't last forever, and this lawsuit could take a long time to resolve."

"I see."

"I realize this is presuming on our friendship, but no one in their right mind will hire a woman in the third trimester of pregnancy."

"It's touchy," he admitted.

"I have upper management experience and a lot to offer. If you give me an opportunity, I promise you won't regret it."

"Of course I can help." He didn't even hesitate. "We're always looking for good people."

"Really? Just like that," she said.

"It's the least I can do for a friend. But I have a feeling you'll be doing me a favor in the long run." He took out his cell phone and started tapping into it. "I'm texting my assistant now to check my schedule and then she'll contact you to make an appointment to come by."

Her eyes got a little blurry with grateful tears, but she blinked several times, determined not to get emotional. "I don't know how to thank you."

"Name the baby after me. Jordan works for a girl or a boy."

His teasing smile brought women to their knees, but she was immune. Why was that? Because she had that reaction to another man. Every time she saw Morgan, her heart skipped a beat and her legs wobbled a little. It made her wonder about what combination of factors attracted a certain woman to a certain man.

Before she could decide, their food arrived and she couldn't believe she was hungry again after the big breakfast she'd eaten. Now that the reason for this meeting had been settled, she could relax and enjoy catching up. They reminisced about the short time they'd dated and decided it wasn't a total waste, what with the friendship that came out of it.

She speared a piece of chicken and lettuce. "You know my parents were hoping I'd fall for you and not go away to college."

"Really?" He took a sip of his beer. "I don't think you ever told me that."

"It's true. They wanted me to marry you. Hometown boy."

"Sorry to disappoint," he teased.

"Unless I miss my guess, I think they're still holding on just a little bit to some kind of fantasy that we'll see the error of our ways and get married." She laughed, then looked up from her salad, expecting that he would be laughing, too.

He wasn't. And his expression was a little dark and brooding. "You deserve someone better than me, Erica."

"Don't be ridiculous."

"I don't think I am. I'm not good enough for you." He looked thoughtful. "And you're going to have a baby. That's a special responsibility."

"The fact that you recognize it as such is proof that you're so much better than you think you are."

He shook his head. "You're wrong."

Erica disagreed, but trying to convince him of that would be a waste of time. There was no question that he was flawed, but who wasn't? She considered him a good friend. And she was confident he was a good man.

As good as Morgan?

Since when was he the bar by which she judged other men? Maybe it was talking about the responsibility of a baby that made her think of him now.

It was a darn shame that he didn't want kids and doubted his suitability as a father.

She liked him very much and that kiss at the Harvest Festival said he liked her, too. But this baby had to be her first priority. Sometimes liking someone a lot just wasn't enough.

Chapter Ten

Talking to Jordan the day before had eased Erica's stress level by a lot. As promised, his assistant had called to make an appointment for the following week. He'd assured her there would be a job after the baby was born, and in all the years she'd known him, he'd never lied to her. There was no reason to believe he was now. That morning she'd visited Gramps and tried to coax him to talk. Sadly he didn't say anything. After lunch she was at loose ends and the waiting without anything to fill her time was driving her nuts. She was used to being busy.

Between Malone cooking and hired help with the housekeeping, her mother didn't need any assistance.

So, Erica wandered down to the barn to see what her father was up to. She walked inside and found him cleaning out stalls. The last time she'd seen Morgan, he was doing the same thing. Not too proud to handle a dirty job. Just like her father.

"Hi, Daddy. Don't you pay people to do this?"

He looked up from shoveling horse manure into a wheelbarrow. "It's relaxing. Keeps me from thinking too much." She was probably a big part of what he didn't want to think about. But burying his head in the sand wasn't going to change anything, and she wanted to do what she could to repair their relationship. "I'm looking for something to do to earn my keep. Can I give you a hand with this?"

He frowned at her. "Don't you need to take it easy? With the baby?"

"The doctor says to do whatever I've been doing. Except riding horses. Can't risk a fall."

"Yeah. I remember that from when your mama was pregnant with Gabe and you." He smiled, remembering something. "She's pretty stubborn and missed riding. It was awfully tempting to get on a horse. Lucky she had me to keep her honest."

The subtext of that was Erica had no one. Well, she had herself and was doing all the right things for her health and the baby's. And she had Morgan to help her through the birth. Just thinking about him brought a blush to her face. It was involuntary because if she had any control, it wouldn't happen.

She refused to think about what their relationship would be after the baby was born. Day-to-day survival was her priority now and she didn't have to worry about a job. Everything was falling into place, so she refused to let her father's comment bother her.

"How about you let me sweep up when you finish that part. And I can spread out clean hay. If you lift the bale, I'll just walk back and forth with the pitchfork. Think of it as getting my daily exercise."

"Sounds okay to me." He smiled at her. It was almost the way he used to before she decided to have a baby by herself.

They worked in silence for a while and then Erica asked, "Do you think about retiring, Daddy?"

"Why would I?"

"Running a ranch is a lot of work."

"And if I don't do it, who will?" He shoveled more muck, then met her gaze through the fence dividing the stalls.

"Gabe will."

"I suppose." He leaned on the shovel. "If he doesn't have me to contend with, he can do it his way. We don't see eye to eye on how to run things these days. I don't see any good reason to change. This land has been in the family for generations and we're doing just fine. Your brother is into his real estate deals. That's *his* way of pushing back."

If Erica was the sensitive type, she would have bristled at that remark. As if her having a baby without marriage and a husband was her preferred rebellion strategy. But, again, she made a conscious effort to let that roll off her back.

"What did Gabe want to do that was so revolutionary?"

Her father stopped working and pushed his Stetson off his forehead a little as he thought about the question and looked down at the wheelbarrow. "Well, take this for instance."

"Horse poop?"

"Yeah." He grinned. "He had me read an article and the title was 'What to do with poo.'"

"Catchy." She laughed. "You compost this, right? And spread it in the pasture?"

"We do. But there's something called manure share."

"Do I even want to know about this?" she asked.

"Probably safer than talking about other things," he said, looking down at her belly. "It's a program that connects livestock owners who have excess manure with gardeners, landscapers and large scale composters. According to your brother, it benefits the environment and the economy of local communities."

"Call me crazy, Daddy, but that sounds like a good program."

"Maybe." He didn't look convinced. "But I've got better things to do than coordinate poo pickups."

"I think you're just being stubborn."

"Takes one to know one," he said pointedly.

She ignored that and pitched more hay on the stall floor. "We're talking about you now."

"Okay. I think the terms old-fashioned and set in my ways have been thrown out more than once to describe me." He met her gaze. "There's probably some truth in it."

"They say recognizing a problem is halfway to solving it."

"I never said I had a problem. If it's not broke, don't fix it, I always say. When I'm not running things, this operation will change. And someday this land will belong to Gabe and you and my grandchildren—" He didn't finish the thought, and the silence was—well—pregnant.

She walked over to the opening of the stall next to hers where he was working. "What is it, Daddy? Something other than the obvious is bothering you. Please talk to me."

He looked at her. "The baby you're carrying is my grandchild. Mine and your mother's. It's something we've looked forward to and prayed would happen for a long time now. We've worked hard for all these years to know that everything will pass on to another generation of Abernathys. Whether you want to talk about him or not, that baby has a father. What if he turns up demanding visitation and more? Some cockamamie claim on the Ambling A?"

"That won't happen," she assured him. "I guarantee it."

"How can you? There are stories on the news all the time about courts granting property and all kinds of demands to someone with flimsy paternity claims."

Her father had just admitted he was set in his ways and had no use for new techniques. Her pregnancy via anonymous sperm donation would, in his mind, fall in that category. This was the absolute wrong time to explain how she could be so certain that no one was going to show up and demand anything.

"You're just going to have to trust me, Daddy."

She went back to the stall where she'd been working and finished spreading the hay. Her father didn't say much more, and the awkward silence persisted. More than once it crossed her mind to leave him alone, but there was a lot of truth to that stubborn Abernathy streak. She stuck it out until the job was finished.

Afterward, Erica want back to the main house, left her dirty boots on the back porch then went up to her room to shower away barn dust. She'd thought the spray of warm water would relax her after the conversation with her father, but it didn't. She was still feeling a little raw.

On her way to the stairs she passed her parents'

room and noticed her mother was there, looking at something on the bed. "Mama?"

"Erica. Come on in."

She walked inside the large room and went directly to the king-size, cherrywood sleigh bed.

"Is that your dress?" She looked down at a fancy gown laid out on the duvet. "This is for Denim and Diamonds?"

"Yes." Her mother picked up the hanger and held the dress up in front of her. It was a long-sleeved black sheath with gorgeous beading. "What do you think?"

"It's just beautiful, Mama." She smiled. "That's going to look fabulous on you."

"You don't think it's too young for me?"

"No way. It's classic. Elegant. And besides, you aren't old. Unless it's a miniskirt and boots, you can pull off anything."

"Okay. Good." Her mother sighed. "I just love it, too. So, what about jewelry?"

"It is Denim and Diamonds after all. Don't you have some big, honkin' diamond earrings that Daddy bought you for a significant birthday?"

"Yes. They'd be perfect." Her mother walked to the mirror over the dresser, held the gown up in front of her and assessed the look. She beamed a satisfied smile.

"You're going to be the belle of the ball, Mama."

It felt really good to just talk girl stuff. No undercurrents. Just enjoying feminine conversation.

"It should be something," her mother agreed. She walked over to Erica and started to say something, then pressed her lips tightly together. "So, Malone tells me you had a call from Jordan. Unless you know another one, I assume that's Jordan Taylor?"

"Yes. I had lunch with him yesterday."

"Oh?" Her mother's eyes gleamed with interest. "And?"

"He looks good."

"Of course he does. They don't call him Bronco's most eligible bachelor for nothing." She waited a moment, then prodded a little. "So you just stared at a nice-looking man over a table at lunch?"

"Funny." Erica grinned. "We did some catching up."

"Is he seeing anyone?"

"He didn't say, so the answer to that question is either no or nothing serious."

The gleam in her mother's eyes intensified. It was a spark of hope. "I guess he noticed that you're pregnant."

"Yes. He congratulated me." And didn't ask any questions, which she appreciated.

"Did you make plans to see each other again?" Angela asked.

"As a matter of fact, we did." She was going to hell, but Erica couldn't resist leading her mother on a bit. Served her right for not letting this go.

"Lunch again? Or maybe dinner?"

"I have an appointment to talk to him about a job."

"And?"

"That's it. He said they're always looking for talented people at Taylor Beef, and he was sure there was something for me."

Her mother looked a little startled. "But you're going to have a baby."

"That's not a news flash, Mama. And that's why I really need a job."

"There's no need to rush into anything, Erica. This is your home."

"I appreciate that. More than I can say. But—"

"But nothing. What will you do with the baby after it's born?"

"I'll find child care."

"Babies need their mothers."

"And I will take care of him or her," Erica protested. "Part of that is earning a living so I can support us."

"Like I said, you have a home. Your father and I can take care of you both—"

"Mama, please don't take this wrong. But I only moved in here temporarily. To get on my feet. I appreciate you and Daddy letting me come home so I can do that. Once the baby's born and I'm back at work, I'll find a place for us to live."

"I suppose I can't talk you out of that."

"If I hadn't been fired, that's what I'd be doing in Denver. It was always my plan, Mama."

"I see." Her mother walked past her to the closet. Without turning, she said, "I need to hang this up, then I've got some things to do."

Erica had seen tears in her eyes and heard the break of emotion in her voice. She started to say something, then stopped. It wouldn't do any good. Angela Abernathy had never come to terms with her daughter going away to school, then having a career somewhere so far from home. Being a ranch wife and mother was her career, and she didn't understand Erica's choices any more than her father accepted new ranching ideas. This wasn't the time to point out that at least she would be living close by this time.

Still she felt awful. She didn't want to hurt her parents, but she had to live life on her own terms. She'd kept intending to tell them about the baby but put it off. Maybe in the back of her mind she believed if they held their newborn grandchild and bonded, the circumstances wouldn't be a big deal.

Women plan, God laughs. But she didn't think this was funny. The only thing getting her through was Morgan. They had childbirth class tonight and she would see him. She was looking forward to that very much.

"So, Erica is picking you up again this evening?" Deborah Dalton toyed with the mug of coffee in front of her.

"Yeah." Morgan sat at the round, oak table in his

kitchen, eating the stew his mother had brought over. Her excuse was that she always fixed too much, and that was probably partly true. The other part was, feeding him was a way to stay connected. Better known as pumping him for information.

He figured her question was just the beginning of an inquisition. The innocent expression on her still-beautiful face was a dead giveaway.

"Erica insists on it," he said.

"Usually a gentleman picks up a lady for a date."

"It's not a date, Mom. She says I'm doing her a favor. The least she can do is drive."

His mother looked down for a second, then met his gaze again. "Why *did* you agree to be her labor coach?"

"Actually I offered. She's going through a lot and I can help. That's it." He shrugged.

"But having a baby is an intimate and emotional experience."

One that should be shared with the father of said baby. His mother didn't say that straight out, but it was there all the same. He wished the woman would get off this subject, and he planned to make that happen. "Cops and firefighters and regular civilians deliver babies for perfect strangers all the time. Not that I'm delivering it, but... She's my friend. It's the least I can do."

"You really like her." That wasn't a question.

It was a different subject and he was even less comfortable talking about this one. "As a friend."

"Erica told me that your kindness and sensitivity are the first things she noticed about you."

"I'm a hell of a guy."

"Just like your father." Her unwavering look was a dare for him to convince her she was wrong about the man's character.

Morgan tried to resist the challenge, but just couldn't. "I'm not like him."

She shot an exasperated look in his direction. "There's no getting around the science. He's your father. You have his DNA—the good, bad and handsome. It's been thirty-five years and he still makes my heart flutter and my knees weak."

"I don't want to know that, Mom." He did not like where this conversation was going.

"Tough. If I can forgive him, so can you."

"That's where you're wrong." He loved his mother a lot. He'd do anything for her and proved that when he moved to Dalton's Grange because she'd explained how important it was to her. None of that meant his attitude toward his father had or ever would change.

"Morgan, we're all only human. We have flaws. You. Me. And your father. People don't always make the best choices when they're under stress. That doesn't mean we should disregard the positive parts of them."

"You made your choice. You have to live with

him," he allowed. "I just have to work with him."
He buttered one of the biscuits she baked and took a
bite. It melted in his mouth. "These are really good."

"Your father said the same thing." Again the challenge was in her eyes for him to deny the connection.

"There isn't anyone on the planet who wouldn't
like these. Don't give me that look," he said.

"Okay. Suit yourself. But don't expect me to stop
trying."

"Suit yourself. It's your time to waste." He would
do almost anything for this woman, but letting his
father off the hook wasn't one of them. "I love you,
Mom."

"I know. And I love you, too. Even though you're
stubborn like your father. Although, in all fairness,
you get it from both sides. Truthfully, I'm not sure
whether or not that's a flaw."

"I'm not stubborn," he said. "It's just that I'm always right."

She rolled her eyes. "When did you say Erica is
coming?"

"About a half hour." Morgan was keeping a close
watch on the time and planned to be outside waiting,
so she didn't have to come up to the door and knock.

"I'll get out of here before that. Otherwise she'll
think I lied about you living with your mother."

"Maybe I should hire you to cook," he teased.

"You couldn't afford me." Her grin was equal
parts confidence and self-satisfaction.

She got up and washed the casserole dish she'd brought the food in. Then she said goodbye and headed to the door. Just before she opened it, there was a knock.

"She's really early," Morgan said.

"Hmm." His mother opened it. "Erica. Hi."

"Hello." If she was surprised, it didn't show. "Nice to see you, Mrs. Dalton."

"Oh please. Call me Deborah. Better yet Deb."

"Okay. Thanks. Is Morgan—"

"I'm here." He moved beside his mom. "Come in. It's cold outside."

"Thanks."

"You're really early. I was going to wait for you outside so you didn't have to get out of the car."

"Oh—" She looked first at his mom, then him. "Sorry. I was ready and didn't want to wait around."

He saw tension in her eyes and the set of her mouth. "Is something wrong?"

"No. At least nothing new."

"Come and sit down," his mom said. "And tell us what's bothering you."

"There's plenty of time before the class," he assured her.

She hesitated for several moments, then sighed and nodded. After walking over to the leather sofa, she sat and he settled beside her. Not as close as he wanted to be.

His mother took one of the chairs and set the

empty casserole dish on the matching ottoman. "Okay. How can we help?"

Erica's smile was rueful and sad. "Just don't click your heels three times and say 'there's no place like home.' Or 'you can't go home again.' I found that out."

"That would mean there's no positive movement with your family," he guessed.

She shook her head. "I tried. I was hanging out with my dad in the barn. Helping him. Earning my keep. But he's stubborn."

"There's a lot of that going around." Morgan met his mom's gaze and saw sympathy in her eyes.

"Right." She twisted her fingers together in her lap. "And my mother—" She looked at Deborah. "We were so close before I went to Colorado."

"Letting go of her children is hard on a mother. Especially when they go far away."

Morgan didn't miss the message in his mother's eyes. She wasn't above using her not so long ago health crisis to bring her sons together.

"Well, now I'm back," Erica said. "With a baby on board. But I'm not married, and that's not the way they wanted to be grandparents."

"Oh, honey—" His mother made a sympathetic sound. "They'll come around."

"I don't think so. Apparently I made another mistake." She looked down for a second. "I had the audacity to look for a job. I contacted Jordan Taylor."

She told them about Jordan's promise to find her a position at Taylor Beef.

Morgan had heard about the guy. A newcomer picked up a lot of information hanging out at DJ's Deluxe bar. He'd heard about Jordan Taylor's reputation with the ladies. "Isn't that the guy your folks wanted you to marry?"

"Yes. Even today Mama was hoping and hinting there might still be a chance with him. The thing is, she said I don't need a job because they can take care of me and the baby." She clasped her hands so tightly her knuckles turned white. "I don't want that. It's my responsibility to support us. My mother's always been a ranch wife. She doesn't understand that I want to do it on my own. And I can."

His mother's expression was kind and concerned. "Women have hard decisions to make when it comes to family and career. I know all about that."

"Really?" Erica's eyes widened.

She nodded. "Before I met my husband, I was a career woman. On my way to top-tier management. Or possibly the first female president of the company."

"Wow. What happened?"

"Neal Dalton happened." She got a soft look on her face and shrugged. "I was a city girl and met him at a rodeo, of all things. He was kind and caring. One look at him, his smile, and I fell in love. I knew he had a ranch and that was his life, in his blood. It wasn't as if he could relocate to the city and find a job with his skill set. Ultimately I couldn't live without him."

"That's so romantic," Erica said.

"My parents and family were professional people and less than thrilled with my decision. But I love him, and love is worth every sacrifice. If you're not willing to do what it takes to be with that person for the rest of your life, it's probably not love. I chose to be a ranch wife and never regretted it." She met Morgan's gaze. "Not once."

"Mama never understood my passion for a career. But I also want very much to be a mother."

"Every mother is a working mother. It's just that some women have jobs outside the home, too." His mother's tone was firm and supportive. "But attitudes have changed, and women have more options and support than ever before."

Erica nodded. "I know they'd like for me to be married with a baby coming because they're concerned about the difficulties of being a single mom."

"They love you, that's all. They just want what's best for you."

"I know that. But—" She hesitated a moment, then waved a hand in front of her face. "I'm sorry to talk about my problems."

"I don't mind listening. But trust me on this. Things will be fine. You wait and see." His mother smiled. "Now I have to go. And so do you two. Go learn something." She stood, grabbed her casserole dish, then let herself out the door.

Morgan was alone with Erica. "You feeling better?"

"Yes, actually." She smiled. "It really was nice talking to someone who understands what I'm dealing with. I've probably said this before, but you're lucky to have her, Morgan."

"I won't argue that. But we have our blind spots, too."

She was staring at the door where his mom had just left. "She sure does love your dad."

"Yeah."

Morgan was well aware that the part of her motivational speech about never regretting her choice had been for his benefit. He thought about the woman he'd proposed to and finding out she was pregnant with another man's baby. Oddly, he realized that he hadn't been that shocked. He felt betrayed and angry about the lie, but he wasn't really hurt. In hindsight, letting her go was the easiest thing he'd ever done. And he never regretted it.

He'd met his fair share of women since then. They were sweet, pretty, bold and sassy. Blondes, brunettes and redheads. Shy, forward, fun and serious. But not a single one of them stuck in his mind or heart when he looked in his rearview mirror.

Not until Erica.

He stared at her now. The tension in her eyes and

around her mouth was gone. She was glowing, and no, that wasn't the sun shining through the window. She got to his heart in a way he'd never been gotten to before. She was becoming awfully important to him, but…

Why did there always have to be a *but*?

She had moved heaven and earth to be a mother, have a baby. He had doubts. Not only whether or not he wanted kids, but also about being a good father. Unless he could be sure about both, he had no business saying anything to Erica about his feelings.

Chapter Eleven

"Mama, thank you so much for taking me shopping."

"You are so welcome, sweetie."

Her mother's suggestion had come out of the blue that morning. The olive branch gave her hope that this was the beginning of better times.

Erica burrowed into the butter-soft leather passenger seat of her mother's luxury SUV. They were finally on their way back to the ranch in the late afternoon. More than once after buying a dress for Denim and Diamonds, Erica had suggested it was time to head home but her mother insisted they browse just one more store—a baby store. How could she resist?

"And the thing is," her mother said, chattering on, "Denim and Diamonds isn't that far off. We had to find you a dress."

"A tent, you mean. Just because it has sequins doesn't make that much material less than a parachute," Erica teased. "Seriously, Mom, it's gorgeous. And I can't believe you whipped out your credit card faster than me."

"I wanted to. So I did."

"And the sleepers you got for the baby are—" Emotion cut off the words. But the tiny outfits were too sweet for words anyway. This surprise shopping spree was her mother's way of mending fences, and Erica was happy that Morgan's mother was right about her coming around. "Thank you again, Mama, for everything."

"You're very welcome. It was fun." Angela drove down the road toward the main house. "I don't know about you, but I can't wait to sit and have a tall glass of iced tea."

"Sounds like heaven."

Her mother parked by the front door and they exited the car. Erica grabbed her dress and the bags of baby things out of the back.

"I'll open the front door for you." Her mother hurried to it, then stood back to let her go in first.

Erica had barely crossed the threshold when she heard, "Surprise!"

"What—" She looked around the entryway decorated with blue and pink balloons that said Baby. Streamers were hanging from the ceiling, and fresh flower arrangements graced the tables. "What is this?"

"A baby shower," her mom said. "Mel's idea."

"My friend Brittany did all the work," Melanie explained. "She's an event planner and very good at it."

Erica looked at her mother. "You knew about this and kept it a secret?"

"Of course. My job was to get you out of the house while everything was being set up." Her mother took the dress and bags from her.

"You played the part perfectly. And I quote, 'just one more store.'" She was completely surprised. "I can't believe this is for me."

"You're the only one here who's pregnant." Mel grinned at her.

Erica glanced at the women gathered there and smiling at her. She recognized Amanda, who was engaged to Morgan's brother Holt.

Deborah Dalton stood beside her. "I love baby showers."

"I'm glad you're here." Erica smiled at her just before her gaze landed on Daphne Taylor, Jordan's sister. "Thank you all for coming."

"Now that our mother-to-be is here, it's my job to make sure everyone has a good time." Mel's friend Brittany was a statuesque woman with light brown skin and beautiful, long dark curls. She wore a form-fitting red dress with a shiny black belt and matching patent leather four-inch heels with a red suede insert. "We haven't officially met yet. I'm Brittany Brandt Dubois, BFF to Amanda and Mel, so I feel as if I know you."

"It's nice to meet you," Erica said. "I never expected to have a shower."

Brittany grinned. "My husband Daniel and I are raising his niece, Hailey. I love her to pieces. She's nine months old and so adorable, but babies are a responsibility. This party is a chance for you to be carefree and have fun before your bundle of joy arrives."

"I don't know what to say. Thank you all." Erica looked ruefully at her outfit, trying not to compare her large sweater, black leggings and cowboy boots to the chicly dressed Brittany. "If I'd known, I'd have dressed up."

"It's not called a surprise for nothing."

She looked up and saw Malone standing at the back of the group. He was the only man there and looked completely fearless. "The food is all set out on the dining room table. So if you ladies will move this party into the other room, I'll start taking drink orders."

There was a rousing sound of agreement, then Mel escorted her to the seat of honor in the great room. Brightly wrapped packages decorated with rattles and pacifiers were stacked around the wing chair.

The women settled on the leather sofa and temporary chairs set up for the occasion.

Brittany took charge in a firm but charming way. They played games and then it was time for food. Malone was on duty to serve.

"We'll have cake soon," Brittany said afterward, "but now it's time for presents."

Erica opened a seemingly endless line of boxes of disposable diapers, baby lotions, tiny sleepers, receiving blankets, a baby monitor, even a thermometer.

She looked around at this incredibly generous group of women who'd come together for her. Even though she'd only known them a short time. "This is so wonderful. I don't know how to thank you all. I'm speechless—"

"Wait. There's one more." Her mother brought over an unwrapped white box and handed it to her.

"What's this?"

"Open it and see."

Erica lifted the lid and pushed aside the protective tissue paper to reveal a small, white dress, delicate lace-covered booties and a stretchy headband with floral appliqués. "Mama? This is gorgeous."

"That was your christening gown. I saved it for you. For your baby."

Erica couldn't count how many times today she'd been overwhelmed, but this was right at the top. She hugged her mom. "Thank you."

"You're welcome." Her mother gently tucked a strand of hair behind her ear and looked at her with love shining in her eyes. "Now, enjoy the rest of your party."

"That's excellent advice because pretty soon it will be all baby, all the time," Amanda said.

"It's a good thing they're cute, adorable and cuddly when they're born," Deborah chimed in. "Because for the first few weeks it's all about changing diapers, trying to interpret the different cries and getting up in the middle of the night to feed them."

"That's true." Her mother sat next to Morgan's mom on the sofa and smiled at the other woman. "You can't even get a smile out of them for the first few weeks. And don't even get me started on teething."

"Oh goodness." Deb rolled her eyes. "The first time Morgan got sick he was about three months old. There's nothing scarier than a sick baby—" She must have seen something in Erica's face because she added, "But babies are incredibly resilient. A little runny nose barely slows them down."

Erica looked at the open packages piled on the floor beside her and fixated on the thermometer. The baby chose that moment to move and stretch. Something, probably a foot, lodged up against her ribs and made her sit up a little straighter.

Suddenly the enormity of the challenge she was facing became all too real. Whatever had possessed her to think it was a good idea to have a baby all by herself? She alone would be responsible for raising this tiny human. Oh dear God...

Somehow she managed to keep the panic at bay through cutting the cake and the random girl talk that followed until the shower was over. She said all the right things, thanked everyone again for coming.

Since Deborah had been dropped off and had to wait for a ride home, she insisted on helping Malone put away leftover food in the kitchen. Amanda and Brittany were pitching in, too. Erica was alone with her mother and just couldn't hold back the anxiety any longer. She burst into tears and almost instantly was wrapped in a familiar, warm embrace.

"What's the matter, sweetie?"

"Oh, Mama, I don't think I can do this."

"I'm pretty sure this is your hormones talking, but let's sit down and you can tell me what's wrong." Her mother led her back to the sofa, where she sat and held her hand. "Now, talk to me."

Erica met her mother's gaze through a blur of tears and was glad she couldn't see the disappointment that was no doubt there. "I'm scared."

"About the birth?" She squeezed the hand still in her own. "You're preparing for that with your class. When the time comes, you'll be ready with all the tools you'll need to make it a positive experience."

Including Morgan, she thought. But after the baby

was born he'd be gone. She looked at the infant thermometer again.

"No, Mama, it's not the birth I'm worried about. It's when I have to take care of a newborn. I'm so afraid I'll do it all wrong and mess this child up. I'm scared that I'll disappoint my baby the way I have you and Daddy."

"Oh, Erica—" Her mother looked astonished. "Is that really what you think?"

"That's how it felt every time I picked my own path instead of yours."

"I didn't realize—" Angela pressed her lips together for a moment. "It never occurred to me that we didn't tell you often enough how proud we are of you. We constantly tell other people how wonderful you are."

"Really?"

She nodded. "We could not be prouder of you. And I can't stress this enough. You are not alone. Your brother and Mel. Your dad and me. Grandpa Alex. Malone. We're all here for you. I'm truly sorry you feel judged. Although, in all fairness, when you came home it was a shock to see you so pregnant when we had no idea about the baby. It was an adjustment and that takes time."

"I'm sorry, Mama. I knew there would be questions about the baby's father, but I should have told you. I just didn't know how."

"Tell us what?"

Erica just had to get this off her chest and hope she had the words to explain in a way that her mother would understand. "Promise me you won't tell Daddy. I know you tell him everything, but you have to swear you won't say anything about this."

There was a wary expression on her mother's face, and she was silent for several moments, obviously conflicted. Finally, and reluctantly, she nodded. "I won't say anything."

"Okay. The thing is, I went to a sperm bank and was inseminated. I've never met the father of this baby, but I have a medical history and a lot of information." Erica took a breath and blew it out. "Daddy's worried about him showing up to try to get something out of us. That will never happen."

"I see. And you felt you couldn't tell us?" Angela asked.

"I was afraid you guys would think I was crazy or foolish, or both. But I felt it was my only choice. My relationship with Peter ended. There was no one in my life and I was pushing thirty. I couldn't help feeling it was now or never, after what you went through…"

"The miscarriages. My bout with depression after."

"Yes."

Her mother sighed and it was a sad sound. "After the miscarriages, my heart broke when the doctor finally told me that I just couldn't carry a baby.

First I felt as if I had done something wrong. Then it felt wrong to not be content with the two beautiful, healthy children I already had. I was only a little older than you are now."

"I was so scared, Mama. I remember that you didn't even want to eat. You weren't sleeping and didn't want to get out of bed. I was afraid you were going to die."

"I'm so sorry you were afraid for me." Angela's eyes teared up. "You brought me peanut butter sandwiches and read to me. You tried so hard to help. I think the only reason I snapped out of it was you, Erica. You made me push myself to put one foot in front of the other."

"You couldn't help it, Mama. And I understand a little better how you felt now that I'm going to be a mother, too."

"And I made you afraid you might never be one." Angela sighed. "That's why you moved heaven and earth to get pregnant."

"Yes." Erica smiled, knowing her mother understood. "But I'm not sure Daddy will get it. Please, don't say anything to him."

"There's something you need to understand, sweetie."

"What?"

"Your father and I want so very much to be grandparents. You know we have for a very long time."

"Yes. You guys aren't subtle." Erica was glad when her mother smiled at that.

"It doesn't matter how this baby came to be, he or she will be loved to the moon and back. Fair warning, though, if you let us be grandparents, I can't promise we won't spoil our grandbaby."

"Oh, Mama—" Erica put a hand over her mouth and nodded. "Yes, please. I would like that very much."

They cried and hugged and laughed. It was cleansing and so very freeing to get all of the hurt out in the open.

"You know—" Her mother brushed a tear from her cheek. "You're going to find out all the joys and challenges of raising a child. And it is joyous."

"I'm glad you'll have my back."

"I absolutely will. In that spirit, here's a piece of motherly advice, just something to tuck away. You may not always understand or approve of your child's choices, but that doesn't mean you won't support and love them unconditionally. Always."

"Like you do me?"

"Yes. And your brother, too." Her mother nodded. "The hardest part is letting go. Standing back without being able to make things better when your children get hurt. In good times and bad, you'll be there for them. No matter what."

"I'll remember that from now on, Mama."

"And one more thing. You took care of me when

you were just a little girl and managed to help me out of that downward spiral. Even then your maternal instincts were working overtime. Never doubt that you're going to be a fantastic mother."

Tears blurred Erica's eyes and she sniffled. "That means so much to me coming from you. Thank you."

It was a relief to finally unburden herself. Her mother would somehow make her father understand there was nothing to worry about from the baby's father. She remembered Morgan had asked if she was in love with the guy. Maybe he was a little jealous?

Wishful thinking. All she knew was that if Morgan hadn't been there for her from the moment they met, she would have been so completely lost. Counting on him had come fast and easy. But she still couldn't decide whether that was a good thing.

Morgan parked his truck outside of Erica's house and waited for his mother. His dad had dropped her off because her car was in the shop and Morgan had volunteered to pick her up when his father got sucked into a spirited game of Go Fish with Robby. Morgan told himself it was about helping out his parents and that was true. But there was another reason. Getting even a glimpse of Erica wouldn't bother him a bit. His mom texted that she'd be a few minutes, so he got out of the truck and leaned against the front of it.

The house lights were on making it almost as bright as day out here. And he focused all his attention on the front door. That's why he didn't see Gabe Abernathy approaching and wasn't braced for the usual confrontation.

"Morgan Dalton. Just the man I wanted to see."

"Oh?" He straightened away from the truck.

"What do you want with my sister? Why are you going out of your way for her? She's having a baby soon. Most guys would be running away as if her hair was on fire. You must have an angle. What is it?"

"You think I'm after something just because my family doesn't go back generations like yours? Because we bought the land instead of inheriting it? That doesn't make us bad people."

"You should see someone about that chip on your shoulder. I never said you were bad people."

"You didn't have to say it." But Morgan wondered if the guy had a point about him being overly critical.

Gabe shook his head. "My sister has enough to deal with. She doesn't need some guy taking advantage of her."

"You're dead wrong and way out of line. Erica is my friend. That's it." Friend fell far short of what he felt for her, but Morgan didn't understand it completely himself. He wasn't going to try to put it into words to appease her overprotective brother.

"I don't believe that's all there is to it."

"Not my problem to convince you otherwise."

Morgan shrugged and slid his hands into the pockets of his sheepskin jacket.

Gabe looked more concerned than hostile. "I just don't understand. What do you want with my sister?"

Her. I just want her.

The truth was that he really couldn't blame Gabe for asking. If he had a pregnant sister and some guy who wasn't the father was hanging around her, he would want to know why. On the other hand, what would Gabe say if Morgan confessed that he had feelings for Erica that were more than friendly? He was having trouble wrapping his own head around that.

Just then the front door opened and he saw Amanda and her best friend Brittany. But Morgan only had eyes for Erica, who was walking out with them, looking radiant and happy. His heart seemed to skid sideways in his chest in the most unsettling and extraordinary kind of way.

"Hi, Gabe," Amanda said. "How are you? What are you doing here?"

He smiled and the protective expression disappeared. "I was hoping to catch you. I was wondering if your internet search has turned up anything new on my great-grandfather's daughter."

She shook her head. "I'd have called right away if it had. Without more information, something to go on, I'm stuck. Wish I had better news."

"I'm going to see Gramps again tomorrow," Erica said. "Maybe this time he'll say something to me."

"Would you like me to go with you?" Gabe asked.

Morgan didn't miss the look the other man slid in his direction. As if he'd expected Morgan to offer and beat him to it. The fact was he'd been about to. She told him seeing her grandfather unresponsive wasn't easy, and he wanted to be there for her. He had no idea why, but helping Erica seemed to be hardwired into him.

"Thanks, Gabe," she said. "I'd really appreciate that."

"Of course."

"Mel will be out momentarily. Are you ready to go?" Brittany asked Amanda. "We came together."

"I am. But since Morgan is here I can hitch a ride back with him and Deborah," Amanda answered. "Come to think of it, why are you here? I thought Neal was going to pick her up."

"I volunteered because he and Robby were playing a game, and I wasn't doing anything important."

"Hmm," Erica said wryly, "Could one surmise that you think an adult spending time with a child is important?"

"Yes." Morgan suspected she was trying to make a point, but he wasn't going there. "That and my dad has a cold. Best if he stays in where it's warm."

"Okay, then. I'll ride back with you, Morgan."

Amanda hugged her friends one last time. "I'll get Deborah."

"And I'll go inside with you to get Mel," Gabe said.

"And I'll say good night." Brittany waggled her fingers at everyone and walked to her car.

Suddenly it was just Morgan and Erica. He resisted the urge to say "alone at last."

"So, how was the shower?"

"I was completely surprised," she admitted. "My mom was actually in on it. She even took me shopping and bought some adorable little clothes for the baby. And she gave me my christening outfit. I was just blown away."

"I'm glad it went well." And he got to see her, although he could have skipped the confrontation with her brother.

She must have heard something in his voice because her eyebrows drew together. "What were you and Gabe discussing a few minutes ago? When I walked outside?"

"Just small talk."

"Really? Because I'd swear you were looking at him as if he was a cattle thief and horse rustler all rolled into one."

"I didn't know I was," he hedged.

"Come on, Morgan. This is me. I've gotten to know you pretty well. My brother said something to make you angry. I'm betting it was about me."

So much for bluffing. She was way too smart and observant for that. "He asked me what I wanted from you."

"What did you tell him?"

"That we're friends."

"Hmm." She frowned. "From the look on his face, I'm guessing he didn't buy that."

"Not even a little bit."

She sighed. "Just give it time. He'll come around."

"I won't hold my breath."

"I didn't think my mother would come around either," she said.

"Even though you preached hope and giving people a chance?"

"Even though." Her expression was sheepish. "The thing is, I didn't really believe what I was saying. And I was wrong. Today all the little infant things made me freak out about raising this baby by myself. My mother gave me a great pep talk and I ended up telling her about going to the sperm bank."

"Really?" That surprised him.

She nodded. "She understood why I did it. If she can do that, my brother will eventually understand that you're a good man. You'll see."

He was skeptical. Her brother had already made up his mind that Morgan was using Erica for some underhanded reason. Truthfully Morgan couldn't wrap his own mind around what was going on with him. Why he would do anything for her and couldn't seem to help himself. If he had this under control, he wouldn't have kissed her. That touch of his mouth to hers had opened the dam and he wasn't sure how to stop wanting her.

Chapter Twelve

It had been a hard day. Erica had gone to see her great-grandfather again and he still didn't know her at all. Feelings of helplessness and disappointment gave way to recurring guilt for having lived far away and not making an effort to see him while he was still responsive. The family dinner that followed with Gabe, Mel and her folks had been a little sad, but the food was fantastic.

Maybe sensing that the Abernathys needed comfort, Malone had outdone himself with a roast and all the trimmings. As they ate, they told stories of Gramps during healthier, happier times that made them laugh. And if all that wasn't enough for big-time comfort, there was cheesecake for dessert.

Now she was sitting beside Gabe at the kitchen table while Malone finished putting away leftovers and washing pots and pans. Mel had excused herself because she had work to do. The folks were watching TV in another room. She and her brother stayed put for some reason. Maybe he felt the need to bond. She sure did.

"Thanks for going with me today." Erica wrapped her hands around the mug of tea Malone had insisted on giving her. "It's hard to see him, but I'm glad I wasn't alone. Having you there made the whole thing so much easier."

He took a sip of his coffee, then smiled. "What kind of a big brother would I be if I didn't support my little sister?"

"Well, it's much appreciated." She reached over and touched his forearm for a moment. "And speaking of the whole big brother thing, you can stand down with Morgan Dalton. He's not a threat to me."

"Do you know that for sure?" Her brother's eyes narrowed. "Have you asked yourself why he's around? Always there for you?"

"Maybe because he's a nice person. What other reason could there be?"

"He wants something."

"What could he possibly want?" She laughed. "I

don't have much money and even if I did, his family is pretty wealthy."

"The rumor is that his father won it gambling."

The rumor was true. "So what does it matter where the money came from? It's not ill-gotten gain. And doesn't change the fact that Morgan is a wealthy man."

"What about the baby?"

"Oh please. My life is a soap opera but not to the point where he'd kidnap my child and sell it to a desperate couple who couldn't have one of their own." She laughed again, and it was a welcome relief from the sad day. "Look, he's a really good guy. Trust me. You'll see."

"I don't know." There was doubt in his voice.

"Seriously, Gabe, it's not about the baby. And—"

"What?" he asked when she stopped.

Erica looked at him. "He's not sure he wants children. So what could he possibly want from me except to be my friend?"

Gabe studied her and a gleam stole into his eyes. "Are you in love with him?"

"Of course not," she said. The response was automatic, but the question made her think.

She liked everything about Morgan, from his sense of humor to his loyalty and friendship. It didn't hurt either that he was awfully good-looking. And she couldn't deny that every time she saw him, her heart just swelled with something wonderful that she refused to name. When she wasn't with him, she longed to be. At the Harvest Festival, when he kissed her, it was the most magical kiss ever.

But was she in love? She sure hoped not. When the baby was born, his promise would be fulfilled. She would be immersed in raising her baby, and he would still be an eligible bachelor. Their relationship would be nothing but a memory, and that made her sad.

Malone finished drying the big pot he'd used for the mashed potatoes and set it on the stove. "More coffee, Gabe?"

"Yes. Thanks, Malone."

"Sure thing." The cook brought over the pot and refilled the mug. "How about you, Erica? More tea?"

"No. Thanks." She smiled at him before he nodded and walked back to scour the roasting pan. She was glad he'd interrupted the conversation because she had no answers for her brother. "Gramps sure didn't say much," she commented, deliberately turning the conversation away from herself.

"I really hoped he would." Gabe shook his head. "You did your best, chattering away about all kinds of things. I was hoping that the two of us there together might jar him out of wherever he is. But he was the same."

"It's hard to picture Gramps as a young man," Erica said. "And to have the responsibility of a baby when he was hardly more than a boy himself."

"Yeah."

"It must have been agonizing for him to give up his baby girl."

Gabe nodded. "He didn't have any family support. In fact just the opposite. Grandpa Alex hardly remembers his grandparents except that they were not the warm and fuzzy type."

"That must have been awful for Gramps. I know you and Mama and Daddy aren't doing the dance of joy about my baby, but no one is pressuring me to give him or her up for adoption."

"We would never do that," he protested.

"Well, I wouldn't—I couldn't give up my child even if there was pressure to. I love this baby so much already. I can't imagine not being there for the first smile, first steps, first word. The thought of it makes me so angry that Gramps was forced to give up his baby girl." Her brother was suddenly staring at her as if she had fire coming out of her eyes. "What?"

"I'm such an idiot."

"Well, I've always suspected as much," she teased. "But what makes you so sure?"

"It just hit me." There was wonder in his expression. "I'm going to be an uncle."

"Really?" she said wryly. "Imagine that. It's what happens when your sister has a baby. You just now figured that out?"

"Of course I knew. I just—" He shrugged. "I just

didn't think about it that way. Too busy resenting you for living so far away. Blowing through on holidays."

"I truly regret that."

"You had your reasons, I guess. And it really doesn't matter now. You're having a baby. Bringing a new life into the world." He looked at her pregnant belly and a warmth stole into his eyes. "I'm going to be an uncle."

"You are."

"I'm going to be the best uncle you've ever seen," Gabe said grinning.

"I know you will because you've always been the best big brother a girl could ask for." She swallowed the lump of emotion in her throat. "I've missed you. Been so busy proving my independence that I didn't realize how much I missed you until I got home. I love you."

"I love you back. And I'm going to love this baby so much. In case you aren't aware, you should prepare for the reality that our parents are going to spoil this kid rotten."

"I'm not so sure. Mama maybe. She's come around. But Daddy—" She shook her head, wishing things could be different.

"Give him time. A boy will be hard enough for him to resist. But a girl? Forget about it." Gabe grinned. "If you have a daughter, she'll wrap him around her little finger."

"You think?"

"I know so. If you have a girl who looks like you, she'll be the prettiest little girl in the world."

"Oh, Gabe—" Her eyes got misty at his compliment.

"What did you say?" Malone shut off the faucet and came over, still holding a saucepan. There was an odd expression on his rugged face.

Gabe gave him a puzzled look. "I said, if Erica has a daughter who looks like her, the baby will be the prettiest little girl in the world."

Erica had forgotten he was there. She'd known this man since she was a kid and had never seen him quite so intense. "Why, Malone? What is it?"

"It just reminded me of something your Gramps said a while back…" There was a strange and thoughtful expression in his eyes, as if he was trying to remember something.

"What did he say?" Gabe prodded.

Malone hesitated for a moment. "It was something like you just said. And I think it was about five years ago. I remember that because it was when his memory was starting to go. A lot of the time he seemed stuck in the past."

"What was it?" Gabe said again.

"I remember him going on and on about 'the prettiest little girl in the world.'" He looked from Erica to Gabe. "And he said a name. It wasn't his wife, Cora. So I thought it might be an old girlfriend."

"Was the name Winona?" Erica asked.

"Nope." Malone shook his head.

"But it was someone from his past." There was excitement in Gabe's voice. "What if he wasn't talking about a woman? What if it was about his daughter? Beatrix?"

Malone thought for a moment. "Nope. That wasn't the name he said."

"Are you sure?" Gabe pushed.

"Yeah." Malone looked apologetic and frustrated with himself. "I just can't recollect what the name was." He tapped his forehead. "It's right there, but I can't grab onto it. I'm sorry, Gabe."

"Don't beat yourself up over it," her brother said. "Sometimes trying too hard just pushes things even more out of reach. It'll come to you."

"Hope so. Sure would like to help find her."

"I know you would."

Although Gabe did his best to hide it, Erica could hear the disappointment in her brother's voice. Like Amanda said, without another clue of some kind, the search for their great-grandfather's daughter was going nowhere. An Abernathy was out there and they all wanted to find her. For just a moment, Malone's comment stirred hope that things would break their way. A name from the past that would unlock a mystery.

Then, just as fast, that hope was gone because there was no way to force a memory. Gramps too had some memories of his lost baby girl buried so deep in his mind they couldn't be reached, and it was frustrating.

Memories were funny and precious and bittersweet. Pretty soon Morgan would be only a memory. When she was as old as Gramps, would she remember him? After she gave birth, the time she spent with him would become the past. That was tearing her apart. She couldn't wait to say hello to her baby, but her heart didn't want to say goodbye to Morgan.

Morgan sat in the passenger seat of his father's old truck. They'd been mending fences at the outermost boundary of Dalton's Grange, and it was a big piece of land. That meant a long ride back with Neal Dalton, the last man on earth he wanted to spend time with. No matter how he grudgingly respected the man's work ethic and his dedication to a physically demanding job, Morgan couldn't forgive the hurt to his mother. And the longer the ride went on, the more awkward the silence became. He was determined not to break it.

But apparently his father had no problem doing it. "Sure is a pretty day. There's nothing like a clear Montana sky. A little cold, though. Winter is coming, so it's a good thing we got this job done while the weather is holding."

Morgan thought about not responding, then changed his mind. But one word was all the man would get. "Yeah."

Neal glanced over, then back to the road in front of him. "Your mom said Erica's baby shower was really nice. She had a good time. Thanks for picking her up."

"No problem." Unless you counted Gabe Abernathy and his suspicious attitude. The guy was way off base. Morgan didn't want anything from her. Not really. Nothing except to spend time with her. Picking up his mom from the baby shower was one way to make that happen.

His father's even-tempered disposition was starting to make Morgan feel like a complete jerk. He could throw the man a bone. "How's your cold? Any better?"

"Yeah. Your mother insisted I take it easy and filled me with liquids and chicken soup. Cold and flu don't stand a chance against her soup. And her, for that matter."

Morgan didn't want to smile but he couldn't help it. "That's Mom."

"Yeah." The man looked over again, just for a moment. "Appreciate you and your brothers picking up the slack for me around the ranch."

"No big deal. Like you said—no one argues with Mom."

After that, neither of them seemed to have anything to say. Morgan just wished this ride would be over.

"How's Erica?" Neal finally said. "Baby's due pretty soon, right?"

"A couple weeks." Morgan smiled to himself just thinking about her. She grumbled about growing big as a house, but he thought she got more beautiful every day.

"She sure is a pretty young woman," his dad said. It was like the man could read minds. "Your mom sure likes her. Said Erica's mom is real nice, too."

"Yeah."

His father waited for more, and when it didn't come he finally said, "Sure is nice of you to support her and be her labor coach. It would be hard to go through that alone."

"I suppose."

"No supposing about it. Bringing a baby into this world is pretty scary." His father maneuvered the truck around a big rut in the unpaved road, then they continued to bounce along. "I remember when your mom was first pregnant. You weren't planned. And I have a confession to make."

"Another one?" Morgan said sarcastically.

Neal ignored that. "I wasn't sure I wanted to be a father. Didn't really know whether I wanted kids."

Wasn't that just great? Morgan took after his unfaithful father. "So why'd you have four more then?"

"Because of you." His dad looked over, then back to the road.

"What about me?"

"You were the first and I worried about everything. Not your mother. She had a knack for knowing when to worry and when to let it go." He laughed and shook his head. "And she loved being pregnant. Was never healthier or more beautiful, but that didn't stop me from being anxious about her. Anything could happen. And she was…"

In spite of himself, Morgan was pulled into this walk down memory lane now. "Mom was what?"

"Everything," Neal said reverently. "She's my whole world and she gave up a successful career and a different kind of life because she loved me. The isolation of ranch life was a lot to ask of her."

"But she did it."

"And I always felt the pressure to give her whatever she wanted so she didn't feel like she made the wrong choice and wasted her life on me."

"And she wanted a baby," Morgan prompted.

"Yeah."

"And you didn't?" he challenged.

"I won't lie. I wasn't fully on board." He suddenly grinned at a memory. "Not until I saw you for the first time." He glanced over, probably to see how Morgan reacted to that statement. "Don't take this the wrong way, but you were not all that good-looking right after you were born. Neither were your brothers. All red and scrunchy. But I had a son. And from that day on the feelings were, are—"

"What?" Morgan asked.

"Bigger than anything I'd ever felt in my life. I loved your mom, but the son we made was—" Hands on the steering wheel, he shrugged. "I can't even describe the love. Maybe as big as this Montana sky."

Morgan looked out the truck window at the blue that seemed to go on forever. That was a lot of love. One of his earliest memories was this man putting him on a horse, patiently teaching him to ride it. Letting Morgan follow him around the ranch. He never raised his voice, even when his brothers came along one by one and the chaos multiplied.

Morgan had a clear memory of resenting Holt for stealing his own time with their father. As the oldest he was expected to share his mother, but he wasn't in the mood to graciously share his father, the man he hero-worshiped.

"If you love mom so much, how could you cheat on her?"

His father pressed his lips together and shook his head slightly. "I messed up big-time. It wasn't a pattern, but happened more than once."

"Slipups," Morgan said angrily.

"Too much liquor was always involved."

"That's just an excuse. The least you can do is be honest and take responsibility."

"Maybe you can't understand, but I have to say this. I was always stressed about money. Ranch operations depended on cash flow. I had doctor bills for my family. The price of beef went up and down. Too much rain or snow could affect the cost of hay, loss of livestock. It was all about keeping the ranch going for you boys and your mom. Sometimes the strain got to be too much. Drink took the edge off."

Morgan remembered several times when his mom had tried to hide that she'd been crying. The man he'd looked up to above all others had broken his mother's heart. Morgan had been hurt and angry the first time. A couple of slipups later and his anger had boiled over.

He'd been the first to leave the family ranch and hire on with another outfit. One by one his brothers all followed him. And for the same reason. They couldn't stand to see their mother with the man who treated her that way.

"Tell me one thing," he snapped.

"Okay." There was no hesitation in his father's voice.

"Why did she forgive you? Why in hell did she take you back?"

"You'll have to ask her that, son. But I thank God every day that she did." Neal let out a long breath. "The money I won to buy this ranch was the second-luckiest thing that ever happened to me."

"What was the first?"

"The day the minister asked your mother if she would honor and cherish me and she said, 'I will.'" He looked over for a moment. "The day I won that money I vowed it would be a new beginning for Deborah and me and our boys. I could finally give the family I love the lifestyle they deserve."

Morgan stared at the man's profile. "You do know that my brothers and I are only here to work the ranch because Mom asked us to, right? That, and we needed to make sure she'd be okay."

"I'm aware." There was sadness and acknowledgment of the fault in his tone. "I know none of you trust me."

"How can we?"

He made the turn onto the road that led to the barn. "I don't expect you to believe this after what I've done, but I love her, too. I'd give my life for hers. I'm going to make it up to her."

"You're right. I don't believe you." He huffed out a breath. "I used to look up to you and you let me down. Tell me why in the name of God I should believe what you're saying now."

"I don't drink anymore, Morgan. Not at all." He glanced over and the resolve in his eyes was unmistakable. "Marriage has its ups and downs, but if a man and woman really love each other, they can work through tough times and make it to the other side. Stronger than before. I swear on everything I hold dear that I only have eyes for your mother. I'm so grateful that she loves me enough to give me another chance. And, son, I hope you and your brothers will follow her lead and do the same."

His father drove up to the barn and parked. "I'm just asking you to keep an open mind."

When he got out of the truck Morgan's mind

wasn't necessarily open but it was sure spinning. As he helped unload the tools, he thought back to the day he'd come to Dalton's Grange. From that day on he couldn't recall seeing his father consume alcohol. Because of his anger and resentment, he'd never noticed before.

He'd never seen his mother happier, and more than once she'd told them this was the best time of her life. Having her sons nearby was such a blessing. And his parents were like newlyweds, always touching, exchanging secret looks, kissing like teenagers when they thought no one was watching. And now this. His dad had come out and asked for another chance.

Morgan remembered Erica saying more than once that they both should give their families an opportunity to patch up relationships. The night of the baby shower, she'd told him she and her mom were on the mend.

It occurred to him that everyone made mistakes, but attempting to right those wrongs was the foundation of character. Maybe Erica was right about second chances.

When the truck bed was empty, Morgan lifted the tailgate and made sure the thing was securely latched. His father stood beside him and their gazes met. There was no mistaking the sincerity in the other man's eyes.

Morgan stuck out his hand. "I believe you, Dad."

Neal's mouth trembled just for a second, and there

was a suspicious moisture in his eyes. Then he shook hands and pulled Morgan in for a hug. "Thank you, son."

Morgan nodded and felt his own throat tighten as a weight lifted from him. Holt seemed at peace with their father, but the rest of his brothers would have to figure out where they stood with him. Morgan wouldn't interfere or influence them one way or the other. But ending hostilities was the right decision for him.

And he had Erica to thank for putting cracks in his attitude in order to give understanding and common sense a way in.

It was a relief to know the man loved being a dad and was a good one. That meant there was hope for Morgan. If—

He pulled up short. For such a small word, *if* had awfully big consequences. Did he want complications? A baby? All he knew for sure was that he couldn't shake the feeling of wanting Erica, and he had no idea what he was going to do about it.

Chapter Thirteen

Erica checked her appearance in the mirror over the bathroom sink and nodded with satisfaction. Her hair was in a ponytail for tonight's childbirth class in which they would be practicing breathing and relaxation techniques. She hadn't seen Morgan since that brief, unsatisfying encounter after her baby shower. There had been barely enough time to say hello, and she wanted more.

She was very aware of the time limit on their involvement and wasn't trying to fight it anymore. Trying to turn off her feelings to avoid emotional messiness was pointless. After the baby was born, she would have Morgan withdrawal and would fall back on her memories, but for now she was going to enjoy the time she had left with him.

After applying lipstick, she headed downstairs and found her mom in the great room reading. It was cozy with a fire crackling, and she had a few minutes to visit before leaving to pick up Morgan. "Hey, Mama. Is that a good book?"

"Yes." She marked her place, then set the book aside. "You're going to class?"

"Pretty soon." It was such a relief to be on good terms again. Up front and honest about her situation. If only she could talk to her dad, too. "I'm picking up Morgan."

Angela nodded. "I invited his mother to join the Bronco Valley Assistance League and she seemed eager to be a part of it. I liked her very much."

"I do, too. And I like Mel, too. I talk to her almost every day. She's becoming the sister I never had. My brother chose wisely."

"I feel the same way. And they're meant to be together, although when they first met there was tension, not all of it the good kind." Her mom smiled. "But they worked it out."

"I'm glad." Erica was so happy for her brother, but also wistful for herself. It was possible that she and Morgan were meant to be together, but her pregnancy made that too big a hurdle.

"You and Morgan seem to get along pretty well.

And you have from the very beginning, I hear." Her mother didn't look upset.

"We definitely clicked," Erica admitted. "As friends. We're not like Mel and Gabe. Not romantic."

"Really?" There was a gleam of speculation in her mother's eyes. "You're sure?"

"Yes. Completely." Because he had doubts about being a father. Her family had doubts about him. "And you don't trust him. Why would you think there's anything serious between us?"

"Because of Deborah Dalton. I got a sense about her that she's a good person who raised her boys to be good men. She and I were talking. She knows her son and I know my daughter." Angela shrugged. "We were just playing 'what if.'"

"You know Morgan had words with Gabe that night," Erica said.

"He's protective. And if I hadn't met Deborah, I might agree with your brother's doubts. She's good people. I'd be really surprised if Morgan isn't, too."

"Well, he's certainly been a good friend to me." She looked at her watch. "I have to go or I'll be late for class."

"Can't have that."

"See you later." She leaned over to kiss her mother's cheek, then straightened and headed for the door.

After driving to Dalton's Grange, she saw Morgan waiting for her outside his house. He walked over to the driver's side of the SUV and she opened the window.

"I know you insisted on picking me up, but at least let me drive from here."

"What? You don't trust me?"

"That's not it at all." He leaned over and rested his arms on the doorframe, his face not far from hers. "It seems to me that my job in all this is to take care of you. Driving you there checks that box."

"Okay." She turned off the engine and stepped out. "I'm not too stubborn to accept a generous offer of assistance."

Especially when the man offering it tugged at her heart in a way no man ever had. Telling him no just might not be possible. She took his outstretched hand and walked to the passenger side of her car. He held the door open for her to get in.

"Thank you," she said.

"Don't mention it." He closed her door and walked around the front of the vehicle, then got in behind the wheel. "And we're off."

Erica had to admit it was nice to sit back and be driven. She could get used to this. As soon as that thought popped into her head, she pushed it away. She couldn't let herself think about getting used to anything with Morgan.

"So, what's new?" he asked.

"You mean since my brother practically took your

head off?" She looked over at him, and the dashboard lights revealed the humor on his face.

"Yeah, since then," he said.

"Well, my mom said she really liked your mom. And I quote, 'she's good people.' And she invited your mother to join the Bronco Valley Assistance League."

"What do you know? It's only been a year. And all it took to be accepted by the old guard was you having a baby." He grinned.

"It's a miracle, all right. Along with the fact that my mother and I are still getting along. And you should know that she doesn't seem to object anymore to you being my coach." In fact, Erica strongly suspected her mother of going in the opposite direction. She'd been doing a little matchmaking tonight. It was a sweet thought but doomed to failure.

"Speaking of getting along…" He glanced over at her for a second. "I had a talk with my dad."

"An actual conversation that consisted of more than yup, nope and livestock feed?"

He laughed. "This will shock you. But we discussed our feelings."

"Gasp." She pressed a hand to her chest in mock surprise. "I thought I felt a ripple in the fabric of the cosmos."

"I know."

Erica listened as he told her about his father taking responsibility for his actions, his vow to make it up to his wife and family and especially his promise to Deborah to love her and make her happy.

"So, you and your dad are really speaking to each other?"

"Thanks to you, yes."

"I don't understand," she said. "I didn't do anything."

"You were the one preaching second chances," he reminded her. "Although I don't think your brother is willing to give me even a first chance."

"Gabe is a good man and normally fair, too." She sighed. "But something about you pushes his buttons."

"Yeah, something. Your brother wants to rip my head off, and I've never even touched you."

Except for that kiss. He hadn't done it again, but every innocent touch—helping her into the car. When their arms brushed or he took her hand—it felt like more. And, right or wrong, she wanted this to be more.

She didn't quite trust her voice not to give away her yearning and didn't talk for several moments. After a deep breath she finally said, "Be patient, Morgan. Gabe will come around. I can see you two becoming good friends."

"That's just crazy talk."

She laughed. "You'll see I'm right about this."

"Agree to disagree," he said. "Change of subject. Did you get lots of good stuff at the shower?"

"I did. All I need now is a crib. And a car seat. Can't bring the baby home from the hospital without one."

"I guess so."

He turned the car into the lot at the Women's Health Center and parked. As they walked to the building, Erica had an almost overwhelming urge to slide her hand into his, but managed to hold back. That's not what a friend would do.

When they reached the conference room, only Carla was there. They were the first ones to arrive.

"Hey, you two." The nurse/educator smiled. "How are you?"

"Good." Erica looked up at Morgan as he nodded.

"Your due date isn't too far away," Carla said. "You both must be getting excited."

"I can't wait to hold this little one." She rested her hands on her belly, then she glanced up and saw the expression on Morgan's face, something that looked a lot like longing. Was it possible that he might not want to say good-bye after she had the baby?

By anyone's measure, what he was doing fell into going above and beyond the call of duty. She'd been drawn to him the first time they met at DJ's Deluxe and the feelings had escalated since then. She'd never met anyone like him and had never felt about a man the way she did about Morgan. Before she could take that thought further the other three couples walked into the room.

"Hi, everyone," Carla said. "We're in the pregnancy home stretch now. I hope you've all been practicing your breathing at home, but let's go over it again. So, if you'll all settle on the floor, we'll get started."

Morgan unrolled the mat and she sat on it with him behind her. She could feel the heat of his body all around her and barely resisted the urge to curl into him. He had her back. He'd always had her back and she loved that he did. Before she could think too much about that, Carla explained what they were doing.

"Okay. First stage of labor. Organizing breath. Take in a deep breath as the contraction starts, then slowly breathe out releasing tension from your head to your toes. Slowly inhale through your nose. Exhale slowly through your mouth. Every time you do this, focus on relaxing a different body part."

Morgan spoke quietly into her ear, reminding her of what the instructor had said. "Okay, now you're in active labor. Keep breathing as slowly as possible, speeding it up as the intensity of the contraction increases."

"Okay."

Moments later he gently rubbed her arms. "You're tensing up. Concentrate on your right leg, relaxing your toes, your foot and ankle, up your calf and thigh."

Erica tried her best to follow his directions but

the feel of his breath on her cheek and the sound of his deep voice in her ear made her feel as if he was actually touching her everywhere. And she wanted that so much.

Carla looked at each of them, nodding enthusiastically. "Okay, you're all doing great. Now transition breathing."

"Okay," Morgan said, "Focus on that picture on the wall. You're having a contraction. Breathe in and out through your mouth, Carla said it should be at a rate of one to ten breaths every five seconds. Every fourth or fifth breath blow out a longer one."

"This is really complicated," she said. "I'm really glad you're here."

"Nowhere else I'd rather be."

Morgan put his big hand at the small of her back and began to gently caress. "Okay. Deep breath."

Erica nodded, even though she wasn't certain she could breathe at all with him touching her. The feel of his warm fingers shorted out her brain and made her want to melt into him. Somehow his deep, steady voice penetrated her mental slide, and she followed his instructions.

"Doing great," he said.

His breath was warm on her cheek and her breathing escalated, but not in any kind of controlled way.

"Good job, everyone." Carla smiled at the group. "You're all here to prepare for a positive birth experience. Relaxation is important. If you tense up, discomfort is magnified. Dads, this is where you can step in. If you feel her tensing, give her a big bear hug."

Without hesitation, Morgan wrapped his muscular arms around her and squeezed gently. The embrace was sure and strong and made her feel so safe she could have stayed there forever. His lips were so near her cheek and she felt him hesitate, as if he was going to kiss her but he didn't. Then Carla started giving them more pointers.

As instructed, Morgan gently stroked her forehead, jaw and hands. Rhythmically, he kneaded her shoulders and neck, and she thought she'd died and gone to heaven. He used firm pressure with the palm of his hand to rub her from shoulder to hip, then from thigh to knee.

Erica was fairly certain nothing she'd ever experienced had felt quite so perfect as Morgan's touch. And she didn't think there was a breathing technique in the world that could control her reaction to the exquisite sensation of his hands on her body.

She glanced up at his face and recognized the intensity that turned his eyes a darker shade of blue than normal. At first she thought it was only concentration. Then she saw the pulse throbbing in his neck and knew. He was feeling something for her, too, and it was more than just being her support partner. It was the scariest, most exciting feeling she'd ever had. But where did they go from here?

* * *

Holy crap! Morgan couldn't believe how close he'd come to kissing Erica in that class. Her skin was so soft and she was so beautiful. Time after time, he caught himself and stopped, but there was something in her eyes. Something he'd never seen before. But he couldn't identify it, and she didn't help. She hadn't said a word since he started driving them back to Dalton's Grange.

It was time to break the silence. "Do you want to stop for something to eat? Are you hungry?"

"No, thanks." Her voice was soft and the tone a little unsure, as if she had something on her mind.

"Okay."

He was thinking hard about what to say but could only come up with an apology for wanting her. But he wasn't really sorry at all. God help him.

She was pregnant and he most likely was crazy. But she was the most beautiful, sexiest woman he'd ever met. And if he was being honest with himself, it was more than that. She was sweet, caring, friendly, kind and funny. He'd never met a woman who had it all. Not until Erica.

And now he'd made it weird.

He turned onto the road where Dalton land started, and Erica still hadn't said anything besides no thanks. If he didn't fix this, she was going to let him off, then drive home, and there would be this unspoken, awkward thing between them.

He pulled up in front of his house, but didn't turn off the car's ignition. "You're awfully quiet. Everything okay?"

"Yes—" She sighed. "No."

"I knew it." He shook his head. "It's me, isn't it? I did something—"

"Morgan, no." She released her seat belt and put her hand on his arm. "It's me. I—"

"What?" he asked when she hesitated.

"I haven't been practicing my breathing, and tonight I guess Carla really got through to me how important it will be."

"So, we'll practice," he said.

He nodded toward his house with the light shining in the front window. "In fact, why not now while the class is still fresh in our minds?"

"Really? Are you sure? I know you get up early—"

"It's fine." He put his hand over hers and tried not to notice the heat that shot through him. "I can see that you're stressed about this. That's not good. The best way to deal with it is to practice. What do you say?"

"Okay."

Morgan turned the key and shut off the car. He got out and went around to open Erica's door, then offered his hand to help her out. When her fingers touched his palm, his whole body went tight with need, and fire licked through him. The heat threatened to consume him.

Get a grip, Dalton. Don't be a jerk.

They walked into the house and she looked around. "This is awfully tidy for a single guy."

"If you don't look in the kitchen, my halo will stay all shiny and bright." Teasing cut the tension and that was a relief. "Can I get you anything? Water? Iced tea? Beer?" He held up a hand. "Just kidding."

"I knew that. Water would be great."

"Coming right up." But he was having a beer. It might take the edge off his wanting her more than his next breath. That thought was ironic considering they were here to practice breathing.

On his way to the kitchen he said over his shoulder, "Make yourself comfortable."

"I guess we should sit on the floor like we do in class," she called back.

"Whatever you want."

Morgan grabbed the drinks, brought them into the living room and set them on a table beside the leather sofa. Erica was sitting on the floor.

She glanced over her shoulder and smiled. "Whenever you're ready."

He was so ready. And, damn it, why couldn't he stop thinking in double entendres? *Focus*, he ordered himself. It would be hard to do that since he had to sit behind her. So close. Touching her. Breathing in the scent of her. But this wasn't about him. For her, he would be the best coach on the planet or die trying.

He assumed his position and couldn't help thinking for the hundredth time how good she smelled. How soft and delicate and graceful her neck looked. How much he wanted to see for himself if her skin tasted as sexy as he thought it would.

"Okay—" He braced himself. "Organizing breath. Slow and deep as the contraction starts, then let it out, releasing all the tension from your shoulders, legs and all the way to your toes."

She did as instructed, but he could feel that she wasn't responding to the technique. He wasn't sure what to do except continue instructing and counting. So, that's what they did and went through all the different stages of breathing.

"Do you want to start over again?" he asked.

"No." She said that a little too quickly. Oddly enough, after all that breathing she'd just done, there was a sexy, breathless quality to her voice. "That went okay. I think we work pretty well together."

"Yes, we do." And he could really get used to the nearness of her. The warmth of her burrowing deep inside him, thawing out a place that had been frozen for a long time.

She glanced over her shoulder and said, "How can I ever thank you?"

"By not hating me for how much I still want to kiss you." Morgan wasn't sure he'd actually said that out loud.

Her eyes widened and she blinked up at him. A

couple of seconds passed before she said, "Does that mean you wanted to kiss me before now?"

There was no way to dodge this, so he didn't try. "In class tonight. So many times I came very close to kissing you. It's official. I'm a jerk. I know it. Right there in front of everyone I wanted to just—"

"I wasn't completely sure I didn't imagine that." She turned around to face him and smiled softly. "There's no one here now except you and me."

"What?"

"If you're a jerk, then so am I. It was so hard to concentrate when all I could think about was you touching me and how good it felt." Definitely that was a breathless whisper.

"Erica—"

Morgan saw that his hand was shaking a little as he traced the curve of her cheek with one finger, then kissed where he'd touched. Her eyes closed, and she shuddered just before the sound of her throaty moan burned through him. She leaned toward him, and this time he didn't hesitate, but took her mouth with his own. The touch sparked a bone-melting fire that spread through his blood.

Not here, he thought. Not on the floor.

Without a word, he stood and held out his hand, helping her to her feet before leading her to his bedroom. Both of them were breathing hard when they sat side by side on the bed.

He kissed her again and let his mouth wander over

her cheekbones, her eyes, her chin. He nuzzled her ear and nipped her neck. Settling his hand on her thigh, he moaned with satisfaction as he remembered how badly he'd been wanting to do this.

He slid his fingers underneath her sweater, over her soft skin and found her breast, cupping it in his palm. She was perfect, the most beautiful, most sensuous woman he'd ever held in his arms. He brushed his thumb over the tip and heard her gasp of pleasure.

She leaned her head against his shoulder. "Oh, Morgan. That feels so good."

"I want you, Erica."

"Yes, please," she whispered.

Mindless with desire, he wanted to touch her everywhere and slid his hand over her belly. There was a rippling movement beneath his palm and he froze. As he hesitated, he felt it again, a rolling motion across her abdomen. If ever there was a cold shower moment, this was it. He pulled his hand away as if he'd touched a hot coal. And maybe he had.

Erica was having a baby. That made her a package deal and sleeping with her was not a step to be taken lightly.

"Morgan?" She was frowning at him.

"I felt the baby move."

"I know." She stared at him and not in a good way. "What's wrong?"

In her eyes he saw the exact moment when she shut down emotionally. "It's not what you think."

"And what do I think?" She slid sideways, a bruised look on her face.

"It's just—" He dragged his fingers through his hair, searching for the words to explain. "I don't want you to think I—"

"I don't think anything except—" She stood up and headed for the door. "I need to go."

"Erica, wait. Let me explain."

She'd stopped in the living room and was looking around. "Where did you put my keys?"

"Just wait a damn minute. We need to talk about this," he said.

"There's nothing to talk about. You've made your feelings crystal clear. So it's better to stop this before either one of us gets hurt." She picked up her purse and looked around the room, anywhere but at him. "I'll go."

Morgan wasn't so sure they weren't already in territory where one of them could get hurt. And, for crying out loud, he needed to take fifteen seconds to process everything. She was bringing a life into the world and that was huge. If he was going to be a part of that, he needed to be sure. He never wanted her to think he'd used her.

He'd thought they had a special connection. Was this just an overreaction to his hesitation? Or something else? Maybe he really was just a friend. A rebound guy from Peter and she was still in love with her ex.

"I need my keys, Morgan."

Damn it, were those tears in her eyes? He didn't think he could take it if she cried. Then he remembered he'd put her keys in his jeans pocket and fished them out. He dropped them into the hand she was holding out and managed to do it without touching her.

She walked to the door and opened it. "Good night, Morgan."

"Erica?"

She brushed a hand across her cheek before looking at him. "What?"

"I'm sorry."

She nodded and without another word walked out the door.

Morgan really felt like putting his fist through a wall. Before she came inside things were weird, but he could have worked with that. If he'd just kept his hands to himself, everything would have been fine, but he hadn't. Now he didn't think there was any coming back from this.

Chapter Fourteen

Erica was hurt and disappointed, but she couldn't be mad at Morgan, and that was super annoying. From the beginning he'd been honest about his doubts, but she'd fallen in love with him anyway. *Love.* Four letters italicized. Capital *L.* In a very short time she'd realized he was a forever-after kind of guy and he cared about her, too. She could tell in everything he did. Especially his kisses. She'd hoped he would change his mind about having kids. Being a father. Being a father to her kid. But last night hope died.

When he felt her baby move, the look on his face had told her everything she needed to know. The man wanted no part in her child's life. That meant Morgan could have no part in hers either.

The tears started again and she was exasperated with herself. She couldn't believe that, after crying most of the night, there could still be any left.

Unable to sleep, she'd gotten up early this morning and showered. Did her hair and put on a little makeup. It was her plan to act as if nothing was wrong. Her family had warned her about Morgan. Her mother, father and Gabe had been afraid he wanted something from her. Ha! It was just the opposite. He wanted nothing to do with her. Only Mel had worried about her getting hurt.

And hurt she was. When she and Peter broke up, she'd been frustrated that her plans for marriage and family had fallen apart. In the end, though, the split felt right. With Morgan there was an ache, an emptiness and a feeling that no other man could ever fill up her heart the way he did.

A tear trickled down her cheek, and impatiently she brushed it away. "Oh, for crying out loud..." Not funny.

She slid off the bed she'd made before the sun came up. If she sat there much longer, she was in real danger of dehydrating. Sooner or later she was going to have to go downstairs and put on a brave face for everyone. Best get it over with.

She took one more look in the mirror and winced at her reflection—the red, puffy eyes. Probably there wasn't enough concealer in the world to hide the evidence of her broken heart, but she applied it anyway. Maybe no one would notice. And it was always possible no one would be there.

Apparently luck abandoned her, because only her father and Malone were missing. Her mother and Gabe were sitting at the kitchen table having coffee. The smell of cooked sausage and eggs filled the air. Not even that made her hungry.

Since her brother was here, that probably meant Mel was out of town for work. Gabe did a double take when he saw her. "You look terrible."

"Thank you." She glared at him, then poured herself half a cup of coffee and sat down at the table.

"Aren't you going to have some breakfast? Malone fixed a plate for you and is keeping it warm in the oven," her mother said.

"I'm not hungry."

"You have to eat something, sweetie. Think about the baby."

Everything she did was for this baby. After making the decision to use a sperm bank, she'd reconciled herself to doing the parent thing alone. But that was before Morgan. Couldn't she feel just a little sorry for herself that things hadn't worked out?

"I don't feel like eating breakfast, Mama. I think the baby will be just fine."

Gabe's eyebrows rose as he sipped his coffee. "Someone is grumpy this morning."

"I'm not," she said, "But keep it up and I'm happy to show you just what grumpy looks like."

"I had cravings when I was pregnant," her mother said. "With Gabe it was candy and chips. Junk."

Erica gave him a smirk. "You are what Mama ate."

Their mother held up a hand to cut off his retort. "He's fine, in spite of what I ate. And with you," she said to Erica, "I wanted avocados and fresh melon."

"Nothing sounds good."

"How was your childbirth class last night?" Her mother met her gaze over the mug of coffee as she took a sip.

"It was good. Lots of information." Afterward sucked. Well, not the kissing Morgan part. That was pretty perfect. So was the touching. Right up until the baby moved.

"I'm surprised the guy hasn't backed out of this labor coach thing yet."

Erica slowly looked up at her brother as the reality hit her. She'd been so caught up in Morgan pulling away when the baby moved, she'd forgotten about everything else. After the way she left his house last night, she wasn't sure if he'd back out. Why wouldn't he? And then what would she do for a coach?

Gabe's expression went from easygoing to concerned as he studied her. "Is something wrong?"

"I don't want to talk about it."

"What happened?" her brother demanded. "Did he come on to you?"

If only.

She tamped down that reaction and speared her brother with a hard look. "He's a good man, and someday you're going to realize that. I predict that you two will be good friends."

Her brother snorted. "Fat chance."

"Ask anyone about him. You won't hear a bad word."

"Uh-huh." Gabe shook his head.

"I don't even know what to say to you right now. If I was ten, I'd call you a butthead. And Mama would scold me and tell me not to call you names."

"Okay, then. That's my cue." He pushed back his chair and stood. "You're crabby. That's not calling her names, Mama. It's an adjective. And I have to go."

"Have a good day, Gabe." Angela smiled at him as he walked out the door, then looked at Erica. "Your brother is right. You are in a mood. What's going on?"

"I'm pregnant, Mama." *And the man I love can't handle it. That's what's wrong.*

"You know, honey, it's completely natural for a pregnant woman to feel uncomfortable. Your body is supporting life. Your ankles are retaining enough water to float a cruise ship. Sleeping is hard because there's no comfortable position and bedtime is usually when your little unborn angel decides to do the backstroke."

Erica couldn't help smiling at the exaggerated but all too accurate description. "And your point is?"

"It's no secret we haven't been as supportive of your pregnancy as we could have been. I wonder if you feel that if you complain about being uncomfortable, we'll think you regret your decision. Or that we'll think this is what you get for making your choice. We don't."

"But, Mama—"

Her mother held up a hand to stop her words. "I'm not finished." She took a deep breath. "It also doesn't mean that we'll think you don't love your baby. Or that we won't love your baby. This is our first grandchild."

A tear rolled down Erica's cheek. "Damn hormones."

"I remember it well." A smile teased Angela's lips.

"The thing is, Mama, I know you understand. But you're a mother. I'm afraid Daddy will never be able to forgive me for doing the motherhood thing the way I have."

"Don't sell your father short. He understands more than you give him credit for."

"But more than once I've heard him criticize technology, newfangled contraptions. If it wasn't for science and a little bit of a miracle, I wouldn't be having a baby. Women do it all the time and that choice is widely accepted. But I don't know if he can get over his daughter taking that path."

Her mother didn't respond to that for several moments. She looked thoughtful, then seemed to come to a decision and stood. "Come with me."

"What? Where?" Erica questioned, but stood anyway.

"There's something you need to see. Get your jacket. It's cold outside."

Erica grabbed her poncho from the hook by the back door, then put it on and followed her mother outside. "Where are we going?"

"To the barn."

"Why?"

"Because one picture is worth a thousand words." That cryptic statement was all she would say.

They walked to the ranch outbuildings and into the barn. Erica kept pace with her mother past the hay-filled stalls and to the tack room in a far corner of the structure where her father was working. He was down on one knee and his back was to them as he dragged a paintbrush across something. The smell of wood sealer was faint in the air.

"George," her mother said. "I think it's time you show Erica what you're doing."

He stood and turned toward them. "Angela, it's supposed to be a surprise. I asked you to keep her away while I finish this."

"What's going on, Daddy? What are you doing?"

She moved closer until she was standing right beside him. When she saw it, her heart melted and she pressed a hand to her chest. "Oh my gosh. You made a cradle."

"Yeah." He set the brush on the open can beside him, then looked at her. His gaze narrowed and concern replaced his tender expression. "Are you all right? Is there something wrong with the baby?"

She laughed, although the sound came out a little like a sob, what with hormones and emotions clogging her throat. "I'm fine. So is the baby. Gabe told me flat out that I look terrible. I guess it's unanimous."

"I didn't say that," her father protested.

She moved closer to the sweet little bed suspended between two supports that allowed it to rock. "I can't believe you made this. It's completely wonderful."

She recognized the grain of the wood as what she'd picked up for him that day she'd run into Morgan at the building supply store. Her father had planned this very soon after he'd learned she was pregnant.

She burst into tears and covered her face with her hands. A moment later she felt strong arms come around her.

"Don't cry, honey. Your mama told me about how the baby came to be," he said gently.

"I guess I knew she couldn't keep a secret from you," she blubbered.

"No," he confirmed. "And I don't keep things from her. It's just how we are."

"It's a good way." She looked up at him. "Please try to understand why I had to have a baby this way, Daddy. I know it's not what you pictured for me, but in time I hope you'll be okay with my decision and with me."

"What?" He took her arms and held her away as he stared at her. There was shock on his face as he met her gaze. "How could you even think that? You're my daughter. My flesh and blood. And your child is, too. I love you. Nothing can change that. And I will love him—"

"Or her." His wife smiled at him.

"Right." He grinned. "I'm looking forward to holding this child. Being a grandfather. Don't you ever doubt that for a second."

"I won't. And thank you. For the cradle, too. I love it. And I love you."

She was sad that Morgan would never see this sweet little bed. When she put the baby down to sleep, she would remember her own father's love and be sorry that Morgan would never know what a good father he'd be. She would think of him and regret that he wasn't with her when they could have made a family together, something real and satisfying and wonderful.

Then she looked at her own amazing father and her mother. "Because of how I chose to conceive my child, there's no father in the picture. But he or she will have you guys. And Uncle Gabe and Aunt Mel. We're family. The baby will always be a part of my life and yours. Not like Gramps's daughter. I can't even imagine how he felt not just without support, but pressured to give his child away. This baby is loved and wanted."

Erica held out her arms and drew her mother and father into a group hug. She really did have so much to be grateful for and felt selfish for wishing she could have Morgan, too.

Erica had spent the morning with her brother and the two of them went to see Gramps. It was becoming their habit to go together. And her secret was out. The whole family knew how the baby had been conceived and assured her of their support. That was a great weight lifted from her. She needed that, because what happened with Morgan still hurt a lot.

He kept calling her cell, but she let it go to voice mail. She didn't think there was anything left to say. She would never forget the expression on his face when the baby moved, and it made her sad. The outing this morning helped a little to take her mind off what might have been.

She'd had lunch with her brother, and now she was taking her afternoon walk. Exercise was important, even near the end of her pregnancy when all she wanted to do was sit and feel like a slug. Gabe insisted on keeping her company, and now they were moving past the barn, heading for the corral and the path beyond it.

"How did you think Gramps was today?" she asked.

"Seemed about the same to me. Why?" He slid his hands into the pockets of his down vest.

"I don't know. It just seemed like there was a spark of something in his eyes. And when I put his hand on my belly and the baby moved, I think he might have smiled."

Gabe's expression was sad as he shook his head. "That's just wishful thinking, Erica. It would be great if he was still in there somewhere, but I'm not hopeful."

"Maybe if we could find his daughter…"

"To do that we need a break. Some piece of information that would send us in the right direction." He met her gaze for a moment. "If Malone could just remember the name Gramps said when he was talking about the prettiest little girl in the world…"

"I know," she agreed. "It's human nature to gloss over things. If we knew how important a piece of information would be later, we'd pay more attention."

"Yeah." They strolled along the white fence where a couple of the horses were hanging around. "I've been meaning to ask. Have you heard anything from your attorney about the Barron Enterprises lawsuit?"

"She called the other day to let me know she'd

heard from their legal department. They received the paperwork and were reviewing it. She warned me again that the process could drag on indefinitely. So, I'm glad Jordan Taylor is going to give me a job."

"Hmm."

Erica glanced up at him. "What?"

"He doesn't exactly have a reputation as a guy with a soft heart."

"I've been gone for a lot of years so I don't know much about him lately. But he's always been straight with me."

"Okay." Gabe's tone had a healthy dose of skepticism. "Then I hope he keeps his word and hires you."

"I've already filled out the employee paperwork. And I have a tentative start date." Before she could say more, her cell phone vibrated in her pocket. She fished it out and looked at the caller ID. Speaking of the devil, she thought, and she didn't mean Jordan. She stopped walking and said to her brother, "I have to take this." When Gabe nodded, she hit the green Accept button on the screen. "Peter. Why are you calling me?"

"How are you, Erica?"

The familiar deep voice used to be one that made her happy when she heard it. Not now. "I'm fine. What do you want? My attorney advised me not to speak to anyone from Barron."

"I'm just asking for a few minutes of your time," he said.

Erica noted that her brother's frown deepened. He shook his head slightly but she was curious enough not to hang up. "Okay."

"First of all I want to apologize for my father. He's not used to employees pushing back, and he lost his temper. Firing you was a knee-jerk reaction."

"Your father is a jackass." She saw Gabe grin and give her a thumb-up. "Feel free to tell him I said that."

"He has his moments." Peter cleared his throat. "The thing is, when someone's employment is terminated, there's a procedure and legal is involved. He didn't consult with the company attorneys when he took that action with you."

"So, you're saying that I have grounds for a lawsuit? Since pregnant women are part of a protected class." She wasn't really asking.

And Peter didn't directly respond to the question. "Barron Enterprises is putting together a generous severance package for you."

"A severance package," she repeated for Gabe's benefit. His eyes widened.

"Yes. I would consider it a favor if you would seriously contemplate accepting it."

"And dropping the lawsuit would be a condition." Again she wasn't asking.

"I won't deny that we would like to avoid any negative publicity." That was his lawyer voice.

"I'm sure you would." That was her "you're not going to push me around" voice.

"It's not just that, Erica." There was a sigh on the other end of the line. "I personally want to make sure you're taken care of."

"Really?" The sarcasm in that single word was laced with a good deal of anger. "Funny how it took filing a lawsuit to bring out your sensitive and caring side."

"You're not going to make this easy, are you?"

"Is there some reason I should?"

If he responded, she didn't hear, what with the blood pounding in her ears. She was shaking with anger. No matter how much she told herself it wasn't good for the baby, she couldn't suppress the feeling. In his father's office that day, her life had been thrown into chaos.

It was all about this man's new, pregnant wife, who didn't want to see Erica every day and be reminded that she'd dated her husband first. No one seemed to care that Erica was pregnant, too. She'd had a viable plan and it would have worked. But his father's power trip put her in a position of extreme stress wondering how she was going to support not just herself, but the baby she was carrying.

Finally she calmed down enough to say, "There's no way in hell I'm going to make this easy for you."

"Okay. We deserve that." There was silence for a moment. "Erica, I don't expect you to believe this, but I'm sorry things didn't work out between the two of us. That's my fault," he added quickly. "But I do care about you. And I truly do want to make sure you're going to be okay."

"You're right, Peter. I don't believe you."

"Erica, please—"

"Send the severance package to my attorney. You have her contact information."

"Seriously, Erica, I'm sincerely sorry about everything. It would mean a lot to me if you'd accept my apology."

There was a retort on the tip of her tongue, but she held it back. It occurred to her that she didn't care about this man. In fact, marrying him would have been a very big mistake. She should, in fact, be grateful to him for breaking things off. For being honest about not wanting children, although that turned out to be a lie, since he was expecting with the new wife. So, he just didn't want children with her. But feeling gratitude for his actions was a work in progress.

What she realized was that being angry over her termination was about fairness in business and a yearning for justice. But being angry on a personal level would mean she still had feelings for Peter, and that just wasn't the case.

This was a time for neutrality and generosity of spirit. "I accept your apology, Peter."

"Thank you. And I'll contact your attorney as soon as we hang up."

"Okay. Goodbye, Peter." She ended the call.

She looked at Gabe, who was grinning from ear to ear. "I guess you got the general picture of what's going on."

"The Barrons blinked. They want to pay you off. If you go to court, they're going to take a beating financially and in the media."

"That's the way I see it, too," she said.

Gabe hugged her. "You did great, sis. Way to keep your cool and tell him to go to hell, without actually saying it. Class act."

"Thank you."

She should have felt triumphant as her brother obviously did. But in reality, she felt deflated. Because there was only one person she wanted to share the news with. And she'd walked away from him. Ever since that night with Morgan she'd been wondering if she should have stayed to hear him out. Now it was too late.

That thought made her burst into tears. She looked helplessly at her brother. "I'm sorry. Hormones."

"Is it?" Gabe gave her a challenging look. "You've been in a mood. Ever since the last time you saw Morgan."

"How do you know?" Before he could answer she said, "Mom."

"Something happened with him."

"I don't want to discuss it."

"I don't need a blow-by-blow," Gabe said. "But there's something I do know."

"What?"

"You care about him. And he cares about you. Before you ask how I know that, it's obvious. Why else would he volunteer to be your labor coach?" Gabe shrugged as if it was a no-brainer. "I could see it that first night you met him at DJ's Deluxe. It's why I got so ticked off. You had stars in your eyes, and he had that look a guy gets when he's met a special woman. I don't know him so I didn't like it."

"Really?" She brushed the moisture from her cheeks. "But it wasn't—"

"Don't try to rationalize. It's a big brother thing. Plus, I wasn't subtle," he admitted. "But I *was* wrong. You two care about each other, and you need to talk to him."

That startled her. "Who are you and what have you done with my brother?"

"I deserve that." He looked sheepish. "Shouldn't a person be allowed to change his mind?"

"Of course. I'm just wondering what changed yours."

"I talked to Morgan after the baby shower. I'm a pretty good judge of people and I believed him, that he cares about you," he said. "And I trust your judgment." He leaned over and kissed her forehead. "You know your own mind and you're smart. I love you, sis. And I just want you to be happy."

"Okay—" Emotion choked off her words.

He pointed at her. "Don't you dare cry. It drives guys crazy because we can't fix it. So, just stop."

"I love you, too. And I'll try—" Who was she trying to kid? There was no way that was going to happen. She burst into tears again, and he pulled her in for a hug.

"It's okay. Just talk to Morgan. Do as your big brother says, and everything will be all right."

She wanted to believe that. The problem was, she didn't think Morgan would give her another chance. And she couldn't blame him.

Chapter Fifteen

Morgan glanced into the office in the big house where Neal Dalton was sitting at his desk, scrutinizing the ranch spreadsheets on his computer.

The door was open but he knocked on it and said, "Dad, can I talk to you?"

His father looked up, then removed his reading glasses and set them down on some file folders. "Have a seat."

Morgan closed the door, then walked over and sat in one of the chairs. After taking a big breath he said, "I screwed up with Erica."

"And you're here because out of everyone you know I've had the most experience screwing up?"

"Look, I'm not here to bust you about that—"

"It was a joke. Guess I'll have to work on my delivery." The man sighed. "What did you do?"

Morgan told him about kissing Erica. "Everything was fine and then I felt the baby move. It was awesome, Dad. But it hit me. There's a real baby in there. That sounds so dumb, but it's the honest to God truth."

"I get it. Believe me."

"That changed everything. It wasn't just about the two of us. There's another life involved, and I needed to take that into consideration before moving forward, before, you know—"

"Yeah. So what did you do then?" his dad asked. "After you felt the baby?"

"Nothing. I froze."

Neal looked puzzled. "I'm not seeing the problem, son."

"Erica jumped to a conclusion. She took my reaction to mean that I didn't want her because of the baby. But I just needed a minute to process." He met his father's gaze. "She walked out without giving me a chance to explain why I was hesitating."

"Okay." The other man nodded thoughtfully. "I don't think this is a screw-up. More a misunderstanding. When did it happen?"

"A couple of days ago. I've tried calling her, but it goes straight to voice mail." He lifted his hands, a gesture of pure frustration. "I don't know what to do."

"You have two choices, son. You can let her go—"

"No," Morgan said firmly. That response came straight from the gut, by way of his heart. "That's not an option."

"You're sure?" His dad studied him. "You haven't known her very long."

"I'm absolutely sure. Don't ask me why—"

"Never crossed my mind," the other man said. "With your mom I knew pretty much from the moment I met her that she was the one. Holt proposed to Amanda pretty fast. It might take us Dalton men a while to find the right woman, but when we do, we move to seal the deal right away. But—"

"What?" Morgan asked sharply.

"That means you'll be a father right away. I know that gave you pause not so long ago. And you're right. It's not just you and her to consider. There's another life involved. If you can't accept that fully, best back off now. Otherwise there's a lot of heartache down the road."

"I hear you, Dad. I can't let her go." He shrugged as if to say he just knew. "So, how do I get her back?"

"You need to find a way to show her you're all in. For her *and* the baby. A big gesture. When you figure that out, you drive over there and show her you really mean it."

A gesture. All in for her and the baby. Morgan's

mind was racing, then suddenly he had an idea and it was perfect.

He met his father's gaze, then stood and headed for the door. "Can you spare me for the rest of the day? I've got some stuff to do."

"Of course. And Morgan?"

He stopped with his hand on the doorknob and turned to look at his father. "Yeah?"

"Good luck. If there's anything else I can do, you only have to ask."

"No offense, Dad, but I hope I won't need you." Morgan smiled. If there was one positive thing to come out of this, it was getting back a relationship with his father. "Thanks, Dad."

After the talk, Morgan jumped in his truck and headed downtown. He needed to purchase two things, and the first one was easy, what with just buying the highest consumer rated and most expensive one on the market. The second item took longer. Part of the reason was him calling Erica's cell every half hour to let her know he was picking her up for childbirth class later. And every half hour he got her voice mail. His guts were in a knot, and the uncertainty was killing him.

It was early, but he couldn't wait any longer to see her. He drove to the Ambling A and went up to the brightly lighted porch. He rang the bell, then nervously waited for someone to answer.

When the door was opened, he was surprised to

see Gabe Abernathy. In his mind he'd been running possible speeches to Erica and was unprepared to see anyone else. "What are you doing here?"

"The better question is why are *you* here?"

"I came to pick up Erica." Morgan braced for hostilities. He planned to stand his ground even though he knew the Abernathys didn't trust him. They were just going to have to suck it up and get used to him being around. Oddly enough, her brother didn't look hostile.

"Did she know you were coming to get her?" Gabe's amusement disappeared.

"We have class tonight. And I left messages that I'd be here." Morgan glanced down for a moment. "Would you please let her know?"

"I would be happy to except she left already."

The words felt like a punch to the gut, and Morgan hadn't braced himself for that. "Where did she go?"

"I heard her tell my mom that she was going to her class. Doesn't she usually pick you up?"

"Yeah." But that was before.

"Maybe there's a miscommunication and she thought you were meeting her at the class."

"No. But we will be meeting." Morgan touched his fingers to the brim of his Stetson. "Thanks, Gabe. Sorry to bother you."

"No problem. And, Morgan?"

He stopped and looked over his shoulder. "Yeah?"

"For what it's worth, I'm rooting for you, Coach."

"Thanks."

Morgan wouldn't have thought anything could make him smile, but that did. It helped knowing her brother was on his side, and right this minute he was in no mood to question what had happened to make him change his mind. His focus was on making his case to the person who mattered most to him.

He drove the now familiar route to the Women's Health Center and realized this was the first time he'd come alone. He didn't much like that and hoped it wasn't a bad omen for the rest of his life. When he arrived at his destination, he went up and down the rows of cars until he found Erica's. For a desperate man in need of some hope, he took the empty space beside her SUV as a good sign.

He exited his vehicle, then opened the rear passenger door of his truck, removed the brand-new infant car seat and headed for the building's lobby and the elevator.

His heart was racing as he walked down the carpeted hallway and into the conference room. Carla was there at the lectern. The other three expectant couples sat at the U-shaped tables. When he walked in, all conversation ceased and everyone stared at him. He only had eyes for Erica.

He walked over to her. "Hi. I'd have been here sooner but I stopped at your place to pick you up. Gabe said you'd already left."

Eyes wide as saucers, she nodded. "I didn't think you wanted to do this with me anymore."

"You thought wrong." He set the carrier on the table in front of her. "We're going to need one of these for the baby."

She stared at it for several seconds, then ran a finger over the small harness. "I don't know what to say."

"It's easy to hook up," he said. "Just takes seconds. An indicator goes from red to green when it's installed correctly." He couldn't tell whether she liked it. "Unlike me, it's idiot proof. But if you want something else, we can return it."

"No," she said quickly. "It's fantastic. The one I wanted. But I don't understand. What does this mean? You keep saying 'we,' but—"

It was time for part two of his screw-up redemption plan. "Erica, I have a million questions about how to be a good father, but zero doubts about you and me."

"But I thought the other night— You made it clear you didn't want this."

He shook his head. "You assumed that and then walked out before we could talk about it."

"You're not wrong." Her hazel eyes were huge as she looked at him, then glanced at the others in the room who were watching this conversation unfold with undisguised curiosity. "But you want to talk about this *now*?"

"Yes. I've waited too long already." He sat in the chair beside hers. "I'm not bailing on you. Not walking away from you. Not now, not ever. I want to be a father to this baby."

"Really?" Her expression was hopeful, but she didn't seem convinced he was all in.

"Yes, really. I've had feelings for you since the first moment I saw you. I was falling for you before I even realized you were pregnant. Love at first sight." He couldn't believe he hadn't put his feelings into words before now. And it was way past time. "I love you, Erica. I love the baby you're carrying. And that makes it my baby, too. I want to be your husband, and I very much want to be his or her father."

"Morgan—" Her voice caught and she swallowed. "I don't know what to say."

"That's because I haven't asked you anything yet." He took the velvet jeweler's box from the front pocket of his jeans. He opened it to reveal the ring he'd picked out at the jewelry store. Angelique, the jewelry designer, had assured him this was the one that would dazzle any woman. He needed the dazzle and a little razzle to convince Erica he was worth taking a chance on.

So, he went down on one knee and said, "Will you make me the happiest man on the planet and marry me? Make a family with me? In case there's any question, the only correct answer is yes."

"Oh, Morgan—"

He waited for her to finish that statement, then couldn't stand it. "Is that an 'Oh, Morgan, I wish you hadn't asked'? Or, 'Oh, Morgan, that's a big fat yes'?"

"It's an 'Oh, Morgan, I love you so much' followed by a heartfelt and unqualified 'absolutely yes.' Nothing would make me happier than to marry you and be a family."

"Thank you, God." He stood and pulled her up and into his arms. The baby kicked just then, and the miracle of it took his breath away. This time there was no doubt or hesitation when he put his hand on her belly. He smiled into her eyes. "I believe our daughter approves."

"Oh? You think we're having a girl?"

"There are five boys in my family. Six with Robby. We're definitely having a girl."

She smiled tenderly. "You are a remarkable man, Morgan Dalton. And I am the luckiest woman in the world. I love you so much."

"I love you more."

And he kissed her, trying to prove just how deeply he meant those words. When they finally came up for air, the expectant dads shook his hand and their wives were sniffling. All of them blamed hormones, but Carla was brushing tears off her cheeks, too, and she wasn't pregnant. The fact of the matter was that everyone loved a happily ever after.

Epilogue

The first Saturday in November, Erica was in her childhood bedroom getting ready for her wedding. She and Morgan wanted to be married before the baby came. Her dream of marriage then baby was coming true after all, though not in the most traditional sense.

Her dress was ivory silk with a lace bodice and long sleeves. The skirt was empire and fell over her tummy and gracefully to the floor. A simple lace veil trailed down her back, secured by a comb in her hair.

Mel, her maid of honor, was fussing with it, making sure the material lay perfectly. She was wearing a lacy, tea-length royal blue dress with a flirty, flared skirt. When she straightened, they stood side by side and looked in the mirror together. And grinned.

"You look beautiful," her almost sister-in-law said.

"Being completely happy does that to a girl."

"This whole bridal thing really suits you."

"When it's right, it's right." She sighed. "With Morgan it was love at first sight. Somehow I knew I would love him forever and beyond."

Mel nodded. "I mean, how can you not be crazy about a guy who proposes with a very impressive diamond ring in one hand and an infant carrier in the other?"

Erica laughed. "He's very special and I'm a lucky girl."

Mel took her hands and squeezed them. "You so deserve the best, and Morgan is that for you."

There was a knock on the door just before her mother opened it. When she saw her daughter, her expression turned achingly tender as her eyes glistened with tears. "Oh, sweetie, you look so beautiful."

"Thank you, Mama."

"And you're not the least bit nervous."

"No room for nerves. Not when I'm so full of happiness. I can't wait to be Mrs. Morgan Dalton."

"Okay, then. Let's get this show on the road. I came up here to let you know the car just arrived to take us to the church." Her mother headed to the door. "Your father and Gabe are already there waiting for us."

"Mama, just real quick before we go—"

"What, sweetie?"

Erica moved close and pulled her into a hug. "I just want to thank you for making today happen. For putting up with me through good and bad. And for being the best mom in the world." She pressed a hand to her belly. "If I'm half as good as you are, I'll do right by this little one."

"You're going to be a wonderful mother. I love you." Angela smiled but her mouth trembled for just a moment. "You're going to make me cry and ruin my makeup."

"I'm sorry, but I needed to say it."

Over the years there'd been ups and downs in their relationship. But the bonds between them were stronger now than ever.

"Okay, ladies," her mom said, "let's get moving."

Erica followed the other two women down the stairs. The house was decorated with flowers for a small reception following the ceremony. Her mother had hired Brittany to handle the event, and Erica already knew that woman could make a feast out of bread and water.

She picked up her bouquet from the box on the entryway table. It was made up of greens and white roses with several orange ones to add a pop of fall color. Mel took her own bouquet, a smaller version of Erica's and they left the house, then stepped into the waiting town car.

A short time later the three of them arrived at the small white church with its graceful, elegant spire. It was charming and traditional and completely perfect. In the vestibule Brittany was waiting for them, looking tall and chic in a pale pink sheath dress with her hair smoothly pulled back into a side bun. Robby was by her side, dapper in his little dark suit and tie, and holding a pillow with two rings. They were symbolic since Morgan's best man had the real ones. And then she saw her father, so handsome in his black suit and tie.

"Hi, Daddy."

"Baby girl—" He stopped and swallowed. "I'm not sure I can give you away."

She moved closer, then stood on tiptoe and kissed his cheek. "You're not. You're just relieved of duty. I have a good man who will be there for me every day, every step of the way."

"I know. Otherwise I wouldn't be able to part with you."

"Okay," Brittany said, taking charge as she gave them all a critical once-over. "Believe it or not, so far everything has gone off without a hitch."

"Of course," Erica said. "You wouldn't accept anything less."

"Darn right." She gave Erica a final approving look. "You ready?"

"Absolutely." She grinned at the boy who would very soon be her nephew. "Robby Dalton, you look awfully handsome."

"Grandma says it runs in the family." The boy gave Brittany a wary look. "My dad and Uncle Morgan told me I have to do everything *she* says."

"They're right." But Brittany smiled at him. "You're going to do great."

Just then the vestibule doors opened, and Gabe walked in. When he saw Erica, a tender look of approval slid into his eyes. But when his gaze settled on his fiancée, he was speechless. Finally he said to her, "Next summer this will be us."

Mel blew him a kiss. "I can't wait."

"Hold that thought, you two. It's time to do *this* wedding," Brittany said. "The groom's mother is already seated. Gabe, escort your mother down the aisle."

He held out his arm and Angela took it. The doors remained open when he walked her down to the front row.

"You ready, Robby?"

The boy looked up at Brittany. "Yes, ma'am."

The organist in the choir loft started playing the traditional "Wedding March," and Robby confidently walked down the aisle, followed by Mel.

"You're up, bride." Brittany hugged her quickly, then brushed away a tear. "You look radiant. Go be happy."

"Thank you. For everything."

Erica took her father's arm, and he put his hand over hers as they matched their steps to the music. She smiled at people as she passed them on her way to the altar. Her groom stood there with his father by his side. Morgan had asked him to be best man, and his mother had cried more than a few happy tears over that.

Then she looked only at Morgan, and he was looking back at her as if she was the most beautiful woman in the world. He sure made her feel that way. In his dark suit and royal blue silk tie, the man defined the word *handsome*, but he was and always would be her cowboy. Eagerly they said their vows and made forever promises that felt so very right.

After pictures, everyone came back to the Ambling A for the reception. Furniture had been moved out of the living and great rooms and tables set up. There were white tablecloths and flowers and a cocktail hour before dinner.

At the family table Malone looked a little uncomfortable being a guest instead of doing the cooking. But Erica had insisted he enjoy her wedding, too. And he'd pronounced the catered food not bad.

There was a dance area on the patio where they shared their first dance as husband and wife. Morgan held out his hand, and she put hers in his palm, knowing somehow that this would never get old.

Afterward he led her back to the family table,

where Gabe and Mel were sitting with her parents and Grandpa Alex. She took the seat beside Malone, who she swore was trying to hide that he was brushing away a tear.

"Sure do wish Josiah could be here to see how pretty his great-granddaughter is."

"I believe he's here in spirit." She leaned her head against his shoulder for a moment.

Then the DJ started talking. "The bride requested a song, a real oldie. It's a tradition at Abernathy weddings. Her great-grandfather, Josiah Abernathy, had it played at his wedding to Cora. Her grandfather did the same as did her parents, George and Angela. So, without further ado, here we go."

The strains of the music began and when the lyrics kicked in, all the guests began to sing along.

"Daisy, Daisy, give me your answer do—" They finished with a rousing, "But you'll look sweet upon the seat of a bicycle built for two."

"Holy cow." Malone sat up straight and sounded very excited. "Holy cow, that's it!"

Erica had never heard that tone from the normally reserved, unflappable man. "What's it?"

"The name I couldn't remember. The name Josiah said when he was talking about the prettiest little girl in the world. It was Daisy."

Erica let that sink in for a moment, then she quivered with excitement. She looked at Gabe and Mel, whose expressions mirrored her own. "Call me crazy, but I don't think he was talking about a girlfriend."

Her brother nodded. "Unless I miss my guess, that's his daughter's name. Her adoptive name."

Erica gripped her new husband's hand. "And I bet Gramps had that song at his wedding as a way to keep his daughter a part of him and his family in any way he could."

"This may be the piece of information we needed," Gabe said. "I'll clue Amanda in right away and we can continue the search." He and Melanie went to find her.

"Way to go, Malone," Erica said.

"Glad I could help. Finally. I need a drink." He got up and went to the bar, and the rest of her family followed.

So, Erica was alone with her new husband and grinned at him. "Do I know how to clear a table, or what?"

"It's your superpower." He smiled, then kissed her.

She was breathless when he stopped. "I aim to please."

"So that song is a family tradition?"

"It is. And I wanted all the Abernathy customs today, because we didn't start out in the most traditional way."

"That song worked in more ways than one." Then he put his hand on her abdomen and smiled at the baby's movement. "And you'd look sweet anywhere, but we need something more family friendly than a bicycle built for two."

"I like the way you think."

It took a very special man to so completely embrace raising a child he didn't make, and her heart was full of emotion. "I love the man you are. You have a heart as big as the Montana sky, Morgan Dalton, and you really stepped up. You'll be an incredible daddy."

"I had no choice," he said. "I made a promise to you. And then I fell in love." He kissed her softly, then met her gaze. "And this cowboy always keeps his promises."

* * * * *

MILLS & BOON

Coming next month

THEIR ROYAL BABY GIFT
Kandy Shepherd

The woman's wet dress clung to her body making no
secret of her curves. She was a scandal in the making.

He grabbed a striped towel from a stack on a nearby
lounger and threw it around her shoulders, another one
around himself. "Keep your head down and walk as
quickly as you can," he said.

She attempted a faster pace but stumbled and he had
to put his arm around her to keep her upright. He scarcely
broke his stride to pick up the phone she'd dropped
when she'd fallen.

"Are you hurt?"

"Only...only my pride."

"Are you staying at this hotel?"

She shook her head and wet strands flew around her
face, sending droplets of water on him. "I...I only came
here for lunch. My hotel is in the older part of town."

"I'm in the penthouse here. There's a private elevator
down to my suite. I'll take you there."

"Please." She was still shivering, and her eyes didn't
look quite focused.

He had to get her—and himself—out of here. Edward
kept his arm around Ms Mermaid as he ushered her to
the discreet private elevator. If people didn't recognise
him, a scandal could be averted.

Within minutes they were in the expansive suite where he was living while his Singapore house was being gutted and refurbished. He slammed the door behind them and slumped in relief. No one with a camera could follow him here. He turned back into the room. Then realised he had swapped one problem for another. Standing opposite him, dripping water on the marble floor of his hotel suite was a beautiful stranger—and her presence here could so easily be misconstrued.

"Thank you," she said. "I could have drowned." Her eyes were huge, her lush mouth trembled. Hair wet and dripping, makeup smudged around her eyes she was breathtakingly lovely. A red-blooded male, no matter how chivalrous, could not fail to feel a stirring of attraction. "I…I can't swim, not enough to save myself. But you…you saved me."

Continue reading
THEIR ROYAL BABY GIFT
Kandy Shepherd

Available next month
www.millsandboon.co.uk

LET'S TALK
Romance

For exclusive extracts, competitions
and special offers, find us online:

f facebook.com/millsandboon

🐦 @MillsandBoon

📷 @MillsandBoonUK

Get in touch on 01413 063232

MILLS & BOON

THE HEART OF ROMANCE

A ROMANCE FOR EVERY KIND OF READER

MODERN

Prepare to be swept off your feet by sophisticated, sexy and seductive heroes, in some of the world's most glamourous and romantic locations, where power and passion collide.
8 stories per month.

HISTORICAL

Escape with historical heroes from time gone by. Whether your passion is for wicked Regency Rakes, muscled Vikings or rugged Highlanders, awaken the romance of the past.
6 stories per month.

MEDICAL

Set your pulse racing with dedicated, delectable doctors in the high-pressure world of medicine, where emotions run high and passion, comfort and love are the best medicine.
6 stories per month.

True Love

Celebrate true love with tender stories of heartfelt romance, from the rush of falling in love to the joy a new baby can bring, and a focus on the emotional heart of a relationship.
8 stories per month.

Desire

Indulge in secrets and scandal, intense drama and plenty of sizzling hot action with powerful and passionate heroes who have it all: wealth, status, good looks…everything but the right woman.
6 stories per month.

HEROES

Experience all the excitement of a gripping thriller, with an intense romance at its heart. Resourceful, true-to-life women and strong, fearless men face danger and desire - a killer combination!
8 stories per month.

DARE

Sensual love stories featuring smart, sassy heroines you'd want as a best friend, and compelling intense heroes who are worthy of them.
4 stories per month.

To see which titles are coming soon, please visit

millsandboon.co.uk/nextmonth

MILLS & BOON

HISTORICAL

Awaken the romance of the past

Escape with historical heroes from time gone by. Whether your passion is for wicked Regency Rakes, muscled Viking warriors or rugged Highlanders, indulge your fantasies and awaken the romance of the past.

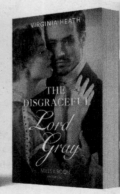

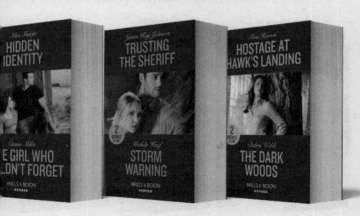

MILLS & BOON
MEDICAL
Pulse-Racing Passion

Set your pulse racing with dedicated, delectable doctors in the high-pressure world of medicine, where emotions run high and passion, comfort and love are the best medicine.